P9-CFV-865

Deighton, Len, 1929—
London match   FEB 3 1986

C. 2

WITHDRAWN
Baldwinsville Public Library
Baldwinsville, New York

8182 02 64343 8   02 7   (IC=1)
DEIGHTON, LEN
LONDON MATCH
(1) 1986 F

Also by Len Deighton

London Match

LONDON MATCH

LEN DEIGHTON

ALFRED A. KNOPF

NEW YORK

1985

WITHDRAWN

Baldwinsville Public Library
Baldwinsville, New York 13027

THIS IS A BORZOI BOOK
PUBLISHED BY ALFRED A. KNOPF, INC.

FEB 3 1986

Copyright © 1985 by Len Deighton

All rights reserved under International and Pan-American
Copyright Conventions. Published in the United States by
Alfred A. Knopf, Inc., New York. Distributed by Random House,
Inc., New York. Originally published in Great Britain by
Hutchinson & Co. (Publishers) Ltd.

Grateful acknowledgment is made to Peer International
Corporation for permission to reprint an excerpt from the lyrics
to *Frensi*. Original words and music by Alberto Dominguez.
English words by Ray Charles and S. K. Russell. Copyright 1939
and 1941 by Peer International Corporation. Copyright renewed.
International Copyright Secured. All Rights Reserved. Used by
Permission.

Library of Congress Cataloging in Publication Data

Deighton, Len, [date]   London match.

Sequel to: Mexico set.
I. Title.
PR6054.E37L6   1986   823'.914   85-40454
ISBN 0-394-54937-6

Manufactured in the United States of America

FIRST EDITION

London Match

Chapter 1

C HEER up, Werner. It will soon be Christmas," I said.

I shook the bottle, dividing the last drips of whisky between the two white plastic cups that were balanced on the car radio. I pushed the empty bottle under the seat. The smell of the whisky was strong. I must have spilled some on the heater or on the warm leather that encased the radio. I thought Werner would decline it. He wasn't a drinker and he'd had far too much already, but Berlin winter nights are cold and Werner swallowed his whisky in one gulp and coughed. Then he crushed the cup in his big muscular hands and sorted through the bent and broken pieces so that he could fit them all into the ashtray. Werner's wife, Zena, was obsessionally tidy and this was her car.

"People are still arriving," said Werner as a black Mercedes limousine drew up. Its headlights made dazzling reflections in the glass and paintwork of the parked cars and glinted on the frosty surface of the road. The chauffeur hurried to open the door and eight or nine people got out. The men wore dark cashmere coats over their evening suits, and the women a menagerie of furs. Here in Berlin-Wannsee, where furs and cashmere are everyday clothes, they are called the *Hautevolee* and there are plenty of them.

"What are you waiting for? Let's barge right in and arrest him now." Werner's words were just slightly slurred and he

3

grinned to acknowledge his condition. Although I'd known Werner since we were kids at school, I'd seldom seen him drunk, or even tipsy as he was now. Tomorrow he'd have a hangover, tomorrow he'd blame me, and so would his wife, Zena. For that and other reasons, tomorrow, early, would be a good time to leave Berlin.

The house in Wannsee was big; an ugly clutter of enlargements and extensions, balconies, sun deck, and penthouse almost hid the original building. It was built on a ridge that provided its rear terrace with a view across the forest to the black waters of the lake. Now the terrace was empty, the garden furniture stacked, and the awnings rolled up tight, but the house was blazing with lights and along the front garden the bare trees had been garlanded with hundreds of tiny white bulbs like electronic blossoms.

"The BfV man knows his job," I said. "He'll come and tell us when the contact has been made."

"The contact won't come here. Do you think Moscow doesn't know we have a defector in London spilling his guts to us? They'll have warned their network by now."

"Not necessarily," I said. I denied his contention for the hundredth time and didn't doubt we'd soon be having the same exchange again. Werner was forty years old, just a few weeks older than I was, but he worried like an old woman and that put me on edge too. "Even his failure to come could provide a chance to identify him," I said. "We have two plainclothes cops checking everyone who arrives tonight, and the office has a copy of the invitation list."

"That's if the contact is a guest," said Werner.

"The staff are checked too."

"The contact will be an outsider," said Werner. "He wouldn't be *dumm* enough to give us his contact on a plate."

"I know."

"Shall we go inside the house again?" suggested Werner. "I get a cramp these days sitting in little cars." I opened the door and got out.

Werner closed his car door gently; it's a habit that comes with years of surveillance work. This exclusive suburb was mostly villas amid woodland and water, and quiet enough for me to hear the sound of heavy trucks pulling into the Border Controlpoint at Drewitz to begin the long haul down the auto-bahn that went through the Democratic Republic to West Germany. "It will snow tonight," I predicted.

Werner gave no sign of having heard me. "Look at all that wealth," he said, waving an arm and almost losing his balance on the ice that had formed in the gutter. As far as we could see along it, the whole street was like a parking lot, or rather like a car showroom, for the cars were almost without exception glossy, new, and expensive. Five-liter V-8 Mercedes with car-phone antennas and turbo Porsches and big Ferraris and three or four Rolls-Royces. The registration plates showed how far people will travel to such a lavish party. Businessmen from Hamburg, bankers from Frankfurt, film people from Munich, and well-paid officials from Bonn. Some cars were perched high on the pavement to make room for others to be double-parked alongside them. We passed a couple of cops who were wander-ing between the long lines of cars, checking the registration plates and admiring the paintwork. In the driveway—stamping their feet against the cold—were two *Parkwächter* who would park the cars of guests unfortunate enough to be without a chauffeur. Werner went up the icy slope of the driveway with arms extended to help him balance. He wobbled like an overfed penguin.

Despite all the double-glazed windows, closed tight against the cold of a Berlin night, there came from the house the faint syrupy whirl of Johann Strauss played by a twenty-piece orches-tra. It was like drowning in a thick strawberry milk shake.

A servant opened the door for us and another took our coats. One of our people was immediately inside, standing next to the butler. He gave no sign of recognition as we entered the flower-bedecked entrance hall. Werner smoothed his silk eve-ning jacket self-consciously and tugged the ends of his bow tie as he caught a glimpse of himself in the gold-framed mirror that covered the wall. Werner's suit was a hand-stitched custom-made silk one from Berlin's most exclusive tailors, but on Werner's thickset figure all suits looked rented.

Standing at the foot of the elaborate staircase were two elderly men in stiff high collars and well-tailored evening suits that made no concessions to modern styling. They were smoking large cigars and talking with their heads close together because of the loudness of the orchestra in the ballroom beyond. One of the men stared at us but went on talking as if we weren't visible to him. We didn't seem right for such a gathering, but he looked away, no doubt thinking we were two heavies hired to protect the silver.

Until 1945 the house—or *Villa,* as such local mansions are known—had belonged to a man who began his career as a minor official with the Nazi farmers organization—and it was by chance that his department was given the task of deciding which farmers and agricultural workers were so indispensable to the economy that they would be exempt from service with the military forces. But from that time onward—like other bureaucrats before and since—he was showered with gifts and opportunities and lived in high style, as his house bore witness.

For some years after the war the house was used as transit accommodation for U.S. Army truck drivers. Only recently had it become a family house once more. The paneling, which so obviously dated back to the original nineteenth-century building, had been carefully repaired and reinstated, but now the oak was painted light gray. A huge painting of a soldier on a horse dominated the wall facing the stairs and on all sides there were carefully arranged displays of fresh flowers. But despite all the careful refurbishing, it was the floor of the entrance hall that attracted the eye. The floor was a complex pattern of black, white, and red marble, a plain white central disc of newer marble having replaced a large gold swastika.

Werner pushed open a plain door secreted into the paneling and I followed him along a bleak corridor designed for the inconspicuous movement of servants. At the end of the passage there was a pantry. Clean linen cloths were arranged on a shelf, a dozen empty champagne bottles were inverted to drain in the sink, and the waste bin was filled with the remains of sandwiches, discarded parsley, and some broken glass. A white-coated waiter arrived carrying a large silver tray of dirty glasses. He emptied them, put them into the service lift together with the empty bottles, wiped the tray with a cloth from under the sink, and then departed without even glancing at either of us.

"There he is, near the bar," said Werner, holding open the door so we could look across the crowded dance floor. There was a crush around the tables where two men in chef's whites dispensed a dozen different sorts of sausages and foaming tankards of strong beer. Emerging from the scrum with food and drink was the man who was to be detained.

"I hope like hell we've got this right," I said. The man was not just a run-of-the-mill bureaucrat; he was the private secretary to a senior member of the Bonn parliament.

I said, "If he sticks his heels in and denies everything, I'm not sure we'll be able to make it stick."

I looked at the suspect carefully, trying to guess how he'd take it. He was a small man with crew-cut hair and a neat Vandyke beard. There was something uniquely German about that combination. Even amongst the overdressed Berlin social set his appearance was flashy. His jacket had wide silk-faced lapels and silk also edged his jacket, cuffs, and trouser seams. The ends of his bow tie were tucked under his collar and he wore a black silk handkerchief in his top pocket.

"He looks much younger than thirty-two, doesn't he?" said Werner.

"You can't rely on those computer printouts, especially with listed civil servants or even members of the Bundestag. They were all put onto the computer when it was installed, by copy typists working long hours of overtime to make a bit of spare cash."

"What do you think?" said Werner.

"I don't like the look of him," I said.

"He's guilty," said Werner. He had no more information than I did, but he was trying to reassure me.

"But the uncorroborated word of a defector such as Stinnes won't cut much ice in an open court, even if London will let Stinnes go into a court. If this fellow's boss stands by him and they both scream blue murder, he might get away with it."

"When do we take him, Bernie?"

"Maybe his contact will come here," I said. It was an excuse for delay.

"He'd have to be a real beginner, Bernie. Just one look at this place—lit up like a Christmas tree, cops outside, and no room to move—no one with any experience would risk coming into a place like this."

"Perhaps they won't be expecting problems," I said optimistically.

"Moscow knows Stinnes is missing and they've had plenty of time to alert their networks. And anyone with experience will smell this stakeout when they park outside."

"He didn't smell it," I said, nodding to our crew-cut man as he swigged at his beer and engaged a fellow guest in conversation.

"Moscow can't send a source like him away to their training school," said Werner. "But that's why you can be quite certain that his contact will be Moscow-trained: and that means wary. You might as well arrest him now."

"We say nothing; we arrest no one," I told him once again. "German security are doing this one; he's simply being detained for questioning. We stand by and see how it goes."

"Let me do it, Bernie." Werner Volkmann was a Berliner by birth. I'd come to school here as a young child, my German was just as authentic as his, but because I was English, Werner was determined to hang on to the conceit that his German was in some magic way more authentic than mine. I suppose I would feel the same way about any German who spoke perfect London-accented English, so I didn't argue about it.

"I don't want him to know any non-German service is involved. If he tumbles to who we are, he'll know Stinnes is in London."

"They know already, Bernie. They must know where he is by now."

"Stinnes has got enough troubles without a KGB hit squad searching for him."

Werner was looking at the dancers and smiling to himself as if at some secret joke, the way people sometimes do when they've had too much to drink. His face was still tanned from his time in Mexico and his teeth were white and perfect. He looked almost handsome despite the lumpy fit of his suit. "It's like a Hollywood movie," he said.

"Yes," I said. "The budget's too big for television."

The ballroom was crowded with elegant couples, all wearing the sort of clothes that would have looked all right for a ball at the turn of the century. And the guests weren't the desiccated old fogies I was expecting to see at this fiftieth birthday party for a manufacturer of dishwashers. There were plenty of richly clad young people whirling to the music of another time in another town. *Kaiserstadt*—isn't that what Vienna was called at a time when there was only one Emperor in Europe and only one capital for him?

It was the makeup and the hair-dos that sounded the jarring note of modernity, that and the gun I could see bulging under Werner's beautiful silk jacket. I suppose that's what was making it so tight across the chest.

The white-coated waiter returned with another big tray of glasses. Some of the glasses were not empty. There was the sudden smell of alcohol as he tipped cherries, olives, and abandoned drinks into the warm water of the sink before putting the glasses into the service lift. Then he turned to Werner and said respectfully, "They've arrested the contact, sir. Went to the car just as you said." He wiped the empty tray with a cloth.

"What's all this, Werner?" I said.

The waiter looked at me and then at Werner and, when

Werner nodded assent, said, "The contact went to the suspect's parked car . . . a woman at least forty years old, maybe older. She had a key that fitted the car door. She unlocked the glove compartment and took an envelope. We've taken her into custody but the envelope has not yet been opened. The captain wants to know if he should take the woman back to the office or hold her here in the panel truck for you to talk to."

The music stopped and the dancers applauded. Somewhere on the far side of the ballroom a man was heard singing an old country song. He stopped, embarrassed, and there was laughter.

"Has she given a Berlin address?"

"Kreuzberg. An apartment house near the Landwehr Canal."

"Tell your captain to take the woman to the apartment. Search it and hold her there. Phone here to confirm that she's given the correct address and we'll come along later to talk to her," I said. "Don't let her make any phone calls. Make sure the envelope remains unopened; we know what's in it. I'll want it as evidence, so don't let everybody maul it about."

"Yes, sir," said the waiter and departed, picking his way across the dance floor as the dancers walked off it.

"Why didn't you tell me he was one of our people?" I asked Werner.

Werner giggled. "You should have seen your face."

"You're drunk, Werner," I said.

"You didn't even recognize a plainclothes cop. What's happening to you, Bernie?"

"I should have guessed. They always have them clearing away the dirty dishes; a cop doesn't know enough about food and wine to serve anything."

"You didn't think it was worth watching his car, did you?"

He was beginning to irritate me. I said, "If I had your kind of money, I wouldn't be dragging around with a lot of cops and security men."

"What would you be doing?"

"With money? If I didn't have the kids, I'd find some little pension in Tuscany, somewhere not too far from the beach."

"Admit it; you didn't think it was worth watching his car, did you?"

"You're a genius."

"No need for sarcasm," said Werner. "You've got him now. Without me you would have ended up with egg on your face." He burped very softly, holding a hand over his mouth.

"Yes, Werner," I said.

"Let's go and arrest the bastard . . . I had a feeling about that car—the way he locked the doors and then looked round like someone might be waiting there." There had always been a didactic side to Werner; he should have been a schoolteacher, as his mother wanted.

"You're a drunken fool, Werner," I said.

"Shall I go and arrest him?"

"Go and breathe all over him," I said.

Werner smiled. Werner had proved what a brilliant field agent he could be. Werner was very, very happy.

HE MADE a fuss of course. He wanted his lawyer and wanted to talk to his boss and to some friend of his in the government. I knew the type only too well; he was treating us as if *we'd* been caught stealing secrets for the Russians. He was still protesting when he departed with the arrest team. They were not impressed; they'd seen it all before. They were experienced men, brought in from the BfV's "political office" in Bonn.

They took him to the BfV office in Spandau but I decided they'd get nothing but indignation out of him this night. Tomorrow perhaps he'd simmer down a little and get nervous enough to say something worth hearing before the time came when they'd have to charge him or release him. Luckily it was a decision I wouldn't have to make. Meanwhile, I decided to go and see if there was anything to be got out of the woman.

Werner drove. He didn't speak much on the journey back

to Kreuzberg. I stared out of the window. Berlin is a sort of history book of twentieth-century violence, and every street corner brought a recollection of something I'd heard, seen, or read. We followed the road alongside the Landwehr Canal, which twists and turns through the heart of the city. Its oily water holds many dark secrets. Back in 1919, when the Spartakists attempted to seize the city by an armed uprising, two officers of the Horse Guards took the badly beaten Rosa Luxemburg—a Communist leader—from their headquarters at the Eden Hotel, next to the Zoo, shot her dead, and threw her into the canal. The officers pretended that she'd been carried off by angry rioters, but four months later her bloated corpse floated up and got jammed into a lock gate. Now, in East Berlin, they name streets after her.

But not all the ghosts go *into* this canal. In February 1920 a police sergeant pulled a young woman out of the canal at the Bendler Bridge. Taken to the Elisabeth Hospital in Lützowstrasse, she was later identified as the Grand Duchess Anastasia, the youngest daughter of the last Czar of All the Russias and only survivor of the massacre.

"This is it," said Werner, pulling in to the curb. "Good job there's a cop on the door, or we'd come back to find the car stripped to the chassis."

The address the contact had given was a shabby nineteenth-century tenement in a neighborhood virtually taken over by Turkish immigrants. The once imposing gray stone entrance, still pitted with splinter damage from the war, was defaced by brightly colored graffiti sprays. Inside the gloomy hallway there was a smell of spicy food and dirt and disinfectant.

These old houses have no numbered apartments, but we found the BfV men at the very top. There were two security locks on the door, but not much sign of anything inside to protect. Two men were still searching the hallway when we arrived. They were tapping the walls, prizing up floorboards, and poking screwdrivers deep into the plaster with that sort of inscrutable delight that comes to men blessed by governmental authority to be destructive.

It was typical of the overnight places the KGB provided for the faithful. Top floors: cold, cramped, and cheap. Perhaps they chose these sleazy accommodations to remind all concerned about the plight of the poor in the capitalist economy. Or perhaps in this sort of district there were fewer questions asked about comings and goings by all kinds of people at all kinds of hours.

No TV, no radio, no soft seats. Iron bedstead with an old gray blanket, four wooden chairs, a small plastic-topped table and upon it black bread roughly sliced, electric ring, dented kettle, tinned milk, dried coffee, and some sugar cubes wrapped to show they were from a Hilton Hotel. There were three dog-eared German paperback books—Dickens, Schiller, and a collection of crossword puzzles, mostly completed. On one of the two single beds a small case was opened and its contents displayed. It was obviously the woman's baggage: a cheap black dress, nylon underwear, low-heeled leather shoes, an apple and orange, and an English newspaper—*The Socialist Worker.*

A young BfV officer was waiting for me there. We exchanged greetings and he told me the woman had been given no more than a brief preliminary questioning. She'd offered to make a statement at first and then said she wouldn't, the officer said. He'd sent a man to get a typewriter so it could be taken down if she changed her mind again. He handed me some Westmarks, a driving license, and a passport; the contents of her handbag. The license and passport were British.

"I've got a pocket recorder," I told him without lowering my voice. "We'll sort out what to type and have it signed after I've spoken with her. I'll want you to witness her signature."

The woman was seated in the tiny kitchen. There were dirty cups on the table and some hairpins that I guessed had come from a search of the handbag she now held on her lap.

"The captain tells me that you want to make a statement," I said in English.

"Are you English?" she said. She looked at me and then at Werner. She showed no great surprise that we were both in dinner suits complete with fancy cuff links and patent-leather shoes. She must have realized we'd been on duty inside the house.

"Yes," I said. I signaled with my hand to tell Werner to leave the room.

"Are you in charge?" she asked. She had the exaggerated upper-class accent that shop girls use in Knightsbridge boutiques. "I want to know what I'm charged with. I warn you I know my rights. Am I under arrest?"

From the side table I picked up the bread knife and waved it at her. "Under Law 43 of the Allied Military Government legislation, still in force in this city, possession of this bread knife is an offense for which the death sentence can be imposed."

"You must be mad," she said. "The war was almost forty years ago."

I put the knife into a drawer and slammed it closed. She was startled by the sound. I moved a kitchen chair and sat on it so that I was facing her at a distance of only a yard or so. "You're not in Germany," I told her. "This is Berlin. And Decree 511, ratified in 1951, includes a clause that makes information gathering an offense for which you can get ten years in prison. Not spying, not intelligence work, just collecting information is an offense."

I put her passport on the table and turned the pages as if reading her name and occupation for the first time. "So don't talk to me about knowing your rights; you've got no rights."

From the passport I read aloud: "Carol Elvira Miller, born in London 1930, occupation: schoolteacher." Then I looked up at her. She returned my gaze with the calm, flat stare that the camera had recorded for her passport. Her hair was straight and short in pageboy style. She had clear blue eyes and a pointed nose, and the pert expression came naturally to her. She'd been pretty once, but now she was thin and drawn and —in dark conservative clothes and with no trace of makeup— well on the way to looking like a frail old woman.

"Elvira. That's a German name, isn't it?"

She showed no sign of fear. She brightened as women so often do at personal talk. "It's Spanish. Mozart used it in *Don Giovanni.*"

I nodded, "And Miller?"

She smiled nervously. She was not frightened, but it was the smile of someone who wanted to seem cooperative. My hectoring little speech had done the trick. "My father is German . . . was German. From Leipzig. He emigrated to England long before Hitler's time. My mother is English . . . from Newcastle," she added after a long pause.

"Married?"

"My husband died nearly ten years ago. His name was Johnson, but I went back to using my family name."

"Children?"

"A married daughter."

"Where do you teach?"

"I was a substitute teacher in London, but the amount of work I got grew less and less. For the last few months I've been virtually unemployed."

"You know what was in the envelope you collected from the car tonight?"

"I won't waste your time with excuses. I know it contained secrets of some description." She had the clear voice and pedantic manner of schoolteachers everywhere.

"And you know where it was going?"

"I want to make a statement. I told the other officer that. I want to be taken back to England and speak to someone in British security. Then I'll make a complete statement."

"Why?" I said. "Why are you so anxious to go back to England? You're a Russian agent; we both know that. What's the difference where you are when you're charged?"

"I've been stupid," she said. "I realize that now."

"Did you realize it before or after you were taken into custody?"

She pressed her lips together as if suppressing a smile. "It was a shock." She put her hands on the table. Her hands were white and wrinkled with the brown freckle marks that come with middle age. There were nicotine stains, and the ink from a leaky pen had marked finger and thumb. "I just can't stop trembling. Sitting here watching the security men searching through my luggage, I've had enough time to consider what a fool I've been. I love England. My father brought me up to love everything English."

Despite this contention she soon slipped back into speaking German. She wasn't German; she wasn't British. I saw the rootless feeling within her and recognized something of myself.

I said, "A man was it?" She looked at me and frowned. She'd been expecting reassurance, a smile in return for the smiles she'd given me and a promise that nothing too bad would happen to her. "A man . . . the one who enticed you into this foolishness?"

She must have heard some note of scorn in my voice. "No," she said. "It was all my own doing. I joined the Party fifteen years ago. After my husband died I wanted to keep myself occupied. So I became a very active worker for the teachers' union. And one day I thought, well, why not go the whole hog."

"What was the whole hog, Mrs. Miller?"

"My father's name was Müller; I may as well tell you that because you will soon find out. Hugo Müller. He changed it to Miller when he was naturalized. He wanted us all to be English." Again she pressed her hands flat on the table and looked at them while she spoke. It was as if she was blaming her hands for doing things of which she'd never really approved.

"I was asked to collect parcels, look after things, and so on. Later I began providing accommodation in my London flat. People were brought there late at night—Russians, Czechs, and so on—usually they spoke no English and no German either. Seamen sometimes, judging by their clothing. They always seemed to be ravenously hungry. Once there was a man dressed as a priest. He spoke Polish, but I managed to make myself understood. In the morning someone would come and collect them."

She sighed and then looked up at me to see how I was taking her confession. "I have a spare bedroom," she added, as if the propriety of their sleeping arrangements was more important than her services to the KGB.

She stopped talking for a long time and looked at her hands.

'They were fugitives," I said, to prompt her into talking again.

"I don't know who they were. Afterwards there was usually an envelope with a few pounds put through my letterbox, but I didn't do it for the money."

"Why did you do it?"

"I was a Marxist; I was serving the cause."

"And now?"

"They made a fool of me," she said. "They used me to do their dirty work. What did they care what happened to me if I got caught? What do they care now? What am I supposed to do?"

It sounded more like the bitter complaint of a woman abandoned by her lover than of an agent under arrest.

"You're supposed to enjoy being a martyr," I said. "That's the way the system works for them."

"I'll give you the names and addresses. I'll tell you everything I know." She leaned forward. "I don't want to go to prison. Will it all have to be in the newspapers?"

"Does it matter?"

"My married daughter is living in Canada. She's married to a Spanish boy she met on holiday. They've applied for Canadian citizenship but their papers haven't come through yet. It would be terrible if this trouble I'm in ruined their lives; they're so happy together."

"And this overnight accommodation you were providing for your Russian friends—when did that all stop?"

She looked up sharply, as if surprised that I could guess that it had stopped.

"The two jobs don't mix," I said. "The accommodation was just an interim task to see how reliable you were."

She nodded. "Two years ago," she said softly, "perhaps two and a half years."

"Then?"

"I came to Berlin for a week. They paid my fare. I went through to the East and spent a week in a training school. All the other students were German, but as you see I speak German well. My father always insisted that I kept up my German."

"A week at Potsdam?"

"Yes, just outside Potsdam, that's right."

"Don't miss out anything important, Mrs. Miller," I said.

"No, I won't," she promised nervously. "I was there for ten days learning about shortwave radios and microdots and so on. You probably know the sort of thing."

"Yes, I know the sort of thing. It's a training school for spies."

"Yes," she whispered.

"You're not going to tell me you came back from there without realizing you were a fully trained Russian spy, Mrs. Miller?"

She looked up and met my stare.

"No, I've told you, I was an enthusiastic Marxist. I was perfectly ready to be a spy for them. As I saw it, I was doing it on behalf of the oppressed and hungry people of the world. I suppose I still am a Marxist-Leninist."

"Then you must be an incurable romantic," I said.

"It was wrong of me to do what I did; I can see that, of course. England has been good to me. But half the world is starving and Marxism is the only solution."

"Don't lecture me, Mrs. Miller," I said. "I get enough of that from my office." I got up so that I could unbutton my overcoat and find my cigarettes. "Do you want a cigarette?" I said.

She gave no sign of having heard me.

"I'm trying to give them up," I said, "but I carry the cigarettes with me."

She still didn't answer. Perhaps she was too busy thinking about what might happen to her. I went to the window and looked out. It was too dark to see very much except Berlin's permanent false dawn: the greenish white glare that came from the floodlit "death strip" along the east side of the Wall. I knew this street well enough; I'd passed this block thousands of times. Since 1961, when the Wall was first built, following the snaky route of the Landwehr Canal had become the quickest way to get around the Wall from the neon glitter of the Kudamm to the floodlights of Checkpoint Charlie.

"Will I go to prison?" she said.

I didn't turn round. I buttoned my coat, pleased that I'd resisted the temptation to smoke. From my pocket I brought the tiny Pearlcorder tape machine. It was made of a bright silver metal. I made no attempt to hide it. I wanted her to see it.

"Will I go to prison?" she asked again.

"I don't know," I said. "But I hope so."

IT HAD taken no more than forty minutes to get her confession. Werner was waiting for me in the next room. There was no heating in that room. He was sitting on a kitchen chair, the fur collar of his coat pulled up round his ears so that it almost touched the rim of his hat.

"A good squeal?" he asked.

"You look like an undertaker, Werner," I said. "A very prosperous undertaker waiting for a very prosperous corpse."

"I've got to sleep," he said. "I can't take these late nights anymore. If you're going to hang on here, to type it all out, I'd rather go home now."

It was the drink that had got to him, of course. The ebullience of intoxication didn't last very long with Werner. Alcohol is a depressant and Werner's metabolic rate had slowed enough to render him unfit to drive.

"I'll drive," I said. "And I'll make the transcription on your typewriter."

"Sure," said Werner. I was staying with him in his apartment at Dahlem. And now, in his melancholy mood, he was anticipating his wife's reaction to us waking her up by arriving in the small hours of the morning. Werner's typewriter was a very noisy machine and he knew I'd want to finish the job before going to sleep. "Is there much of it?" he asked.

"It's short and sweet, Werner. But she's given us a few things that might make London Central scratch their heads and wonder."

"Such as?"

"Read it in the morning, Werner. We'll talk about it over breakfast."

IT WAS a beautiful Berlin morning. The sky was blue despite all those East German generating plants that burn brown coal so that pale smog sits over the city for so much of the year. Today the fumes of the *Braunkohle* were drifting elsewhere, and outside the birds were singing to celebrate it. Inside, a big wasp, a last survivor from the summer, buzzed around angrily.

Werner's Dahlem apartment was like a second home to me. I'd known it when it was a gathering place for an endless stream of Werner's oddball friends. In those days the furniture was old and Werner played jazz on a piano decorated with cigarette burns, and Werner's beautifully constructed model planes were hanging from the ceiling because that was the only place where they would not be sat upon.

Now it was all different. The old things had all been removed by Zena, his very young wife. Now the flat was done to her taste: expensive modern furniture and a big rubber plant and a rug that hung on the wall and bore the name of the "artist" who'd woven it. The only thing that remained from the old days was the lumpy sofa that converted to the lumpy bed on which I'd slept.

The three of us were sitting in the "breakfast room," a counter at the end of the kitchen. It was arranged like a lunch counter with Zena playing the role of bartender. From here there was a view through the window, and we were high enough to see the sun-edged treetops of the Grunewald just a block or two away. Zena was squeezing oranges in an electric juicer, and in the automatic coffee-maker the coffee was dripping, its rich aroma floating through the room.

We were talking about marriage. I said, "The tragedy of marriage is that while all women marry thinking that their man will change, all men marry believing their wife will never change. Both are invariably disappointed."

"What rot," said Zena as she poured the juice into three glasses. "Men do change."

She bent down to better see the level of the juice and ensure that we all got precisely the same amount. It was a legacy of the Prussian family background of which she was so proud, despite the fact that she'd never even seen the old family homeland. For Prussians like to think of themselves not only as the conscience of the world, but also its final judge and jury.

"Don't encourage him, Zena darling," said Werner. "That contrived Oscar Wilde-ish assertion is just Bernard's way of annoying wives."

Zena didn't let it go; she liked to argue with me. "Men change. It's men who usually leave home and break up the marriage. And it's because they change."

"Good juice," I said, sipping some.

"Men go out to work. Men want promotion in their jobs and they aspire to the higher social class of their superiors. Then they feel their wives are inadequate and start looking for a wife who knows the manners and vocabulary of that class they want to join."

"You're right," I admitted. "I meant that men don't change in the way that their women want them to change."

She smiled. She knew that I was commenting on the way she had changed poor Werner from being an easygoing and somewhat bohemian character into a devoted and obedient husband. It was Zena who had got him to stop smoking and made him diet enough to reduce his waistline. And it was Zena who approved everything he bought to wear, from swimming trunks to tuxedo. In this respect Zena regarded me as her opponent. I was the bad influence who could undo all her good work, and that was something Zena was determined to prevent.

She climbed up onto the stool. She was so well proportioned that you only noticed how tiny she was when she did such things. She had long, dark hair and this morning she'd clipped it back into a ponytail that reached down to her shoulder blades. She was wearing a red cotton kimono with a wide black sash around her middle. She'd not missed any sleep that night and her eyes were bright and clear; she'd even found time enough to put on a touch of makeup. She didn't need makeup —she was only twenty-two years old and there was no disputing her beauty—but the makeup was something from behind which she preferred to face the world.

The coffee was very dark and strong. She liked it like that, but I poured a lot of milk into mine. The buzzer on the oven sounded and Zena went to get the warm rolls. She put them into a small basket with a red-checked cloth before offering them to us. *"Brötchen,"* she said. Zena was born and brought up in Berlin, but she didn't call the bread rolls *Schrippe* the way the rest of the population of Berlin did. Zena didn't want to be identified with Berlin; she preferred keeping her options open.

"Any butter?" I said, breaking open the bread roll.

"We don't eat it," said Zena. "It's bad for you."

"Give Bernie some of that new margarine," said Werner.

"You should lose some weight," Zena told me. "I wouldn't even be eating bread if I were you."

"There are all kinds of other things I do that you wouldn't do if you were me," I said. The wasp settled in my hair and I brushed it away.

She decided not to get into that one. She rolled up a newspaper and aimed some blows at the wasp. Then with unconcealed ill-humor she went to the refrigerator and brought me a plastic tub of margarine.

"Thanks," I said. "I'm catching the morning flight. I'll get out of your way as soon as I'm shaved."

"No hurry," said Werner to smooth things over. He had already shaved, of course; Zena wouldn't have let him have breakfast if he'd turned up unshaven. "So you got all your typing done last night," he said. "I should have stayed up and helped."

"It wasn't necessary. I'll have the translation done in London. I appreciate you and Zena giving me a place to sleep, to say nothing of the coffee last night and Zena's great breakfast this morning."

I overdid the appreciation I suppose. I'm prone to do this when I'm nervous, and Zena was a great expert at making me nervous.

"I was damned tired," said Werner.

Zena shot me a glance, but when she spoke it was to Werner. "You were drunk," she said. "I thought you were supposed to be working last night."

"We were, darling," said Werner.

"There wasn't much drinking, Zena," I said.

"Werner gets drunk on the smell of a barmaid's apron," said Zena.

Werner opened his mouth to object to this put-down. Then he realized that he could only challenge it by claiming to have drunk a great deal. He sipped some coffee instead.

"I've seen her before," said Werner.

"The woman?"

"What's her name?"

"She says it's Müller, but she was married to a man named Johnson at one time. Here? You've seen her here? She said she lives in England."

"She went to the school in Potsdam," said Werner. He smiled at my look of surprise. "I read your report when I got up this morning. You don't mind, do you?"

"Of course not. I wanted you to read it. There might be developments."

"Was this to do with Erich Stinnes?" said Zena. She waved the wasp away from her head.

"Yes," I said. "It was his information."

She nodded and poured herself more coffee. It was difficult to believe that not so long ago she'd been in love with Erich Stinnes. It was difficult to believe that she'd risked her life to protect him and that she was still having physiotherapy sessions because of injuries she'd suffered in his defense.

But Zena was young, and romantic. For both of those reasons, her passions could be of short duration. And for both those reasons, it could well be that she had never been in love with him, but merely in love with the idea of herself in love.

Werner seemed not to notice the mention of Erich Stinnes's name. That was Werner's way—*honi soit qui mal y pense.* Evil to him who evil thinks—that could well be Werner's motto, for Werner was too generous and considerate to ever think the worst of anyone. And even when the worst was evident, Werner was ready to forgive. Zena's flagrant love affair with Frank Harrington—the head of our Berlin Field Unit, the Berlin Resident—had made me angrier with her than Werner had been.

Some people said that Werner was the sort of masochist who got a perverse pleasure from the knowledge that his wife had gone off to live with Frank, but I knew Werner too well to go in for that sort of instant psychology. Werner was a tough guy who played the game by his own rules. Maybe some of his rules were flexible, but God help anyone who overstepped the line that Werner drew. Werner was an Old Testament man, and his wrath and vengeance could be terrible. I know, and Werner knows I know. That's what makes us so close that nothing can come between us, not even the cunning little Zena.

"I've seen that Miller woman somewhere," said Werner. "I never forget a face."

He watched the wasp. It was sleepy, crawling slowly up the wall. Werner reached for Zena's newspaper, but the wasp, sensing danger, flew away.

Zena was still thinking of Erich Stinnes. "We do all the work," she said bitterly. "Bernard gets all the credit. And Erich Stinnes gets all the money."

She was referring to the way in which Stinnes, a KGB major, had been persuaded to come over to work for us and given a big cash payment. She reached for the jug, and some coffee dripped onto the hot plate, making a loud, hissing sound. When she'd poured coffee for herself, she put the very hot jug onto the tiles of the counter. The change of temperature must have made the jug crack, for there was a sound like a pistol shot and the hot coffee flowed across the countertop so that we all jumped to our feet to avoid being scalded.

Zena grabbed some paper towels and, standing well back from the coffee flowing onto the tiled floor, dabbed them around. "I put it down too hard," she said when the mess was cleared away.

"I think you did, Zena," I said.

"It was already cracked," said Werner.

Then he brought the rolled newspaper down on the wasp and killed it.

Chapter 2

IT WAS eight o'clock that evening in London when I finally delivered my report to my immediate boss, Dicky Cruyer, German Stations Controller. I'd attached a complete translation too, as I knew Dicky wasn't exactly bilingual.

"Congratulations," he said. "One up to Comrade Stinnes, eh?" He shook the flimsy sheets of my hastily written report as if something might fall from between the pages. He'd already heard my tape and had my oral account of the Berlin trip so there was little chance that he'd read the report very thoroughly, especially if it meant missing his dinner.

"No one in Bonn will thank us," I warned him.

"They have all the evidence they need," said Dicky with a sniff.

"I was on the phone to Berlin an hour ago," I said. "He's pulling all the strings that can be pulled."

"What does his boss say?"

"He's spending his Christmas vacation in Egypt. No one can find him," I said.

"What a sensible man," said Dicky with admiration that was both sincere and undisguised. "Was he informed of the impending arrest of his secretary?"

"Not by us, but that would be the regular BfV procedure."

"Have you phoned Bonn this evening? What do BfV reckon the chances of a statement from him?"

"Better we stay out of it, Dicky."

Dicky looked at me while he thought about this and then, deciding I was right, tried another aspect of the same problem. "Have you seen Stinnes since you handed him over to London Debriefing Centre?"

"I gather the current policy is to keep me away from him."

"Come along," said Dicky, smiling to humor me in my state of paranoia. "You're not saying you're still suspect?" He stood up from behind the rosewood table that he used instead of a desk and got a transparent plastic folding chair for me.

"My wife defected." I sat down. Dicky's hand removed his visitors' chairs on the pretext of making more space. His actual motive was to provide an excuse for him to use the conference rooms along the corridor. Dicky liked to use the conference rooms; it made him feel important and it meant that his name was exhibited in little plastic letters on the notice board opposite the top-floor lifts.

His folding chairs were the most uncomfortable seats in the building, but Dicky didn't worry about this as he never sat in them. And anyway, I didn't want to sit chatting with him. There was still work to clear up before I could go home.

"That's all past history," said Dicky, running a thin bony hand through his curly hair so that he could take a surreptitious look at his big black wristwatch, the kind that works deep under water.

I'd always suspected that Dicky would be more comfortable with his hair cut short and brushed, and in the dark suits, white shirts, and old school ties that were de rigueur for senior staff. But he persisted in being the only one of us who wore faded denims, cowboy boots, colored neckerchiefs, and black leather because he thought it would help to identify him as an infant prodigy. But perhaps I had it the wrong way round; perhaps Dicky would have been happier to keep the trendy garb and be "creative" in an advertising agency.

He zipped the front of his jacket up and down again and said, "You're the local hero. You are the one who brought Stinnes to us at a time when everyone here said it couldn't be done."

"Is that what they were saying? I wish I'd known. The way I heard it, a lot of people were saying I did everything to avoid bringing him in because I was frightened his debriefing would drop me into it."

"Well, anyone who was spreading that sort of story is now looking pretty damned stupid."

"I'm not in the clear yet, Dicky. You know it and I know it, so let's stop all this bullshit."

He held up his hand as if to ward off a blow. "You're still not clear on paper," said Dicky. "On paper . . . and you know why?"

"No, I don't know why. Tell me."

Dicky sighed. "For the simple but obvious reason that this Department needs an excuse to hold Stinnes in London Debriefing Centre and keep on pumping him. Without an ongoing investigation of our own staff, we'd have to hand Stinnes over to MI5. . . . That's why the Department haven't cleared you yet: it's a departmental necessity, Bernard, nothing sinister about it."

"Who's in charge of the Stinnes debriefing?" I asked.

"Don't look at me, old friend. Stinnes is a hot potato. I don't want any part of that one. Neither does Bret . . . no one up here on the top floor wants anything to do with it."

"Things could change," I said. "If Stinnes gives us a couple more winners like this one, then a few people will start to see that being in charge of the Stinnes debriefing could be the road to fame and fortune."

"I don't think so," said Dicky. "The tip-off you handled in Berlin was just for openers . . . a few quick forays before Moscow tumbles to what's happening to their networks. Once the dust settles, the interrogators will take Stinnes through the files . . . right?"

"Files? You mean they'll be poking into all our past operations?"

"Not *all* of them. I don't suppose they'll go back to determine how Christopher Marlowe discovered that the Spanish Armada had sailed." Dicky permitted himself a smile at this joke. "It's obvious that the Department will want to discover how good our guesses were. They'll play all the games again, but this time they'll know which ones have a happy ending."

"And you'll go along with that?"

"They won't consult me, old son. I'm just German Stations Controller; I'm not the D-G. I'm not even on the Policy Committee."

"Giving Stinnes access to departmental archives would be showing a lot of trust in him."

"You know what the old man's like. Deputy D-G came in yesterday on one of his rare visits to the building. He's enraptured about the progress of the Stinnes debriefing."

"If Stinnes is a plant . . ."

"Ah, if Stinnes is a plant . . ."

Dicky sank down in his Charles Eames chair and put his feet on the matching footstool. The night was dark outside and the windowpanes were like ebony reflecting a perfect image of the room. Only the antique desk light was on; it made a pool of light on the table where the report and transcript were placed side by side. Dicky almost disappeared into the gloom except when the light reflected from the brass buckle of his belt or shone on the gold medallion he wore suspended inside his open-neck shirt. "But the idea that Stinnes is a plant is hard to sustain when he's just given us three well-placed KGB agents in a row."

He looked at his watch before shouting "coffee" loudly enough for his secretary to hear in the adjoining room. When Dicky worked late, his secretary worked late too. He didn't trust the duty-roster staff with making his coffee.

"Will he talk, this one you arrested in Berlin? He had a year with the Bonn Defense Ministry, I notice from the file."

"I didn't arrest him; we left it to the Germans. Yes, he'll talk if they push him hard enough. They have the evidence and—thanks to Volkmann—they're holding the woman who came to collect it from the car."

"And I'm sure you put all that in your report. Are you now the official secretary of the Werner Volkmann fan club? Or is this something you do for all your old school chums?"

"He's very good at what he does."

"And so we all agree, but don't tell me that but for Volkmann, we wouldn't have picked up the woman. Staking out the car is standard procedure. Ye gods, Bernard, any probationary cop would do that as a matter of course."

"A commendation would work wonders for him."

"Well, he's not getting any bloody commendation from me. Just because he's your close friend, you think you can inveigle any kind of praise and privilege out of me for him."

"It wouldn't cost anything, Dicky," I said mildly.

"No, it wouldn't cost anything," said Dicky sarcastically. "Not until the next time he makes some monumental cock-up. Then someone asks me how come I commended him, then it would cost something. It would cost me a chewing out and maybe a promotion."

"Yes, Dicky," I said.

Promotion? Dicky was two years younger than me and he'd already been promoted several rungs beyond his competence. What promotion did he have his eyes on now? He'd only just fought off Bret Rensselaer's attempt to take over the German desk. I'd thought he'd be satisfied to consolidate his good fortune.

"And what do you make of this Englishwoman?" He tapped the roughly typed transcript of her statement. "Looks as if you got her talking."

"I couldn't stop her," I said.

"Like that, was it? I don't want to go all through it again tonight. Anything important?"

"Some inconsistencies that should be followed up."

"For instance?"

"She was working in London, handling selected items for immediate shortwave radio transmission to Moscow."

"Must have been bloody urgent," said Dicky. So he'd noticed that already. Had he waited to see if I brought it up? "And that means damned good. Right? I mean, not even handled through the Embassy radio, so it was a source they wanted to keep very very secret."

"Fiona's material probably," I said.

"I wondered if you'd twig that," said Dicky. "It was obviously the stuff your wife was betraying out of our day-to-day operational files."

He liked to twist the knife in the wound. He held me personally responsible for what Fiona had done; he'd virtually said so on more than one occasion.

"But the material kept coming."

Dicky frowned. "What are you getting at?"

"It kept coming. First-grade material even after Fiona ran for it."

"This woman's transmitted material wasn't all from the same source," said Dicky. "I remember what she said when you played your tape to me."

He picked up the transcript and tried to find what he wanted in the muddle of *humm*s and *hahh*s and "indistinct passage" marks that are always a part of transcripts from such tape recordings. He put the sheets down again.

"Well anyway, I remember there were two assignment

codes: JAKE and IRONFOOT. Is that what's worrying you?"

"We should follow it up," I said. "I don't like loose ends like that. The dates suggest that Fiona was IRONFOOT. Who the hell was JAKE?"

"The Fiona material is our worry. Whatever else Moscow gets—and is still getting—is a matter for Five. You know that, Bernard. It's not our job to search high and low to find Russian spies."

"I still think we should check this woman's statement against what Stinnes knows."

"Stinnes is nothing to do with me, Bernard. I've just told you that."

"Well, I think he should be. It's madness that we don't have access to him without going to Debriefing Centre for permission."

"Let me tell you something, Bernard," said Dicky, leaning well back in the soft leather seat and adopting the manner of an Oxford don explaining the law of gravity to a delivery boy. "When London Debriefing Centre get through with Stinnes, heads will roll up here on the top floor. You know the monumental cock-ups that have dogged the work of this Department for the last few years. Now we'll have chapter and verse on every decision made up here while Stinnes was running things in Berlin. Every decision made by senior staff will be scrutinized with twenty-twenty hindsight. It could get messy; people with a history of bad decisions are going to be axed very smartly."

Dicky smiled. He could afford to smile; Dicky had never made a decision in his life. Whenever something decisive was about to happen, Dicky went home with a headache.

"And you think that whoever's in charge of the Stinnes debriefing will be unpopular?"

"Running a witch-hunt is not likely to be a social asset," said Dicky.

I thought "witch-hunt" was an inaccurate description of the weeding out of incompetents, but there would be plenty who would favor Dicky's terminology.

"And that's not only my opinion," he added. "No one wants to take Stinnes. And I don't want you saying we should have responsibility for him."

Dicky's secretary brought coffee.

"I was just coming, Mr. Cruyer," she said apologetically. She was a mousy little widow whose every sheet of typing was a patchwork of white correcting paint. At one time Dicky had had a shapely twenty-five-year-old divorcée as secretary, but his wife, Daphne, had made him get rid of her. At the time, Dicky had pretended that firing the secretary was his idea; he said it was because she didn't boil the water properly for his coffee. "Your wife phoned. She wanted to know what time to expect you for dinner."

"And what did you say?" Dicky asked her.

The poor woman hesitated, worrying if she'd done the right thing. "I said you were at a meeting and I would call her back."

"Tell my wife not to wait dinner for me. I'll get a bite to eat somewhere or other."

"If you want to get away, Dicky," I said, rising to my feet.

"Sit down, Bernard. We can't waste a decent cup of coffee. I'll be home soon enough. Daphne knows what this job is like; eighteen hours a day lately." It was not a soft, melancholy reflection but a loud proclamation to the world, or at least to me and to his secretary, who departed to pass the news on to Daphne.

I nodded but I couldn't help wondering if Dicky was scheduling a visit to some other lady. Lately I'd noticed a gleam in his eye and a spring in his step and a most unusual willingness to stay late at the office.

Dicky got up from his easy chair and fussed over the antique butler's tray which his secretary had placed so carefully on his side table. He emptied the Spode cups of the hot water and half filled each warmed cup with black coffee. Dicky was extremely particular about his coffee. Twice a week he sent one of the drivers to collect a packet of freshly roasted beans from Mr. Higgins in South Moulton Street—chagga, no blends—and it had to be ground just before being brewed.

"That's good," he said, sipping it with all the studied attention of the connoisseur he claimed to be. Having approved the coffee, he poured some for me.

"Wouldn't it be better to stay away from Stinnes, Bernard? He doesn't belong to us any longer, does he?" He smiled. It was a direct order; I knew Dicky's style.

"Can I have milk or cream or something in mine?" I said. "That strong black brew you make keeps me awake at night."

He always had a jug of cream and a bowl of sugar brought in with his coffee although he never used either. He once told me that in his regimental officers mess, the cream was always on the table but it was considered bad form to take any. I wondered if there were a lot of people like Dicky in the Army; it was a dreadful thought. He brought the cream to me.

"You're getting old, Bernard. Did you ever think of jogging? I run three miles every morning—summer, winter, Christmas, every morning without fail."

"Is it doing you any good?" I asked as he poured cream for me from the cow-shaped silver jug.

"Ye gods, Bernard. I'm fitter now than I was at twenty-five. I swear I am."

"What kind of shape were you in at twenty-five?" I said.

"Damned good." He put the jug down so that he could run his fingers round the brass-buckled leather belt that held up his jeans. He sucked in his stomach to exaggerate his slim figure and then slammed himself in the gut with a flattened hand. Even without the intake of breath, his lack of fat was impressive. Especially when you took into account the countless long lunches he charged against his expense account.

"But not as good as now?" I persisted.

"I wasn't fat and flabby the way you are, Bernard. I didn't huff and puff every time I went up a flight of stairs."

"I thought Bret Rensselaer would take over the Stinnes debriefing."

"'Debriefing,'" said Dicky suddenly. "How I hate that

word. You get briefed and maybe briefed again, but there is no way anyone can be debriefed."

"I thought Bret would jump at it. He's been out of a job since Stinnes was enrolled."

Dicky gave the tiniest chuckle and rubbed his hands together. "Out of a job since he tried to take over my desk and failed. That's what you mean, isn't it?"

"Was he after your desk?" I said innocently, although Dicky had been providing me with a blow-by-blow account of Bret's tactics and his own counterploys.

"Jesus Christ, Bernard, you know he was. I told you all that."

"So what's he got lined up now?"

"He'd like to take over in Berlin when Frank goes."

Frank Harrington's job as head of the Berlin Field Unit was one I coveted, but it meant close liaison with Dicky, maybe even taking orders from him sometimes (although such orders were always wrapped up in polite double-talk and signed by Deputy Controller Europe or a member of the London Central Policy Committee). It wasn't exactly a role that the autocratic Bret Rensselaer would cherish.

"Berlin? Bret? Would he like that job?"

"The rumor is that Frank will get his K. and then retire."

"And so Bret plans to sit in Berlin until his retirement comes round and hope that he'll get a K. too?" It seemed unlikely. Bret's social life centred on the swanky jet-setters of London South West One. I couldn't see him sweating it out in Berlin.

"Why not?" said Dicky, who seemed to get a flushed face whenever the subject of knighthoods came up.

"Why not?" I repeated. "Bret can't speak the language, for one thing."

"Come along, Bernard!" said Dicky, whose command of German was about on a par with Bret's. "He'll be running the show; he won't be required to pass himself off as bricklayer from Prenzlauer Berg."

A palpable hit for Dicky. Bernard Samson had spent his youth masquerading as just such lowly coarse-accented East German citizens.

"It's not just a matter of throwing gracious dinner parties in that big house in the Grunewald," I said. "Whoever takes over in Berlin has to know the streets and alleys. He'll also need to know the crooks and hustlers who come in to sell bits and pieces of intelligence."

"That's what you say," said Dicky, pouring himself more coffee. He held up the jug. "More for you?" And when I shook my head he continued: "That's because you fancy yourself doing Frank's job . . . don't deny it, you know it's true. You've always wanted Berlin. But times have changed, Bernard. The days of rough-and-tumble stuff are over and done with. That was okay in your father's time, when we were a de facto occupying power. But now—whatever the lawyers say—the Germans have to be treated as equal partners. What the Berlin job needs is a smoothie like Bret, someone who can charm the natives and get things done by gentle persuasion."

"Can I change my mind about the coffee?" I said. I suspected that Dicky's views were those prevailing among the top-floor mandarins. There was no way I'd be on a shortlist of smoothies who got things done by means of gentle persuasion, so this was goodbye to my chances of Berlin.

"Don't be so damned gloomy about it," said Dicky as he poured coffee. "It's mostly dregs, I'm afraid. You didn't really think you were in line for Frank's job, did you?" He smiled at the idea.

"There isn't enough money in Central Funding to entice me back to Berlin on any permanent basis. I spent half my life there. I deserve my London posting and I'm hanging on to it."

"London is the only place to be," said Dicky.

But I wasn't fooling him. My indignation was too strong and my explanation too long. A public-school man like Dicky would have done a better job of concealing his bitterness. He would have smiled coldly and said that a Berlin posting would be "super" in such a way that it seemed he didn't care.

I'D ONLY been in my office for about ten minutes when I heard Dicky coming down the corridor. Dicky and I must have been the only ones still working, apart from the night-duty people, and his footsteps sounded unnaturally sharp, as sounds do at night. And I could always recognize the sound of Dicky's high-heeled cowboy boots.

"Do you know what those stupid sods have done?" he asked, standing in the doorway, arms akimbo and feet apart, like Wyatt Earp coming into the saloon at Tombstone. I knew he would get on the phone to Berlin as soon as I left the office; it was always easier to meddle in other people's work than to get on with his own.

"Released him?"

"Right," he said. My accurate guess angered him even more, as if he thought I might have been party to this development. "How did you know?"

"I didn't know. But with you standing there blowing your top it wasn't difficult to guess."

"They released him an hour ago. Direct instructions from Bonn. The government can't survive another scandal, is the line they're taking. How can they let politics interfere with our work?"

I noted the nice turn of phrase: "our work."

"It's all politics," I said calmly. "Espionage is about politics. Remove the politics and you don't need espionage or any of the paraphernalia of it."

"By paraphernalia you mean us, I suppose. Well, I knew you'd have some bloody smart answer."

"We don't run the world, Dicky. We can pick it over and then report on it. After that it's up to the politicians."

"I suppose so."

The anger was draining out of him now. He was often given

to these violent explosions, but they didn't last long providing he had someone to shout at.

"Your secretary gone?" I asked.

He nodded. That explained everything—usually it was his poor secretary who got the brunt of Dicky's fury when the world didn't run to his complete satisfaction. "I'm going too," he said, looking at his watch.

"I've got a lot more work to do," I told him. I got up from my desk and put papers into the secure filing cabinet and turned the combination lock. Dicky still stood there. I looked at him and raised an eyebrow.

"And that bloody Miller woman," said Dicky. "She tried to knock herself off."

"They didn't release her too?"

"No, of course not. But they let her keep her sleeping tablets. Can you imagine that sort of stupidity? She said they were aspirins and that she needed them for period pains. They believed her, and as soon as they left her alone for five minutes she swallowed the whole bottle of them."

"And?"

"She's in the Steglitz Clinic. They pumped her stomach; it sounds as if she'll be okay. But I ask you . . . God knows when she'll be fit enough for more interrogation."

"I'd let it go, Dicky."

But he stood there, obviously unwilling to depart without some further word of consolation.

"And it would all happen tonight," he added petulantly, "just when I'm going out to dinner."

I looked at him and nodded. So I was right about an assignation. He bit his lip, angry at having let slip his secret. "That's strictly between you and me of course."

"My lips are sealed," I said.

And the German Stations Controller marched off to his dinner date. It was sobering to realize that this man in the front line of the Western World's intelligence system couldn't even keep his own infidelities secret.

WHEN Dicky Cruyer had gone I went downstairs to the film department and took a reel of film from the rack that was waiting for the filing clerk. It was still in the wrapping paper with the courier's marks on it. I placed the film in position on the editing bench and laced it up. Then I dimmed the lights and watched the screen.

The titles were in Hungarian and so was the commentary. It was film of a security conference that had just taken place in Budapest. There was nothing very secret; the film had been made by the Hungarian Film Service for distribution to news agencies. This copy was to be used for identification purposes, so that we had up-to-date pictures of their officials.

The conference building was a fine old mansion in a well-kept park. The film crew had done exactly what was expected of them: they'd filmed the big black shiny cars arriving, they'd got pictures of Army officers and civilians walking up the marble steps, and the inevitable shot of delegates round a huge table, smiling amicably at each other.

I kept the film running until the camera panned round the table. It came to a nameplate FIONA SAMSON and there was my wife—more beautiful than ever, perfectly groomed, and smiling for the cameraman. I stopped the film. The commentary growled to a halt and she froze, her hand awkwardly splayed, her face strained, and her smile false. I don't know how long I sat there looking at her. But suddenly the door of the editing room banged open and flooded everything with bright yellow light from the corridor.

"I'm sorry, Mr. Samson. I thought everyone had finished work."

"It's not work," I said. "Just something I remembered."

Chapter 3

So Dicky, having scoffed at the notion that I was being kept away from Stinnes, had virtually ordered me not to go near him. Well, that was all right. For the first time in months I was able to get my desk more or less clear. I worked from nine to five and even found myself able to join in some of those earnest conversations about what had been on TV the previous evening.

And at last I was able to spend more time with my children. For the past six months I had been almost a stranger to them. They never asked about Fiona, but now, when we'd finished putting up the paper decorations for Christmas, I sat them down and told them that their mother was safe and well but that she'd had to go abroad to work.

"I know," said Billy. "She's in Germany with the Russians."

"Who told you that?" I said.

I hadn't told him. I hadn't told anyone. Just after Fiona's defection, the Director-General had addressed all the staff in the downstairs dining room—the D-G was an Army man with undisguised admiration for the late Field Marshal Montgomery's techniques with the lower ranks—and told us that no mention of Fiona's defection was to be included in any written reports, and it was on no account to be discussed outside the building. The Prime Minister had been told, and anyone who mattered at the Foreign Office knew by means of the daily report. Otherwise the whole business was to be "kept to ourselves."

"Grandpa told us," said Billy.

Well, that was someone the D-G hadn't reckoned with: my irrepressible father-in-law, David Kimber-Hutchinson, by his own admission a self-made man.

"What else did he tell you?" I asked.

"I can't remember," said Billy. He was a bright child, academic, calculating, and naturally inquisitive. His memory was formidable. I wondered if it was his way of saying that he didn't much want to talk about it.

"He said that Mummy may not be back for a long time," said Sally. She was younger than Billy, generous but introverted in that mysterious way that so many second children are and closer to her mother. Sally was never moody in the way Billy could be, but she was more sensitive. She had taken her mother's absence much better than I'd feared, but I was still concerned about her.

"That's what I was going to tell you," I said. I was relieved that the children were taking this discussion about their mother's disappearance so calmly. Fiona had always arranged their outings and gone to immense trouble to organize every last detail of their parties. My efforts were a poor substitute, and we all knew it.

"Mummy is really there to spy for *us,* isn't she, Daddy?" said Billy.

"Ummm," I said. It was a difficult one to respond to. I was afraid that Fiona or her KGB colleagues would grab the children and take them to her in East Berlin or Moscow or somewhere, as she once tried to. If she tried again, I didn't want to make it easier for her to succeed, and yet I couldn't bring myself to warn them against their own mother. "No one knows," I said vaguely.

"Sure, it's a secret," said Billy with that confident shrug of the shoulders used by Dicky Cruyer to help emphasize the obvious. "Don't worry, I won't tell."

"It's better just to say she's gone away," I said.

"Grandpa said we're to say Mummy's in hospital in Switzerland."

It was typical of David to invent his own loony deception story and involve my children in it.

"The fact is that Mummy and I have separated," I said in a

rush. "And I've asked a lady from my office to come round and see us this afternoon."

There was a long silence. Billy looked at Sally and Sally looked at her new shoes.

"Aren't you going to ask her name?" I said desperately.

Sally looked at me with her big blue eyes. "Will she be staying?" she said.

"We don't need anyone else to live here. You have Nanny to look after you," I said, avoiding the question.

"Will she use our bathroom?" said Sally.

"No. I don't think so," I said. "Why?"

"Nanny hates visitors using our bathroom."

This was a new insight into Nanny, a quiet plump girl from a Devon village who spoke in whispers, was transfixed by all TV programmes, ate chocolates by the truckload, and never complained. "Well, I'll make sure she uses my bathroom," I promised.

"Must she come today?" said Billy.

"I invited her for tea so that we could all be together," I said. "Then, when you go to bed, I'm taking her to dinner in a restaurant."

"I wish we could all go out to dinner in a restaurant," said Billy, who had recently acquired a blue blazer and long trousers and wanted to wear them to good effect.

"Which restaurant?" said Sally.

"The Greek restaurant where Billy had his birthday."

"The waiters sang 'Happy Birthday' for him."

"So I heard."

"You were away."

"I was in Berlin."

"Why don't you tell them it's your girlfriend's birthday," said Sally. "They'll be awfully nice to her, and they'd never find out."

"She's not my girlfriend," I said. "She's just a friend."

"She's his boyfriend," said Billy. Sally laughed.

"She's just a friend," I said soberly.

" 'All my lovers and I are just good friends,' " said Sally, putting on her "Hollywood" voice.

"She heard that in a film," Billy explained.

"Her name is Gloria," I said.

"We've nothing for tea," said Sally. "Not even biscuits."

"Nanny will make toast," said Billy to reassure me. "She always makes toast when there's nothing for tea. Toast with butter and jam. It's quite nice really."

"I believe she'll be bringing a cake."

"Auntie Tessa brings the best cakes," said Sally. "She gets them from a shop near Harrods."

"That's because Auntie Tessa is very rich," said Billy. "She has a Rolls-Royce."

"She comes here in a Volkswagen," said Sally.

"That's because she doesn't want to be flash," said Billy. "I heard her say that on the phone once."

"I think she's *very* flash," said Sally in a voice heavy with admiration. "Couldn't Auntie Tessa be your girlfriend, Daddy?"

"Auntie Tessa is married to Uncle George," I said before things got out of hand.

"But Auntie Tessa isn't faithful to him," Sally told Billy. Before I could contradict this uncontradictable fact, Sally after a glance at me added, "I heard Daddy tell Mummy that one day when I shouldn't have been listening."

"What kind of cake will she bring?" said Billy.

"Will she bring chocolate layer cake?" said Sally.

"I like rum babas best," said Billy. "Especially when they have lots of rum on them."

They were still discussing their favorite cakes—a discussion that can go for a very long time—when the doorbell rang.

Gloria Zsuzsa Kent was a tall and very beautiful blonde whose twentieth birthday was soon approaching. She was what the service called an "Executive Officer," which meant in theory that she could be promoted to Director-General. Armed with good marks from school and fluent Hungarian learned from her parents, she joined the Department on the vague promise of being given paid leave to go to university. It probably seemed like a good idea at the time. Dicky Cruyer had got his Army service—and Bret his studies at Oxford—credited toward promotion. Now financial cutbacks made it look as if she was stuck with nothing beyond a second-rate office job.

She took off her expensive fur-lined suede coat and the children gave whoops of joy on discovering that she'd brought the rum baba and chocolate layer cake that were their favorites.

"You're a mind reader," I said. I kissed her. Under the children's gaze I made sure it was no more than the sort of peck you get along with the Legion of Honor.

She smiled as the children gave her a kiss of thanks before they went off to set the table for tea. "I adore your children, Bernard."

"You chose their favorite cakes," I said.

"I have two young sisters. I know what children like."

She sat down near the fire and warmed her hands. Already the afternoon light was fading and the room was dark. There was just a rim of daylight on her straw-colored hair and the red glow of the fire's light on her hands and face.

Nanny came in and exchanged amiably noisy greetings with Gloria. They had spoken on the phone several times and the similarity in their ages gave them enough in common to allay my fears about Nanny's reaction to the news that I had a "girlfriend."

To me Nanny said, "The children want to make toast by the fire in here, but I can easily do it in the toaster."

"Let's all sit by the fire and have tea," I said.

Nanny looked at me and said nothing.

"What's wrong, Nanny?"

"It would be better if we eat in the kitchen. The children will make a lot of crumbs and mess on the carpet, and Mrs. Dias won't come in again to clean until Tuesday."

"You're a fuss pot, Nanny," I said.

"I'll tidy up, Doris," Gloria told Nanny. Doris! Good grief, those two were getting along too nicely!

"And Mr. Samson," said Nanny tentatively. "The children were invited to spend the evening with one of Billy's school friends. The Dubois family. They live near Swiss Cottage. I promised to phone them before five."

"Sure, that's okay. If the children want to go. Are you going too?"

"Yes, I'd like to. They have *Singin' in the Rain* on video, and they'll serve soup and a snack meal afterwards. Other children will be there. We'd be back rather late, but the children could sleep late tomorrow."

"Well, drive carefully, Nanny. The town's full of drunk drivers on a Saturday night."

I heard cheers from the kitchen when Nanny went back and announced my decision. And tea was a delight. The children recited *If* for Gloria, and Billy did three new magic tricks he'd been practicing for the school Christmas concert.

"As I remember it," I said, "I'd promised to take you to the Greek restaurant for dinner, have a drink or two at Les Ambassadeurs, and then drive you home to your parents."

"This is better," she said. We were in bed. I said nothing. "It is better, isn't it?" she asked anxiously.

I kissed her. "It's madness and you know it."

"Nanny and the children won't be back for hours."

"I mean you and me. When will you realize that I'm twenty years older than you are?"

"I love you and you love me."

"I didn't say I loved you," I said.

She pulled a face. She resented the fact that I wouldn't say I loved her, but I was adamant; she was so young that I felt I was taking advantage of her. It was absurd, but refusing to tell her that I loved her enabled me to hang onto a last shred of self-respect.

"It doesn't matter," she said. She pulled the bedclothes over our heads to make a tent. "I know you love me but you don't want to admit it."

"Do your parents suspect that we're having an affair?"

"Are you still frightened that my father will come after you?"

"You're damned right I am."

"I'm a grown woman," she said. The more I tried to explain my feelings to her, the more amused she always got. She laughed and snuggled down in the bed, pressing against me.

"You're only ten years older than little Sally."

She grew tired of the tent game and threw the bedclothes back. "Your daughter is eight. Apart from the inaccurate mathematics of that allegation, you'll have to come to terms with the fact that when your lovely daughter is ten years older she will be a grown woman too. Much sooner than that, in fact. You're an old fogy, Bernard."

"I have Dicky telling me that I'm fat and flabby and you telling me that I'm an old fogy. It's enough to crush a man's ego."

"Not an ego like yours, darling."

"Come here," I said. I hugged her tight and kissed her.

The truth was that I was falling in love with her. I thought of her too much; soon everyone at the office would guess what was between us. Worse, I was becoming frightened at the prospect of this impossible affair coming to an end. And that, I suppose, is love.

"I've been filing for Dicky all week."

"I know, and I'm jealous."

"Dicky is such an idiot," she said for no apparent reason. "I used to think he was so clever, but he's such a fool." She was amused and scornful, but I didn't miss the element of affection in her voice. Dicky seemed to bring out the maternal instinct in all women, even in his wife.

"You're telling me. I work for him."

"Did you ever think of getting out of the Department, Bernard?"

"Over and over again. But what would I do?"

"You could do almost anything," she said with the adoring intensity and the sincere belief that are the marks of those who are very young.

"I'm forty," I said. "Companies don't want promising 'young' men of forty. They don't fit into the pension scheme and they're too old to be infant prodigies."

"I shall get out soon," she said. "Those bastards will never give me paid leave to go to Cambridge, and if I don't go up next year I'm not sure when I'll get another place."

"Have they told you they won't give you paid leave?"

"They asked me if unpaid leave would suit me just as well. Morgan, actually; that little Welsh shit who does all the dirty work for the D-G's office."

"What did you say?"

"I told him to get stuffed."

"In those very words?"

"No point in beating about the bush, is there?"

"None at all, darling," I said.

"I can't stand Morgan," she said. "And he's no friend of yours either."

"Why do you say that?"

"I heard him talking to Bret Rensselaer last week. They were talking about you. I heard Morgan say he felt sorry for you really because there was no real future for you in the Department now that your wife's gone over to the Russians."

"What did Bret say?"

"He's always very just, very dispassionate, very honorable and sincere; he's the beautiful American, Bret Rensselaer. He said that the German Section would go to pieces without you. Morgan said the German Section isn't the only section in the Department and Bret said, 'No, just the most important one.'"

"How did Morgan take that?"

"He said that when the Stinnes debriefing is complete, Bret might think again."

"Jesus," I said. "What's that bastard talking about?"

"Don't get upset, Bernie. It's just Morgan putting the poison in. You know what he's like."

"Frank Harrington said Morgan is the Martin Bormann of London South West One." I laughed.

"Explain the joke to me."

"Martin Bormann was Hitler's secretary, but by controlling the paperwork of Hitler's office and by deciding who was permitted to have an audience with Hitler, Bormann became the power behind the throne. He decided everything that happened. People who upset Bormann never got to see Hitler and their influence and importance waned and waned."

"And Morgan controls the D-G like that?"

"The D-G is not well," I said.

"He's as nutty as a fruitcake," said Gloria.

"He has good days and bad days," I said. I was sorry for the D-G; he'd been good in his day—tough when it was necessary, but always scrupulously honest. "But by taking on the job of being the D-G's hatchet man—a job no one else wanted—Morgan has become a formidable power in that building. And he's done it in a very short time."

"How long has he been in the Department?"

"I don't know exactly—two years, three at the most. Now he's talking to old-timers like Bret Rensselaer and Frank Harrington as man to man."

"That's right. I heard him ask Bret about taking charge of the Stinnes debriefing. Bret said he had no time. Morgan said it wouldn't be time-consuming; it was just a matter of holding the reins so that the Department knew what was happening, from day to day, over at London Debriefing Centre. You'd have thought Morgan was the D-G the way he was saying it."

"And how did Bret react to that?"

"He asked for time to think it over, and it was decided that he'd let Morgan know next week. And then Bret asked if anyone knew when Frank Harrington was retiring, and Morgan said nothing was fixed. Bret said, 'Nothing?' in a funny voice and they laughed. I don't know what that was about."

"The D-G has a knighthood to dispose of. Rumor says it will go to Frank Harrington when he retires from the Berlin office. Everyone knows that Bret would give his right arm for a knighthood."

"I see. Is that how people get knighthoods?"

"Sometimes."

"There was something else," said Gloria. "I wasn't going to tell you this, but Morgan said the D-G had decided it would be just as well for the Department if you didn't work in Operations as from the end of this year."

"Are you serious?" I said in alarm.

"Bret said that Internal Security had given you a clean bill of health—that's what he said, 'a clean bill of health.' And then Morgan said it was nothing to do with Internal Security; it was a matter of the Department's reputation."

"That doesn't sound like the D-G," I said. "That sounds like Morgan."

"Morgan the ventriloquist," said Gloria.

I kissed her again and changed the subject. It was all getting too damned depressing for me.

"I'm sorry," she said, responding to my change of mood. "I was determined not to tell you."

I hugged her. "How did you know the children's favorite cakes, you witch?"

"I phoned Doris and asked her."

"You and Nanny are very thick," I said suspiciously.

"Why don't you call her Doris?"

"I always call her Nanny. It's better that way when we're living in the same house."

"You're such a prude. She adores you, you know."

"Don't avoid my question. Have you been plotting with Nanny?"

"With Nanny? About what?"

"You know about what."

"Don't do that. Oh, stop tickling me. Oh oh oh. I don't know what you're talking about. Oh stop it."

"Did you connive with Nanny so that she and the children were out for the evening? So that we could go to bed?"

"Of course not."

"What did you give her?"

"Stop it. Please. You beast."

"What did you give her?"

"A box of chocolates."

"I knew it. You schemer."

"I hate Greek food."

Chapter 4

TAKING the children to see Billy's godfather was an excuse for a day in the country, a Sunday lunch second to none, and a chance to talk to "Uncle Silas," one of the legends of the Department's golden days. Also it gave me a chance to tie up some loose ends in the arrested woman's evidence. If Dicky didn't want it done for the Department, then I would do it just to satisfy my own curiosity.

The property had always fascinated me; Whitelands was as surprising as Silas Gaunt himself. From the long drive, with its well-tended garden, the ancient stone farmhouse was as pretty as a calendar picture. But over the years it had been adapted to the tastes of many different owners. Adapted, modified, extended, and defaced. Across the cobbled yard at the back there was a curious castellated Gothic tower, its spiral staircase leading up to a large, ornately decorated chamber which once had been a mirrored bedroom. Even more incongruous in this cottage with its stone floors and oak beams was the richly paneled billiards room, with game trophies crowding its walls. Both architectural additions dated from the same time, both installed by a nineteenth-century beer baron to indulge his favorite pastimes.

Silas Gaunt had inherited Whitelands from his father, but Silas had never been a farmer. Even when he left the Department and came to live here in retirement, he still let his farm manager make all the decisions. Little wonder that Silas got lonely amid his six hundred acres on the edge of the Cotswolds. Now all the soft greenery of summer had gone. So had the crisp browns of autumn. Only the framework of landscape remained: bare tangles of hedgerow and leafless trees. The first snow had whitened rock-hard ridges of the empty brown fields: cross-hatched pieces of landscape where magpies, rooks, and starlings scavenged for worms and insects.

Silas had had few guests. It had been a hermit's life, for the conversation of Mrs. Porter, his housekeeper, was limited to recipes, needlework, and the steadily rising prices of groceries in the village shop. Silas Gaunt's life had revolved round his library, his records, and his wine cellar. But there is more to life than Schiller, Mahler, and Margaux, which trio Silas claimed as his "fellow pensioners." And so he'd come to encourage these occasional weekend house parties at which departmental staff, both past and present, were usually represented along with a sprinkling of the artists, tycoons, eccentrics, and weirdos whom Silas had encountered during his very long and amazing career.

Silas was unkempt, the wispy white hair that made a halo on his almost bald head did not respond to combs or to the clawing gesture of his fingers that he made whenever a strand of hair fell forward across his eyes. He was tall and broad, a Falstaffian figure who liked to laugh and shout, could curse fluently in half a dozen languages, and who'd make reckless bets on anything and everything and claimed—with some justification—to be able to drink any man under the table.

Billy and Sally were in awe of him. They were always ready to go to Whitelands and see Uncle Silas, but they regarded him as a benevolent old ruffian whose sudden moods they should constantly be wary of. And that was the way I saw him myself. But he'd had a fully decorated Christmas tree erected in the entrance hall. Under it there was a little pile of presents for both children, all of them wrapped in bright paper and tied neatly with big bows. Mrs. Porter's doing no doubt.

Like all old people, Silas Gaunt felt a need for unchanging ritual. These guest weekends followed a long established pattern: a long country walk on Saturday morning (which I did my best to avoid), roast beef lunch to follow, billiards in the afternoon, and a dress-up dinner on Saturday evening. On Sunday morning his guests were shepherded to church and then to the village pub before coming back to lunch, which meant locally obtained game or, failing that, poultry. I was relieved to find that duckling was on the menu this week. I did not care for Silas's selection of curious little wild birds, every mouthful with its portion of lead shot.

"Surprised to see Walter here?" Uncle Silas asked me again as he sharpened his long carving knife with the careless abandon of a butcher.

I had registered my surprise on first arriving, but apparently I'd inadequately performed my allotted role. "Amazed!" I said, putting all my energies into it. "I had no idea . . ." I winked at von Munte. I knew him even better than I knew Uncle Silas; once long ago he'd saved my life by risking his own. Dr. Walter von Munte smiled, and even the staid old Frau Doctor gave the ghost of a smile. Living with extroverted, outspoken Silas must have come as something of a shock after their austere and tight-lipped life in the German Democratic Republic, where even the von in their name had been taken from them.

I knew that the von Muntes were staying there—it was my job to know such things. I'd played a part in bringing them out of the East. Their presence was, to some extent, the reason for my visit, but their whereabouts was considered a departmental secret and I was expected to register appropriate surprise.

Until a few short weeks ago this lugubrious old man had been one of our most reliable agents. Known only as Brahms Four, he'd supplied regular and carefully selected facts and figures from the Deutsche Notenbank, through which came banking clearances for the whole of East Germany. From time to time he'd also obtained for us the decisions and plans of COMECON—the East Bloc Common Market—and memos from the Moscow Narodny bank too. At the receiving end, Bret Rensselaer had built an empire upon the dangerous work of von Munte, but now von Munte had been debriefed and left in the custodial care of his old friend Uncle Silas and Bret was desperately seeking new dominions.

Silas stood at the end of the long table and dismembered the duck, apportioning suitable pieces to each guest. He liked to do it himself. It was a game he played: discussing and arguing what each and every guest should have. Mrs. Porter watched the cameo with an expressionless face. She arranged the pile of warmed plates, positioned the vegetables and gravy, and, at exactly the right psychological moment, brought in the second roasted duckling. "Another one!" said Silas as if he hadn't ordered the meal himself and as if he didn't have a third duckling in the oven for extra portions.

Before pouring the wine, Silas lectured us about it. Château Palmer 1961, he said, was the finest claret he'd ever tasted, the finest perhaps of this century. He still hovered, looking at the wine in the antique decanter as if now wondering whether it would be wasted on the present company.

Perhaps von Munte sensed the hesitation for he said, "It's generous of you to share it with us."

"I was looking through my cellar the other day." He stood up straight, looking out across the snow-whitened lawn as if oblivious of his guests. "I found a dozen bottles of 1878 port down there. My grandfather bought them for me, to mark my tenth birthday, and I'd completely forgotten them. I've never tasted it. Yes, I've got a lot of treasures there. I stocked up when I had the money to afford it. It would break my heart to leave too much magnificent claret behind when I go."

He poured the wine carefully and evoked from us the sort of compliments he needed. He was like an actor in that and many other respects—he desperately needed regular and earnest declarations of love. "Label uppermost, always label uppermost; when you store and when you pour," he demonstrated it. "Otherwise you'll disturb it."

I knew it would be a predominantly masculine lunch, a departmental get-together, Silas had warned me beforehand, but I still came. Bret Rensselaer and Frank Harrington were both there. Rensselaer was in his mid-fifties, American-born, he was trim almost to the point of emaciation. Although his hair was turning white, there was still enough of the blond coloring left to prevent him looking old. And he smiled a lot and had good teeth and a face that was bony so that there weren't many wrinkles.

Over lunch there was the usual seasonal discussion about how quickly Christmas was approaching and the likelihood of more snow. Bret Rensselaer was deciding upon a place to ski. Frank Harrington, our senior man in Berlin, told him it was too early for good snow, but Silas advised Switzerland.

Frank argued about the snow. He liked to think he was an authority on such matters. He liked skiing, golfing, and sailing and generally having a good time. Frank Harrington was waiting for retirement, something for which he'd been strenuously practicing all his life. He was a soldierly-looking figure with a weather-beaten face and a blunt-ended stubble mustache. Unlike Bret, who was wearing the same sort of Savile Row suit he wore to the office, Frank had come correctly attired for the upper-class English weekend: old Bedford cord trousers and a khaki sweater with a silk scarf in the open neck of his faded shirt.

"February," said Frank. "That's the only time for any decent skiing anywhere worth going."

I observed the way Bret was eying von Munte, whose stream of high-grade information had taken Bret into the very top ranks of the Department. Bret's desk was now closed down and his seniority had been in peril ever since the old man had been forced to flee. No wonder the two men watched each other like boxers in a ring.

Talk became more serious when it touched upon that inevitable subject in such company, the unification of Germany. "How deeply ingrained in East Germans is the philosophy of Communism?" Bret asked von Munte.

"Philosophy," said Silas, interrupting sharply. "I'll accept that Communism is a perverted sort of religion—infallible Kremlin, infallible Vatican—but philosophy, no." He was happier with the Muntes here, I could tell from the tone of his voice.

Von Munte didn't take up Silas's semantic contention. Gravely he said, "The way in which Stalin took from Germany Silesia, Pomerania, and East Prussia made it impossible for many of us Germans to accept the U.S.S.R. as a friend, neighbor, or example."

"That's going back a long while," said Bret. "Which Germans are we talking about? Are young Germans interested in the tears and cries of pain we hear about the lost territories?" He smiled. This was Bret being deliberately provocative. His charming manner was frequently used like this—the local anesthetic that accompanied the lancet of his rude remarks.

Von Munte remained very calm; was it a legacy of years of banking or years of Communism? Either way, I'd hate to play poker against him. "You English equate our eastern lands with Imperial India. The French think we who talk about reasserting Germany's border to the frontiers of East Prussia are like the *pieds-noirs,* who hope once again to have Algeria governed from Paris."

"Exactly," said Bret. He smiled to himself and ate some duckling.

Von Munte nodded. "But our eastern provinces have always

been German and a vital part of Europe's relationship with the East. Culturally, psychologically, and commercially, Germany's eastern lands, not Poland, provided the buffer and the link with Russia. Frederick the Great, Yorck, and Bismarck—and indeed all those Germans who instituted important alliances with the East—were *ostelbisch*, Germans from the eastern side of the River Elbe." He paused and looked round the table before going on with what was obviously something he'd said time and time again. "Czar Alexander I and Nicholas who succeeded him were more German than Russian, and they both married German princesses. And what about Bismarck, who was continually defending Russian interests even at the expense of Germany's relations with the Austrians?"

"Yes," said Bret sardonically. "And you have yet to mention the German-born Karl Marx."

For a moment I thought von Munte was going to reply seriously to the joke and make a fool of himself, but he'd lived amid signals, innuendos, and half-truths long enough to recognize the joke for what it was. He smiled.

"Can there ever be lasting peace in Europe?" said Bret wearily. "Now, if I'm to believe my ears, you say Germany still has territorial aspirations." For Bret it was all a game, but poor old von Munte could not play it.

"For our own provinces," said von Munte stolidly.

"For Poland and pieces of Russia," said Bret. "You'd better be clear on that."

Silas poured more of his precious Château Palmer in a gesture of placation for all concerned. "You're from Pomerania, aren't you, Walter?" It was an invitation to talk rather than a real question, for by now Silas knew every last detail of von Munte's family history.

"I was born in Falkenburg. My father had a big estate there."

"That's near the Baltic," said Bret, feigning interest to make what he considered a measure of reconciliation.

"Pomerania," said von Munte. "Do you know it, Bernard?"

he asked me, because I was the closest person there to being a fellow countryman.

"Yes," I said. "Many lakes and hills. They call it Pomeranian Switzerland, don't they?"

"Not any longer."

"A beautiful place," I said. "But as I remember it, damned cold, Walter."

"You must go in the summer," said von Munte. "It's one of the most enchanting places in the world." I looked at Frau Doctor von Munte. I had the feeling that the move to the West was a disappointment for her. Her English was poor and she keenly felt the social disadvantage she suffered as a refugee. With the talk of Pomerania she brightened and tried to follow the conversation.

"You've been back?" Silas asked.

"Yes, my wife and I went there about ten years ago. It was foolish. One should never go back."

"Tell us about it," said Silas.

At first it seemed as if the memories were too painful for von Munte to recount, but after a pause he told us about his trip. "There is something nightmarish about going back to your homeland and finding that it's occupied exclusively by foreigners. It was the most curious experience I've ever had—to write 'birthplace Falkenburg' and then 'destination Złocieniec.'"

"The same place, now given a Polish name," said Frank Harrington. "But you must have been prepared for that."

"I was prepared in my mind but not in my heart," said von Munte. He turned to his wife and repeated this in rapid German. She nodded dolefully.

"The train connection from Berlin was never good," von Munte went on. "Even before the war we had to change twice. This time we went by bus. I tried to borrow a car, but it was not possible. The bus was convenient. We went to Neustettin, my wife's hometown. We had difficulty finding the house in which she'd lived as a child."

"Couldn't you ask for directions?" said Frank.

"Neither of us speaks much Polish," said von Munte. "Also, my wife had lived in Hermann-Göring-Strasse and I did not care to ask the way there." He smiled. "But we found it eventually. In the street where she lived as a girl we even found an old German woman who remembered my wife's family. It was a remarkable stroke of luck, for there are only a handful of Germans still living there."

"And in Falkenburg?" said Silas.

"Ah, in my beloved Złocieniec, Stalin was more thorough. We could find no one there who spoke German. I was born in a house in the country, right on the lake. We went to the nearest village and the priest tried to help us, but there were no records. He even lent me a bicycle so that I could go out to the house, but it had completely disappeared. The buildings have all been destroyed and the area has been made into a forest. The only remains I could recognize were a couple of farm buildings a long way distant from the site of the house where I was born. The priest promised to write if he found out any more, but he never did."

"And you never went back again?" asked Silas.

"We planned to return, but things happened in Poland. The big demonstrations for free trade unions and the creation of Solidarity were reported in our East German newspapers as being the work of reactionary elements supported by Western fascists. Very few people were prepared to even comment on the Polish crisis. And most of the people who did talk about it said that such 'troubles,' by upsetting the Russians, made conditions worse for us East Germans and other peoples in the Eastern Bloc. Poles became unpopular and no one went there. It was as if Poland ceased to exist as a next-door neighbor and became some land far away on the other side of the world."

"Eat up," said Silas. "We're keeping you from your lunch, Walter."

But soon von Munte took up the same subject again. It was as if he had to convert us to his point of view. He had to remove our misunderstandings. "It was the occupation zones that created the archetype German for you," he said. "Now the French think all Germans are chattering Rhinelanders, the Americans think we are all beer-swilling Bavarians, the British think we are all icy Westphalians, and the Russians think we are all cloddish Saxons."

"The Russians," I said, having downed two generous glasses of Silas's magnificent wine as well as a few aperitifs, "think you are all brutal Prussians."

He nodded sadly. "Yes, *Saupreiss,*" he said, using the Bavarian dialect word for Prussian swine. "Perhaps you are right."

After lunch the other guests divided into those who played billiards and those who preferred to sit huddled round the blazing log fire in the drawing room. My children were watching TV with Mrs. Porter.

Silas, giving me a chance to speak privately with von Munte, took us to the conservatory to which, at this time of year, he had moved his house plants. It was a huge glass palace, resting against the side of the house, its framework gracefully curved, its floor formed of beautiful old decorative tiles. In these cold months the whole place was crammed full of prehensile-looking greenery of every shape and size. It seemed too cold in there for such plants to flourish, but Silas said they didn't need heat so much as light. "With me," I told him, "it's exactly the opposite."

He smiled as if he'd heard the joke before, which he had because I told it to him every time he trapped me into one of these chats amid his turnip tops. But Silas liked the conservatory, and if he liked it, everyone else had to like it too. He seemed not to feel the cold. He was jacketless, with bright red braces visible under his unbuttoned waistcoat. Walter von Munte was wearing a black suit of the kind that was uniform for a German government official in the service of the Kaiser. His face was gray and lined and his whitening hair cropped short. He took off his gold-rimmed glasses and polished them on a silk handkerchief. Seated on the big wicker seat under the large and leafy plants, the old man looked like some ancient studio portrait.

"Young Bernard has a question for you, Walter," said Silas. He had a bottle of Madeira with him and three glasses. He put them on the table and poured a measure of the amber-colored wine for each of us, then lowered his weight onto a cast-iron garden chair. He sat between us, positioned like a referee.

"It is not good for me," said von Munte, but he took the glass and looked at the color of it and sniffed it appreciatively.

"It's not good for anyone," said Silas cheerfully, sipping his carefully measured portion. "It's not *supposed* to be good for you. The doctor cut me down to one bottle per month last year." He drank. "This year he told me to cut it out altogether."

"Then you are disobeying orders," said von Munte.

"I got myself another doctor," said Silas. "We live in a capitalist society over here, Walter. I can afford to get myself a doctor who says it's okay to smoke and drink." He laughed and sipped a little more of his Madeira. "Cossart 1926, bottled fifty years later. Not the finest Madeira I've ever encountered, but not at all bad, eh?"

He didn't wait for our response, but selected a cigar from the box he'd brought under his arm. "Try that," he said, offering the cigar to me. "That's an Upmann grand corona, one of the best cigars you can smoke and just right for this time of day. Walter, what about one of those petits that you enjoyed last night?"

"Alas," said von Munte, holding up his hand to decline. "I cannot afford your doctor. I must keep to one a week."

I lit the cigar Silas had given me. It was typical of him that he had to select what he thought suitable for us. He had well-defined ideas about what everyone should have and what they shouldn't have. For anyone who called him a "fascist"—and there were plenty who did—he had the perfect response: scars from Gestapo bullets.

"What do you want to ask me, Bernard?" said von Munte.

I got the cigar going and then I said, "Ever hear of MAR-TELLO, HARRY, JAKE, SEE SAW, or IRONFOOT?" I'd put in a couple of extra names as a means of control.

"What kind of names are these?" said von Munte. "People?"

"Agents. Code names. Russian agents operating out of the United Kingdom."

"Recently?"

"It looks as if one of them was used by my wife."

"Yes, recently. I see." Von Munte sipped his port. He was old-fashioned enough to be embarrassed at the mention of my wife and her spying. He shifted his weight on the wicker seat and the movement produced a loud creaking sound.

"Did you ever come across those names?" I asked.

"It was not the policy to let my people have access to such secrets as the code names of agents."

"Not even source names?" I persisted. "These are probably not agent names; they're the code names used in messages and for distribution. No real risk there, and the material from any one source keeps its name until identified and measured and pronounced upon. That's the KGB system and our system too."

I glanced round at Silas. He was examining one of his plants, his head turned away as if he weren't listening. But he was listening all right; listening and remembering every last syllable of what was being said. I knew him of old.

"Source names. Yes, MARTELLO sounds familiar," said von Munte. "Perhaps the others too, I can't remember."

"Two names used by one agent *at the same time,*" I said.

"That would be unprecedented," said von Munte. He was loosening up now. "Two names, no. How would we ever keep track of our material?"

"That's what I thought," I said.

"This was from the woman arrested in Berlin?" said Silas suddenly. He dropped the pretense of looking at his plants. "I heard about that." Silas always knew what was happening. In earlier days, while the D-G had been settling in, he'd even asked Silas to monitor some of the operations. Nowadays Silas and the D-G kept in touch. It would be foolish of me to imagine that this conversation would not get back to the Department.

"Yes, the woman in Berlin," I said.

Walter von Munte touched his stiff white collar. "I was never allowed to know any secrets. They gave me only what they thought I should have."

I said, "Like Silas distributing his food and cigars, you mean?"

I kept wishing that Silas would depart and leave me and von Munte to have the conversation I wanted. But that was not Silas's way. Information was his stock in trade, it always had been, and he knew how to use it to his own advantage. That's why he'd survived so long in the Department.

"Not as generously as Silas," said von Munte. He smiled and drank some of the Madeira and then shifted about, deciding how to explain it all. "The bank's intelligence staff went over to the Warschauer Strasse office once a week. They would have all the new material in trays waiting for us. Old Mr. Heine was in charge there. He'd produce for us each item according to subject."

"Raw?" I said.

"Raw?" said von Munte. "What does that mean?"

"Did they tell you what the agent said or did they merely tell you the content of his message?"

"Oh, the messages were edited, but otherwise as received. They had to be; the staff handling the material didn't know enough about economics to understand what it was about."

"But you identified different sources?" I asked yet again.

"Sometimes we could, sometimes that was easy. Some of it was total rubbish."

"From different agents?" I persisted. My God, but it was agony to deal with old people. Would I be like this one day?

"Some of their agents sent only rumors. There was one who never provided a word of good sense. They called him 'Grock.' That wasn't his code name or his source name; it was our joke. We called him 'Grock,' after the famous clown, of course."

"Yes," I said. But I'm glad von Munte had told me it was a

joke; that gave me the cue to laugh. "What about the good sources?" I said.

"You could recognize them from the quality of their intelligence and from the style in which it was presented." He sat back in his chair. "Perhaps I should explain what it was like in the Warschauer Strasse office. It wasn't our office. It is supposed to be an office belonging to Aeroflot, but there are always police and security guards on the door, and our passes were carefully scrutinized no matter how often we visited there. I don't know who else uses the building, but the economic intelligence staff met there regularly, as I said."

"And you were included in 'economic intelligence staff'?"

"Certainly not. They were all KGB and security people. My superior was only invited to attend when there was something directly affecting our department. Other bank officials and Ministry people came according to what was to be discussed."

"Why didn't the briefing take place at the KGB offices?" I asked. Silas was sitting upright on his metal chair, his eyes closed as if he were dozing off to sleep.

"The Warschauer Strasse office was—perhaps I should say, is—used at arm's length by the KGB. When some Party official or some exalted visitor has enough influence to be permitted to visit the KGB installation in Berlin, they are invariably taken to Warschauer Strasse rather than to Karlshorst."

"It's used as a front?" said Silas, opening his eyes and blinking as if suddenly coming awake from a deep slumber.

"They wouldn't want visitors tramping through the offices where the real work was being done. And Warschauer Strasse has a kitchen and dining room where such dignitaries can be entertained. Also there is a small lecture hall where they can see slide shows and demonstration films and so on. We liked going over there. Even the coffee and sandwiches served were far better than anything available elsewhere."

"You said you could tell the source from the quality and the style. Could you enlarge on that?" I asked.

"Some communications would begin an item with a phrase

such as 'I hear that the Bank of England' or whatever. Others would say 'Last week the Treasury issued a confidential statement.' Others might put it 'Fears of an imminent drop in American interest rates are likely to bring . . .' These different styles are virtually sufficient for identification, but correlated with the proved quality of certain sources, we were soon able to recognize the agents. We spoke of them as people and joked about the nonsense that certain of them sometimes passed on to us."

"So you must have recognized the first-grade material that my wife was providing."

Von Munte looked at me and then at Silas. Silas said, "Is this official, Bernard?" There was a note of warning in his voice.

"Not yet," I said.

"We're sailing a bit close to the wind for chitchat," Silas said. The choice of casual words, and the softness of his voice, did nothing to hide the authority behind what he said; on the contrary, it was the manner in which certain classes of Englishmen give orders to their subordinates. I said nothing and von Munte watched Silas carefully. Then Silas drew on his cigar reflectively and, having taken his time, said, "Tell him whatever you know, Walter."

"As I told you, I only saw the economic material. I can't guess what proportion of any one agent's submissions that might be." He looked at me. "Take the material from the man we called 'Grock.' It was rubbish, as I said. But for all I know, Grock might have been sending wonderful stuff about underwater weaponry or secret NATO conferences."

"Looking back at it, can you now guess what my wife was sending?"

"It's only a guess," said von Munte, "but there was one tray of material that was always well written and organized in a manner one might call academic."

"Good stuff?"

"Very reliable but inclined toward caution. Nothing very alarming or exciting; mostly confirmations of trends that we could guess at. Useful, of course, but from our point of view not wonderful." He looked up at the sky through the glass roof of the conservatory. *"Eisenguss,"* he said suddenly and laughed. *"Nicht Eisenfuss; Eisenguss.* Not ironfoot but cast iron or pig iron; *Gusseisen.* Yes, that was the name of the source. I remember at the time I thought he must be some sort of government official."

"It means poured iron," said Silas, who spoke a perfect and pedantic German and couldn't tolerate my Berlin accent.

"I know the word," I said irritably. "The audiotypist was careless, that's all. None of them are really fluent." It was a feeble excuse and quite untrue. I'd done it myself. I should have listened more carefully when I was with the Miller woman or picked up my mistranslation when typing from the tape recording.

"So now we have a name to connect Fiona with the material she gave them," said Silas. "Is that what you wanted?"

I looked at von Munte. "Just the one code word for Fiona's tray?"

"It all came under the one identification," said von Munte. "Why would they split it up? It wouldn't make sense, would it?"

"No," I said. I finished my drink and stood up. "It wouldn't make sense."

Upstairs I could hear the children growing noisy. There was a limit to the amount of time that TV kept them entertained. "I'll go and take charge of my children," I said. "I know they tire Mrs. Porter."

"Are you staying for supper?" said Silas.

"Thanks, but it's a long journey, Silas. And the children will be late to bed as it is."

"There's plenty of room for you all."

"You're very kind, but it would mean leaving at the crack of dawn to get the children to school and me to the office."

He nodded and turned back to von Munte. But I knew there was more to it than simple hospitality. Silas was determined to have a word with me in private. And on my way downstairs, after I'd told the children that we'd be leaving soon after tea, he emerged from his study and, with one hand on my shoulder, drew me inside.

He closed the study door with great care. Then, in a sudden change of mood that was typical of him, he said, "Do you mind telling me what the bloody hell this is all about?"

"What?"

"Don't what me, Bernard. You understand English. What the hell are you cross-questioning von Munte about?"

"The arrested woman . . ."

"Mrs. Miller," he interrupted me, to show how well informed he was.

"Yes, Mrs. Carol Elvira Johnson, née Miller, father's name Müller, born London 1930, occupation schoolteacher. That's the one."

"That was quite uncalled for," said Silas, offended at my reply. "Well, what about her?"

"Her testimony doesn't fit what I know of KGB procedures and I wanted to hear about von Munte's experience."

"About using multiple code names? Did the Miller woman say they used multiple code names?"

"She handled two lots of exceptionally high-grade intelligence material. There were two code names, but the Department are happy to believe that it all came from Fiona."

"But you incline to the view that it was two lots of material from two different agents?"

"I didn't say that," I said. "I'm still trying to find out. It can't hurt to improve upon our knowledge, can it?"

"Have you spoken to anyone at the office about this?"

"Dicky Cruyer knows."

"Well, he's a bright lad," said Silas. "What did he say?"

"He's not interested."

"What would you do in Dicky Cruyer's place?"

"Someone should check it with Stinnes," I said. "What is the point of debriefing a KGB defector if we don't use him to improve upon what we already know?"

Silas turned to the window; his lips were pressed tight together and his face was angry. From this second-floor room there was a view across the paddock all the way to the stream that Silas called his "river." For a long time he watched the flecks of snow spinning in the air. "Drive slowly. It will freeze hard tonight," he said without looking round at me. He'd suppressed his anger and his body relaxed as the rage went out of him.

"No other way to drive in that old banger of mine."

When he turned to me he had his smile in place. "Didn't I hear you telling Frank that you're buying something good from your brother-in-law?" He never missed anything. He must have had superhuman hearing and, in defiance of the laws of nature, it improved with every year he aged. I had been telling Frank Harrington about it, and, in keeping with our curious father-son sort of relationship, Frank had told me to be very careful when I was driving it.

"Yes," I said. "A Rover 3500 saloon that a couple of tearaways souped up to do one hundred fifty miles an hour."

"With a V-8 engine that shouldn't be too difficult." His eyes narrowed. "You'll surprise a few Sunday drivers with that one, Bernard."

"Yes, that's what Tessa's husband said. But until it's ready I have to manage with the Ford. And in that I can't surprise anyone."

Silas leaned close and his manner was avuncular. "You've come out of the Kimber-Hutchinson business with a smile on your face, Bernard. I'm pleased." I couldn't help noticing that his distant relative Fiona was now referred to by her maiden name, thus distancing both of us from her.

"I don't know about the smile," I said.

He ignored my retort. "Don't start digging into that all over again. Let it go."

"You think that's best?" I said, to avoid giving him the reassurance he was asking for.

"Leave all that to the people at Five. It's not our job to chase spies," said Silas and opened the door of his study to let me out onto the landing.

"Come along, children," I called. "Tea and cake and then we must leave."

"The Germans have a word for the results of such overenthusiasm, don't they," said Silas, who never knew when to stop. *"Schlimmbesserung,* an improvement that makes things worse." He smiled and patted my shoulder. There was no sign of anger now. Silas had become Uncle Silas again.

Chapter 5

WHY DOES *anyone* have to go to Berlin?" I asked Dicky resentfully. I was at home: warm and comfortable and looking forward to Christmas Day.

"Be sensible," said Dicky. "They're getting this Miller woman's body out of the Hohenzollern Canal. We can't leave it to the Berlin cops. And a lot of questions will have to be answered. Why was she being moved? Who authorized the ambulance? And where the hell was she being moved to?"

"It's Christmas, Dicky," I said.

"Oh, is it?" said Dicky, feigning surprise. "That accounts for the difficulty I seem to be having getting anything done."

"Don't Operations know that we have something called the Berlin Field Unit?" I said sarcastically. "Why isn't Frank Harrington handling it?"

"Don't be peevish, old boy," said Dicky, who I think was enjoying the idea of ruining my Christmas. "We showed Frank how important this was by sending you over to supervise the arrest. And you interrogated her. We can't suddenly decide that BFU must take over. They'll say we're unloading this one onto them because it's the Christmas holiday. And they'd be right."

"What does Frank say?"

"Frank isn't in Berlin. He's gone away for Christmas."

"He must have left a contact number," I said desperately.

"He's gone to some relatives in the Scottish Highlands. There have been gales and the phone lines are down. And don't say send the local constabulary to find him because when I track him down, Frank will point out that he has a deputy on duty in Berlin. No, you'll have to go, Bernard. I'm sorry, but there it is. And after all, you're not married."

"Hell, Dicky. I've got the children with me and the nanny has gone home for Christmas with her parents. I'm not even on stand-by duty. I've planned all sorts of things over the holiday."

"With gorgeous Gloria, no doubt. I can imagine what sort of things you planned, Bernard. Bad luck, but this is an emergency."

"Who I spend my Christmas with is my personal business," I said huffily.

"Of course, old chap. But let me point out that you introduced the personal note into this conversation. I didn't."

"I'll phone Werner," I said.

"By all means. But you'll have to go, Bernard. You are the person the BfV knows. I can't get all the paperwork done to authorize someone else to work with them."

"I see," I said. That was the real reason, of course. Dicky was determined that he would not go back into the office for a couple of hours of paperwork and phoning.

"And who else could I send? Tell me who could go and see to it."

"From what you say, it's only going to be a matter of identifying a corpse."

"And who else can do that?"

"Any of the BfV men who were in the arrest team."

"That would look very good on the documentation, wouldn't it," said Dicky with heavy irony. "We have to rely on a foreign police service for our certified identification. Even Coordination would query that one."

"If it's a corpse, Dicky, let it stay in the icebox until after the holiday."

There was a deep sigh from the other end. "You can wriggle and wriggle, Bernard, but you're on this hook and you know it. I'm sorry to wreck your cozy little Christmas, but it's nothing of my doing. You have to go and that's that. The ticket is arranged, and cash and so on will be sent round by security messenger tomorrow morning."

"Okay," I said.

"Daphne and I will be pleased to entertain the children round here, you know. Gloria can come round too, if she'd like that."

"Thanks, Dicky," I said. "I'll think about it."

"She'll be safe with me, Bernard," said Dicky, and did nothing to disguise the smirk with which he said it. He'd always lusted after Gloria. I knew it and he knew I knew it. I think Daphne, his wife, knew it too. I hung up the phone without saying goodbye.

AND SO it was that, on Christmas Eve, when Gloria was with my children, preparing them for early bed so that Santa Claus could operate undisturbed, I was standing watching the Berlin police trying to winch a wrecked car out of the water. It wasn't exactly the Hohenzollern Canal, Dicky had got that wrong; it was Hakenfelde, that industrialized section on the bank of the Havel River not far from where the Hohenzollern joins it.

Here the Havel widens to become a lake. It was so cold that the police doctor insisted the frogmen must have a couple of hours rest to thaw out. The police inspector had argued about it, but in the end the doctor's opinion prevailed. Now the boat containing the frogmen had disappeared into the gloom and I was left with only the police inspector for company. The two policemen left to guard the scene had gone behind the generator truck, the noise of which never ceased. The police electricians had put flood lamps along the wharf to make light for the winch crew, so that the whole place was lit with the bright artificiality of a film set.

I stepped through the broken railing at the place where the car had gone into the water. Looking down over the edge of the jetty I could just make out the wobbling outline of the car under the dark oily surface. The winch and two steadying cables held it suspended there. For the time being, the car had won the battle. One steel cable had broken, and the first attempts to lift the car had ripped its rear off. That was the trouble with cars, said the inspector—they filled with water, and water weighs a ton per cubic meter. And this was a big car, a Citroën ambulance. To make it worse, its frame was bent enough to prevent the frogmen from getting its doors open.

The inspector was in his mid-fifties, a tall man with a large white mustache, its ends curling in the style of the Kaiser's soldiers. It was the sort of mustache a man grew to make himself look older. "To think," said the inspector, "that I transferred out of the Traffic Department because I thought standing on point duty was too cold." He stamped his feet. His heavy jackboots made a crunching sound where ice was forming in the cracks between the cobblestones.

"You should have kept to traffic," I said, "but transferred to the Nice or Cannes Police Department."

"Rio," said the inspector. "I was offered a job in Rio. There was an agency here recruiting ex-policemen. My wife was all in favor, but I like Berlin. There's no town like it. And I've always been a cop; never wanted to be anything else. I know you from somewhere, don't I? I remember your face. Were you ever a cop?"

"No," I said. I didn't want to get into a discussion about what I did for a living.

"Right from the time I was a child," he continued. "I'm going back a long time now to the war and even before that. There was a traffic cop, famous all over Berlin. Siegfried they called him, I don't know if that was his real name but everyone knew Siegfried. He was always on duty at the Wilhelmplatz, the beautiful little white palace where Dr. Goebbels ran his Propaganda Ministry. There were always crowds of tourists there, watching the well-known faces that went in and out, and if there was any kind of crisis, big crowds would form to try and guess what was going on. My father always pointed out Siegfried, a tall policeman in a long white coat. And I wanted a big white coat like the traffic police wear. And I wanted to have the ministers and the generals, the journalists and the film stars say hello to me in that friendly way they always greeted him. There was a kiosk there on the Wilhelmplatz which sold souvenirs and they had postcard photos of all the Nazi bigwigs and I asked my father why there wasn't a photo card of Siegfried on sale there. I wanted to buy one. My father said that maybe next week there would be one of Siegfried, and every week I looked but there wasn't one. I decided that when I grew up I'd be the policeman in the Wilhelmplatz and I'd make sure they had my photo on sale in the kiosk. It's silly, isn't it, how such unimportant things change a man's life?''

"Yes," I said.

"I know you from somewhere," he said, looking at my face and frowning. I passed the police inspector my hip flask of brandy. He hesitated and took a look round the desolate yard. "Doctor's orders," I joked. He smiled, took a gulp, and wiped his mouth on the back of his hand.

"My God, it's cold," he said as if to explain his lapse from grace.

"It's cold and it's Christmas Eve," I said.

"Now I remember," he said suddenly. "You were in that football team that played on the rubble behind the Stadium. I used to take my kid brother along. He was ten or eleven; you must have been about the same age." He chuckled at the recollection and with the satisfaction of remembering where he'd seen me before. "The football team; yes. It was run by that crazy English colonel—the tall one with glasses. He had no idea about how to play football; he couldn't even kick the ball straight, but he ran round the pitch waving a walking stick and yelling his head off. Remember?"

"I remember," I said.

"Those were the days. I can see him now, waving that stick in the air and yelling. What a crazy old man he was. After the match he'd give each boy a bar of chocolate and an apple. Most of the kids only went to get the chocolate and apple."

"You're right," I said.

"I knew I'd seen you somewhere before." He stood looking across the water for a long time and then said, "Who was in the ambulance? One of your people?" He knew I was from London and guessed the rest of it. In Berlin you didn't have to be psychic to guess the rest of it.

"A prisoner," I said.

It was already getting dark. Daylight doesn't last long on clouded Berlin days like this in December. The warehouse lights made little puff balls in the mist. Round here there were only cranes, sheds, storage tanks, crates stacked as high as tenements, and rusty railway tracks. Facing us far across the water were more of the same. There was no movement except the sluggish current. The great city round us was almost silent and only the generator disturbed the peace. Looking south along the river I could see the island of Eiswerder. Beyond that, swallowed by the mist, was Spandau—world-famous now, not only for its machine guns but for the fortress prison inside which the soldiers of four nations guarded one aged and infirm prisoner: Hitler's Deputy.

The police inspector followed my gaze. "Not Hess," he joked. "Don't say the poor old fellow finally escaped?"

I smiled dutifully. "Bad luck getting Christmas duty," I said. "Are you married?"

"I'm married. I live just round the corner from here. My parents lived in the same house. Do you know I've never been out of Berlin in all my life?"

"All through the war too?"

"Yes, all through the war I was living here. I was thinking

of that just now when you gave me the drink." He turned up the collar of his uniform greatcoat. "You get old and suddenly you find yourself remembering things that you haven't recalled in almost forty years. Tonight for instance, suddenly I'm remembering a time just before Christmas in 1944 when I was on duty very near here: the gasworks."

"You were in the Army?" He didn't look old enough.

"No. Hitler Youth. I was fourteen and I'd only just got my uniform. They said I wasn't strong enough to join a gun crew, so they made me a messenger for the air defense post. I was the youngest kid there. They only let me do that job because Berlin hadn't had an air raid for months and it seemed so safe. There were rumors that Stalin had told the Western powers that Berlin mustn't be bombed so that the Red Army could capture it intact." He gave a sardonic little smile. "But the rumors were proved wrong, and on December fifth the Americans came over in daylight. People said they were trying to hit the Siemens factory, but I don't know. Siemensstadt was badly bombed, but bombs hit Spandau, and Pankow and Oranienburg and Weissensee. Our fighters attacked the *Amis* as they came in to bomb —it was a thick overcast but I could hear the machine guns— and I think they just dropped everything as soon as they could and headed home."

"Why do you remember that particular air raid?"

"I was outside and I was blown off my bicycle by the bomb that dropped in Streitstrasse just along the back of here. The officer at the air-raid post found another bike for me and gave me a swig of schnapps from his flask, like you did just now. I felt very grown up. I'd never tasted schnapps before. Then he sent me off on my bike with a message for our headquarters at Spandau station. Our phones had been knocked out. Be careful, he said, and if another lot of bombers come, you take shelter. When I got back from delivering the message there was nothing left of them. The air defense post was just rubble. They were all dead. It was a delayed-action bomb. It must have been right alongside us when he gave me the schnapps, but no one felt the shock of it because of all the racket."

Suddenly his manner changed, as if he was embarrassed at having told me his war experiences. Perhaps he'd been chafed about his yarns by men who'd come back from the Eastern Front with stories that made his air-raid experiences seem no more than minor troubles.

He tugged at his greatcoat like a man about to go on parade. And then, looking down into the water at the submerged car again, he said, "If the next go doesn't move it, we'll have to get a big crane. And that will mean waiting until after the holiday; the union man will make sure of that."

"I'll hang on," I said. I knew he was trying to provide me with an excuse to leave.

"The frogmen say the car is empty."

"They wanted to go home," I said flippantly.

The inspector was offended. "Oh, no. They are good boys. They wouldn't tell me wrong just to avoid another dive." He was right, of course. In Germany there was still a work ethic.

I said, "They can't see much, with the car covered in all that oil and muck. I know what it's like in this sort of water; the underwater lamps just reflect in the car's window glass."

"Here's your friend," said the inspector. He strolled off toward the other end of the wharf to give us a chance to talk in private.

It was Werner Volkmann. He had his hat dumped on top of his head and was wearing his long heavy coat with the astrakhan collar. I called it his impresario's coat, but today the laugh was on me, freezing to death in my damp trench coat. "What's happening?" he said.

"Nothing," I said. "Nothing at all."

"Don't bite my head off," said Werner. "I'm not even getting paid."

"I'm sorry, Werner, but I told you not to bother to drag out here."

"The roads are empty, and to tell you the truth, being a Jew I feel a bit of a hypocrite celebrating Christmas."

"You haven't left Zena alone?"

"Her sister's family are with us—four children and a husband who works in the VAT office."

"I can see why you came."

"I like it all up to a point," said Werner. "Zena likes to do the whole thing right. You know how it is in Germany. She spent all the afternoon decorating the tree and putting the presents out, and she has real candles on it."

"You should be with them," I said. In Germany the evening before Christmas Day—*heiliger Abend*—is the most important time of the holiday. "Make sure she doesn't burn the house down."

"I'll be back with them in time for the dinner. I told them you'd join us."

"I wish I could, Werner. But I'll have to be here when it comes out of the water. Dicky put that in writing and you know what he's like."

"Are they going to try again soon?"

"In about an hour. What did you find out at the hospital this morning?"

"Nothing very helpful. The people who took her away were dressed up to be a doctor and hospital staff. They had the Citroën waiting outside. From what the people in the reception office say, the ambulance was supposed to be taking her to a private clinic in Dahlem."

"What about the cop guarding her?"

"For him they had a different story. They told him they were clinic staff. They said they were just taking her downstairs for another X ray and would be back in about thirty minutes. She was very weak and complained bitterly about being moved. She probably didn't realize what was going to happen."

"That she was going into the Havel, you mean?"

"No. That they were a KGB team, there to get her away from police custody."

I said, "Why didn't the clinic reception phone the police before releasing her?"

"I don't know, Bernie. One of them said that she was taken out using the papers of a patient who was due to be moved that day. Another one said there was a policeman outside with the ambulance, so it seemed to be all in order. We'll probably never find out exactly what happened. It's a hospital, not a prison; the staff don't worry too much about who's going in and out."

"What do you make of it, Werner?"

"They knew she was talking, I suppose. Somehow what she was telling us got back to Moscow and they decided there was only one way of handling it."

"Why not take her straight back into East Berlin?" I said.

"In an ambulance? Very conspicuous. Even the Russians are not too keen on that sort of publicity. Snatching a prisoner from police custody and taking her across the wire would not look good at a time when the East Germans are trying to show the world what good neighbors they can be." He looked at me. I pulled a face. "It's easier this way," added Werner. "They got rid of her. They were taking no chances. If she had talked to us already, they'd be making sure she couldn't give evidence."

"But it's a drastic remedy, Werner. What made them get so excited?"

"They knew she was handling the radio traffic your wife provided."

"Right," I said. "And Fiona is over there. So why would they be worried about what she might tell us?"

"Fiona is behind it? Is that what you mean?"

"It's difficult not to suspect her hand is in it."

"But Fiona is safe and sound. What has she got to worry about?"

"Nothing, Werner, she's got nothing to worry about."

He looked at me as if puzzled. Then he said, "The radio traffic then. What did Dicky think about the multiple codes?"

"Dicky didn't seem to be listening. He was hoping the Miller woman would just fade away, and he's forbidden me to speak with Stinnes."

"Dicky was never one to go looking for extra work," said Werner.

"No one is interested," I said. "I went down to talk to Silas Gaunt and von Munte and neither of them was very interested. Silas waggled his finger at me when I brought the matter up with von Munte. And he told me not to rock the boat. Don't start digging into all that again, he said."

"I don't know old Mr. Gaunt the way you do. I just remember him in the Berlin office at the time when your dad was Resident. We were about eighteen years old. Mr. Gaunt bet me that the Wall would never go up. I won fifty marks from him when they built the Wall. And fifty marks was a lot of money in those days. You could have an evening out with all the trimmings for fifty marks."

"I wish I had one mark for every time you've told me that story, Werner."

"You're in a filthy mood, Bernie. I'm sorry you got this rotten job, but it's not my fault."

"I'd really looked forward to a couple of days with the kids. They're growing up without me, Werner. And Gloria is there too."

"I'm glad that's going well . . . you and Gloria."

"Its bloody ridiculous," I said. "I'm old enough to be her father. Do you know how old she is?"

"No, and I don't care. There's an age difference between me and Zena, isn't there? But that doesn't stop us being happy."

I turned to Werner so that I could look at him. It was dark. His face was visible only because it was edged with light reflected from the array of floodlights. His heavy-lidded eyes were serious. Poor Werner. Was he really happy? His marriage was my idea of hell. "Zena is older than Gloria," I said.

"Be happy while you can, Bernie. It's nothing to do with Gloria's age. You still feel bad about losing Fiona. You haven't got over her running away yet. I know you, and I can tell. She was a sort of anchor for you, a base. Without her you are restless and unsure of yourself. But that's only temporary. You'll get over it. And Gloria is just what you need."

"Maybe." I didn't argue with him; he was usually very perceptive about people and their relationships. That was why he'd been such a good field agent back in the days when we were young and carefree, and enjoyed taking risks.

"What's really on your mind? Code names are just for the analysts and Coordination staff. Why do you care how many code names Fiona used?"

"She used *one,*" I snapped. "They all use one. Our people have one name per source and so do their agents. That's what von Munte confirmed. Fiona was *Eisenguss*—no other names."

"How can you be so sure?"

"I'm not one hundred percent sure," I told him. "Special circumstances come up in this business; we all know that. But I'm ninety-nine percent sure."

"What are you saying, Bernie?"

"Surely it's obvious, Werner."

"It's Christmas, Bernie. I had a few drinks just to be sociable. What is it you're saying?"

"There are two major sources of material that the Miller woman handled. Both top-grade intelligence. Only one of them was Fiona."

Werner pinched his nose between thumb and forefinger and closed his eyes. Werner did that when he was thinking hard. "You mean there's someone else still there? You mean the KGB still have someone in London Central?"

"I don't know," I said.

"Don't just shrug it off," said Werner. "Don't hit me in the face with that kind of custard pie and then say you don't know."

"Everything points to it," I said. "But I've told them at London Central. I've done everything short of drawing a diagram and no one gives a damn."

"It might just be a stunt, a KGB stunt."

"I'm not organizing a lynching party, Werner. I'm just suggesting that it should be checked out."

"The Miller woman might have got it wrong," said Werner.

"She might have got it wrong, but even if she got it wrong, that still leaves a question to be answered. And what if someone reads the Miller transcript and starts wondering if I might be the other source?"

"Ahh! You're just covering your arse," said Werner. "You don't really think there's another KGB source in London Central, but you realized that you'd have to interpret it that way in case anyone thought it was you and you were trying to protect yourself."

"Don't be stupid."

"I'm not stupid, Bernard. I know London Central and I know you. You're just running round shouting fire in case someone accuses you of arson."

I shook my head to say no, but I was wondering if perhaps he was right. He knew me better than anyone, better even than Fiona knew me.

"Are you really going to hang on until they get that motorcar out of the water?"

"That's what I'm going to do."

"Come back for a bite of dinner. Ask the police inspector to phone us when they start work again."

"I mustn't, Werner. I promised Lisl to have dinner with her at the hotel in the unlikely event of my getting away from here in time."

"Shall I phone her to say you won't make it?"

I looked at my watch. "Yes, please, Werner. She's having some cronies in to eat there—old Mr. Koch and those people she buys wine from—and they'll get fidgety if she delays dinner for me."

"I'll phone her. I took her a present yesterday, but I'll phone to say Happy Christmas." He pulled the collar of his coat up and tucked his white silk scarf into it. "Damned cold out here on the river."

"Get back to Zena," I told him.

"If you're sure you're not coming. . . . Shall I bring you something to eat?"

"Stop being a Jewish mother, Werner. There are plenty of places where I can get something. In fact, I'll walk back to your car with you. There's a bar open on the corner. I'll get myself sausage and beer."

IT WAS nearly ten o'clock at night when they dragged the ambulance out of the Havel. It was a sorry sight, its side caked with oily mud where it had rested on the bottom of the river. One tire was torn off and some of the bodywork ripped open where it had collided with the railings that were there to prevent such accidents.

There was a muffled cheer as the car came to rest. But there was no delay in finishing the job. Even while the frogmen were still packing their gear away, the car's doors had been levered open and a search was being made of its interior.

There was no body inside—that was obvious within the first two or three minutes—but we continued to search through the car for other evidence.

By eleven-fifteen the police inspector declared the preliminary forensic examination complete. Although they'd put a number of oddments into clear-plastic evidence bags, nothing had been discovered that was likely to throw any light on the disappearance of Carol Elvira Miller, self-confessed Russian agent.

We were all very dirty. I went with the policemen into the toilet facilities at wharfside. There was no hot water from the tap, and only one bar of soap. One of the policemen came back with a large pail of boiling water. The rest of them stood aside so that the inspector could wash first. He indicated that I should use the other sink.

"What do you make of it?" said the inspector as he rationed out a measure of the hot water into each of the sinks.

"Where would a body turn up?" I asked.

"Spandau locks, that's where we fish them out," he said without hesitation. "But there was no one in that car when it went into the water." He took off his jacket and shirt so that he could wash his arms where mud had dribbled up his sleeve.

"You think not?" I stood alongside him and took the soap he offered.

"The front doors were locked, and the back door of the ambulance was locked too. Not many people getting out of a car underwater remember to lock the doors before swimming away." He passed me some paper towels.

"It went into the water empty?"

"So you don't want to talk about it. Very well."

"No, you're right," I said. "It's probably just a stunt. How did you get the information about where to find it?"

"I looked at the docket. An anonymous phone call from a passerby. You think it was a phony?"

"Probably."

"While the prisoner was taken away somewhere else."

"It would be a way of getting our attention."

"And spoiling my Christmas Eve," he said. "I'll kill the bastards if I ever get hold of them."

"Them?"

"At least two people. It wasn't in gear, you notice; it was in neutral. So they must have pushed it in. That needs two people: one to push and one to steer."

"Three of them, according to what we heard."

He nodded. "There's too much crime on television," said the police inspector. He signaled to the policeman to get another bucket of water for the rest of them to wash up with. "That old English colonel with the kids football team . . . he was your father, wasn't he?"

"Yes," I said.

"I realized that afterwards. I could have bitten my tongue off. No offense. Everyone liked the old man."

"That's okay," I said.

"He didn't even enjoy the football. He just did it for the German kids; there wasn't much for them in those days. He probably hated every minute of those games. At the time, we didn't see that; we wondered why he took so much trouble about the football when he couldn't even kick the ball straight. He organized lots of things for the kids, didn't he. And he sent you to the neighborhood school instead of to that fancy school where the other British children went. He must have been an unusual man, your father."

Washing my hands and arms and face had only got rid of the most obvious dirt. My trench coat was soaked and my shoes squelched. The mud along the banks of the Havel at that point is polluted with a century of industrial waste and effluents. Even my newly washed hands still bore the stench of the riverbed.

The hotel was dark when I let myself in by means of the key that certain privileged guests were permitted to borrow. Lisl Hennig's hotel had once been her grand home, and her parents' home before that. It was just off Kantstrasse, a heavy gray stone building of the sort that abounds in Berlin. The ground floor was an optician's shop and its bright façade partly hid the pockmarked stone that was the result of Red Army artillery fire in 1945. My very earliest memories were of Lisl's house—it wasn't easy to think of it as a hotel—for I came here as a baby when my father was with the British Army. I'd known the patched brown carpet that led up the grand staircase when it had been bright red.

At the top of the stairs there was the large salon and the bar. It was gloomy. The only illumination came from a tiny Christmas tree positioned on the bar counter. Tiny green and red bulbs flashed on and off in a melancholy attempt to be festive. Intermittent light fell upon the framed photos that covered every wall. Here were some of Berlin's most illustrious residents, from Einstein to Nabokov, Garbo to Dietrich, Max Schmeling to Grand Admiral Dönitz, celebrities of a Berlin now gone forever.

I looked into the breakfast room; it was empty. The bentwood chairs had been put up on the tables so that the floor could be swept. The cruets and cutlery and a tall stack of white plates were ready on the table near the serving hatch. There was no sign of life anywhere. There weren't even the smells of cooking that usually crept up through the house at nighttime.

I tiptoed across the salon to the back stairs. My room was at the top—I always liked to occupy the little garret room that had been my bedroom as a child. But before reaching the stairs I passed the door of Lisl's room. A strip of light along the door confirmed that she was there.

"Who is it?" she called anxiously. "Who's there?"

"It's Bernd," I said.

"Come in, you wretched boy." Her shout was loud enough to wake everyone in the building.

She was propped up in bed; there must have been a dozen lace-edged pillows behind her. She had a scarf tied round her head, and on the side table there was a bottle of sherry and a glass. All over the bed there were newspapers; some of them had come to pieces so that pages had drifted across the room as far as the fireplace.

She'd snatched her glasses off so quickly that her dyed brown hair was disarranged. "Give me a kiss," she demanded. I did so and noticed the expensive perfume and the makeup and false eyelashes that she applied only for very special occasions. This *heiliger Abend* with her friends had meant a lot to her. I guessed she'd waited for me to come home before she'd remove the makeup. "Did you have a nice time?" she asked. There was repressed anger in her voice.

"I've been working," I said. I didn't want to get into a conversation. I wanted to go to bed and sleep for a long time.

"Who were you with?"

"I told you, I was working." I tried to assuage her annoyance. "Did you have dinner with Mr. Koch and your friends? What did you serve them—carp?" She liked carp at Christmas; she'd often told me it was the only thing to serve. Even during the war they'd always somehow managed to get carp.

"Lothar Koch couldn't come. He has influenza and the wine people had to go to a trade party."

"So you were all alone," I said. I bent over and kissed her again. "I'm so sorry, Lisl." She'd been so pretty. I remember as a child feeling guilty for thinking she was more beautiful than my mother. "I really am sorry."

"And so you should be."

"There was no way of avoiding it. I had to be there."

"Had to be where—Kempinski or the Steigenberger? Don't lie to me, *Liebchen*. When Werner phoned me I could hear the voices and the music in the background. So you don't have to pretend you were working." She gave a little hoot of laughter, but there was no joy in it.

So she'd been in bed here working herself up into a rage about that. "I was working," I repeated, "I'll explain tomorrow."

"There's nothing you have to explain, *Liebchen*. You are a free man. You don't have to spend your *heiliger Abend* with an ugly old woman. Go and have fun while you are young. I don't mind."

"Don't upset yourself, Lisl," I said. "Werner was phoning from his apartment because I was working."

By this time she'd noticed the smell of the mud on my clothes, and now she pushed her glasses into place so that she could see me more clearly. "You're filthy, Bernd. Whatever have you been doing? Where have you been?" From her study there came the loud chimes of the ornate ormolu clock striking two-thirty.

"I keep telling you over and over again, Lisl. I've been with the police on the Havel getting a car from the water."

"The times I've told you that you drive too fast."

"It wasn't anything to do with me," I said.

"So what were you doing there?"

"Working. Can I have a drink?"

"There's a glass on the sideboard. I've only got sherry. The whisky and brandy is locked in the cellar."

"Sherry will be just right."

"My God, Bernd, what are you doing? You don't drink sherry by the tumblerful."

"It's Christmas," I said.

"Yes, it's Christmas," she said, and poured herself another small measure. "There was a phone message, a woman. She said her name was Gloria Kent. She said that everyone sent you their love. She wouldn't leave a phone number. She said you'd understand." Lisl sniffed.

"Yes, I understand," I said. "It's a message from the children."

"Ah, Bernd. Give me a kiss, *Liebchen*. Why are you so cruel to your Tante Lisl? I bounced you on my knee in this very room, and that was before you could walk."

"Yes, I know, but I couldn't get away, Lisl. It was work."

She fluttered her eyelashes like a young actress. "One day you'll be old, darling. Then you'll know what it's like."

Chapter 6

CHRISTMAS morning. West Berlin was like a ghost town; as I stepped into the street the silence was uncanny. The Ku-damm was empty of traffic and, although some of the neon signs and shop lights were still shining, there was no one strolling on its wide pavements. I had the town virtually to myself all the way to Potsdamer Strasse.

Potsdamer Strasse is Schöneberg's main street, a wide thoroughfare that is called Hauptstrasse at one end and continues north to the Tiergarten. You can find everything you want there and a lot of things you've been trying to avoid. There are smart shops and slums, kabob counters and superb nineteenth-century houses now listed as national monuments. Here is a neobaroque palace—the Volksgerichtshof—where Hitler's judges passed death sentences at the rate of two thousand a year, so that citizens found guilty of telling even the most feeble anti-Nazi jokes were executed.

Behind the Volksgerichtshof—its rooms now echoing and empty except for those used by the Allied Travel Office and the Allied Air Security Office (where the four powers control the air lanes across East Germany to Berlin)—was the street where Lange lived. His top-floor apartment overlooked one of the seedier side streets. Lange was not his family name, it was not his name at all. "Lange"—or "Lofty"—was the descriptive nickname the Germans had given to this very tall American. His real name was John Koby. Of Lithuanian extraction, his grandfather had decided that "Kubilunas" was not American enough to go over a storefront in Boston.

The street door led to a grim stone staircase. The windows on every landing had been boarded up. It was dark, the stairs illuminated by dim lamps protected against vandals by wire mesh. The walls were bare of any decoration but graffiti. At the top of the house the apartment door was newly painted dark gray and a new plastic bell push was labeled JOHN KOBY— JOURNALIST. The door was opened by Mrs. Koby and she led me into a brightly lit, well-furnished apartment. "Lange was so glad you phoned," she whispered. "It was wonderful that you could come right away. He gets miserable sometimes. You'll cheer him up." She was a small thin woman, her face pale like the faces of most Berliners when winter comes. She had clear eyes, a round face, and a fringe that came almost down to her eyebrows.

"I'll try," I promised.

It was the sort of untidy room in which you'd expect to find a writer or even a "journalist." There were crowded bookshelves, a desk with an old manual typewriter, and more books and papers piled on the floor. But Lange had not been a professional writer for many years, and even in his newspaper days he'd never been a man who referred to books except as a last resort. Lange had never been a journalist; Lange had always been a streetwise reporter who got his facts at firsthand and guessed the bits in between. Just as I did.

The furniture was old but not valuable—the random mixture of shapes and styles that's to be found in a saleroom or attic. Obviously a big stove had once stood in the corner, and the wall where it had been was covered in old blue-and-white tiles. Antique tiles like those were valuable now, but these must have been firmly affixed to the wall, for I had the feeling that any valuable thing not firmly attached had already been sold.

He was wearing an old red-and-gold silk dressing gown. Under it there were gray flannel slacks and a heavy cotton button-down shirt of the sort that Brooks Brothers made famous. His tie bore the ice-cream colors of the Garrick Club, a London meeting place for actors, advertising men, and lawyers. He was over seventy, but he was thin and tall and somehow that helped to give him a more youthful appearance. His face was drawn and clean-shaven, with a high forehead and gray hair neatly parted. He had a prominent bony nose and teeth that were too yellow and irregular to be anything but his own natural ones.

I remembered in time the sort of greeting that Lange gave to old friends—the *Handschlag,* the hands slapped together in that noisy handshake with which German farmers conclude a sale of pigs.

"A Merry Christmas, Lange," I said.

"It's good to see you, Bernie," he said as he released my hand. "We were in the other house the last time we saw you. The apartment over the baker's shop." His American accent was strong, as if he'd arrived only yesterday. And yet Lange had lived in Berlin longer than most of his neighbors. He'd come here as a newspaperman even before Hitler took power in 1933, and he'd stayed here right up to the time America got into World War II.

"Coffee, Bernard? It's already made. Or would you prefer a glass of wine?" said Gerda Koby, taking my coat. She was a shy withdrawn woman, and although I'd known her since I was a child, she'd never called me "Bernie." I think she would have rather called me "Herr Samson," but she followed her husband in this matter as in all others. She was still pretty. Rather younger than Lange, she had once been an opera singer famous throughout Germany. They'd met in Berlin when he returned here as a newspaperman with the U.S. Army in 1945.

"I missed breakfast," I said. "A cup of coffee would be great."

"Lange?" she said. He looked at her blankly and didn't answer. She shrugged. "He'll have wine," she told me. "He won't cut down on it." She looked too small for an opera singer, but the ancient posters on the wall gave her billing above the title: Wagner in Bayreuth, *Fidelio* at the Berlin State Opera, and in Munich a performance of *Mongol Fury,* which was the Nazis' "Aryanized" version of Handel's *Israel in Egypt.*

"It's Christmas, woman," said Lange. "Give us both wine." He didn't smile and neither did she. It was the brusque way he always addressed her.

"I'll stick to coffee," I said. "I have a lot of driving to do. And I have to go to Police HQ and sign some forms later today."

"Sit down, Bernie, and tell me what you're doing here. The last time we saw you you were settled in London, married, and with kids." His voice was hoarse and slurred slightly in the Bogart manner.

"I am," I said. "I'm just here for a couple of days on business."

"Oh, sure," said Lange. "Stuffing presents down the chimneys; then you've got to get your reindeer together and head back to the workshops."

"The children must be big," said Mrs. Koby. "You should be with them at home. They make you work at Christmas? That's terrible."

"My boss has a mean streak," I said.

"And you haven't got a union, by the sound of it," said

Lange. He had little love for the Department and he made his dislike evident in almost everything he said about the men in London Central.

"That's right," I said.

We sat there exchanging small talk for fifteen minutes or maybe half an hour. I needed a little time to get used to Lange's harsh, abrasive style.

"Still working for the Department, eh?"

"Not any longer," I said.

He ignored my denial; he knew it counted for nothing. "Well, I'm glad I got out of it when I did."

"You were the first man my dad recruited in Berlin, at least that's what people say."

"Then they've got it right," said Lange. "And I was grateful to him. In 1945 I couldn't wait to kiss the newspaper business goodbye."

"What was wrong with it?"

"You're too young to remember. They dressed reporters up in fancy uniforms and stuck 'War Correspondent' badges on us. That was so all those dumb jerks in the Army press departments could order us about and tell us what to write."

"Not you, Lange. No one told you what to do."

"We couldn't argue. I was living in an apartment that the Army had commandeered. I was eating U.S. rations, driving an Army car on Army gas, and spending Army occupation money. Sure, they had us by the balls."

"They tried to stop Lange seeing me," said Mrs. Koby indignantly.

"They forbade all Allied soldiers to talk to any Germans. Those dummies were trying to sell the soldiers their crackpot non-fraternization doctrine. Can you imagine me trying to write stories here while forbidden to talk to Germans? The Army fumed and threw kids into the stockade, but when you've got young German girls walking past the G.I.s patting their asses and shouting '*Verboten,*' even the Army brass began to see what a dumb idea it was."

"It was terrible in 1945 when I met Lange," said Gerda Koby. "My beautiful Berlin was unrecognizable. You're too young to remember, Bernard. There were heaps of rubble as tall as the tenement blocks. There wasn't one tree or bush left in the entire city; the Tiergarten was like a desert—everything that would burn had long since been cut down. The canals and waterways were all completely filled with rubble and ironwork, pushed there to clear a lane through the street. The whole city stank with the dead, the stench from the canals was even worse."

It was uncharacteristic of her to speak so passionately. She came to a sudden stop as if embarrassed. Then she got up and poured coffee for me from a vacuum flask and poured a glass of wine for her husband. I think he'd had a few before I arrived.

The coffee was in a delicate demitasse that contained no more than a mouthful. I swallowed it gratefully. I can't get started in the morning until I've had some coffee.

"Die Stunde Null," said Lange. "Germany's hour zero—I didn't need anyone to explain what that meant when I got here in 1945. Berlin looked like the end of the world had arrived." Lange scratched his head without disarranging his neatly combed hair. "And that's the kind of chaos I had to work in. None of these Army guys, or the clowns who worked for the so-called Military Government, knew the city. Half of them couldn't even speak the language. I'd been in Berlin right up until 1941 and I was able to renew all those old contacts. I set up the whole agent network that your dad ran into the East. He was smart, your dad, he knew I could deliver what I promised. He assigned me to work as his assistant and I told the Army where to stick their 'War Correspondent' badge, pin and all." He laughed. "Jesus, but they were mad. They were mad at me and mad at your dad. The U.S. Army complained to Eisenhower's intelligence big shots. But your dad had a direct line to Whitehall and that trumped their ace."

"Why did you go to Hamburg?" I said.

"I'd been here too long." He drank some of the bright red wine.

"How long after that did Bret Rensselaer do his 'fact-finding mission'?" I asked.

"Don't mention that bastard to me. Bret was just a kid when he came out here trying to 'rationalize the administration.'" Lange put heavy sarcastic emphasis on the last three words. "He was the best pal the Kremlin ever had, and I'll give you that in writing anytime."

"Was he?" I said.

"Go to the archives and look . . . or better still, go to the 'yellow submarine.'" He smiled and studied my face to see if I was surprised at the extent of his knowledge. "The 'yellow submarine'—that's what I hear they call the big London Central computer."

"I don't know . . ."

"Sure, sure," said Lange. "I know, you're not in the Department anymore; you're over here to conduct a concert of Christmas carols for the British garrison."

"What did Bret Rensselaer do?"

"Do? He dismantled three networks that I was running into the Russian Zone. Everything was going smoothly until he arrived. He put a spanner into the works and eventually got London to pack me off to Hamburg."

"What was his explanation?" I persisted.

"Bret didn't provide any explanations. You know him better than that. No one could stop him. Bret was only on temporary attachment to us at that time but he'd been given some piece of paper in London Central that said he could do anything."

"And what did my father do?"

"Your father wasn't here. They got him out of the way before Bret arrived. I had no one to appeal to; that was part of the setup."

"Setup? Were you set up?" I said.

"Sure I was set up. Bret was out to get me. Mine was the only desk in Berlin that was getting good material from the Russians.

Jesus. I had a guy in Karlshorst who was bringing me day-to-day
material from the Russian commandant's office. You can't do
better than that."

"And he was stopped?"

"He was one of the first we lost. I went across to the U.S.
Army to offer them what I had left, but Bret had already been
there. I got the cold shoulder. I had no friends there because
of the showdown I'd had with them during the early days. So
I went to Hamburg just as London Central wanted."

"But you didn't stay."

"In Hamburg? No, I didn't stay in Hamburg. Berlin is my
town, mister. I just went to Hamburg long enough to work my
way through my resignation and then I got out. Bret Rensselaer
had got what he wanted."

"What was that?"

"He'd showed us what a big shot he was. He'd denazified
the Berlin office and wrecked our best networks. 'Denazified'—
that's what he called it. Who the hell did he think we could find
who would risk their necks prying secrets from the Russkies—
Socialists, Communists, left-wing liberals? We had to use ex-
Nazis; they were the only pros we had. By the time your dad
came back and tried to pick up the pieces, Bret was reading
philosophy at some fancy college. Your dad wanted me to work
with him again. But I said, 'No dice.' I didn't want to work for
London Central, not if I was going to be looking over my
shoulder in case Bret came back to breathe fire all over me
again. No, sir."

"It was my fault, Bernard," said Mrs. Koby. Again she spoke
my name as if it was unfamiliar to her. Perhaps she always felt
self-conscious as a German amongst Lange's American and
British friends.

"No, no, no," said Lange.

"It was my brother," she persisted. "He came back from the
war so sick. He was injured in Hungary just before the end. He
had nowhere to go. Lange let him stay with us."

"Nah!" said Lange angrily. "It was nothing to do with
Stefan."

"Stefan was a wonderful boy." She said it with heartfelt earnestness, as if she was pleading for him.

"Stefan was a bastard," said Lange.

"You didn't know him until afterwards. . . . It was the pain, the constant pain that made him so ill-natured. But before he went off to the war he was a kind and gentle boy. Hitler destroyed him."

"Oh, sure, blame Hitler," said Lange. "That's the style nowadays. Everything was Hitler's fault. How would Germans manage without the Nazis to blame everything on?"

"He was a sweet boy," said Mrs. Koby. "You never knew him."

Lange gave a sardonic laugh that ended as a snort. "No, I never knew any sweet boy named Stefan, and that's for sure."

Mrs. Koby turned all her attention to me and said, "Lange gave him a bedroom. At that time Lange was working for your people. We had a big apartment in Tegel, near the water."

"He came there," said Lange. "Bernie came there many times."

"Of course you did," said Mrs. Koby. "And you never met my brother Stefan?"

"I'm not sure," I said.

"Bernie wouldn't remember Stefan," said Lange. "Bernie was just a kid when Stefan died. And for years Stefan hardly ever left that damned bedroom."

"Yes, poor Stefan. His life was so short and time passes so quickly," said Mrs. Koby.

Lange explained to me, "My wife thinks that everybody cut her dead because Stefan had been a Waffen-SS officer. But in those days most Germans were too damned busy trying to find a handful of potatoes to feed their families. No one cared about their neighbors' regimental histories."

"They cared," said Mrs. Koby feelingly. "I am a German. People said things to me that they wouldn't have said to you or to any American or British officer. And there were looks and murmurs that only a German would understand."

"Stefan was in the SS," said Lange contemptuously.

"He was a major . . . what did they call SS majors—*Obergruppen-führer* . . . ?"

"*Sturmbannführer,*" supplied Mrs. Koby wearily. Lange knew what an SS major was called, but he preferred a word that sounded cumbersome and comical to his ears. "They picked on Stefan because he was once an adjutant at Sepp Dietrich's headquarters."

"Nah!" said Lange. "He was only there a couple of weeks. He was an artillery man."

"They wanted Stefan to give evidence at the trial of General Dietrich, but he was too sick to go." It had become an argument now, the sort of quiet ritualistic dispute that couples indulge in only when visitors are there to sit in judgment.

"Your brother had the bad luck to be in a division that bore the name of Adolf Hitler. Had he been in some other SS division, such as *Prinz Eugen* or the SS cavalry division *Maria Theresia,* he wouldn't have attracted any comment at all." He smiled and drank some more of his blood-red wine. "Have a glass of wine, Bernie. Plum wine; Gerda makes it. It's delicious."

"People can be so cruel," said Mrs. Koby.

"She means all those wonderful 'liberals' who crawled out of the woodwork when Germany lost the war."

"It hurt Lange too," said Mrs. Koby. "Bret Rensselaer came to the apartment one day and told him to get rid of Stefan. But Lange was brave; he told Rensselaer to go to hell. I loved him for that." She turned to her husband. "I loved you for that, Lange." I had the feeling that in all the years that had passed, she'd never told him before.

"I don't have creeps like Bret Rensselaer telling me who I can have in my apartment," growled Lange. "And where would Stefan have gone? He needed attention all the time. Sometimes Gerda was up all night with him."

Mrs. Koby said, "It was a terrible row . . . shouting. I thought Lange would hit him. Bret Rensselaer never forgave Lange after the argument. He said that Allied officers shouldn't be sheltering SS war criminals. But Stefan wasn't a criminal, he was just a soldier, a brave soldier who'd fought for his country."

"Bret loses his temper sometimes, Mrs. Koby," I said. "He says things he doesn't really mean."

"He was just a kid," said Lange again. Bret's youthfulness had obviously added to Lange's humiliation. "Having a rich father got junior a fancy intelligence assignment."

"It was the Russian woman," said Mrs. Koby. "I always said she was behind it."

"Nah," said Lange.

"What Russian woman?" I said.

"She called herself a princess," said Lange. "Tall, dark . . . she'd obviously been a great-looking doll when she was young. She was much older than Bret, but he was the sort of American who goes for all that aristocracy junk. She knew everyone in the city and Bret liked that. He moved her into the apartment he grabbed for himself and lived with her all the time he was here. They had two servants and gave smart little dinner parties and Frank Harrington and Silas Gaunt and the D-G were entertained there. She spoke perfect English and a dozen more languages. Her father had been a Russian general killed in the Revolution. Or so the story went."

"And she was a Nazi," Mrs. Koby prompted.

"That's the real joke," said Lange. "His White Russian 'princess' was a well-known figure in Berlin. She was always being photographed at the night spots and the parties. She was someone the top Nazis always invited along to their parties and balls. Yeah, it was Bret who was really getting close to the Nazis, not me."

"Is any of this stuff on Bret's file?" I said.

With a flash of the insight for which he was famous, Lange said, "Are you vetting Rensselaer? Are you checking the bastard out for some new job?"

"No," I said truthfully.

"This goddamned conversation always seems to get back to

Rensselaer, the way conversations do when people from London Central call here."

I got to my feet. "And a Merry Christmas to you both," I said acidly.

"Sit down, kid, for Christ's sake. You're like your dad; too damned prickly for your own good." He finished his wine and gave his wife the empty glass. "Have a glass of wine, Bernie. No one can make it like Gerda. I didn't mean *you*, kid. Shit, you were with Max when he died. Max was one of my best guys. Now was he a Nazi?"

"Max was one of the best," I said.

"I never heard how it happened," said Lange.

For a moment or more I hesitated. Then I said, "We'd been in the East nearly three weeks. It was at the time when a lot of things were going wrong for us. A KGB arrest team came for him in a safe house we used in Stendal. I was there with him. It was about nine o'clock in the evening. Max got a car; God knows where he found it. Neither of us had papers; they were in a suitcase at the station."

"You should have got the papers. No one in their right mind tries the Wall."

"Railway station?" I said. "Don't you remember what an East German railway station is like? They're full of cops and soldiers. There's someone asking you for your papers every step of the way. And by that time the luggage office was probably staked out. No, there was no way but through the wire. We decided to try the border down near Wolfsburg. We chose that section because the Wall was being repaired there, and I'd seen a drawing of it. Okay, no one in their right mind tries the Wall, but the guards were getting to feel the same way and they can be slack on a cold night.

"The *Sperrzone* was easy; at that place it was mostly agricultural land still being worked. We spotted the bunkers and the towers and followed the ditch by the road the workers use. We had tools to cut the fences and everything was fine until we were crawling through the *Kontrollstreifen*. And the night was dark, really dark. Everything went fine at the start. But we must have hit a wire or some alarm because suddenly there was a commotion. They began shooting before they could really get a bead on us. You know how they are; they shoot just to show their sergeant that they're on the ball. We were okay until we got to the road that they use for the patrol cars. We stopped worrying about disturbing the pattern in the raked strip and ran across into the mine field. The guards chasing us stopped at the edge of the mine field. It was too dark for them to see us so they had to get the searchlight—we were too far into the mine field for their hand lamps to be much use to them. We crawled and stopped. Crawled and stopped. Max was an old man; the crawling was difficult for him. A couple of times the big light in the tower came across us without stopping. We stayed still for a few minutes, but then they got systematic about it and began to sweep the area bit by bit. Max took careful aim and took out the light with two shots. But they saw the flash of his gun. The machine gunner in the tower just fired at the place he'd seen the flash. He kept his finger on the trigger so that Max must have been torn to pieces. I ran. It was a miracle. In the darkness and the general confusion I got right through."

Just thinking about it made me tremble.

"Months later, Frank Harrington got hold of the Vopo guard commander's report. It confirmed that Max had been killed by the machine gunner. They'd decided to say there was only one escaper, and thus make their success rate one hundred percent." I took a drink of coffee. "Max saved my life, Lange. He must have guessed what would happen. He saved me." Why had I suddenly blurted out this story to Lange? I hadn't talked about it to anyone since it happened in 1978.

"Hear that, Gerda?" said Lange softly. "You remember dear old Max, don't you? What a drinker. Remember how angry you used to get because he never wanted to go home? Then next day he always sent flowers and you forgave him."

"Of course I do, darling," she said. I understood now why I'd suddenly had to say it. I couldn't say it to Max. Max was dead. The next best thing was to say it to Lange, who loved him.

"He was a good man," said Lange. "He was a Prussian of the old school. I recruited him back in 1946."

Mrs. Koby gave me a glass of her bright red homemade plum wine and gave another one to Lange.

"Didn't you ever feel like going back to the States, Lange?" I said. I drank some of the wine. It was a fierce fruity concoction that made me purse my lips.

"Nah. Berlin is where I want to be." He watched me drinking the wine without commenting. I had the feeling that drinking a glass of Gerda's plum wine was a test that visitors were expected to endure without complaining.

"They wouldn't let us go to America, Bernard," said Mrs. Koby in contradiction to her husband's bluff dismissal of the idea. "We got all ready to leave, but the Embassy wouldn't give us a visa."

"But you're a citizen, Lange," I said.

"No, I'm not. When I started working for your dad, he rushed through a British passport for me. Even if they let me in, we'd both be aliens in the U.S. I'm not sure I'd even get Social Security payments. And when I talked to one of our Embassy people he had the nerve to tell me that 'working for a foreign intelligence service' would count against me with the Immigration Department. How do you like that?"

"He was kidding you, Lange," I said. Lange looked at me and said nothing and I didn't press it. I drained my wineglass and got to my feet again. "I must go," I said.

"I didn't mean anything, Bernie. I know you weren't sent here by London Central."

"No offense taken, Lange. But I'm taking Lisl to Werner Volkmann's place for a meal. You know how Lisl is about people being late."

"It's going to be a Jewish Christmas, is it? What's he serving you—gefilte fish and turkey noodle soup?"

"Something like that," I said. I didn't care for Lange's jokes.

Lange got up too. "I hear Frank is retiring," he said. It was an obvious attempt to draw me out. "Jesus, he's said goodbye enough times, hasn't he?"

"Sinatra?" I said facetiously.

"Frank *Harrington*," said Mrs. Koby, to put me right.

Lange gave his snorty little laugh and said, "And I hear that some guy named Cruyer is calling the shots in London these days."

I pulled my trench coat on. "Cruyer?" I said. "That name doesn't ring any bells for me."

"You've got a great sense of humor, Bernie," said Lange, without disguising the bitterness he felt at being excluded from the latest gossip about London Central.

Chapter 7

IT WAS still early when I left Lange and walked north to the Tiergarten and what is the most mysterious part of the present-day city of Berlin. The park was empty, its grass brown and dead and glazed with frost. The trees were bare, like scratchy doodles upon the low gray sky. Rising from behind the trees, like a gilt-tipped rocket set for launching, the *Siegessäule* column. Its winged Victoria—which Berliners call "golden Elsie"—celebrates the last war that Germany won, some hundred and ten years ago.

And as you turn the corner, you see them—stranded along the edge of the Tiergarten like the gigantic hulks of a rusting battlefleet. They are the Embassy buildings that until 1945 made this "diplomatic quarter" the centre of Berlin's most exclusive and extravagant social life—Berlin is not the capital of West Germany; Bonn enjoys that distinction. These roofless, derelict buildings, standing on the sacrosanct foreign ground of other governments, have been left untouched for almost forty years.

The ruined embassies had always fascinated me, ever since we had trespassed there to play dangerous games in my school days. There was the window from which Werner launched his model glider and fell thirty feet into the stinging nettles. Through the broken shell I could see the rafters I'd climbed as a dare and won from a boy named Binder one out of his coveted collection of forbidden Nazi badges. The roof was high and the rafters rickety. I looked at the dangers now and shuddered. I looked at many such previously encountered dangers now and shuddered; that's why I was no longer suitable for employment as a field agent.

I went round the *Diplomatenviertel* not once but twice. I wanted to be quite sure that I was being followed; it's so easy to become paranoid. He was not a real professional; he wasn't quick enough, for one thing, and what professional would wear a distinctive beard and short tartan-patterned coat? He was carrying a large brown-paper parcel, trying to look like someone taking a Christmas present across town, but he wasn't delivering a present to somewhere across town; he was following me; there was no doubt about that. I stopped and peered up at the old Italian Embassy. Some rooms at the back seemed to be occupied, and I wondered who would live in such a place. The bearded man stopped and seemed to wonder too.

My decision to visit Lange this morning was a spontaneous one, so my follower must have been with me since I left Tante Lisl's before breakfast, and that meant he'd probably been outside the hotel all night. All night on Christmas Eve; where do you find such dedication these days? From Tante Lisl's he must have used a car, otherwise I would have spotted him earlier. He'd have found it easy enough to anticipate the speed and direction of a solitary walker in the almost empty streets. I should have noticed the car right from the start. I was becoming too old and too careless. He stopped again; he must have guessed he'd been spotted, but he was still sticking to the book, ducking out of sight and keeping his distance. He was inexpert but diligent. It was easy to guess that he'd hoped to do the whole job from inside a car, hence the brightly colored car coat, but now that I'd come poking about in the Tiergarten, he'd had to get out of the car and earn his money. Now he was conspicuous, especially with that big parcel under his arm.

I looked back. I couldn't see his car but he hadn't had many alternatives about where to leave it. I walked west, uncertainly changing direction but heading southward enough to keep him hoping that I would return to where he'd left the car. Was he alone? I wondered. Surely no professional would try to tail a suspect without any assistance whatsoever. But it was Christmas and perhaps all he had to do was to report my movements. He wasn't a private eye; whatever their shortcomings, they can all follow an errant husband and stay out of sight. And if he wasn't a KGB man and he wasn't a private eye, what was left? One of our own people from the Berlin Field Unit? Even my advanced paranoia couldn't believe that one of those lazy bastards could be persuaded into action on Christmas Day. Now I strolled back toward the park. I stopped to examine the trunk of a tree where someone had carved a hammer and sickle that was bent to become a swastika. I used the chance to watch him out of the corner of my eye. The parcel slipped from his grasp and he took his time about picking it up. He was right-handed; well, that was a useful thing to bear in mind.

I paused again at the little river in the park. But today the famous *Berliner Luft* was too cold for water to survive in. There were two people skating on the ice. A man and a woman, elderly judging by their stately posture and the way they skated side by side, long overcoats, flowing scarfs, and heads held high, like an illustration from some nineteenth-century magazine.

I hurried along the path as if suddenly remembering an appointment. Then I stooped down to hide. It wouldn't have worked with anyone more experienced, so it was really a test of his expertise. I still had no measure of him and couldn't guess what his motives might be. As it was, he walked right into it. That is to say, he walked right into me. It was the hurrying that did it; it often stampedes the pursuer into incautious and impulsive actions. That was how Hannibal won the Battle of Lake Trasimene after crossing the Apennines. All it needed was that sudden dash toward Rome to make Flaminius chase after him and blunder right into his ambush. Hannibal would probably have had the makings of a good field agent.

"Don't move," I said. I had him from behind, my arm round his throat and the other twisting hell out of his right arm while he was still looking for me far down the path. He grunted. I was holding his neck too tight. "I'm going to release you," I said, "but if you move carelessly after that, I'll have to really hurt you. You understand, don't you?"

He still didn't answer properly so I relaxed my hold on his throat a bit more to let him breathe. When I let him go he bent double and I thought he was going to collapse on me. I looked at him with surprise. The arm seam of his coat was torn and his hat was knocked off. He was making terrible noises. I suppose I'd grabbed him too tightly; I was out of practice. But he shouldn't have been gasping; a young man like him, well under thirty, should have been in better physical shape. Still bent over, he clutched his middle, taking very deep breaths.

"Who the hell are you?" I said.

"We'll ask the questions, Mr. Samson!"

There was another of them, a slim bespectacled man in a flashy brown-suede overcoat with fur collar. He was holding a gun and not bothering too much about who saw it.

"Hands behind your back, Samson. You know how these things are done." I cursed my stupid overconfidence. I should have guessed that such clumsiness as the bearded man displayed was all part of the trick. They'd now made me play Flaminius to their Hannibal.

The bearded one—still gasping for breath—rubbed me down quickly and expertly and said, "He has nothing."

"No gun, Samson? This is not the expert we've heard so much about. You're getting old and careless."

I didn't answer. He was right. I'd chosen not to go to Lange with a gun under my arm because it would have made it harder to deny my connection with London Central.

"Here he comes," said the man. "It took him long enough, didn't it." He was watching a dented panel truck trundling over the brown grass. The skaters were nowhere to be seen now: they were all part of the same team sent to get me.

The rear doors of the van opened to reveal a gleaming wheel chair. They pushed me up onto the chair and strapped my ankles and neck to the steel framework. Then they blindfolded me as the van drove away. It was all over in five minutes.

The roads were empty. The journey took no more than twenty minutes. The blindfold was good enough to prevent me seeing where I was, but I was bumped up steps and the gates of a lift were carelessly slammed against my arm.

They unstrapped me and locked me in a room. I was left to remove my own blindfold, not so easy when one's arms are cuffed behind one's back. It was impossible not to admire their efficiency and to deplore my own unpreparedness. There was no doubt where they'd brought me: I was in East Berlin, just a few minutes' walk from Checkpoint Charlie. But from this side of the Wall, it's a long walk back.

There were two windows. It was an anteroom—really a place where people waited. But the people who waited here had to have bars on the windows and heavy locks on the doors, and the window glass was frosted to make it difficult to see out. At the top of each window there was a small ventilation panel. I could reach that far only by putting a stool on the tabletop. With hands cuffed behind me I almost toppled as I scrambled up. Now through the narrow gap—the panel opened only as far as the bars permitted—I could see across the city. There was no movement: no cars, no trucks, no people. I recognized the massive U.S.S.R. Embassy in the Linden from the shape of the roof. Nearby there was the last remaining section of the Adlon Hotel; a few cramped rooms in the rear that in the thirties were used only for the personal servants of the hotel's clients. And there were the parking lot and the hillock that marked the site of the *Führerbunker* where Hitler had fought his last battles against marriage and the Red Army and, defeated by both Venus and Mars, blew out his troubled brains. Now I knew where I was: this was Hermann Göring's old Air Ministry, one of the few examples of Nazi architecture to escape both Anglo-American bombers and Soviet planners.

I went back to the hard wooden chair and sat down. It was Christmas Day—not a festival that any sincere Communist cares to celebrate, but there were enough insincere ones to empty the building. It was silent except for the occasional, distant sound of a slammed door or the hum of the lift. I looked round the room: no books or papers, the only printed item a brightly colored poster that was a part of the Kremlin's contribution to the anti-nuke debate. But the missile to be banned was labeled "NATO." There was no mention of Russian missiles—just a handsome young Communist and a snarling G.I. There was a second door in the room. It had a glass panel over which had been stuck patterned translucent paper. Such paper was commonly used in the East Bloc where frosted glass was sometimes in short supply. Standing with my back to the door I was able to peel a little of it back from the corner. A sticky compound remained on the glass, but I scratched it away with my fingernail.

By resting my face close against the glass it was possible to see into the next room. There were two people there, a man and a woman. Both wore white linen: a doctor and nurse. The woman was about forty; over her graying hair she wore a small starched cap. The man was younger, twenty-five or so. His white jacket was unbuttoned and there was a stain on the lapel that might have been blood. A stethoscope hung from his neck. He stood by the door writing in a small notebook. He consulted his wristwatch and then wrote more. The nurse was leaning against a two-tier bunk bed looking at something bundled there on the lower bed. She looked back to catch the doctor's eye. He looked up from his writing and she shook her head. The movement was almost imperceptible, as if she'd been shaking her head all morning. She was Russian, I had no doubt of that. She had the flat features, narrowed eyes, and pale coloring that is typical of people from Russia's eastern Arctic. She turned back to the bundle of clothes and touched it tenderly. It was too small to be a person—except a very small person. She leaned closer, fussing in the way that mothers do when babies sleep face down. But this was too big for a baby. She moved back a trifle. It was a child—a red, woolly striped hat had slipped from its head. Swaddled in thick blankets an elbow protruded from between. A yellow sleeve—an anorak. And shiny boots. Jesus Christ, they had Billy! Little Billy. Here in Berlin.

The scene wobbled, my pulse raced, and my throat was suddenly dry. Only by steadying myself against the wall was I able to prevent myself fainting. Billy! Billy! Billy! I leaned close to the peephole again. The nurse moved away to get a small enamel tray from the table. She carried it carefully to the sink and took from it a hypodermic syringe. She put the needle into a glass of pink-colored liquid. I felt ill. No matter how much my brain told me to remain calm, my emotions took over. Now I knew why men with wives and families were so seldom used as field agents.

They are watching, they are watching you, now, at this moment, I told myself for the hundredth time. This is all a well-prepared act to disorient you and soften you up for what comes next. But it didn't help much. I could think of nothing except my son and what these bastards might do to him. Surely to God, Fiona knows about this. Surely she would stop them hurting her own son. But suppose Fiona doesn't know?

There was the sudden noise of a key being inserted into the lock. Someone was entering from the corridor. There was enough time for me to get back to the bench and sit down. There was enough time for me to look relaxed and unconcerned, but I'm not sure I managed that.

"Herr Samson!"

We knew each other. He was a great bull of a man, about fifty years old, with a big peasant frame upon which years of manual labor had layered hard muscle. His skull shone through close-cropped hair. His large nose was surmounted by a big broad forehead. Pavel Moskvin. The London Central computer described him as a KGB "political adviser." That could mean anything. Political advisers were sometimes the brightest of bright graduates, multilingual polymaths who could quote Groucho as readily as Karl Marx. Such men used a stretch with the KGB as a finishing school. But Moskvin was long past all that. I had him marked down as the sort of untalented plodder who'd graduated from the factory floor having discovered that the Party always looks after its own. The U.S.S.R. was filled with men like him; their unthinking loyalty was what held the whole creaky system together.

"Where is my wife?" I asked him. It wasn't a textbook opening or anything that London Central would have approved, but I knew they'd have me on a tape and there seemed a good chance that Fiona would be monitoring the dialogue.

"Your wife? Why would you want to know that, Herr Samson?" said Moskvin mockingly. His German was awkward and ungrammatical but his manner said everything.

"My people know I'm here, Moskvin," I said. "They'll be putting out a red alert any time now."

"Are you trying to frighten me?" he said. "Your people know nothing, and they don't care. It is Christmas. You are all alone, Herr Samson, all alone. Your people in London will be eating pudding, watching your Queen speaking on television and getting drunk!"

"We'll see," I muttered ominously, but his version of what London Central might be doing sounded only too likely.

"Why don't you behave sensibly, Samson?"

"For instance?"

There were footsteps in the corridor. He half turned toward the door, his head cocked to listen. The break in his attention gave me the chance I'd been praying for. With both hands cuffed behind me, I grasped the backrest of the chair. Then, with head bowed low to counter the weight, I twisted my body and with all my force heaved the chair in his direction.

It was too heavy for me. It hit him in the legs instead of on the side of the head, but the violence of it caught him unprepared so that he staggered back cursing and spluttering with rage.

He kicked the chair aside. "I'll teach you . . . ," he said and stepped forward to punch me. He didn't aim anywhere; he hit me as an angry drunk might pound a wall. But Moskvin was a heavyweight. His blows didn't have to be aimed; they hit like sledgehammers and I was slammed against the wall so hard that I lost my balance and slid to the floor.

"You crazy fool!" he growled and wiped his mouth with the reddened knuckles of his fist. "If you want a fight I'll take you downstairs and kill you with my bare hands."

Slowly I scrambled to my feet and he kicked the chair over to me again with the side of his boot. I sat down on it and closed my eyes. I had a terrible pain inside me, as though molten lead was pouring through my lungs.

When Moskvin spoke again, he'd recovered some of his former composure. "Be sensible. Face the truth. Your wife has chosen to work with us of her own free will. Do you really believe that we are holding her captive? Is that what your bosses in London have told you? Forget it. She is one of us, Samson. She does not wish to return to the West; she will never go back there. Never." He watched me carefully and I stared back at him. "Do you want a cigarette?" he asked finally.

"No," I said, although I needed one desperately. We both knew the way it went; you accept a cigarette, you say thank you, and the next thing you're chatting away and reaching for the writing paper. "I don't smoke."

He smiled. He knew all about me. With Fiona working for the KGB, there was little about me that they couldn't find out. The pain lessened a little as I shifted my position and controlled my breathing, but one of his punches seemed to have torn a ligament and the big trapezius muscle of my back sent sharp pains right up to my neck.

"Why make life miserable for both of you?" said Moskvin in what he obviously thought a friendly manner. His German was better now; perhaps this was a text he'd prepared and practiced. "While you are working for the German Stations Controller in London and your wife is here in Berlin, the two of you must be permanently unhappy."

"What are you proposing?" I said. I tried not to look at the glass-paneled door but it was difficult.

Moskvin watched me carefully. He knew I'd seen into the next room. His arrival was too prompt to be anything but a reaction from a man watching what I did. Yes, I could see it now; the camera was behind that damned anti-nuke poster. A circular patch of the lettering was dull—open-weave cloth through which a focused camera could see clearly.

"There would be nothing for you here, Samson. We know everything you could tell us."

I nodded. Had they really given up hope of enrolling me, or was this some subtle way of trying to get me to prove I knew more than they thought? "You're right," I said.

"So why not an overseas posting?" said Moskvin. He had both hands in the pockets of his greatcoat, fidgeting with something metallic that clanked. When he brought his hands into view there were three clips of pistol ammunition in his fingers. He fiddled with them. When he saw me looking at him he said, "Don't have any more of those stupid ideas, Samson. The gun is downstairs in my safe." Lots of bullets; it was characteristic of this violent primitive.

"Overseas?"

"You know Washington; you like Americans."

"Lots of people want to go to Washington," I said to gain time. "Who knows when a vacancy will come."

Moskvin continued to play with the clips. "Washington gossip says London Central will fill two vacancies in the next month or two. Two senior jobs—that's what our Washington office tells us."

Through the blur of pain my memory said he was right:

sickness and a promotion had created two unexpected vacancies in the Washington Embassy. I'd seen the signal on Bret's desk. I was senior enough to apply for either. "No," I said.

"Think about it," said Moskvin. Under his silky voice I could hear the hatred and contempt that he was trying to hide.

"Or what?"

"No threats," said Moskvin. "But surely it would be more civilized?"

"More civilized than staying in London to undo some of the harm of my wife's treachery?"

"Be more sophisticated and less arrogant, Herr Samson. Can you really believe that your contribution to the work at London Central will make any difference?"

I shrugged—but it hurt.

"What are you trying to prove, Samson? We've got an operations file on you that's that thick." He indicated with finger and thumb. "And that's without all the dangerous tricks you've done undetected. How long can you go on trying to prove you're a field agent? Until you get yourself killed, is that it?"

"You wouldn't understand," I said.

"Because I'm a deskman?" He almost lost control over his rage. "Vanity, is that it? Prove yourself over and over again so you can be sure you're not a coward? Just as the repressed homosexual becomes a womanizer to prove he's really a man?" Was that some reference to his ex-colleague Stinnes? If it was, he gave no further evidence of it.

He put away his playthings and stood, hands on hip, his long black greatcoat open to reveal an ill-fitting gray suit and dark roll-neck sweater. He looked like someone who'd dressed in response to a fire alarm.

"Start life again, Herr Samson. Forget the pain of the past." He saw me glance toward the door. "What do I have to do to persuade you?" He smiled and I could see the sadistic glee in his face. He knew I'd seen into the next room.

"I'll think about it," I told him. Was Billy still there? I wondered. It was torture carrying on this conversation.

"Don't think about it," said Moskvin softly. His voice rose to a shout as he added, "Do it!"

"I said I'd think about it."

"Then think about this too," he yelled. He snatched the door open and stood in the doorway. With hands cuffed, I'd stand no chance against him—he'd already proved that. But I pushed close to see over his shoulder.

"Billy!" I called but the bundled figure made no response. "Why drug the child?" I said. I couldn't keep the weariness and defeat from my voice. The doctor and nurse had gone. Even the disinfectant, the hypodermic, and the enamel tray had gone. "Where's the doctor?" I asked.

"Doctor?" said Moskvin. "What doctor? Are you mad?" He went striding across the room to the bunk bed. "Think about this, Samson," he yelled over his shoulder. He raised his arm, his massive fist clenched over the bed.

"No, don't!" It was a plea now, the fight had gone out of me. But he paid no heed to my call. His punch almost broke the wooden frame of the bed, with such force did it descend. The terrible blow swept everything across the room: blankets, the pathetic woolen hat, the boots and anorak. It all clattered to the floor in a heap.

Moskvin laughed. "What did you think, Samson? Did you think we had your son in here?" Now I could see that these were not Billy's clothes: just clothes like them.

I leaned against the wall. I felt the bile rising in my throat. I closed my lips tight, determined not to give him the satisfaction of seeing me throw up. But it was not possible. I leaned forward and vomited my breakfast across the floor along with a generous measure of Mrs. Koby's homemade wine.

Moskvin really laughed then. It was the first spontaneous human reaction I'd ever seen from him. He unlocked my handcuffs. "We'll get a car and take you back to the West, Samson. Where would you like to go, Frau Hennig's hotel?"

I nodded and used a handkerchief to wipe my face and my clothes. The sweet-sour smell of the vomit was in my nostrils.

"You'll need to wash and change," said Moskvin. "But you just remember this, clever Mr. Field Agent: anytime we want you, we'll pick you up as easily as we did today. And not just you, Samson; your children, your mother, your friend Volkmann . . . anytime we want you. You remember that, my friend." He laughed again.

I could hear him laughing as he marched off down the corridor and shouted for the driver. I looked back at the TV monitor. Was Fiona watching? And did she feel proud of herself?

WHEN I got back to Tante Lisl's I took a long hot bath and examined my cuts and bruises. Then I changed my clothes to take Lisl to the Volkmanns' for what we both thought was to be a quiet sit-down meal. We were wrong.

It was a ferocious event; the sort of frantic party you find only in Berlin and New York. The hi-fi was playing "Hello, Dolly!" as I went in, and the guests were in that restrained sort of fancy dress that provides a chance to wear jewelry and expensive hair-dos. It was noisy and crowded and the air was blue with tobacco smoke and there was the fragrance of French perfumes and Havana cigars.

Tante Lisl showed little surprise at the mad scene to which I'd brought her. She'd brought up little Werner after his parents died, and she felt for him that compassionate condescension that motherhood brings. She sat in the corner on the thronelike chair that Werner had thoughtfully placed there for her. She sipped her champagne and surveyed the antics of the guests with a wry superiority, like a tribal chief watching the sort of ceremonial dances that end in human sacrifice. She'd prepared carefully for the party: false eyelashes and real pearls; Tante Lisl's ultimate accolade.

I went to the buffet table in the dining room to assemble a plate of food for her. The room, like every other room in the apartment, was crowded. In front of me there was a tall thin

Mephistopheles. He was engaged in earnest conversation with a man in a white silk roll-neck sweater. He said in uncertain English, "We Germans are so very like you Americans! That's why there is this constant friction. Both our countrymen respond to ideology, both seek always to improve the world, and both often want to improve it by means of military crusades."

"And both like clean toilets," said the American in the roll-neck sweater. "Germany is the only goddamned country in Europe that doesn't have filthy bathrooms."

"Anal oriented, we psychiatrists say," Mephistopheles told him. "In other countries people just want to get in there, do what has to be done, and get out again as soon as possible. But you Americans and we Germans like to have toilets we can spend time in. One glance in any of these home improvement magazines will confirm that."

A movement of the crowd round the buffet allowed me to push forward to the table near the window and reach the stack of empty plates and silverware. I looked round me. Only in Berlin would they have a party like this in daylight. Outside it was gloomy, but to the west there was even a little sunlight breaking through the clouds. The food was disorienting too. It was not exactly what I'd think of as Christmas Day lunch, but it was a magnificent display of luxuries. Although a great deal had already been eaten, new plates of food kept appearing, brought by waitresses in neat black dresses and fancy lace aprons. This was a *Fresserei*, a feast where people gobble like animals. There were lobster tails in mayonnaise and crab claws in wine sauce. There was caviar and cold salmon, foie gras with truffles, and a dozen types of sliced sausage.

"There's blood on your face," said a woman with diamond-studded spectacles, reaching past me to get more *Leberwurst* and potato salad. "Naughty boy. You look as if you'd been fighting."

"I have," I said. "I found Santa Claus in my sitting room helping himself to my whisky." In the Tiergarten the bearded man's sleeve buttons had cut my cheek, and when I dabbed the place, I found it had been bleeding again.

The diamond spectacles discovered a dish of smoked eel garnished with jelly. Uttering a whoop of joy she heaped her plate with eel and black bread and moved away.

I put a selection of food onto two plates and, balancing them carefully, moved off through the crowd. Enough space had been cleared in the centre of the floor for a dozen or more people to dance, but they had to hug really close. Berliners give themselves wholeheartedly to everything they do: Berlin opera and concert audiences cheer, boo, jeer, or applaud with a mad tenacity unknown elsewhere. And so it was with parties; they sang, they danced, they gobbled and guzzled, hugging, arguing, and laughing as if this party were the final expression of everything they'd ever lived for.

A very handsome young black man, dressed in the shiny silk shorts and brightly colored singlet of a boxer—and with gloves suspended from his neck in case anyone missed the point—was talking to Zena Volkmann, his hostess, while both were picking at one plate of food.

Zena Volkmann was wearing glittering gold pants and a close-fitting black shirt upon which a heavy gold necklace and a gold flower brooch showed to good effect, as did her figure. Her face was still tanned dark from her recent trip to Mexico and her jet-black hair was loose and long enough to fall over her shoulders. She saw me and waved a fork.

"Hello, Zena," I said. "Where's Werner?"

"I sent him to borrow ice from the people downstairs," she answered. And immediately turned back to her companion, saying, "Go on with what you were saying."

I saw other people I knew. In the corner there was Axel Mauser, who'd been at school with me and Werner. He was wearing a beautifully tailored white silk jacket with black pants, bow tie, and frilly shirt. He was talking to a woman in a silver sheath dress and waving his hands as he always did when telling a story. "Tante Lisl's here," I told him as I went past. "She'd love you to say hello, Axel."

"Hello, you old bastard," said Axel, getting me into focus. "You look terrible. Still up to your tricks?"

"Just say hello," I said. "She'll be hurt if you forget her."

"Okay, Bernd, I won't forget. You know my wife, don't you?"

I said hello. I hadn't recognized the woman in the silver dress as Axel's wife. Every other time I'd seen her she'd been in a grimy apron with her hands in the sink.

By the time I took the plates of food, cutlery, and black bread to Lisl, I was too late. Old Lothar Koch had already brought a plate for her. He was sitting beside her, embarrassed perhaps to see her here and explaining his sudden recovery from the influenza that had prevented him dining with her the previous evening. Koch was a shrunken little man in his mid-eighties. His ancient evening suit was far too big for him, but he'd long ago declared that his life expectancy precluded him wasting money on new clothes. I said hello to him.

"Miracle drugs," said Lothar Koch to me and to Lisl and to the world at large. "I was at death's door last night, Bernd. I was just telling Frau Hennig the same thing." I called her "Lisl" and he called her "Lisl," but when he talked to me about her she had to be "Frau Hennig," even when she was sitting there with us. He was like that. He wiped his large nose on a crisp linen handkerchief.

I decided to abandon both plates of food. What I really needed was a drink. I joined a big crowd at the table where an overworked waitress was dispensing champagne.

"That's a bloody good costume," remarked a very young sheriff doffing his ten-gallon hat to a man dressed as a Berlin cop. But the man dressed as the cop was not amused. He *was* a Berlin cop, desperately trying to find someone who'd left a light-blue Audi blocking the entrance to the underground garage.

"Cocktails to the right, champagne to the left," said a waitress trying to disperse the crowd.

I moved forward and got a bit nearer to the drinks. In front of me there was an elderly architecture lecturer talking with a delicate-looking female student. I knew them both as people I'd met with the Volkmanns. The lecturer was saying ". . . leaving politics to one side, Hitler's plans for a new Berlin were superb."

"Really," said the pale girl; she was a history student. "I think the plans were grotesque."

"The Anhalter and Potsdam railway stations were to be rebuilt to the south of Tempelhof so that the centre of the city could have an avenue three miles long. Palaces, magnificent office buildings, and a huge triumphal arch. On the northern side there was to be a meeting hall with a dome eight hundred and twenty-five feet across with space inside for one hundred and fifty thousand people."

"I know. I went to your lectures about it," said the girl in a bored voice. "Afterwards I went to the library. Did you know that the only part of Hitler's plan ever put into effect was the planting of deciduous trees in the Tiergarten? And that only restored the old mixed forest that Frederick the Great had felled to help pay for the Silesian Wars."

The lecturer seemed not to have heard. He said, "City planning needs firm central government. The way things are going, we'll never see a properly planned town anywhere."

"Thank God for that," said the bored girl. She picked up two glasses of champagne and moved away. He recognized me and smiled.

As soon as I'd got my champagne I began looking for somewhere to sit. Then I saw Werner. He was standing in the doorway that led to his bedroom. He was looking harassed. I went across. "Quite a party, Werner," I said in admiration. "I was expecting a small sit-down for eight or ten."

He ushered me into the bedroom. Now I saw how enough space had been cleared for the dancing. Furniture was packed into the bedroom so that it was piled almost to the ceiling. There was only just space enough for Werner and me to stand. He closed the bedroom door.

"I just have to have a few minutes to myself," he explained. "Zena says we need more ice, but we've got tons of ice."

"Well, it's a hell of a spread, Werner. I saw Axel . . . Axel Mauser dressed up like I'd never believe. Is he still working for the police?"

"Axel's wife got a big promotion in AEG. She's some kind of executive now and they're moving out of that lousy apartment in Märkisches Viertel to a place near the forest in Hermsdorf."

"You'd better give Tante Lisl a kiss and a formal greeting," I said. "She keeps asking where you are. In her day, the host and hostess stood at the door and shook hands with everyone as they were announced."

"Zena loves this sort of party," said Werner, "but it's too noisy for me. I come and hide. I don't know half those people out there. Would you believe that?" He wrung his hands and said, "Did you go and see Lange?" He straightened some of the dining-room chairs that were stacked one upon the other. Then he looked at me, "Are you all right?"

"I phoned him and went across there this morning."

Werner nodded mournfully. "He's still the same, isn't he? Still bad-tempered. Remember how he used to shout at us when we were kids?" Werner wasn't looking at me. Stuck under the seats of the dining chairs there were manufacturers' labels. Werner suddenly began reading one as if deeply interested in the dates and codes.

"I didn't realize how much he hates Bret Rensselaer," I said. "Lange still blames Bret for his having to leave the Department."

Werner abandoned his study of the label and gave me a little smile that showed no sympathy for Lange. "He only says that because he's been on the shelf ever since. When Lange resigned from the Department he thought he was going to get a wonderful job somewhere else and go back and show your dad and all the rest of them what a big success he was."

"I don't know what he lives on," I said.

"His wife inherited her parents' apartment in Munich. They lease it out and live on the income from it."

"I was followed this morning, Werner," I said. I drank the rest of my champagne. What I needed was something stronger.

He looked up sharply and raised his eyebrows. I told him about the bearded man and the way I'd been kidnapped and held in East Berlin.

"My God!" said Werner. He went white. "And then they released you?"

"I wasn't really worried," I told him untruthfully. "It was obviously just to throw a scare into me."

"Perhaps taking a job in Washington would be the best course."

"You've never worked in an Embassy," I reminded him. "Those people live in a fantasy world . . . Ritz Crackers, white wine, and randy wives. I had six months of that; never again."

"Do you think it was Fiona's idea? What was behind it?"

"I just can't decide," I said.

"A doctor and a nurse . . . pretending they had your son . . . too bizarre for Fiona. It smells like Moscow."

"I'd prefer to think that."

"You'll report it, of course," said Werner.

"I don't come out of it too well, do I?"

"You must report it, Bernie."

"How did they get to hear about the vacancies coming up in Washington?" I said.

"The word gets round quickly," said Werner cautiously. He guessed what I was going to say.

"You know who automatically gets first notice of any changes in Washington, don't you?" I said.

Werner came closer to where I was standing and lowered his voice. "You're not getting some sort of obsession about Bret Rensselaer, are you?" he asked.

"Obsession?"

"You keep on about him. First it was these code names . . . about how no agent ever had two names. And you try to persuade me that there is still a KGB man in London Central."

"I've told you no more than facts," I said.

"No one can argue with facts, Bernie. But the Bret Rensselaer role you're trying to write into this script of yours is not something that has emerged from calm and rational reasoning; it's personal."

"I don't give a damn about Bret," I said.

"You know that's not true, Bernie," said Werner in a sweet and reasonable voice. "You went round to Lange knowing that he hates Bret. You wanted to hear someone say that Bret was some kind of monster who deliberately wrecked the early networks. You knew what Lange was going to say before you went; we've both heard all that rigmarole from him a hundred times. If you're trying to put a noose round Bret's neck, you'll need something a damn sight more reliable than Lange's gossip or news about vacancies in Washington. You try and prove Bret a bad security risk and you're going to make a fool of yourself."

"Why would I want to do that?" I protested.

"There was a time when you suspected he was having an affair with Fiona . . ."

"I was wrong," I said quickly. Werner looked up; I'd said it too damned quickly. "There was no substance in that," I added, more calmly this time.

"You resent Bret. No matter how irrational that might be, you resent him."

"Why should I?"

"I don't know. He's rich and charming and something of a ladies' man. I resent him too; he's too damned smooth, and he has a cruel streak in him. But keep your head, Bernie."

"I'll keep my head."

Werner was not convinced. "Bret has everything going for him. Bret is an Anglophile: everything British is wonderful. The British like hearing that kind of praise—it's exactly what they believe—and so Bret is very popular. You won't find it easy to move against him."

"I've already discovered that," I said. "For all Silas Gaunt's caustic remarks and Dicky Cruyer's bitter envy of him, neither of them would be happy to see Bret facing a board of enquiry."

"Bret's an old-fashioned U.S. gentleman—honest and brave."

"Is that the way you see him?"

"It's the way he is, Bernie. He's not KGB material. Promise me you'll think about what I'm telling you, Bernie. I don't give a damn about Bret. It's you I'm thinking of. You know that, don't you?"

"Sure I do, Werner. Thanks. But I'm not gunning for Bret. I just want to talk with Stinnes and get a few ends tidied away."

"Did you wonder if the Stinnes defection might be a KGB stunt?"

"Yes, lots of times, but he's given us some good ones; not wonderful, but good," I said. "And now it looks like the Miller woman was murdered. She was a long-term agent, Werner. Would they really kill one of their own just to make Stinnes look kosher?"

"We haven't found her body yet," said Werner.

"Leaving it inside the ambulance would make it too easy for us," I said. But Werner was right: until we had an identified corpse, there was always the chance that she was alive.

"Then what about the chances of Brahms Four being a KGB plant?"

I thought about it before answering. "I don't think so."

But Werner noticed my hesitation and followed it up. "Did von Munte really need to be brought out of the East? He was an old man and so was his wife. How long before he'd be old enough to make one of those permitted visits to the West?"

"Don't be stupid, Werner. Officials with his sort of confidential information are not permitted to come West on visits, even if they live to be a hundred years old."

"But suppose von Munte *was* a plant? Sent to give us dud information. You said Silas Gaunt was difficult and protective when you tried to question him. Suppose London Debriefing Centre have already detected that he's a KGB plant. Suppose they've lodged him with Silas Gaunt to keep him on ice and make sure he doesn't do any damage."

"That would require a faith in the brilliance of the London Debriefing Centre staff that I just can't muster," I said.

"That's what I mean, Bernie. You're determined to see it the way you want it."

Chapter 8

CHRISTMAS was gone but, having been on duty, I had my Christmas leave to come. I took the children to the circus and to the theatre. We did the things they wanted to do. We inspected the model ships and real planes on the top floors of the Science Museum, the live reptiles in the Regent's Park zoo, and the plaster dinosaur skeleton in the hall of the Natural History Museum. The children had seen it all before, over and over again, but they were creatures of habit and they chose the things they knew so well so that they could tell me about them, instead of me telling them. I understood this pleasure and shared it. The only thing that marred these delightful events was that Gloria had no leave days to enjoy and I missed her.

I took the children to see George Kosinski, their uncle and my brother-in-law. The place we visited wasn't one of his swanky motorcar showrooms but a dirty cobbled yard in Southwark. One-time marshland, the district was now a grimy collection of slums and sooty factories interspersed with ugly new office blocks as rent increases drive more and more companies south of the River Thames.

George Kosinski's repair yard was a derelict site; a place that had been hit by a German bomb in 1941 and never subsequently built upon. Next to the yard was a heavy and ornate block of Victorian flats that had become slums. Across the road, more recent municipal housing was even worse.

George's yard was protected by a high wall into which broken glass had been cemented to discourage uninvited callers. For those more difficult to discourage there were two guard dogs. Along the other side of the yard there was a railway viaduct. Two arches of the viaduct had been bricked up and converted to repair shops, but one section of the arched accommodation had been made into an office.

George was sitting behind a table. He was wearing his hat and overcoat, for the small electric fan-heater did little to warm the cold damp air. The ceiling curved over his head and nothing had been done to disguise or insulate the ancient brickwork of the arch. In a cardboard box in the corner there were empty beer and wine bottles, cigarette butts, broken glass, and discarded Christmas decorations. Through the thin partition that separated this makeshift office from the workshop there came the sound of rock music from a transistor radio.

George Kosinski was thirty-six years old, although most people would have thought him five or even ten years older than that. He was a small man with a large nose and a large mustache, both of which looked inappropriate, if not false. The same could be said of his strong cockney accent to which I had to get freshly attuned each time I saw him. His suit was expensive: Savile Row, with the lapels stitched a little too tight so as to make the handwork evident. His shirt, his shoes, which were resting on the table amid the paperwork, and his tie were all as expensive as can be. His hair was curly and graying at the temples to give him the distinguished appearance that is the result of regular visits to the hairdresser. Whatever he economized on, it was not his clothes or his transport, for outside there stood his gleaming new Rolls.

"Well, here we are. You've come to beard your Uncle George in his den, have you?" He took his feet off the table with a sigh. I had the feeling that he'd contrived that posture for our entrance. He liked to think of himself as unconventional.

The children were too awed to reply. Leaning back in his chair George banged on the wall with the side of his fist. Someone next door responded to this command, for the radio was immediately turned down.

"Your father's come to buy a beautiful car from me—did he tell you that?" He looked up at me and added, "It's not arrived yet." A glance at his watch. "Any minute now."

"We're a bit early, George," I said.

"Can't give you a drink or anything. I don't keep anything of any value here. You can see what it's like here."

I could see. The cracked lino on the floor and the bare walls said it all. As well as that, there was a notice that said WE DON'T BUY CAR RADIOS. He saw me looking at it and said, "All day long there are people in and out of here trying to sell me radios and tape recorders."

"Stolen?"

"Of course. What would these tearaways be doing with an expensive car stereo except that they've ripped it out of some parked car? I never touch anything suspect."

"Do you spend much time here?" I asked.

He shrugged. "I call in from time to time. You run a business, any sort of business, you have to see what's happening. Right, Bernard?"

"I suppose so." George Kosinski was a rich man, and I wondered how he endured such squalor. He wasn't mean—his generosity was well known and admitted even by those with whom he struck the tough bargains for which he was equally well known.

"Rover 3500; you'll not be sorry you bought it, Bernard. And if I'm wrong, bring it back to me and I'll give you your money back. Okay?"

"Okay," I said. He was saying it to the children as much as to me. He liked children. Perhaps his marriage would have been happier if he'd had children of his own.

"I saw it yesterday morning. Dark green, a beautiful respray, just like a factory finish, and the people doing the waxing job are the best in the country. You've got a vintage car there, Bernard. Better than that: a special. The V-8 engine has scarcely been used."

"It's not another one of those cars that's been owned by that old lady who only used it to go shopping once a week and was too nervous to go more than twenty miles an hour?" I said.

"Naughty," said George with a smile. "Your dad is naughty," he told the children. "He doesn't believe what I'm telling him. And I've never told a fib in my life." Suddenly there came a thunderous roar. Billy flinched and Sally put her hands to her head. "It's just the trains," said George. "They're only just above our heads."

But George's boast had captured Billy's imagination and when the sound of the train diminished he said, "Have you really never told a fib, Uncle George? Never ever?"

"Almost never," said George. He turned to me. "I have a friend of yours calling in this morning. I told him you'd be here."

"Who?"

"It's not a secret or anything?" said George. "I won't get into trouble for telling somebody where you are, will I?" It was a jest, but not entirely a jest. I'd heard the same sort of resentment in the voices of other people who had only a rough idea of what I did for a living.

He screwed his face up in an expression that was somewhat apologetic. "There are people who know I know you . . . people who seem to know more about what you do for a living than I know." Nervously George pushed his glasses up, using his forefinger. He was always doing that when he became agitated. The spectacle frames were too heavy, I suppose, or perhaps it was perspiration.

"People try to guess what I do," I said. "Better they're not encouraged, George. Who is it?"

"Posh Harry they call him. Do you know who I mean? He's something in the CIA, isn't he? He seems to know you well enough. I thought it would be all right to say I was seeing you."

"It was a long time ago that he worked for the CIA," I said. "But Harry is all right. He's coming here, you say?"

"He wants to see you, Bernard. He reckons he's got something you'll like."

"We'll see," I said. "But you know what he's like, George. I never meet him without wondering if he's going to wind up selling me a set of encyclopedias."

POSH Harry arrived on time. He was a pristine American, whose face, like his suits and linen, seemed never to wrinkle. He was of Japanese-Hawaiian extraction, and although in a crowd he would pass as European, he had the flat features, small nose, and high cheekbones of Oriental peoples. He spent half his life on planes and had no address except hotels, shared offices, and box numbers. He was an amazing linguist and he always knew what was happening to whom, from Washington to Warsaw and back again. He was what the reporters call "a source" and always had something to add about the latest spy scandal or trial or investigation whenever the media ran short of comment. His brother—much older than Harry—was a CIA man whose career went back to OSS days in World War II. He'd died in some lousy CIA foul-up in Vietnam. Sometimes it was suggested that Harry was a recognized conduit through whom the CIA leaked stories they wanted to make public, but it was difficult to reconcile that with Harry's family history. Harry was not an apologist for the CIA; he'd never completely forgiven them for his brother's death.

Harry was exactly the kind of man that Hollywood casts as a CIA agent. His voice was just right too. He had the sort of low, very soft American voice that is crisp, clear, and attractive, the voice that sports commentators use for games that are very slow and boring.

Harry arrived wearing those English clothes you can only find in New York City. A dark-gray cotton poplin raincoat, calfskin oxford shoes, tweedy jacket, and a striped English old-school tie that had been invented by an American designer. The hat was a giveaway, though; a plaid sports cap that few Englishmen would wear, even on a golf course.

"Good to see you again, George," he said as he took

George's hand. Then he gave me the same sort of greeting, in that low gravelly voice, and shook my hand with a firm, sincere grip.

"I'll go and see if your motorcar has arrived," said George. "Come on, kids."

"I spoke on the phone to Lange," explained Harry. "He really enjoyed meeting with you again."

"What did Lange have to say?"

"Nothing I didn't already know. That you're still working hard, following up orders from London Central."

"What else?"

"Something about Bret Rensselaer," said Harry. "I didn't pay too much attention."

"That's the best way with Lange," I agreed. "He has a bee in his bonnet about Bret Rensselaer."

"So it's not true that Bret's being specially vetted?"

"Not as far as I know," I said.

"I'm no special buddy of Bret's, as you probably know. But Bret is one hundred percent okay. There's no chance Bret would do anything disloyal."

"Is that so?" I said, keeping it all very casual.

"For years your people kept Bret away from any U.S. sensitive material in case it compromised his loyalty, but he was never any kind of undercover man for the Agency. Bret is your man, you can rest assured on that one."

I nodded and wondered where Posh Harry had got the idea that Bret was suspected of leaking to the Americans. Was that Lange's misinterpretation or Harry's? Or was it simply that no one could start to envisage him doing anything as dishonorable as spying for the Russians? And if that was it, was I wrong? And, if he was guilty of such ungentlemanly activities, who was going to believe it?

"What have they got against Bret anyway?" asked Harry.

"Better you contact me through the office, Harry," I said. "I don't like getting my relatives involved."

"Sure, I'm sorry," said Harry, giving no sign of being sorry.

"But this is something better done away from the people across the river there." He gave a nod in the vague direction of Westminster and Whitehall.

"What is it?"

"I'm going to give you something on a plate, Bernard. It will give you a lot of kudos with your people."

"That's good," I said without sounding very keen. I'd suffered some of Harry's favors in the past.

"And that's the truth," said Harry. "Take a look at that." He passed me a photocopy of a typewritten document. There were eight pages of it.

"Do I have to read it? Or are you going to tell me what it's all about?"

"That's a memo that was discussed by the Cabinet about three or four months ago. It concerns the security of British installations in West Germany."

"The British Cabinet? This is a British Cabinet memo?"

"Yessir."

"Is there anything special about it?"

"The special thing about it was that one copy at least ended up in the KGB files in Moscow."

"Is that where this photocopy came from?"

"KGB; Moscow. That is exactly right." He smiled. It was the salesman's smile, broad but bleak.

"What has this got to do with me, Harry?"

"This could be the break you need, Bernard."

"Do I need a break?"

"Come on, Bernard. Come on! Do you think it's a secret that your people are nervous about employing you?"

"I don't know what you're talking about, Harry," I said.

"Okay. When your wife defected it was swept under the carpet. But don't imagine there were no off-the-record chats to the boys in Washington and Brussels. So what do you think those people were likely to say? What about the husband, they asked. I'm not going to baby you along, Bernie. Quite a few people—people in the business, I mean—know what happened to your wife. And they know that you are under the microscope right now. Are you going to deny it?"

"What's your proposition, Harry?" I said.

"This memo is a hot potato, Bernie. What son of a bitch leaked that one? Leaked it so that it didn't stop moving until it got to Moscow?"

"An agent inside Ten Downing Street? Is that what you're selling me?"

"Number Ten is your neck of the woods, old buddy. I'm suggesting you take this photocopy and start asking questions. I'm saying that a big one like this could do you a power of good right now."

"And what do you want out of it?"

"Now come on, Bernie. Is that what you think of me? It's a present. I owe you a couple of favors. We both know that."

I folded the sheets as best I could and put it all into my pocket. "I'll report it, of course."

"You do whatever you choose. But if you report it, that paper will go into the box and you'll never hear another thing about it. The investigation will be directly handed over to the security service. You know that as well as I do."

"I'll think about it, Harry. Thanks anyway."

"A lot of folks are rooting for you, Bernard."

"Where did you get it, Harry?"

Posh Harry had a foot on the chair and was gently scraping a mud spot from his shoe with his fingernail. "Bernard!" he said reproachfully. "You know I can't tell you that." He wet his fingertips with spittle and tried a second time.

"Well, let's eliminate a few nasties," I said. "This wasn't taken from any CIA office, was it?"

"Bernard, Bernard." He still was looking at his shoe. "What a mind you've got!"

"Because I don't want to carry a parcel that's ticking."

He finished the work on his shoe and put his feet on the floor and looked at me. "Of course not. It's raw, it's hot. It hasn't been on any desks."

"Some kind of floater then?"

"What do you think I am, Bernard? A part-time pimp for the KGB? Do you think I've lasted this long without being able to smell a KGB float?"

"There's always a first time, Harry. And any one of us can make a mistake."

"Well, okay, Bernard. I've got no real provenance on this one, I'll admit that. It's a German contact who's given me nothing but gold so far."

"And who pays him?"

"He's not for sale, Bernard."

"Then it's no one I know," I said.

He gave a little mirthless chuckle as a man might acknowledge the feeble joke of a valuable client. "You're getting old and embittered, Bernard. Do you know there was a time when you'd get angry at hearing a crack like that? You'd have given your lecture about idealism, and politics, and freedom, and people who have died for what they believe in. Now you say it's no one you know." He shook his head. It was mockery, but we both knew he was right. We both knew plenty of people who had never been for sale, and some of them had died proving it.

"Is George selling you a car?" I said to change the subject.

"I lease from George. I've done that for years. He lets me change cars, see? You knew that, didn't you?" He meant that George let him have a succession of cars when he was keeping someone under observation and didn't want the car he used recognized.

"No," I said. "George observes the discretion of the confessional. I didn't even know he knew you."

"And nice kids, Bernie." He slapped me on the back. "Don't look so worried, pal. You've got a lot of good friends. A lot of people owe you. They'll see you through."

Posh Harry was in the middle of saying all this when the door of the office crashed open. In the doorway there was a woman, thirtyish and pretty in the way that women become pretty if they use enough expensive makeup. She wore a full-length fur coat and hugged a large handbag to herself as if it contained a lot of valuables.

"Hon-ee," she called petulantly. "How much longer do I have to sit around in this dump?"

"Coming, sweetheart," said Posh Harry.

"Har-reee! We're going to be so late," she said. Her voice was laden with magnolia blossoms, the sort of accent that happens to ladies who watch *Gone With the Wind* on TV while eating chocolates.

Harry looked at his watch. Then we went through the usual routine of exchanging phone numbers and promising to meet for lunch, but neither of us put much enthusiasm into it. After Harry had finally said goodbye, George Kosinski returned with the kids.

"Everything all right, Bernard?" he said. He looked at me expectantly. I suppose for George all meetings were deals or potential deals.

"Yes, it was all right," I said.

"Your Rover is here. The kids like it." He put his briefcase on the table and began to rummage through it to find the registration book, but he only found it after dumping the contents of his case on the table. There was a bundle of mail ready to be posted, a biography of Mozart, and an elaborately bound Bible. "A present for my nephew," he said, as if the presence of the Bible required some sort of explanation. He also found a copy of *The Daily Telegraph,* an assortment of car keys with large labels attached, an address book, some foreign coins, and a red silk scarf. He waved the Mozart book at me. "I've become interested in music lately," he said. "I've been going to concerts with Tessa. Mozart had a terrible life, did you know that?"

"I'd heard rumors," I said.

"If ever you wanted to prove that there is no relationship between effort and reward in this world, you've only got to read the life of Mozart."

"You don't even have to do that," I said. "You can come and work in my office and find that out."

"The piano concertos," said George. He pushed his glasses up again. "It's the piano concertos that I really like. I've gone right off pop music since discovering Mozart. This morning I've ordered the complete quintets from the record shop. Wonderful music, Bernard. Wonderful."

"Is Tessa sharing this musical enthusiasm?" I asked.

"She goes along with it," said George. "She's an educated woman, of course. Not like me; left school at fourteen hardly able to write. Tessa knows about music and art and that sort of thing. She learned it at school."

He saw me glancing out of the window at what was going on in the yard. "The children are all right, Bernard. My foreman is letting them help him with a decoking job. All kids are keen on mechanical things; you probably know that already. You just can't keep boys away from motorcars. I was like that when I was young. I loved cars. Most of the cars pinched are taken by kids too young to get a driving license." He sighed. "Yes, Tessa and me are getting along. We've got to, Bernard. She's getting too old for running after other men; she's realized that herself."

"I'm glad," I said. "I've always liked Tessa."

George stopped this rambling conversation. He looked at me and spent a moment thinking about what he was going to say. "I owe you an apology, Bernard. I know that."

He'd virtually accused me of having an affair with his wife, Tessa, at a time when he was suspecting every man who knew her of the same thing. Now he'd had a chance to see things in perspective.

"It's never been like that," I said. "In fact, I never really knew her until Fiona left me. Then Tessa did everything to help . . . with the children and getting the house sorted out and arguing with her father and so on. I appreciate it and I like her, George. I like her very much. I like her so much that I think she deserves a happy marriage."

"We're trying," said George. "We're both trying. But that father of hers. He hates me, you know. He can't bear anyone he knows hearing that I'm his son-in-law. He's ashamed of me. He calls himself a socialist, but he's ashamed of me because I don't have the right accent, the right education, or the right family background. He really hates me."

"He's not exactly crazy about me," I said.

"But you don't have to meet him in your club or fall over him in restaurants when you've got a client in tow. I swear he's screwed up a couple of good deals for me by barging in when I'm in the middle of lunch and making broad hints about my marriage. Life's difficult enough, Bernie. I don't need that kind of treatment, especially when I'm with a client."

"He may not have done it deliberately," I said.

"Of course he does it deliberately. He's teaching me a lesson. I go round telling everyone that I'm his son-in-law, so he goes round telling everyone that I can't control my wife."

"Does he say that?"

"If I caught him . . ." George scowled as he thought about it. "He hints, Bernard. He hints. You know what that man can imply with a wink and a nod."

"He's got some strange ideas," I said.

"You mean he's dead stupid. Yes, well I know that, don't I. You should hear his ideas about how I should run my business." George stopped putting his possessions back into the briefcase, placed his hands on his hips, and cocked his head to one side in the manner of my father-in-law. His voice was that of David Kimber-Hutchinson too: "Go public, George. Look for export opportunities, George. Better still, create a chance to merge with one of the really big companies. Think big. You don't want to be a car salesman all your life, do you?" George smiled.

The egregious David Kimber-Huchinson was inimitable, but it was a good impersonation. And yet there is no better opportunity of seeing deep into a person's soul than to watch him impersonate someone else. A deep hurt had produced in George a resentment that burned bright. If it came to a showdown, I wouldn't care to be in Kimber-Hutchinson's shoes.

And because I was already ranged against my father-in-law, I noted this fact with interest.

"And yet he makes a lot of money," I said.

"They look after each other, the Davids of this world."

"He wanted the children. He thought he'd adopt them . . ."

"And make them into little Kimber-Hutchinsons. I know. Tessa told me all about it. But you'll fight him, Bernard?"

"Every inch of the way."

My enemy's enemy . . . there is no finer basis for friendship, according to the old proverb. "Do you see him often?" I asked.

"Too damned often," said George. "But I'm determined to be nice to Tessa so I go down there with her and listen to the old man rabbiting on about what a big success he is." George put his Mozart book into his case. "He wants to buy a new Roller from me and he's determined to trade in the old one at a good price. He's taken me all round the paintwork and upholstery three times. Three times!"

"Wouldn't that be good business, George? A new Rolls-Royce must cost quite a packet."

"And have him on my doorstep whenever it didn't start on the first turn of the key? Look, I'm not a Rolls dealer, but I buy and sell a few in the course of the year. They're good, the ones I sell, because I won't touch a dodgy one. It's a tricky market; a customer can't deduct much of the price from his tax allowances these days. But you know, and I know, that no matter what kind of brand new Rolls I get for that old bastard, it will start giving him trouble from the moment I deliver it. Right? It's some kind of law of nature; the car I get for him will give trouble. And he'll immediately decide that it's not straight from the factory at all; he'll say it's one I got cheap because there was something wrong with it." He snapped the case shut. "I don't want all that hassle, Bernard. I'd rather he went off and bought one in Berkeley Square. I've told him that, but he won't bloody well believe that there's anyone in this world who turns down a business opportunity."

"Well, it's not like you, George."

He grinned ruefully. "I suppose not, but it's the way I feel about him."

"Let's go and look at my new car," I said. But he didn't move from behind the table.

"Posh Harry said you're in trouble. Is that right, Bernard?"

"Posh Harry makes his living by selling snippets of information. What he doesn't know he guesses, what he can't guess he invents."

"Money trouble? Woman trouble? Trouble at work? If it's money I might be able to help, Bernard. You'd be better borrowing from me than from a High Street bank. I know you don't want to move from the house. Tessa explained all that to me."

"Thanks, George. I think I'm going to manage the money end. Looks like they're going to give me some special allowance to help with the kids and the nanny and so on."

"Couldn't you take the children away for a bit? Get a leave of absence and have a rest? You look damned tired these days."

"I can't afford it," I said. "You're rich, George. You can do whatever you fancy doing. I can't."

"I'm not rich enough to do anything I want to do. But I know what you mean; I'm rich enough to avoid doing the things I don't want to do." George took off his heavy spectacles. "I asked Posh Harry what he had to see you about. He didn't want to tell me, but I pressed him. He has to keep in with me, I do him a lot of favors one way and the other. And he wouldn't find many people who'd wait so patiently to be paid. I said, 'What do you want with Bernard?' He said, 'I'm helping him; he's in trouble.' 'What kind of trouble,' I said. 'His people think he's working for the other side,' said Harry. 'If they prove it, he'll go to jail for about thirty years; they can't let him walk the streets; he knows too damned much about the way his people work.'" George stopped for a moment. "'Bernard Samson wouldn't work for the Russians,' I said. 'I know him well enough to know that, and if the people he works for can't see that, they must be stupid.'" George scratched his neck as he decided how to go on with his story. "'Well, his wife worked for them,' said Harry, 'and if he's not working for them too, the Russians are not going to leave him alone either.' 'What do you mean?' I asked Posh Harry. 'That's the bind he's in,' said Posh Harry, 'that's why he needs help. Either the Brits will jail him for thirty years or the Russians will send a hit team to waste him.' " George put his glasses on again and looked at me as if seeing me for the first time.

"Posh Harry earns a living selling stories like that, George. It's good dramatic stuff, isn't it? It's like the films on TV."

"Not when you know one of the cast," said George. Another train rolled slowly across the viaduct, its noise enough to prevent any conversation. "Bloody trains," said George after the sound had died away. "We had trains making that kind of a racket right alongside the house where I grew up. I swore I'd never have to endure that kind of thing again once I made enough money . . . and here I am." He looked round his squalid little office as if seeing it through the eyes of a visitor. "Funny, isn't it?"

"Let's go and look at my car," I suggested again.

"Bernard," said George, fixing me with a serious stare. "Do you know a man named Richard Cruyer?"

"Yes," I said, vaguely enough to suddenly deny it if that became necessary.

"You work with him, don't you?"

I tried to remember if George and Tessa had ever had dinner at my home with the Cruyers as fellow guests. "Yes, I work with him. Why?"

"Tessa has had to see him a couple of times. She says it was in connection with this children's charity she's doing so much work for."

"I see," I said, although I didn't see. I'd never heard Tessa mention any sort of charity she was doing any work for and I couldn't imagine what role Dicky Cruyer would play in any charity that wasn't devoting its energies to his own well-being.

"I can't help being suspicious, Bernard. I've forgiven her

and removed from my mind a lot of the bad feeling that was poisoning our relationship. But I still get suspicious, Bernard. I'm only human."

"And what do you want to know?" I asked, although what he wanted to know was only too evident. He wanted to know if Dicky Cruyer was the sort of man who would have an affair with Tessa. And the only truthful answer was an unequivocal "Yes."

"What's going on? I want to know what's going on."

"Have you asked Tessa?"

"It would mean a flare-up, Bernard. It would destroy all the work we've both done trying to put the marriage together. But I've got to know. It's racking me; I'm desperate. Will you find out for me? Please?"

"I'll do what I can, George," I promised.

Chapter 9

IDENTIFIED with Stinnes. He was a cold fish and yet I thought of him as someone like myself. His father had been a Russian soldier with the occupation forces in Berlin and he'd been brought up like a German, just as I had. And I felt close to him because of the way our paths had overlapped since that day he had me arrested in East Berlin. I'd talked him into coming over to us; I'd reassured him about his treatment, and I'd personally escorted him to London from Mexico City. I respected his professionalism, and that colored all my thoughts and my actions. But I didn't really like him, and that affected my judgment too. I couldn't completely understand the undoubted success he enjoyed with women. What the devil did they see in him? Women were always attracted by purposeful masculine strength, organizing ability, and the sort of self-confidence that leaves everything unsaid. Stinnes had all that in abundance. But there were none of the other things one usually saw in womanizers: no fun, no flamboyance, no amusing stories, none of the gesturing or physical movements by which women so often remember the ones they once loved. He had none of those warm human characteristics that make a love affair so easy to get into and so hard to escape, no self-mockery, no admitted failings; just the cold eyes, calculating mind, and inscrutable face. He seemed especially cold-blooded about the work he did. Perhaps that was something to do with it. For the womanizer is destructive, the rock upon which desperate women dash themselves to pieces.

But there was no denying the dynamic energy that was evident in that seemingly inert body. Stinnes had an actor's skill, an almost hypnotic will that is turned on like a laser beam. Such heartless dedication is to be seen in the great Hollywood stars, in certain very idealistic politicians, and even more often as a brutal streak in comedians who frighten their audience into laughing at their inadequate jokes.

I didn't feel like that about Bret Rensselaer, who was an entirely different personality. Bret wasn't the hard-eyed pro that Stinnes was. Quite apart from his inadequate German, Bret could never have been a field agent; he would never have been able to endure the squalor and discomfort. And Bret could never have been a good field agent for the same reason that so many other Americans failed in that role: Bret liked to be seen. Bret was a social animal who wanted to be noticed. The self-effacing furtiveness that all Europeans have been taught, in a society still essentially feudal, does not come readily to Americans.

Bret seemed to have had endless women since his wife left him, but his ability to charm was easy to understand, even for those who were impervious to it. Despite his age, he was physically attractive, and he was generous with money and was amusing company. He liked food and wine, music and movies. And he did all those things that rich people always know how to do:

he could ski and shoot and sail and ride a horse; and get served in crowded restaurants. I'd had my share of differences with Bret; I'd suffered his insulting outbursts and grudgingly admired his stubbornness, but he was not a heartless apparatchik. If you got him at the right moment, he could be informal and approachable in a way that none of the other senior staff were. Most important of all, Bret had the uniquely American talent of flexibility, the willingness to try anything likely to get the job done. Yes, Bret got jobs done, and for that I gave him due credit; it was on that account that I trod warily when I first began to wonder about his loyalties.

Bret Rensselaer had the jutting chin and the rugged ageless features of a strip-cartoon hero. Like most Americans, Bret was concerned with his weight and his health and his clothes to an extent that his English colleagues regarded as unacceptably foreign. The public-school senior staff at London Central spent just as much money on their Savile Row suits and handmade shirts and Jermyn Street shoes, but they wore them with a careless scruffiness that was a vital part of their snobbery. A real English gentleman never tries; that was the article of faith. And Bret Rensselaer tried. But Bret had a family that went back as far as the Revolutionary War, and what's more, Bret had money, lots of it. And with any kind of snob, money is the trump card if you play it right.

Bret was already in his office when I arrived. He always started work very early—that was another of his American characteristics. His early arrival and punctuality at meetings were universally admired, though I can't say he started a trend. This morning a meeting had been arranged between me, Dicky Cruyer, Morgan—the D-G's stooge—and Bret Rensselaer in Bret's office. But when I arrived on time—growing up in Germany produces in people a quite unnatural determination to be punctual—Morgan was not there and Dicky hadn't even arrived in his office, let alone in Bret's office.

Bret Rensselaer's office accommodated him on the top floor along with all the other men who mattered at London Central.

From his desk there was a view across that section of London where the parks are: St. James's Park, Green Park, the garden of Buckingham Palace, and Hyde Park were all lined up to make a continuous green carpet. In the summer it was a wonderful view. Even now, in winter, with a haze of smoke from the chimneys and the trees bare, it was better than looking at the dented filing cabinets in my room.

Bret was working. He was sitting at his desk, reading his paperwork and trying to make the world conform to it. The jacket of his suit, complete with starched white linen handkerchief in his top pocket, was placed carefully across the back of a chair that Bret seemed to keep for no other purpose. He wore a gray silk bow tie and a white shirt with a monogram placed so that it could be seen even when he wore his waistcoat. The waistcoat—"vest," he called it, of course—was unbuttoned and his sleeves rolled back.

He'd had his office furnished to his own taste—that was one of the perquisites of senior rank—and I remember the fuss there'd been when Bret brought in his own interior decorator. A lot of the obstructive arguments about it had come from someone in Internal Security who thought interior decorators were large teams of men in white coveralls with steam hammers, scaffolding, and pots of paint. In the event it was a delicate bearded man, wearing a denim jacket embroidered with flower patterns over a "No Nukes" sweatshirt. It took a long time to get him past the doorman.

But the result was worth it. The centrepiece of the office was a huge, chrome, black-leather-and-glass desk, specially ordered from Denmark. The carpet was dark gray and the walls were in two shades of gray too. There was a long black chesterfield for visitors to sit on while Bret swiveled and rocked in a big chair that matched the chrome and leather of the desk. The theory was that the clothes of the occupants of the room provided all the necessary color. And as long as the colorful bearded designer was in the room, it worked. But Bret was a monochrome figure and he blended into the decor as a chameleon matches its natural habitat, except that chameleons only match their surroundings when they're frightened.

"I'm taking over Stinnes," he announced when I went into the room.

"I heard they were trying to hang that on you," I said.

He grinned to acknowledge my attempt to put him down. "No one hung it on me, buddy. I'm very happy to handle this end of the Stinnes debriefing."

"Well, that's just great then," I said. I looked at my watch. "Have I arrived too early?"

We both knew that I was just poisoning the well for Dicky Cruyer and Morgan, but Bret went along with it. "The others are late," he said. "They're always goddamned late."

"Shall we start?" I said. "Or shall I go and have a cup of coffee?"

"You sit where you are, smart ass. If you need coffee so urgently, I'll get some brought here." He pressed a button on his white phone and spoke into a box while staring at the far side of the room with his eyes unfocused.

They sent coffee for four and Bret got to his feet and poured out all four cups so that Cruyer's coffee and Morgan's coffee were getting cold. It seemed a childish revenge, but perhaps it was the only one Bret could think of. While I drank my coffee Bret looked out of his window and then looked at things on his desk and tidied it up. He was a restless man who, despite an injured knee, liked to duck and weave and swing like a punch-drunk boxer. He came round and sat on the edge of his desk to drink his coffee; it was a contrived pose of executive informality, the kind that chairmen of big companies adopt when they're being photographed for *Forbes* magazine.

Even after Bret and I had been sitting there for ten minutes drinking in silence the other two had still not turned up. "I saw Stinnes yesterday," Bret finally volunteered. "I don't know what they do to people at that damned Debriefing Centre, but he was in a lousy uncooperative mood."

"Where have they put him, Berwick House?"

"Yes. Do you know that the so-called London Debriefing Centre has premises as far away as Birmingham?"

"They were using a place in Scotland until last year, when the D-G said we couldn't spare the traveling time for our staff going backward and forward."

"Well, Stinnes isn't having a ball. He did nothing but complain. He said he's given us all he's going to give us until he gets a few concessions. The first concession is to go somewhere else. The Governor—the one you don't like: Potter—says Stinnes has threatened to escape."

"How would you feel, restricted to Berwick House for week after week? It's furnished like a flophouse and the only outdoor entertainment is walking round the garden close to the walls to see how many alarms you can trigger before they order you back inside again."

"It sounds as if you've been locked up there," said Bret.

"Not there, Bret, but places very like it."

"So you wouldn't have put him there?"

"Put him there?" I couldn't help smiling, it was so bloody ridiculous. "Have you taken a look at the staff of the London Debriefing Centre lately?" I asked. "Do you know where they recruit those people? Most of them are redundant ex-employees of Her Majesty's famous Customs and Excise Department. That fat one who is now officially designated the Governor—stop me if you're laughing so much it hurts—came from the Income Tax office in West Hartlepool. No, Bret, I wouldn't have put the poor bastard into Berwick House. I wouldn't have put Stalin there either."

"So let's have it," said Bret with studied patience. He slid off the edge of the desk and stretched his back as if he was getting stiff.

"I haven't given it a lot of thought, Bret. But if I wanted anyone to cooperate, I'd put him somewhere where he felt good. I'd put him into the Oliver Messel suite at the Dorchester Hotel."

"You would, eh?" He knew I was trying to needle him.

"And do you know something, Bret? The Dorchester would cost only a fraction of what it's costing the taxpayer to hold him at Berwick House. How many guards and clerks do they have there nowadays?"

"And what's to stop him walking out of the Dorchester Hotel?"

"Well, Bret, maybe he wouldn't want to escape from the Dorchester Hotel the way he wants to get out of Berwick House."

Bret leaned forward as if trying to see me better. "I listen to everything you say, but I'm never quite sure how much of this crap you believe," he said. I didn't reply. Then Bret said, "I don't remember hearing any of these theories when Giles Trent was being held in Berwick House. You're the one who said he mustn't be allowed to smoke and arranged for him to have small-size pajamas with buttons missing and a patched cotton dressing gown without a cord."

"That's all standard drill for people we're interrogating. Jesus, Bret, you know the score, it's to make them feel inadequate. It wasn't my idea; it's old hat."

"Stinnes gets the Oliver Messel suite and Trent didn't even get buttons for his pj's? What are you giving me?"

"Stinnes isn't a prisoner. He's come over to us voluntarily. We should be flattering him and making him feel good. We should be getting him into a mood so that he wants to give us one hundred percent."

"Maybe."

"And Stinnes is a pro. . . . He's an ex–field agent, not a pen pusher like Trent. And Stinnes knows his job from top to bottom. He knows that we're not going to rip out his fingernails or give him the live electrodes where it hurts most. He's sitting pretty, and until we play ball with him he'll remain *stumm.*"

"Have you discussed this with Dicky?" asked Bret.

I shrugged. Bret knew that Dicky didn't want to hear about Stinnes; he'd made that clear to everyone. "No sense in letting the rest of the coffee get cold," I said. "Mind if I take Dicky's cup?"

He pushed the coffee toward me and looking at the door again said, "It wouldn't have to be a great idea to be an improvement on what's happening at present."

"Isn't he talking at all?"

"The first two weeks were okay. The senior interrogator—Ladbrook, the ex-cop—knows what he's doing. But he doesn't know much about our end of the business. He got out of his depth and since the Berlin arrest Stinnes's become very difficult. He is very disillusioned, Bernard. He's been through the honeymoon and now he is in that post-honeymoon gloom."

"No, don't tell me, Bret." I held one hand to my head as if on the verge of remembering something important. "The 'honeymoon' and the 'post-honeymoon gloom' . . . I recognize the magical syntax . . . there's a touch of Hemingway there, or is it Shelley? What golden-tongued wordsmith told you that Stinnes was in the—how was it he put it?—'post-honeymoon gloom'? I must write that down in case I forget it. Was that the Deputy Governor, the bearded one with the incontinent dachshund that craps on his carpet? Jesus, if I could only get stuff like that into my reports, I'd be D-G by now."

Bret looked at me and chewed his lip in fury. He was mad at me, but he was even madder at himself for repeating all that garbage that London Debriefing staff trot out to cover their manifold incompetence. "So where can we move him to? Technically, London Debriefing have custody of him."

"I know, Bret. And this is the time that you tell me again about how necessary it is to keep up the pretense that he's being questioned about my loyalty, in case the Home Office start making noises about him being transferred to MI5 facilities."

"It's the truth," said Bret. "Never mind how much you don't like it, the truth is that you're our only excuse for holding onto Stinnes."

"Bullshit," I said. "Even if the Home Office started asking for him today, the paperwork would take three months going through normal channels, four or five months if we were deliberately slow."

"That's not so. I could tell you of three of four people handed over to Five within two or three weeks of entering the U.K."

"I'm talking about the paperwork, Bret. Until now we've mostly let them go because we don't want them. But the paperwork that makes the transfer necessary takes an average of three months."

"I won't argue with you," said Bret. "I guess you see more of the paperwork from where you sit."

"Oh boy, do I."

He looked at his watch. "If they don't arrive by nine, we'll have to do this later in the day. I'm due at a meeting in the conference room at nine forty-five."

But as he said it, Dicky Cruyer and Morgan came through the door, talking animatedly and with exhilarant friendliness. I was disconcerted by this noisy show, for I detested Morgan in a way I didn't dislike anyone else in the building. Morgan was the only person there whose patronizing superiority came near driving me to physical violence.

"And what happens if I get you home later than midnight?" said Dicky with that fruity voice he used after people had laughed at a couple of his jokes. "Do you turn into a pumpkin or something?" They both laughed. Perhaps he wasn't talking about Tessa, but it made me sick at my stomach to think of her being with Dicky Cruyer and of George being miserable about it.

Without a word of greeting Bret pointed a finger at the black leather chesterfield and the two of them sat down. This seemed to sober them and Dicky was even moved to apologize for being late. Morgan had a blue cardboard folder with him; he balanced it on his knees and brought out a plain sheet of paper and a slim gold pencil. Dicky had the Gucci zipper case that he'd brought back from Los Angeles. From the case he brought a thick bundle of mixed papers that looked like the entire contents of his in-tray. I suspected that he intended dumping it upon me; it was what he usually did. But he spent a moment getting them in order to show how prepared he was for business.

"I have an important appointment in just a little while," said Bret, "so never mind the road show; let's get down to business." He reached for the agenda sheet and, after adjusting his spectacles, read it aloud to us.

Bret was determined to establish control of the meeting right away. He had unchallenged seniority, but he had everything to fear from both of them. The insidious tactics of Morgan, who used his role of assistant to the D-G to manipulate all and sundry, were well known. As for Dicky Cruyer, Bret had been trying to take over the German desk from him and been rebuffed at every stage. Watching the way that Dicky was ingratiating himself with Morgan, I began to see how Bret had been outmaneuvered.

"If you have to get away, Bret, we can adjourn to my office and finish off," offered Morgan affably. His face was very pale and rotund, with small eyes, like two currants placed in a bowl of rice pudding. He had a powerful singsong Welsh accent. I wondered if it had always been like that or whether he wanted to be recognized as the local boy who'd made good.

"Who would sign the minutes?" said Bret in an elegant dismissal of Morgan's attempt to shed him. "No, I'll make certain we'll finish off in the allotted time."

It was a run-of-the-mill meeting to decide some supplementary allocations to various German Stations. They'd been having a tough time financially, since appropriations hadn't been revised through countless upward revaluations of the Deutschemark. Bret put on his glasses to read the agenda and pushed the meeting along at breakneck speed, cutting into all Dicky's digressions and Morgan's questions. When it was all over, Bret got to his feet. "I've accepted the D-G's invitation to supervise the Stinnes interrogation," he announced, although by that time everyone in the room—if not everyone in the building—knew that. "And I'm going to ask for Bernard to assist me."

"That's not possible," said Dicky, reacting like a scalded cat. Dicky suddenly glimpsed the unwelcome prospect of actually having to do the work of the German desk, instead of passing it over to me while he tried to find new things to insert into his expense accounts. "Bernard has a big backlog of work. I couldn't spare him."

"He'll have time enough for other work as well," said Bret calmly. "I just want him to advise me. He's got some ideas I like the sound of." He looked at me and smiled, but I wasn't sure what he was smiling about.

Morgan said, "When I offered help, I didn't mean senior staff. Certainly not technical people such as Bernard."

"Well, I didn't know *you* ever offered me anything," said Bret coldly. "I was under the impression that the D-G still ran the Department."

"A slip of the tongue, Bret," said Morgan smoothly.

"Bernard is the only person who can unlock the problems Debriefing Centre is having with Stinnes." Bret was establishing the syntax. The problems with Stinnes would remain LDC's problems, not Bret's, and a continuing failure to unlock those problems would be my failure.

"It's just not possible," said Dicky Cruyer. "I don't want to seem uncooperative, but if the D-G keeps pushing this one, I'll have to explain to him exactly what's at stake." Translated, this meant that if Bret didn't lay off, he'd get Morgan to pretend the order to lay off came from the D-G.

"You'll have to tackle your problem by getting some temporary help, Dicky," said Bret. "This particular matter is all settled. I talked to the D-G at the Travellers' Club yesterday—I ran into him by accident and it seemed a good chance to talk over the current situation. The D-G said I could have anyone. In fact, I've not sure it wasn't Sir Henry who first brought Bernard's name into the conversation." He looked at his watch and then smiled at everyone and removed his speed-cop glasses. He got to his feet, and Dicky and Morgan stood up too. "Must go. This next one is a really important meeting," said Bret. Not like this meeting he was leaving, which by implication was a really unimportant one.

It was Morgan's turn to be obstructive. "There are one or two things you are overlooking, Bret," he said, his lilting Welsh accent more than ever in evidence. "Our story to the world at large is that we are holding Stinnes only in order to investigate Bernard's possible malfeasance. How can we explain Bernard's presence at Berwick House as one of the investigating officers?"

Bret came round from behind his desk. We were all standing close. Bret seemed at a loss for words. He rolled his sleeves down slowly and gave all his attention to pushing his gold cuff links through the holes. Perhaps he'd not reckoned with that sort of objection.

Although until this point I'd had reservations about joining Bret Rensselaer's team, now I saw the need to voice my own point of view, if only for self-preservation. "What lies you are telling in order to hold Stinnes is your problem, Morgan," I said. "I was never consulted about them, and I can't see that operating decisions should be made just to support your insupportable fairy stories."

Bret took his cue from me. "Yes, why should Bernard roll over and play possum to get you out of the hole?" he said. "Bernard's the only one who's been close to Stinnes. He knows the score, like none of the rest of us. Let's not have the tail wagging the dog. Eh?" The "eh" was addressed to Morgan in his role as tail.

"The D-G will be unhappy," threatened Morgan. He smoothed his tie. It was a nervous gesture and so was the glance he gave in Dicky's direction. Or what would have been Dicky's direction, except that Dicky had returned to the sofa and become very busy collecting together, and counting, the bundle of papers that we hadn't got round to discussing. Even if they were just papers that Dicky carried with him in order to look overworked, on contentious occasions like this he knew how to suddenly become occupied and thus keep apart from the warring factions.

Bret went to the chair where his jacket was arrayed and took his time about putting it on. He shot his cuffs and then adjusted the knot of his tie. "I talked this over with him, Morgan," said Bret. He took a deep breath. Until now he'd been very calm and composed, but he was about to blow his top. I knew the signals. Without raising his voice very much Bret said, "I never wanted responsibility for the Stinnes business; you know that better than anyone because you've been the one pestering me to take it on. But I said okay and I've started work." Bret took another breath. I'd seen it all before; he didn't need the deep breath so it gave nervous onlookers the impression that he was about to start throwing punches. In the event, he prodded Morgan in the chest with his forefinger. Morgan flinched. "If you screw this up, I'll rip your balls off. And don't come creeping back here with some little written instruction that the old man's initialed. The only thing you'll succeed in changing is that I'll hand your lousy job right back to you, and it's not the job upon which careers are built. You'll discover that, Morgan, if you're misguided enough to try taking it over."

"Steady on, Bret," said Dicky mildly, looking up briefly from his papers but not coming within range of Bret's wrath.

Bret was really angry. This was something more than just a Bret tantrum, and I wondered what else might be behind it. His face was drawn and his mouth twitched as if he was about to go further, and then he seemed to change his mind about doing so. He reached his fingers into his top pocket to make sure his spectacles were there and strode from the room without looking back at anyone.

Morgan seemed shaken by Bret's outburst. He'd seen these flashes of temper before, but that wasn't the same as being on the receiving end of them, as I well knew. Dicky counted his papers yet again and held on tight to his neutral status. This round went to Bret, but only on points, and Bret was not fool enough—or American enough—to think that a couple of quick jabs to the body would decide a match against these two bruisers. Winning one little argument with the public-school mafia at London Central was like landing a blow on a heavy leather punching sack—the visible effect was slight, and two minutes later the pendulum swung the whole contraption back again and knocked you for six.

There was a silence after Bret departed. I felt like Cinderella abandoned by the fairy godmother to the mercies of the ugly step-sisters. As if to confirm these fears Dicky gave me the papers, which were indeed the contents of his in-tray, and said would I have a look at them and bring them back this afternoon. Then Dicky looked at Morgan and said, "Bret's not himself these days."

"It's understandable," said Morgan. "Poor Bret's had a tough time of it lately. Since he lost the Economics Intelligence Committee he's not been able to find his feet again."

"Rumor says Bret will get Berlin when Frank Harrington resigns," said Dicky.

"Not without your say-so, Dicky," said Morgan. "The D-G would never put into Berlin someone whom you'd find it difficult to work with. Do you want Bret in Berlin?"

Ah! So that was it. It was obvious what Dicky might gain from keeping Morgan sweet, but now I saw what Morgan might want in exchange. Dicky muttered something about that all being a long way in the future, which was Dicky's way of avoiding a question that Morgan was going to ask again and again, until he finally got no for an answer.

Chapter 10

W HEN YOU're felling a forest, the chips must fly," said
Bret. He was quoting Stinnes, but he might have been
referring to the brush he'd had with Morgan that morning and
to what might come of it. We were sitting in the back of his
chauffeur-driven Bentley purring along the fast lane to visit
Stinnes. "Is that a Russian proverb?" he asked.

"Yes," I said. "But a Russian remembers it also as the widely
used excuse for the injustices, imprisonments, and massacres
by Stalin."

"You're a goddamned encyclopedia brain, Samson," said
Bret. "And this guy Stinnes is a tricky little shit."

I nodded and leaned back in the real leather. For security
reasons the senior staff were expected to use the car pool
for duty trips, and the only chauffeur-driven car was that
provided to the Director-General, but Bret Rensselaer cared
nothing for all that. The Belgravia residence his family had
maintained in London since before World War I came complete with servants and motorcars. When Bret became a permanent fixture at London Central there was no way to ask
him to give up his pampered lifestyle and start driving
himself round in some car appropriate to his departmental
rank and seniority.

"And here we are," said Bret. He'd been reading the transcript of his previous talks with Stinnes and now he put the
typewritten pages back into his case. His reading hadn't left him
in a very happy mood.

Berwick House, a fine old mansion of red brick, was built
long before that building material became associated with new
and undistinguished provincial colleges. It was an eighteenth-
century attempt to imitate one of Wren's country mansions.
But the War Office official who chose to commandeer the whole

estate just after World War II started was no doubt attracted by the moat that surrounded the house.

The house couldn't be seen from the road; it only came into view after the car turned in at the weathered sign that announced that Berwick House was a Ministry of Pensions training school. I suppose that was the most unattractive kind of establishment that the occupiers could think of. There was a delay at the gate lodge. We went through the outer gate and then pulled into the gravel patch where there were detection devices to check every vehicle. They knew we were coming and Bret's shiny black Bentley was well known to them, but they went through the formal procedure. Ted Riley even wanted to see our identification and that of Albert the chauffeur. Ted was an elderly man who had long ago worked for my father. I knew him well but he gave no sign of recognition.

"Hello, Ted."

"Good morning, sir." He was not a man who would presume on old friendships.

Ted had been an Intelligence Corps captain in Berlin after the war, but he got involved with some black-market dealers in Potsdamer Platz and my father had transferred him out uncomfortably quickly. Ted had given my mother whole Westphalian hams from time to time, and when my father discovered that Ted had dabbled in the black market, he was furious at what he thought was some kind of attempt to involve us. Ted was white-haired now, but he was still the same man who used to give me his chocolate ration every week when I was small. Ted Riley waved us through. The second man opened the electric gates and the third man phoned to the guard box at the house.

"They're rude bastards," said Bret, as if his definition was something I should write down and consult on future visits.

"They have a bloody awful job, Bret," I said.

"They should use Defence Ministry police down here.

These people are full of crap. Identity. They know me well enough."

"Ministry of Defence police look like cops, Bret. The whole idea is that these people wear civilian clothes and look like civilians."

"This bunch look like civilians, all right," said Bret scornfully. "They look like senior citizens. Can you imagine how they'd handle a real attempt to break into this place?"

"At least they're reliable and don't attract attention locally. They're all carefully vetted, and Ted Riley, who's in charge, is a man I'd stake my life on. The number-one priority here is that we have people on guard duty who won't take bribes from newspaper reporters or smuggle gin for the inmates." When he didn't answer I added, "They're not supposed to be able to repulse an armored division."

"I'm glad you told me," said Bret sarcastically. "That makes me feel much better about them." He stared out as we passed the Nissen huts where the guards lived and at the slab-sided gray structures that were sometimes used for conferences. The landscape was brown and bare, so that in places the alarms and wires had become visible.

We went over the old bridge across the moat. It was only when the car turned into the courtyard at the rear of the building that its true condition could be seen. It was like a film set: the east wing was little more than a façade supported by huge slabs of timber. This side of the house had been burned to the ground by incendiary bombs jettisoned by a Luftwaffe pilot trying desperately to gain height. He'd failed and the Heinkel crashed, six miles away after taking a small section of steeple from the village church.

London Debriefing Centre was an updated version of what used to be called the "London District Cage," the place where the War Crimes Investigation Unit imprisoned important Nazis awaiting trial. Signs of those days hadn't entirely disappeared: there were still the remnants of old wartime posters to be seen in some of the offices, and defacing the walls of some of the subterranean "hard-rooms"—a polite departmental euphemism for prison cells—there were the curious runelike marks that prisoners use to keep track of time.

The LDC senior administration staff were all there when we arrived. Their presence was no doubt due to the fact that Bret had now taken over liaison duties. On my previous visits to Berwick House I'd wandered in and out with only a perfunctory hello and scribbled signature, but Bret was important enough for both the Governor and Deputy Governor to be in their offices.

The Governor, still in his mid-thirties, was a huge man with heavy jowls, black hair brushed tight against his skull, and a carefully manicured hairline mustache, the sort of thing Valentino wore when playing a rotter. To complete the effect, he was smoking a cigarette in an amber cigarette holder. Like his Deputy, he was dressed in black pants, white shirt, and plain black tie. I had the feeling that they would both have preferred the whole staff to be in uniform, preferably one with plenty of gold braid.

The Governor's office was in fact a large paneled room with comfortable armchairs and an impressive fireplace. The only justification for calling it an office was a small desk in the corner together with two metal filing cabinets and a box of small file cards on the windowsill. He offered us a drink and wanted us to sit down and chat about nothing in particular, but Bret declined.

"Let me see," said the Governor, reaching for his little file cards and walking his fingertips along the edges of them as if Stinnes wasn't the only person they were holding. "Sadoff . . . ah, here we are: Sadoff, Nikolai." From the box he plucked a photo of Erich Stinnes and slapped it on the desk top with the air of a man winning a poker game. The photo showed Stinnes staring into the camera and holding across his chest a small board with a number.

"He usually calls himself Stinnes," I said.

The Governor looked up as if seeing me for the first time.

"We don't let people indulge their fantasies here at the Debriefing Centre. Let them use a pseudonym and you invite them to invent the rest of it." He put down his cigarette and pulled a card out of the box far enough to read the handwriting on it, but he'd kept his little finger in position so that he hadn't lost the place. I suppose you learn little tricks like that when you spend a lifetime counting paper clips.

"When was he last interviewed?" Bret asked.

"We are letting him stew for a few days," said the Governor. He smiled. "He began to be very tiresome."

"What did he do?" Bret asked.

The Governor looked at his bearded Deputy who said, "He shouted at me when I took some books away from him. A childish display of temper, no more than that. But you have to let him see who's the boss."

"Is he locked up?" I said.

"He's confined to his room," said the Governor.

"We're trying to get information from him," I explained patiently. "We're in a hurry."

"Life and death, is it?" the Governor asked with a not quite hidden edge of sarcasm in his tone.

"That's right," I said, responding in the same manner.

He was smoking the cigarette in the amber holder again. "It always is with you chaps," said the Governor, smiling like an adult playing along with a children's game. "But you can't hurry these things. The first thing is to establish the relationship between the staff and the prisoner. Only then can you get down to the real nub of the intelligence." He sat down in a chair that was far too small for him and crossed his legs.

"I'll try and remember that," I said.

He didn't look at me; he looked at Bret and said, "If you want to see him, you can, but I prefer him not to be permitted out of his room."

"And there was the medical," the bearded Deputy reminded his boss.

"Ah, yes." The Governor's voice was sad as he put the cards and photo away. "He twice refused to let the doctor examine him. We can't have that. If anything happened to him, there'd be hell to pay, and you chaps would put the blame on me." Big smile. "And you'd be right to do so."

"So what's the position now?" Bret asked.

"The doctor refused to attempt an examination unless Sadoff was willing and cooperative. So we've deferred it until next week. But meanwhile we don't even have a note of his height and weight and so on." He looked up at us. I suppose both Bret and I were looking worried. The Governor said, "It's nothing new to us. We've seen all this before. By next week he'll be willing enough, have no fear."

Bret said, "It sounds as if it's developed into a contest of wills."

"I don't enter into contests," said the Governor with a closed-mouth smile. "I'm in charge here. The detainees do as I say. And certainly I won't allow any one of them to avoid a physical examination."

"We'll have a word with him," said Bret.

"I'll come with you," said the Governor. He heaved himself to his feet.

"That won't be necessary," said Bret.

"I'm afraid it will," said the Governor.

I could see that Bret was becoming more and more angry, so I said to him, "I'm not sure the Governor's security clearance would be sufficient, considering the subject to be discussed."

There was of course no particular subject on the agenda, but Bret got the idea quickly enough. "That's quite true," said Bret. He turned to the Governor and said, "Better we keep to the regulations, Governor. From what you say, Stinnes might well make a written complaint about something or other. If that happens, I'd like to make sure you're completely in the clear."

"In the clear?" said the Governor indignantly. But when

Bret made no supplementary explanation, he sat down heavily, moved some papers round, and said, "I've got a great deal of work to get through here. If you're quite sure you can manage on your own, by all means carry on."

I WENT in alone. Erich Stinnes looked content—as much as anyone locked up in Berwick House and left to the mercies of the Governor and his Deputy could have looked content. I knew which room they'd choose for him. It was up on the second floor; cream-painted wall and a plain metal-frame bed, with a print of a naval battle on the wall. That was the room that had the microphones. And the mirror over the sink could be changed so that a TV camera in the next room could film through it.

They'd replaced the light cotton suit he'd worn in Mexico with a heavier English one. It wasn't a perfect fit but it looked good enough. His spectacles flashed with the light from the window as he turned round to see me. "Oh, it's you," he said with no emotion to reveal whether he was happy or disappointed to see me. He'd been standing near the window sketching.

Stinnes was forty years old, a thin bony figure with Slavic features and circular gold-rimmed glasses behind which quick intelligent eyes glittered, and made an otherwise nondescript face hard. He might have been taken for an absent-minded professor, but Sadoff—who preferred his operational name of Stinnes—had been until a few weeks ago a KGB major. Married twice, with a grown-up son who was trying to get into Moscow University, he'd defected and thus got rid of a troublesome wife and been paid a quarter of a million dollars for his services. For such a man, time was not pressing; he was youngish and he was Russian. It was imbecilic to think that "letting him stew for a few days" would have any effect upon him. I'd never seen him looking more relaxed.

I went to look at his drawing. He must have spent most

of the daylight hours at the window. There was a copy of the *Reader's Digest Book of British Birds* with scraps of paper to mark some of the pages. A school notebook was crammed with his spiky writing. He'd diligently recorded the birds he'd sighted.

A bird identification book was the first thing he'd asked for when he arrived at Berwick House. He'd also asked for a pair of binoculars, a request that was denied. There had been a discussion about whether Erich's bird watching was genuine or whether he had some other reason for wanting the binoculars. If it was a pretense, he'd certainly devoted a lot of time and energy to it. There were sketches of the birds, too, and notes about their songs.

But his observations were not confined to ornithology. He'd pinned a piece of paper to a removable shelf that was propped against the window frame. It made a crude easel so that he could draw the landscape as seen from his room. The paper was some sort of brown wrapping paper, and to draw he was using the stub end of an old pencil and a fountain pen.

"I didn't know you were an artist, Erich . . . the perspective looks spot on. Your trees are a bit shaky though."

"Trees are always difficult for me," he confessed. "The bare ones are easy enough, but the evergreens are difficult to draw." Thoughtfully he added a couple of extra touches to the line of trees that surmounted the hill beyond the village. "Do you like it?" he asked, indicating the drawing with his hand and not looking up from it.

"I love it," I said. "But they won't like it downstairs."

"No?"

"They'll think you're compromising security by making a drawing of the moat and grounds and the walls and what's beyond them."

"Then why put me on the second floor? If you don't want me to see over the wall, why put me here?"

"I don't know, Erich. It's not my idea to hold you here at all."

"You'd put me into a four-star hotel, I suppose?"

"Something like that," I said.

He shrugged to show that he didn't believe me. "This is good enough. The food is good, the room is warm, and I can have as many hot baths as I wish. It is what I expected . . . better than I feared it might be." This was not in line with what Bret had said about Stinnes and his complaints.

Without preamble I said, "They released the male secretary. It was political: Bonn. We had enough evidence, but it was a political decision to let him go. We picked up the courier too. I thought we'd got a case officer at first, but it was just the courier."

"What name?" said Stinnes. He was still looking at his landscape drawing.

"Müller—a woman. Do you know her?"

"I met her once. A Party member, a fanatic. I don't like using people like that." He held up the pencil to show me. "Do you have a penknife?"

"Radio operator," I prompted him. I wondered if he liked holding some bits of information back so that I would feel clever at getting them out of him. Certainly he gave no sign of reticence at telling me the rest of what he knew.

"Correct. She came over to Potsdam for the course. That was when I met her. She didn't know I was from the Command Staff, of course."

"She was working out of London, probably handling my wife's material," I said.

"Are you sure?" He took my Swiss Army knife from me and sharpened his pencil very carefully. "If I use my razor blade, it's no good for shaving. They only give one blade per week and always take the old one away."

"It's a guess," I admitted. "Grow a beard."

"It's probably a good guess. In our system we keep Communications completely separated from Operations, so I can't tell you for sure." He passed the knife back to me and tried out the pencil on the edge of his picture. He made a lot of little scribbles, wearing it down to give the pencil an especially sharp point. Then he had another go at the trees.

"With two code names?" I said. "One agent with two codes? Is that likely?"

Stinnes stopped toying with his drawing and looked at me, frowning, as if trying to understand what I was getting at. "Of course, Communications staff are a law unto themselves. They have all sorts of crazy ideas, but I have never heard of such a thing."

"And material kept coming after my wife defected," I said.

He smiled. It was a grim smile that didn't extend to his cold eyes. "The Müller woman is telling you this?"

"Yes, she is." I kept it in the present tense. I didn't want him to know that the woman was lost to us.

"She is mad." He looked at his drawing again. I said nothing. I knew he was reflecting on it all. "Oh, she might have had more material, but operators never know the difference between top-rate material and day-to-day rubbish. The Müller woman is fooling you. What is it she is trying to get from you?" He made the trees a little taller. It looked better. Then he shaded the wall darker.

"Think, Erich. It's important."

He looked at me. "Important? Are you trying to persuade yourself that there is another one of our people deeply embedded in London Central?"

"I want to know," I said.

"You want to make a name for yourself. Is that what you mean?" He looked into my eyes and smoothed his thinning hair against the top of his head. It was wispy hair and the light from the window made it into a halo.

"That would be a part of it," I admitted.

"I would have been told." He pricked the sharp pencil point against the palm of his hand, not once but again and again like a sapper cautiously feeling for buried mines. "If there was another well-placed agent in London Central, I would have been told."

"Suppose the Müller woman had regular traffic direct with Moscow."

"That's quite possible. But they would have told me. I was the senior man in Berlin. I would have known." He stopped fidgeting with the pencil and put it into his top pocket. "The Müller woman is trying to make you go round and round in circles. I'd advise you to disregard any suggestions about another KGB agent in London. It's the sort of thing that Moscow would like to start you wondering about."

"Do you have enough to read?"

"I have the Bible," he said. "They gave me a Bible."

"Is that what you're reading, the Bible?"

"It's always interested me, and reading it in English helps me learn. I am beginning to think that Christianity has a lot in common with Marxist-Leninism."

"For instance?"

"God is dialectical materialism; Christ is Karl Marx; the Church is the Party, the elect is the proletariat, and the Second Coming is the Revolution." He looked at me and smiled.

"How do heaven and hell fit into all that?" I asked.

He thought for a moment. "Heaven is the socialist millennium, of course. I think hell must be the punishment of capitalists."

"Bravo, Erich," I said.

"You know I used to be with Section 44?"

Section 44 was the KGB's Religious Affairs Bureau. "It was in your file," I said. "You left at the wrong time, Erich."

"Because of Poland, you mean? Yes, the man running Section 44 these days is a general. But I would never have got that sort of promotion. They would have slotted less expert people in above me. Had I stayed there, I would still be a lieutenant. It's the way things are done in Russia."

"It's the way things are done everywhere," I said. "So the Bible is enough for you?"

"A few books would be welcome."

"I'll see what I can do," I said. "And I'll see if I can get you moved to somewhere more comfortable, but it might take time." I took from my pocket five small packets of cheroots. They were evil smelling and I didn't want to give him a chance to light up before I left the room.

"What is time?" He displayed the palms of both hands. There was no humor in his gesture: just contemptuous mockery.

"DID YOU have to tell him that Bonn ordered the release of that guy?" said Bret. He was standing in the surveillance room with a set of headphones in his hands. "That's lousy security, Bernard. We took a lot of trouble keeping that out of the newspapers." It was a tiny dimly lit room with just enough space for the radio and TV equipment, although today there was nothing in use but the bugging equipment wired here from the second floor.

"Maybe you did, but every reporter in town knows about it, so don't think Moscow is puzzling. It's a two-way traffic, Bret. Stinnes has got to feel he's a part of what's going on."

"You should be pushing harder. That's what I wanted you for, to help push the interrogation along faster."

"I will, but I'm not the interrogator and I can't undo weeks of stupidity in one short interview, Bret," I said. "Easy does it. Let me move him out of here and establish a working relationship."

"Hardly worth the journey down here," Bret complained, putting the headphones on the shelf and switching off the light. "I could have got a lot done this afternoon."

"That's what I told you, but you insisted on coming with me."

"I never know what you're likely to get up to when you're on your own." The only light came from a small grimy skylight and Bret's face was completely in shadow. He put his hands into his trouser pockets so that his dark melton overcoat was held open. This aggressive stance, the clothes, and the lighting made him look like a still photo from some old gangster film.

"That makes me wonder why you chose me to work with you on this one," I said. That much was true, very true.

He looked at me as if deciding whether to bother with a proper reply. Then he said, "There's no one in the German Section with field experience comparable to yours. You're bright as hell, despite your lack of proper schooling and the chip you have on your shoulder about it. For most things concerning the German Section, you've got your own unofficial sources of information, and often you dig out material that no one else can get. You are straight. You make up your own mind, and you write your reports without giving a damn what anyone wants to hear. I like that." He paused and just slightly flexed his leg as if his bad knee was troubling him. "On the other hand, you put yourself and your personal problems before the Department. You're damned rude and I don't find your sarcastic remarks as amusing as some of the others do. You're insubordinate to the point of arrogance. You're selfish, reckless, and you never stop complaining."

"You must have been reading my mail, Bret," I said. It was interesting to see that Bret made no comment about what Stinnes had said about the Miller woman or about the suggestion that the KGB had another agent working inside London Central. Perhaps he thought it was just my way of drawing Stinnes out.

Chapter 11

THE SCIENCE Museum was quiet that morning. It was Saturday. The giggling, chewing, chatting, scuffling battalions of schoolchildren who are shepherded through it by glazy-eyed teachers on weekdays do not choose to visit such institutions in their own time. Especially when there's a football match on TV.

I was with the children and Gloria. It had become a regular Saturday routine: a visit to one of the South Kensington museums followed by lunch at Mario's restaurant nearby in Brompton Road. Then she came back home with me and stayed until Sunday night, or sometimes Monday morning.

The aviation gallery on the top floor of the Science Museum was empty. We stood on the overhead walkway that provided a chance to be up among the old planes suspended from the roof. The children had run ahead to stare at the Spitfire, leaving me and Gloria with the dusty old Vickers Vimy that made the first non-stop flight across the Atlantic. We hadn't been talking about work, but I suddenly said, "Do you know the sort of chits they fill out when someone has to go across to the Cabinet Office and ask questions? Pale green chits with lines and a little box for a rubber stamp. You know what I mean?"

"Yes," she said. She leaned over the balcony of the walkway, trying to see where the children were.

"Have you ever dealt with anyone in the Cabinet Office? Do you know anyone over there?"

"From time to time I have to deal with some of them," she said. She still was giving the conversation only perfunctory attention. She had picked up the phone earpiece to get a recorded account of the exhibit and I had to wait until she was finished. Then she offered the phone to me but I shook my head.

"It's going to rain," she said. "I should have brought an umbrella." She had just come from the hairdresser's and rain is the hairdresser's friend. I looked out through the big windows. You could see across the rooftops of West London from here. The clouds were dark gray so that inside the hall it was gloomy. The huge planes were casting dark shadows on the exhibits below us.

When she'd put the earpiece down I said, "Do you know anyone in the Cabinet Office? Do you know anyone I could talk to without official permission?"

"You want to go over there and make enquiries?" she said. She was alert now and turned to watch my face. "I suppose so, if that's what you want." She smiled.

It was her immediate cheerful complaisance that made me feel guilty. "No, forget it," I said. I heard the children clattering down the stairs at the far end and watched them emerge from under the walkway. Billy made straight for the aero engines. He'd always liked the engines, even when he was small.

"Of course I'll do it." Gloria put her arm through mine and hugged me. "Look at me, darling, I'll do it for you. It's the easiest thing in the world."

"No. It's a stupid idea," I said, turning away from her. "If they insist upon having the chit, it could end up with you getting fired." The Cabinet Office was for us the most sensitive of government departments. We were controlled from the Cabinet Office. When the D-G was put upon the carpet—as he was now and again—it was the carpet of the Cabinet Office that he was put on.

"Why not go through ordinary channels?" she said. She touched her pale blond hair. The sky had grown even darker and it was beginning to rain; the raindrops could be heard beating against the glass panels of the roof.

"Shall we just forget it?"

"No need to get angry. I said I'd do it. But tell me why."

"This isn't the time or the place . . . and in any case I don't want to discuss it. Forget it."

She hugged my arm. "Tell me why, Bernard. You'd want to know why if it was you arranging it for someone else, wouldn't you?"

It was reasonable. But it was damned difficult to explain it all to her without sounding like a lunatic. "There's a technical input of material that opens the possibility of another KGB penetration of the Department."

She gave a little laugh. It was a lovely laugh. Her laugh was always enough to make me fall in love with her all over again, even when it contained so much derision. "How very departmental. I've never heard you using all that jargon. You sound like Mr. Cruyer. Is that a very pompous way of saying that the woman you went off to see in Berlin said we have a mole in the office?"

"Yes, it's a pompous way of saying that."

"And you believe her, Bernard? A mole? Who do you think it might be?"

"I don't believe her, but it should be followed up."

"So why not tell Mr. Cruyer. . . . My God, you don't think it's Dicky Cruyer, do you?"

I played it down, of course. "The woman is not a very high-ranking source. She's just a low-grade radio operator. It's a matter of code words and radio procedures. Even if she's told us the whole truth, there could easily be some other explanation."

Gloria was still looking at me and waiting for an answer. "No, it's not Dicky," I said. "But it's no good talking to him about it. Dicky doesn't want to get involved. I've mentioned it to him, but he doesn't want to know."

Of course, she couldn't resist the temptation to play spies. Who can resist it? I can't. "What if his indifference is simply a cover?" she said, like a child guessing the answer to a riddle.

"No. He's too busy with his clubs and his expense-account lunches and his girlfriends to have time for his work, let alone being a double."

"But what if . . . ?"

"Look, sweetheart. How many times have you taken a pile of work into Dicky and had him tell you to bring it straight across to me, without even going through it to see what was there?"

"I see what you mean," she said.

"Don't sound so disappointed," I said. "No, it's not Dicky. The chances are, it's not anyone."

"But if there was someone, that someone would be in the German Section?"

"Yes. I think so."

"So it's Bret." She was quick.

"It's probably not anyone."

"But it's Bret you're concerned about. Your request to go over to the Cabinet Office and ask questions would have to go through Bret. It's him you want to avoid, isn't it?"

"For the time being, yes."

"But that's absurd, darling. Bret is . . . well, he's . . ."

"He's so honorable. I know. That's what everyone says. I'm getting sick of hearing about how honorable he is."

"Do you have anything else that points to Bret?"

"Some silly little things. A man in Berlin reckons that when Bret went there many years ago, he dismantled the networks we were running to the Russian Zone."

"And did he do that?"

"I don't know."

She hugged me and rested her head against my cheek. "Don't be stupid, darling," she whispered. "I know you too well. You must have double-checked that one in the archives. How could you resist it? And you were in there only yesterday."

"The official explanation is that Bret was expediting the de-nazification programme in line with top-level Anglo-American agreements of that time."

"And do you believe that's what Bret was doing?"

"Bret was sent to Berlin to do a job. I can't find any evidence that he did anything wrong."

"But he has lots of little bits of mud sticking to him?"

"That's right," I said.

"And now there's something else," she said. "A bigger piece of mud?"

"What makes you think so?"

"Because so far there's nothing that would account for you wanting to talk to the Cabinet Office staff."

"Yes," I said. "Something else has come up. I've got hold of one of our secret documents. . . . It's suggested that it's come from Moscow."

"And you've got it?"

"A photocopy," I said.

"And you haven't told anyone at the office? That's awfully dangerous, Bernard. Even I know that you can go to prison for that."

"Who should I tell?"

"And it points at Bret?"

"Even if there was a leak, it's not necessarily one of the staff. We lose papers by theft and accident. Material goes astray and winds up on the other side."

"If you did find something against Bret, it wouldn't be difficult to convince Morgan . . . he'd use any little thing to roast Bret. He hates him, you know. They had an argument the other day. Do you know about it?"

"Yes, I know."

"Morgan is determined to bring Bret Rensselaer down."

"Well, I don't want to help Morgan do that. But I have to follow this line to wherever it leads. I don't like Cabinet memos being sent to newspapers and I don't like them going directly to Moscow either."

"What do you want to find out?"

"I want to talk to someone who knows how the Cabinet Office works. Someone who knows how their paperwork circulates."

"I know a woman in the chief whip's office. She's nice and she knows everyone. There'll be no problem. She could tell you all that. That would be easier than the Cabinet Office."

"Look at Billy explaining about the engine to Sally. He looks like an old man, doesn't he?"

"Of course he doesn't," she said. "How sweet the children are together."

"We mustn't be late at Mario's; they get crowded at lunchtime on Saturday."

"Relax. Mario won't turn you away," she said. "But take it easy on that *pappardelle* you keep eating. You're getting plump, darling."

It was only a matter of time. The urge to reform the male

is something no woman can resist. I said, *"Pappardelle con lepre* —they only have it in winter. And they run out of it if you're late."

"Did I say plump?" she said. "I meant big. Have two lots, Bernard. I like my men colossal."

I aimed a playful blow at her, but she was ready for it and jumped aside.

IT WAS still raining when we came out of the Science Museum. There are never any taxicabs available in Exhibition Road at midday on Saturday, they're all working the West End or the airport or taking a day off. Mario's is not very far, but we were all rather wet by the time we arrived.

Mario was there, of course; laughing, shouting, and doing a lot of those things I don't like the schoolkids doing when they're in the museums. We always went to Mario's to eat; that's not quite true, of course—not always but often. There were lots of reasons. I'd known Mario for ages—everyone in London knew him—but his new restaurant had only just opened by the time Fiona defected. I'd never been there with her; it had no unhappy memories for me. And I liked Mario. And I couldn't help remembering the time that little Billy had vomited all over his lovely tiled floor and Mario had laughed and made no fuss about it. They don't make people like Mario anymore, or if they do, they're not running restaurants.

The children ordered *spaghetti carbonara* followed by chicken. It was their regular favorite. Gloria thought I was a bad influence on their eating habits but, as I always pointed out to her, they never demanded salad when I had salad.

When I ordered the *pappardelle,* it was Gloria who said, "Give him a big portion; he hasn't eaten for a couple of days."

Mario's face was inscrutable, but I said, "Mario knows that's not true. I had lunch here yesterday with Dicky Cruyer."

"You swine," said Gloria. "You told me you were going to diet."

"I had to come," I said. "It was work. And Dicky was paying."

Billy went off to the toilet. Mario had imported the urinals at tremendous expense from Mexico, and Billy liked to check them out whenever he visited the place.

Sally went with Mario to choose an avocado for Gloria. Sally considered herself a connoisseur of avocados. It was while we were on our own that Gloria said, "Is Dicky Cruyer having an affair with your sister-in-law?"

"Not as far as I know," I said truthfully, although not totally truthfully since George had told me she might be. "Why?"

"I saw them in a Soho restaurant that night when my father took me to dinner to quiz me about why I wasn't sleeping at home on weekends."

"It couldn't have been Tessa," I said. "She won't eat anywhere except at the Savoy."

"Don't be flippant," she said. She grinned and tried to slap my hand, but I pulled it away so that she made the cutlery jingle. "Answer me. Am I right?"

"What did your father say that evening? You never told me about it."

"Why don't you just answer my question?" she said.

"Why don't you answer *my* question?" I replied.

She sighed. "I should never have fallen in love with a spy."

"Ex-spy," I said. "I gave up spying a long time ago."

"You never do anything else," she said. It was a joke, but it wasn't a joke.

WE HAD to go out to dinner—to George and Tessa Kosinski's —that evening. But you can't go out to dinner after rain has reduced your hair to rat tails. It was a special event, their house-warming, and we'd promised to go; but Gloria wailed that she couldn't. That was the predicament that faced us that Saturday afternoon. Had my wife, Fiona, ever been so childish and petulant, I would have dismissed such protests angrily, or at least with bad-tempered sarcasm. But Gloria was little more than a child, and I found the manner in which she treated such minor incidents as crises both silly and funny. How wonderful to be so young, and so unaware of the terror that the real world holds, that disarrayed hair can bring tears. How gratifying when one quick phone call and the price of a repair job at a crimping salon in Sloane Street can bring such a gasp of joy.

And if you'd told me that my reactions were the sign of a fundamental flaw in our relationship, if you'd told me that these aspects of my love affair with her were only what could be expected when a man of forty falls in love with a woman young enough to be his daughter, I'd have agreed with you. I worried about it constantly, and yet I always ended up asking myself whether such elements of paternalism weren't to be found everywhere. Maybe not in every happy marriage, but certainly in every blissful affair.

I was still careful, not to say wary, about the places I took her to and the people we mixed with. Not that I had an infinity of choices. A man without a wife discovers all kinds of things about his friends. When my wife first left me I'd expected that all my friends and acquaintances would be inviting me out—I'd heard so many wives complaining about how difficult it was to find that "extra man" for dinner. But it doesn't work like that; at least, it didn't for me. A man separated from his lawful wife becomes a leper overnight. People—that is to say one's married friends—act as if a broken marriage is some kind of disease that might prove contagious. They avoid you, the party invitations dry up, the phone doesn't ring, and when you finally do get an invitation, you're likely to find yourself entertained alone on an evening when their attractive teenage daughters are not in the house.

The Kosinkis' housewarming party was amusing enough. I suspected that this was a result of practice, for it was rumored that George and Tessa were staging a series of such gatherings and representing each as the one and only. But the evening was none the worse for that. The guests, like the food, were decorative and very rich. The cooking was elaborate and the wines were old and rare. Tessa was amusing and George was friendly in a way that suggested that he liked to see me with Gloria; perhaps seeing us together removed any last feelings he had about me coveting his wife.

George's Mayfair flat was a glittering display of tasteful extravagance. The old Victorian dining table that had once belonged to George's poor immigrant parents was the only modest item of furniture to be seen. And yet this long table, so necessary for a big family and now fully extended, provided George with a chance to play host to sixteen guests with enough room at each place setting for three large polished wine glasses, lots of solid-silver knives and forks, and a big damask napkin. The other guests were a glamorous mixture that emphasized the different worlds in which George and Tessa moved: a bald stockbroker who, sniffing the claret admiringly, dropped his monocle into it; a heavily lacquered TV actress who would eat only vegetables; a Japanese car designer who drank nothing but brandy; a gray-haired woman who looked like a granny, ate everything, and drank everything and turned out to be a particularly fearless rallye driver; a Horse Guards subaltern with a shrill young deb; and two girls who owned a cooking school and had sent a prize student to cook for Tessa that evening.

None of the women—not even the gorgeous Tessa, flaunting a new green silk dress that was all pleats and fringe—could compare with mine. Gloria's hair was perfect, and she wore a choker of pearls and a very low-cut white dress that was tight-fitting enough to do justice to her wonderful figure. I watched her all the evening as she effortlessly charmed everyone, and I knew beyond a doubt that I was seriously in love with her. Like all such London dinner parties it ended rather early and we were home and undressing for bed before midnight. We didn't read.

.   .   .

IT WAS dark. I looked at the radio clock and saw that it was three-twenty in the morning as I became fully awake. I'd been sleeping badly for some time. I had a recurring dream in which I was swept away in the filthy swirl of some wide tropical river —I could see the palm trees along the distant banks—and as I drowned I choked on the oily scum. And as I choked I woke up.

"Are you all right?" said Gloria sleepily.

"I'm all right."

"I heard you coughing. You always cough when you wake up in the night like this." She switched on the light.

"It's a dream I have sometimes."

"Since that boy MacKenzie was killed."

"Maybe," I said.

"No maybe about it," she said. "You told me that yourself."

"Switch the light off. I'll be all right now. I'll go back to sleep."

I tried to sleep, but it was no use. Gloria was awake too, and after more time had passed she said, "Is it about Bret? Are you worrying about Bret?"

"Why should I worry about him?"

"You know what I mean."

"I know what you mean." It was dark. I wanted a cigarette very badly, but I was determined not to start smoking again. Anyway there were no cigarettes in the house.

"Do you want to tell me about it?"

"Not particularly," I replied.

"Because I might be the mole?"

I laughed. "No, not because you might be the mole," I said. "You've only been in the Department five minutes. You're very recently vetted. And with a Hungarian father you'd get a specially careful scrutiny. You're not the mole."

"Then tell me."

"The Cabinet memo that ended up in Moscow was about the security of certain very sensitive British establishments in West Germany. The Prime Minister had asked how secure they were, and some bright spark got the idea of asking us to attempt penetrations of them. So that's what we eventually did. We assigned reliable people in West Germany to target those establishments. Operation Vitamin they called it. Then there was a report compiled so that security could be improved."

"So what?"

"It was a loony idea, but they say the PM liked the report. It was written up like an adventure story. It was simple. So simple that even the politicians could understand it. No one over here liked it, of course. The D-G was against it all along. He said we were creating a dangerous precedent. He was frightened that we'd be continually asked to waste our resources checking out the security of our overseas installations."

"What then?"

"MI5 were furious. Even though it was all done overseas, they felt we were treading on their toes. The Defence Ministry made a fuss too. They said they had enough problems keeping the Communists and protesters out without us making trouble for them too. And they said that the existence of that report constituted a security risk. It was a blueprint for Moscow, an instruction manual telling anyone how to breach our most secret installations."

"And Bret signed the Vitamin report?"

"I didn't say that." There *were* cigarettes in the house; there was an unopened packet of twenty Benson & Hedges that someone had left on the hall table. I'd put them in the drawer there.

"You didn't have to say it."

"See why it's important? My wife saw the memo probably, but the report was done after she'd gone. Moscow had the memo; but has Moscow seen the full report? We really must know."

She switched the light on and got out of bed. She was wearing a blue nightdress with a lacy top and lots of tiny silk bows. "Would you like a cup of tea? It wouldn't take a minute." The dim glow from the bedside lamp made a golden rim round her. She was very desirable.

"It might wake up the children and Nanny." Maybe one cigarette wouldn't start me off again.

"Even if the report did get to Moscow, it might not have been Bret Rensselaer's fault."

"His fault or not his fault; if that report got to Moscow the blame will be placed on Bret."

"That's not right."

"Yes it is. Not fair, you mean? Maybe not, but he masterminded our end of the Vitamin operation. Any breach in its security will be his, and this one could be the end of Bret's career in the Department." Damn. Now I remembered giving the cigarettes to the plumber who fixed the immersion heater; I'd had no money for a tip for him.

She said, "I'll make tea; I'd like a cup myself." She was very close to me, standing in front of the mirror. She glanced at her reflection as she straightened her hair and smoothed her rumpled nightdress. It was thin, almost transparent, and the light was shining through it.

"Come here, duchess," I said. "I don't feel like tea just yet."

Chapter 12

MY DEPARTMENT has been called a "ministry without a minister." That description is never used by our own staff. It's a description applied to us by envious civil servants suffering at the hands of their own political masters. In any case, it isn't true. Such a condition would equate the D-G with the career permanent secretaries who head up other departments, and permanent secretaries leave when aged sixty. One glance at the D-G and you'd know he was far, far over that hill, and there was still no sign of his departing.

Though in the sense that we didn't have a political boss, that fanciful description was true. But we had something worse; we had the Cabinet Office, and that was not a place I cared to tread uninvited. So I gladly accepted Gloria's suggestion that her friend in the government chief whip's office could answer all my questions about the distribution of Cabinet paperwork.

Downing Street is, of course, not a street of houses. It's all one house—that is to say, it's all part of one big block of government offices, so that you can walk right through it to the Horse Guards, or maybe even to the Admiralty if you know your way upstairs and downstairs and through the maze of corridors.

Number Twelve, where the whip's office was situated, was quiet. In the old days, when the socialists were running things, you could always count on meeting someone entertaining over there. Obscure party officials from distant provincial constituencies, trade union leaders swapping funny stories between mouthfuls of beer or whisky and ham sandwiches, the air full of smoke and slander.

It was more sedate nowadays. The PM didn't like smoking, and Gloria's friend, Mrs. Hogarth, had only weak tea and ginger biscuits to offer. She was about forty, an attractive red-haired woman with Christian Dior spectacles and a hand-knitted cardigan with a frayed elbow.

She took me into one of the rather grand paneled offices at the back, explaining that her own office in the basement was cramped. She normally used this one when the politicians were on holiday, and that meant for much of the year. She gave me tea and a comfortable chair and took her place behind the desk.

"Any of the lobby correspondents could tell you that," she said, in answer to my question about who saw Cabinet memos. "It's not a secret."

"I don't know any lobby correspondents," I said.

"Don't you?" she said, examining me with real interest for the first time. "I would have thought you'd have known a lot of them."

I smiled awkwardly. It was not a compliment. I had a feeling she'd smelled the whisky on my breath. Through the window behind her there was a fine view of the Prime Minister's garden and beyond its wall the parade ground of the Horse Guards, where certain very privileged officials had parked their cars.

"I haven't got a lot of time for chatting," she said. "People think we've got nothing to do over here when the House isn't sitting, but I'm awfully busy. I always am." She smiled as if confessing to some shameful failing.

"It's good of you to help me, Mrs. Hogarth," I said.

"It's all part of my job," she said. She measured one spoon of sugar into her tea, stirred very gently so it didn't spill, and then drank some unhurriedly. "Cabinet memos." She looked at the photocopy I'd given her and read some of it. "There were eight copies of this one. I remember it, as a matter of fact."

"Could you tell me who got them?" I said. I dipped my biscuit into my tea before eating it. I wanted to see how she'd take it.

She saw me, but looked away hurriedly and became engrossed in her notepad. "One for the Prime Minister, of course; one for the Foreign Secretary; one for the Home Secretary; one for Defence; one for the leader of the Commons; one for the government chief whip; one for the Lords; one for the Cabinet secretary."

"Eight?" Two men had come into the garden carrying roses, still wrapped in the nursery packing, in a large box. One of them kneeled down and prodded the soil with a trowel. Then he put some of the soil into his hand and touched it to see how wet it was.

Mrs. Hogarth swung round to see what I was looking at. "It's a wonderful view in the summer," she said. "All roses. The PM's very fond of them."

"It's a bit late to be planting roses," I said.

"It's been too wet," she said. She turned to watch the men. "I planted some in November, but they're not doing well at all. Mind you, I live in Cheam—there's a lot of clay in the soil where

I live." The gardeners decided that the soil was right for planting roses. One of them started to dig a line of holes to put them in, while the second man produced bamboo canes to support the rosebushes that were already established.

Mrs. Hogarth coughed to get my attention again. "This memo was drafted by the Defence Ministry. I don't know who did it, but junior ministers will have seen it in the early stages. Perhaps it was drafted many times. That could add up."

"I'm interested in who saw the document or a copy of it," I said.

"Well, let's look at what might have happened to those eight copies of the memo," she said briskly. "In each minister's private office there is his principal private secretary plus one or two bright young men. Additionally, there will be an executive officer and a couple of clerical officers."

"Would all those people normally see a memo like this?"

"Certainly the PPS would read it. And one of the clerical staff, or perhaps an executive officer, will file it. It depends how keen and efficient the others are. I think you should assume that all of the people in each minister's private office would have a good idea of the content, just in case the minister started shouting for it and they had to find it."

"Sounds like a lot of people," I said. The gardeners were lining up the newly planted roses, using a piece of white string.

"We're not finished yet. The Cabinet Office, the Home Office, and the Foreign Office would all have executive responsibilities arising from this document."

"Not the Home Office," I corrected her gently.

"That's not the way they'd see it," she said. Obviously, she too had had dealings with the Home Office, who assumed executive responsibility over everyone and everything.

"You're right," I said. "Please go on."

"So in those departments the memo would go to the permanent secretary and to his private office, and then to the appropriate branch to be dealt with."

"Two more administrative officials and at least one executive or clerical officer." I said.

"In the Cabinet Office add one private secretary and one executive or clerical officer. From there to the Defence Secretariat, which would mean three administrators and one executive or clerical officer."

"It's quite a crowd," I said.

"It adds up." She drank some tea.

A man came in through the door. "I didn't know you were in here, Mabel. I was just going to use the phone." Then he caught sight of me. "Oh, hello, Samson," he said.

"Hello, Pete," I said. He was a baby-faced thirty-year-old, with light-brown wavy hair and a pale complexion upon which his cheeks seemed artificially reddened. For all his Whitehall attire—pinstripe trousers and black jacket—Pete Barrett was a very ambitious career policeman who'd taken a law degree at night school. He'd adapted to local costume in just the way I would have expected when I'd first met him about five years earlier. Barrett was a Special Branch man who'd been desperate to get into the Department. He'd failed to do so and, despite this soft job he'd found, he was bitter about it.

"Is that man bothering you, Mrs. Hogarth?" he enquired with his ponderous humor. He was cautious about baiting me, but it was a diffidence laced with contempt. He went round to the window, looked out at the garden as if he might be checking on the gardeners, and then looked at the papers on the desk. She closed the spiral notebook in which she'd been doing her figuring. It had a double red stripe on the cover; such notebooks are for classified information with all the pages numbered.

She kept her hand on the closed notebook. "A routine enquiry," she answered, in a studied attempt to discourage his interest.

But he was not to be deterred. "A routine enquiry?" he gave a forced chuckle. "That sounds like Scotland Yard, Mabel. That sounds like what I'm supposed to say." He leaned forward to read the document on the desk in front of her. He held his tie against his chest so that it wouldn't fall against her. This stiff posture, hand flat on chest, his wavy hair and red cheeks made him look more than ever like a puppet.

"If you're after tea, you're unlucky. My girl is off sick. I made it myself this afternoon. And my ginger biscuits are all finished."

Barrett didn't respond to this at all. In other circumstances I would have told him to go away in no uncertain terms, but this was his territory and I had no authority to be asking questions here. And I could think of no convincing reason for having this copy of the memo. Furthermore I had the feeling that Barrett had known I was in the room before coming in.

"A Cabinet memo no less," he said. He looked at me and said, "What exactly is the problem, Bernie?"

"Just passing the time," I said.

He stood upright, a puppet on parade now, chin tucked in and shoulders held well back. He looked at me. "You're on my patch now," he said with a mock severity. Outside, the two gardeners had dug the line of holes for the roses, but one of them was looking up at the sky as if he'd felt a spot of rain.

"It's nothing you'd be interested in," I said.

"My office received no notice that you were coming," he said.

Mrs. Hogarth was watching me. She was biting her lip, but I don't know whether this was in anger or anxiety.

"You know the drill, Bernie," he persisted. "A Cabinet memo . . . that's a serious line of enquiry."

Mrs. Hogarth stopped biting her lip and said, "I wish you'd stop reading the papers on my desk, Mr. Barrett." She put the photocopy memo I'd given her into the tray with other papers. "That particular paper has nothing to do with my visitor and I find your reading it aloud a most embarrassing breach of security."

Barrett went red. "Oh . . . ," he said. "Oh. Oh, I see."

"Use the phone next door. There's no one in there. I really must get on now. Perhaps you're not busy, but I am."

"Yes, of course," said Barrett. "I'll see you around, Bernie."

I didn't answer.

"And please shut the door," Mrs. Hogarth called after him.

"Sorry," he said as he came back to close it.

"Now where were we," she said. "Ah, yes: Number Ten. Here in Number Ten such a memo would be handled by two private secretaries. And one executive or clerical officer must have seen it. And I think you should consider the possibility that the press office and policy unit were interested enough to read it. That would be quite normal."

"I'm losing track."

"I have a note of it. I haven't added the Defence Ministry people. . . ." She paused for a moment to write something on her pad, murmuring as she wrote ". . . private office, let's say two; permanent secretary's office, another two . . . and policy branch, plus clerical. Let's say eleven at the Defence Ministry."

"Eleven at the Defence Ministry? But they had no executive action."

"Don't you think they would want to notify their units in an effort to keep these SIS intruders out?"

"Yes, I suppose they might. But they shouldn't have done it. That wasn't the idea at all. The plan was intended to test the security."

"Don't be silly. This is Whitehall. This is politics. This is power. The Defence Ministry is not going to stand there and wait patiently and do nothing while you cut their balls off." She saw the surprise in my face. She smiled. She was a surprising lady. "And if you're going to do a thorough investigation, you must take into account that some ministers have private secretaries who would handle all papers that cross their minister's desk. And the way that papers are filed in a registry sometimes means that the registry clerks handle them too."

"It's a hell of a lot of people," I said. "So even the most secret secrets are not very secret."

"I'm sure I don't have to mention that papers like this are left on desks and are sometimes seen by visitors to the various offices as well as by the staff. And, I haven't included your own staff who handled this particular one." She tapped the photocopy lightly with her fingertips.

"That particular one? What do you mean?"

"Well, this is a photocopy of the Cabinet secretary's copy. You knew that, didn't you?"

"No, I didn't. The number and date have been blanked out. How can you tell?"

She took a biscuit and nibbled it to gain time. "I'm not sure if I'm permitted to tell you that," she said.

"It's an investigation, Mrs. Hogarth."

"I suppose it's all right, but I can't give you the details. I can only tell you that when sensitive material like this is circulated, the word processor is used so that the actual wording of its text is changed. Just the syntax, you understand; the meaning is not affected. It's a precaution . . ."

"So that if a newspaper prints a quote from it, the actual copy can be identified."

"That's the idea. They don't talk about that very much, of course."

"Of course. And this is the one that went to the Cabinet Office?"

"Yes. I wouldn't have wasted your time with all that detail if I'd known that's all you wanted. I naturally thought you'd photocopied your own copy and were trying to trace one that had been stolen." She passed the photocopy to me.

"It's natural that you'd think that," I said as I put it back into my pocket. "It was stupid of me not to make it all clear."

"Oh yes, that's made from your Department's copy," said Mrs. Hogarth.

She got to her feet, but for a moment I sat there, slowly coming to terms with the idea that the document Bret Rensselaer had been given for action was the one copied for Moscow's KGB archives. I'd gone on hoping that her answer would be different, but now I would have to look the facts straight in the eye.

"I'll come with you to the door," she prompted. "We're

getting very security conscious nowadays. Would you like to go out through the Number Ten door? Most people do, it's rather fun, isn't it?"

"You're quite certain?" I said. "No chance you've got it wrong?"

"No chance at all. I checked it twice against my list. I can't show it to you, I'm afraid, but I could get one of the security people to confirm it . . ."

"No need for that," I said.

It was raining now and the gardeners had abandoned the idea of planting the roses. They'd put the plants back into their box and were heading back into the house for shelter.

Mrs. Hogarth watched them sorrowfully. "It happens every time they start on the garden. It's almost like a rainmaking ceremony."

In the front hall of Number Ten there was a bored-looking police inspector, a woman in an overall distributing cups of tea from a tray, and a man who opened the door for me while holding his tea in one hand. "I appreciate your help, Mrs. Hogarth," I said. "I'm sorry about not having the official chit."

She shook hands as I went out onto that famous doorstep and said, "Don't worry about the chit. I have it already. It came over this morning."

Chapter 13

Iᴛ's ᴏᴜʀ anniversary," said Gloria.

"Is it?" I said.

"Don't sound so surprised, darling. We've been together exactly three months tomorrow."

I didn't know from what event she'd started counting, but

out of delicacy I didn't enquire. "And they said it wouldn't last," I said.

"Don't make jokes about us," she said anxiously. "I don't mind what jokes you make about me, but don't joke about us."

We were in the sitting room of an eleventh-floor flat near Notting Hill Gate, a residential district of mixed races and lifestyles on the west side of central London. It was eight-thirty on a Monday evening. We were dancing very, very slowly in that old-fashioned way in which you clasped each other tight. The radio was tuned to Alan Dell's BBC programme of big-band jazz, and he was playing an old Dorsey recording of "Tea for Two." She was letting her hair grow longer. It was a pale-gold color and now it was breaking over her shoulders. She wore a dark-green ribbed polo-neck sweater, with a chunky necklace and a light-brown suede skirt. It was all very simple, but with her long legs and generous figure the effect was stunning.

I looked round the room: gilded mirror, silk-lined lamp shades, electric-candle wall lights, and red velvet hangings. The hi-fi was hidden behind a row of fake books. It was the same elaborate clutter of vaguely nineteenth-century brothel furnishings that's to be seen in every High Street furniture shop throughout Britain. The curtains were open, and it was better to look through the window and see the glittering patterns of London by night. And I could see us reflected in the windows, dancing close.

Erich Stinnes was thirty minutes overdue. He was to stay here, with Ted Riley in the role of "minder." Upstairs, where Stinnes would spend most of his time, there was a small bedroom and study, and a rather elaborate bathroom. It was a departmental house, not exactly a "safe house" but one of the places used for the clandestine accommodation of overseas departmental employees. It was the policy that such people were not brought into the offices of London Central. Some of them didn't even know where our offices were.

I had come here to greet Stinnes on his arrival, double-check that Ted Riley was in attendance, and take Stinnes out to dinner to celebrate the new "freedom" he'd been so reluctantly granted. Gloria was with me because I'd convinced Bret, and myself, that her presence would make Stinnes more relaxed and soften him up for the new series of interrogations that were planned.

"What happened about that chit for Number Ten?" I said as we danced. "Your friend over there said she'd already had one. How could she have got a chit? I didn't even apply for one."

"I told her a tale of woe. I said that after it was all signed and approved I'd lost it. I told her that I'd get the sack if she didn't cover for me."

"You wicked girl," I said.

"There's so much paperwork. If we didn't bend the rules now and again, we'd never get everything done." As we danced she reached out and stroked my head. I didn't like being stroked like a pet poodle, but I didn't complain. She was only a child and I suppose such corny little manifestations of endearment were what she thought appropriate to her role as a femme fatale. I wondered what she'd really like *me* to do—bury her in long-stemmed red roses and ravish her on a sable rug in front of a log fire in the mountains, with gypsy violins in an adjoining room?

"You're worrying about Bret Rensselaer, aren't you?" she asked softly.

"You're always saying that, and I'm always replying that I don't give a damn about him."

"You're worried about what you discovered," she said. She accepted my little bursts of bad temper with equanimity. I wondered if she realized how much I loved her for doing that.

"I'd feel a hell of a lot better without having discovered it," I admitted. The music came to an end and there was some chat about trumpet and the tenor-sax solos before the next record started: Count Basie playing "Moonglow." She threw her head back, twisting her head so that her long pale hair flashed in the light. We began dancing again.

"What are you going to do about it? Report it?" she asked.

"There's not much I can report. It's all very slight and circumstantial except for the Cabinet memo, and I'm not going to stride into the D-G's office and report that. They'll want to know why I didn't report it when I first got it. They'll ask who gave it to me, and I don't want to tell them. And they'll start digging deep into all kinds of things. And meanwhile I'll be suspended from duty."

"Why not tell them who gave it to you?"

"All my sources of information and goodwill would dry up overnight if I blew one of them. Can you imagine what sort of grilling Morgan would arrange for the man who'd got hold of Bret's copy of the memo?"

"In order to get rid of Rensselaer?"

"Yes, to get rid of Rensselaer."

"He must be a wonderful man, your contact," she said wistfully. I hadn't told her anything about Posh Harry and she resented my secrecy.

"He's a slippery bastard," I said. "But I wouldn't deliver him to Morgan."

"It might be him or you," she said with that ruthless simplicity that women call feminine logic.

"It's not him or me yet. And it's not going to be him or me for a long time to come."

"So you'll do nothing?"

"I haven't decided yet."

"But how can it be Bret?" she asked. It was the beginning of the same circle of questions that whirled round in my head day and night. "Bret takes your advice all the time. He's even agreed to moving Stinnes here from Berwick House at your suggestion."

"Yes, he has," I said.

"And you're having second thoughts about his coming here. I know you are. Are you worried that Bret might try to kill him or something?"

"At Berwick House they have guards and alarms and so on.

They're not installed there solely to keep the inmates in; they keep nasty people out."

"So send him back there."

"He'll be here any minute."

"Send him back tomorrow."

"How can I do that? Think what a damned fool I'd look going into Bret's office, cap in hand, to tell him I've changed my mind about it."

"And think what a damned fool you'd look if something happened to Stinnes."

"I have thought about that," I said with what I thought was masterful restraint.

She smiled. "It *is* funny, darling. I'm sorry to laugh, but you have brought it on yourself by telling Bret how incompetent the Debriefing Centre staff are."

"I'm wondering to what extent Bret maneuvered me into that one," I said.

She hooted. "That'll be the day, beloved. When you're maneuvered into one of your tirades."

I smiled too. She was right, of course; I had walked right into this one, and the consequences were entirely of my own making.

She said, "But if Bret is a KGB agent . . ."

"I've told you there's nothing . . ."

"But let's play 'if,' " she persisted. "He's placed himself into a wonderful position of power." She hesitated.

Her hesitation was because any conjecture about Bret and Stinnes inevitably made me look a fool. "Go on," I said.

"If Bret Rensselaer is a KGB agent, he's done everything just right. He's been pushed into taking over the Stinnes debriefing without showing any desire to get the job. Now he's going to isolate the best intelligence source we've had for years and do it at your suggestion. All the Stinnes intelligence will pass through him, and if anything goes wrong, he has you as the perfect scapegoat." She looked at me but I didn't react. "Suppose Bret Rensselaer knows you have the photocopy of that Cabinet memo? Did you think of that, Bernard? Maybe Moscow knows what's happened. If he's a KGB agent, they would have told him."

"I did think of that," I admitted.

"Oh, Bernard, darling. I'm so frightened."

"There's nothing to be frightened about."

"I'm frightened for you, darling."

I heard the apartment front door bang and an exchange of voices as Ted Riley let Stinnes step past him into the hallway and then double-locked the door.

I let go of Gloria and said, "Hello, Ted."

Ted Riley said, "Sorry we're late. Those bloody Berwick House people can't even understand their own paperwork." He went across to the window and closed the curtains. Ted was right of course; I should have kept them closed when the lights were on. We were high in the sky and not overlooked, but a sniper's rifle could do the job all right. And Moscow would think Stinnes worth that kind of trouble.

Erich Stinnes watched us with solemn and sardonic respect. Even when he was introduced to Gloria his reaction was a polite smile and a bow in the German fashion. Over his gray suit he wore a stiffly new raincoat and a soft felt hat, its brim turned down all round in a way that made him look very foreign.

"You'll probably be anxious to get away to your gut-bash," said Riley, throwing his coat on to a chair and looking at his watch.

"It won't be crowded," I said. "It's just a little family place." Stinnes looked up, realizing that I was warning him not to expect a banquet. My available expenses did not extend to a lavish treat, and with Gloria along, the modest dinner for three was going to have to sound like a big dinner for two if I was going to reclaim it all.

Before we left, I took Stinnes upstairs to show him his study. There was a small desk there with an electric typewriter and a pile of paper. On the wall there was a map of the world and over his desk a map of Russia. There was a shelf of assorted books —mostly Russian-language books including some fiction and

English-Russian and English-German dictionaries. On his desk there was the current copy of *The Economist* and some English and German newspapers. There was a small shortwave radio receiver too, a Sony 2001 with preset and scan tuning. Instead of using batteries it was plugged into the mains via a power adapter and I warned him that if he unplugged it there was a danger that the adapter would burn out, but he seemed to know that already. Not surprising since the 2001 had long since been standard issue for KGB agents.

"Eventually you'll be able to go out alone," I told him. "But for the time being, Ted Riley will have to accompany you wherever you want to go. But if he says no, it's no. Ted's in charge."

"You have gone to a lot of trouble, Samson," Stinnes said as he surveyed the room. The suspicion that was to be seen in his eyes was in his voice too.

"It wasn't easy to arrange, so don't let me down," I said. "If you bolt, I'll get all the blame . . . all the blame." I said it twice to emphasize the truth of it.

"I have no plans to bolt," he said.

"Good," I said, and we went downstairs to where Ted was unpacking his overnight bag and Gloria was holding the curtain aside, staring out at the London skyline. Bad security, but you can't live your entire life by rules and regulations. I know: I'd tried.

"We won't be late, Ted," I promised.

Ted looked at Gloria who closed the curtains and put on her coat. Ted helped her into it. "At midnight he turns into a frog," he told her, indicating me with a movement of his head.

"Yes, I know, but he's seeing someone about it," she said affably.

Ted laughed. He guessed that I'd asked for him to do this job and it seemed to have given him a new lease on life.

To ENTERTAIN Erich Stinnes, my first choice would have been a German restaurant or, failing that, a place that served good Russian food. But London, almost alone among the world's great cities, has neither Russian nor German restaurants. Gloria suggested a Spanish place she knew in Soho, but my dislike of Spanish and Portuguese cooking is exceeded only by my dislike of the fiery stodge of Latin America. So we went to an Indian restaurant. Erich Stinnes needed guidance through the menu. It was an unusual admission; Stinnes was not the sort of man who readily admitted to needing assistance in any circumstance, but he was a great ladies' man and I could see he liked having Gloria describe to him the difference between the peppery *vindaloos* and the milder *kormas*. Gloria was what gossip columnists call a "foodie": she liked talking about food and discussing restaurants and recipes even more than she liked eating. So I let her order the whole spread, from the thick puree of *dhal* to crispy fried *papadoms* and the big bowl of boiled rice that comes decorated with nuts and dried fruit and edible bits of something that looks like silver paper.

I watched them, heads close together, as they went muttering their way through the long menu. For a moment I felt a pang of jealousy. Suppose Erich Stinnes was a KGB plant—I'd never entirely dismissed the idea, even when he was at his most cooperative—then what an extra laugh for Fiona if I lost my girlfriend to one of her field agents. Gloria was fascinated by him, I could see that. It was strange that this sallow-complexioned man with his hard face and balding head could attract women so effortlessly. It was his evident energy, of course, but now and again, when he thought I wasn't observing him, I could see signs of that energy flagging. Stinnes was growing tired. Or old. Or frightened. Or maybe all three. I knew the feeling.

We drank beer. I preferred an Indian meal partly because no one was expected to drink anything strong with a curry. This wasn't going to be the right time to get Stinnes boozed to the point of indiscretion. And it wasn't going to be the right expense account either. At this first outing, Stinnes would be wary of such tactics, but his first sip of the fizzy water that the British call lager allayed all such fears. He pursed his lips in distaste, but didn't complain about the watery beer or anything else.

The decor was typical of such places: red-flocked wallpaper and a dark-blue ceiling painted with stars. But the food was good enough, flavored with ginger and paprika and the milder spices. Erich Stinnes seemed to enjoy it. He sat against the wall with Gloria next to him, and although he supplied his due amount of small talk, his eyes moved constantly, looking to see whether any of the other customers, or even staff, looked like departmental employees. That's the way Moscow would have done it; they always have watchers to watch the watchers.

We had been talking about books. "Erich likes reading the Bible," I announced for no real reason other than to keep the conversation going.

"Is that true?" she said, turning to Erich Stinnes.

Before he could answer, I explained, "He was with Section 44 back in the old days."

"Do you know what that is?" he asked her.

"The KGB's Religious Affairs Bureau," she said. It wasn't easy to catch her out; she knew her way round the files. "But I don't know exactly what they do."

"I'll tell you something they do," I said to her, ignoring the presence of Stinnes for a moment. "They desecrate graves and spray swastikas on the walls of synagogues in NATO countries so that the Western press can make headlines speculating about the latest upsurge of neo-Nazi activity and get a few extra votes for the left-wingers."

I watched Stinnes, wondering if he'd deny such outrages. "Sometimes," he said gravely. "Sometimes."

I'd finished eating, but now she picked up a crisp *papadom* I'd not eaten and nibbled at it. "Do you mean you've become a dedicated Christian?"

"I'm not a dedicated anything," said Stinnes. "But one day I will write a book comparing the medieval Church to applied Marxist-Leninism."

This was just the sort of talk she liked: an intellectual discussion, not the bourgeois chitchat, office gossip, and warmed-up chunks of *The Economist* that I served her. "For instance?" she said. She furrowed her brow; she looked very young and very beautiful in the dim restaurant lighting, or was that British lager stronger than I thought?

"The medieval Church and the Communist state share four basic dictums," he said. "First and foremost comes the instruction to seek the life of the spirit: seek pure Marxism. Don't waste your efforts on other trivial things. Gain is avarice, love is lust, beauty is vanity." He looked round at us. "Two: Communists are urged to give service to the state, as Christians must give it to the Church—in a spirit of humility and devotion, not in order to serve themselves or to become a success. Ambition is bad: it is the result of sinful pride . . ."

"But you haven't . . . ," said Gloria.

"Let me go on," said Stinnes quietly. He was enjoying himself. I think it was the first time I'd seen him looking really happy. "Three: both Church and Marx renounce money. Investment and interest payments are singled out as the worst of evils. Four, and this is the most important similarity, there is the way in which the Christian faithful are urged to deny themselves all the pleasures of this world to get their reward in paradise after they die."

"And Communists?" she asked.

He smiled a hard close-lipped smile. "If *they* work hard and deny themselves the pleasures of this world, then after they die their children will grow up in paradise," said Stinnes. He smiled again.

"Very good," said Gloria admiringly. There wasn't much left on the plates or dishes that covered the table. I'd already had enough to eat—a little curry goes a long way with me—so she picked up the dish of chicken *korma* and divided the last of it onto their two plates. Stinnes took the dishes of the rice and the eggplant and, when I declined, divided the food between them.

"You missed out number five," I said, while they were tucking into their final helpings. Both of them looked at me as if they'd forgotten I was there with them. "Victory over the flesh. Both Church and Communist state preach that."

I was serious, but Gloria dismissed it. "Very funny," she said. She wiped her lips with the napkin. To Stinnes she said, "Was the Church *very* opposed to capitalism? I know it objected to loaning money and collecting interest, but it wasn't opposed to trading."

"You're wrong," said Stinnes. "The medieval Church preached against any sort of free competition. All craftsmen were forbidden to improve tools or change their methods lest they take advantage of their neighbors. They were forbidden to undersell; goods had to be offered at a fixed price. And the Church objected to advertising, especially if any trader compared his goods with inferior goods offered by another trader at the same price."

"It sounds familiar," said Gloria. "Doesn't it, Bernard?" she asked, politely drawing me into the conversation as she looked into a tiny handbag-mirror to see that her lips were wiped clean of curry.

"Yes," I said, *"Homo mercator vix aut numquam potest Deo placare*—a man who is a merchant will never be able to please God —or please the Party Congress. Or please the Trades Union Congress either."

"Poor merchants," said Gloria.

"Yes," said Stinnes.

The waiter came over to our table and began clearing the dishes away. He offered us a selection of those very sweet Indian-style desserts, but no one wanted anything but coffee.

Stinnes waited until the table was completely cleared. It was as if this action prompted him to change the conversation: he leaned forward, arms on the table, and said, "You were asking about code words . . . radio codes . . . two names for one agent." He stopped there to give me time to shut him up if I didn't want Gloria to hear the rest of the conversation.

I told him to go on.

"I said it was impossible. Or at least unprecedented. But I've been thinking about it since then . . ."

"And?" I said after a long pause during which the waiter put the coffee on the table.

"I told you it was nonsense, but now I think you may be correct. There was a line of intelligence material that I was not permitted to see. It was handled by our radio room, but it went directly to Moscow. None of my staff ever saw it."

"Was that unusual?" I asked.

"Very unusual, but there seemed no reason to think that we were missing anything very good. I thought it was some Moscow deskman trying to make a name for himself by working on one narrow field of interest. Senior staff in Moscow do that sometimes; then suddenly—choosing their moment carefully— they produce a very thick file of new material and before the cheers die down they get the promotion they've had their eye on."

"How did you find out about it?"

"It was kept separate, but it wasn't given any special high security rating. That might have been a very cunning idea—it didn't attract so much attention like that. People handling it would just have thought it applied to some boring technical file. How did I come across it? It came onto my desk by accident. It was the second of February of last year. I remember the date because it was my son's birthday. The decoded transcripts were put on my desk with a pile of other material. I looked through it to see what was there and found this stuff with an agent name I didn't recognize but a London coding. I thought it must be a mistake. I thought a typing error had given it the five-letter group for London. It's not often that the typists there make such an error, but it's not unknown. It was only last week that I remembered it in the light of what you were asking me about agents with two code names. Any use to you?"

"It might be," I said. "What else can you remember?"

"Nothing. Except that it was very long and it seemed to be

about some sort of intelligence exercise that your people had carried out in West Germany." He looked at me but I gave no reaction. "You'd sent your own agents breaking into your data-gathering installations. Some sort of security report and a lot of electronics . . . I can't understand electronics, can you?"

"No," I said. So that was it. The long message couldn't be anything other than the full report for the PM that resulted from the Cabinet memo. Bret had supervised and signed that report. If Moscow's copy of the memo had come through Bret's hands—and I had Mrs. Hogarth's evidence that it did—then it was reasonable to suppose that the full report that followed had also been supplied by Bret. My God, it was shattering, even when I was partly prepared for it. More shattering perhaps because when you begin to be convinced of something, you expect some damned law of averages to start providing a bit of contradictory evidence. Bret: Could it be true?

"You've gone very quiet," said Stinnes.

"It's that damned *dhal,*" I said. "It really slows me down."

Gloria glanced at me. She said nothing, but she began looking through her handbag as if looking for something she'd mislaid. It was her attempt to appear bored by the conversation. Maybe Stinnes was fooled, but I doubt it.

Chapter 14

THE RELAXED evening in the curry restaurant with Stinnes brought quick results. By the following Saturday morning I was drinking Bret Rensselaer's gin and tonics and listening to Bret's congratulations. The fact that Bret's congratulations were delivered in a way that could have an inattentive on-looker thinking he was singing his own praises did not distress me. First, because I was accustomed to Bret's habits and manners, and, secondly, because there were no onlookers.

"It sure paid off," said Bret. "Everything I said okay to paid off." He was dressed in casual wear: dark open-neck sports shirt and white linen pants. I'd seldom seen Bret wearing anything other than his Savile Row suits, but then I'd seldom been honored with an invitation to go to his Thames-side mansion in off-duty hours. Bret had his own circle of friends—minor aristocracy, international jet-setters, merchant bankers, and business tycoons. No one from the Department got a regular invitation here except perhaps the D-G and the Deputy and maybe the Cruyers if Bret needed a favor from the German desk. Other than that, the guest list was confined to a few particularly sexy girls from the office who got invited for the weekend to look at Bret's art collection.

I'd driven from London in dry weather with the sun shining through a gap of blue sky, but now the sky was clouding over and the color drained from the landscape. From where I sat there was a view across a long lawn, brown after the harsh winter frosts, and then, at the bottom of his garden, the Thames. Here in Berkshire it was just a weedy stream a few yards across. Despite the river's huge loops, it was difficult to believe that we were in the Thames Valley a short distance from London's dockland where oceangoing ships could navigate on these same waters.

Bret walked round the back of the sofa where I was sitting and poured more gin into my glass. It was a large room. Three soft, gray leather sofas of modern Italian design were arranged round the glass-topped coffee table. There was an unpainted wooden fireplace where a log fire flickered and occasionally filled the room with a puff of wood smoke that made my eyes water. The walls were plain white to provide a background against which Bret's paintings could be seen at their best. One on each wall: a Bratby portrait, a Peter Blake pop-art bearded lady, a Hockney swimming pool, and a wood abstract by Tilson over the fireplace. The best of British painters were there. It would have to be British for him; Bret was the sort of Anglophile who took it all seriously. Other than the sofas, the furniture was English, antique and expensive. There was a Regency chest of dark mahogany with a glass-domed skeleton clock on it and a secretaire-bookcase behind whose glass doors some pieces of Minton porcelain were displayed. No books; all the books were in the library, a room Bret liked to preserve for his own exclusive use.

"The interrogator is pleased, of course. The D-G is pleased. Dicky Cruyer is pleased. Everyone is pleased, except perhaps the staff at London Debriefing Centre, but the D-G is smoothing things over with them. Some sort of letter congratulating them on their skillful preparation is the sort of thing I thought appropriate."

Would this be a time when I could start cross-questioning Bret about his apparent involvement with the KGB? I decided not and drank some more gin and tonic. "Good," I said.

"In just two days Stinnes has given us enough to break a network that's operating out of the Ministry of Defence research laboratory at Cambridge. Apparently they've known there's been a leak for months and months, and this will provide a chance to clear that one up."

"England?" I said. "Cambridge, England? Hold the phone, Bret—we can't go into a KGB network operating in Britain. That's Home Office territory. That's MI5's job. They'll go ape."

He went to the fire and squatted at it to prod the burning log with his fingertips. It made sparks. Then he wiped his fingers on a paper tissue before sinking into the soft leather opposite me. He smiled his wide, charming, Hollywood smile. It was a calculated gesture to make his explanation more dramatic. Everything he did was calculated, and he liked drama to the point of losing his temper with anyone in sight if the mood took him. "We're legitimately holding Erich Stinnes. The Home Office have responded to the D-G's notification and agreed that we do some preliminary interrogations so that we can make sure that our own people are in the clear."

"You mean hold him while I'm being investigated," I said.

"Of course," said Bret. "You know perfectly well we're using you as the excuse. It's wonderful. Don't suddenly go temperamental on me, Bernard. It's just a formality. Hell, do you think they'd let you anywhere near Stinnes if you were really suspect?"

"I don't know, Bret. There are some damned funny people in the Department."

"You're in the clear, so forget it."

"And you're going to infiltrate some poor sod into the Cambridge network and try to blow it? You don't stand a chance. Can't we investigate it on a formal basis—questioning and so on?"

"It would take too long. We've got to move fast. If we go for a formal investigation, MI5 will take it over when Stinnes is transferred and they'll make the arrests and get the glory. No, this is urgent. We'll do it ourselves."

"And you'll get the glory," I said.

Bret didn't take offense. He smiled. "Take it easy, Bernard," he said mildly. "You know me better than that." He spoke to the ceiling for he was sitting deep down in the soft cushions of the sofa, his head resting back, and his suede moccasins plonked on the glass-topped table so that he was stretched as straight as a ruler. Outside the sky was getting darker and even the white walls couldn't stop the room becoming gloomy.

I didn't pursue that particular line. I didn't know him better than that. I didn't know him at all. "You'll have to tell Five," I said.

"I told them last night," he said.

"The night duty officer on a Friday night? That's too obvious, Bret. They'll be hopping mad. When are you putting your man in?"

"Tonight," he said.

"Tonight!" I almost snorted my drink down my nose. "Who's running him? Are Operations in on this? Who gave the okay?"

"Don't be so jittery, Bernard. It will be all right. The D-G gave me the go-ahead. No, Operations are not a party to the plan; it's better that they don't know about it. Secrecy is of paramount importance."

"Secrecy is of paramount importance? And you've left a message with the night duty officer at Five? You realize that probationers—kids just down from college—are likely to get weekend duties like that. Whoever he is, he'll want to cover himself, so now he's phoning everyone in his contact book and trying to think of more names."

"You're becoming paranoid, Bernard," Bret said. He smiled to show me how calm he was remaining. "Even if he is an inexperienced kid from college—and I know kids from college are not high on your all-time Hit Parade—the messages he'll leave with maids, au pair girls, and receptionists at country hotels won't explicitly describe our operation."

He was a sarcastic bastard. "For God's sake, grow up, Bret," I said. "Can't you see that a flurry of activity like that—messages being left in all sorts of non-departmental places for the urgent attention of senior MI5 staff—is enough to compromise your operation?"

"I don't agree," he said, but he stopped smiling.

"Some smart newspaperman is likely to get the smell of that one. If that happens, it could blow up in your face."

"In *my* face?"

"Well, what are those messages going to be saying? They are going to be saying that we're just about to go blundering into matters that don't concern us. They're going to say we're stealing Five's jobs from them. And they'll be right."

"This isn't a hot tip on a horse; they'll be sensible," said Bret.

"It's going to be all over town," I said. "You're putting your man into danger, real danger. Forget it."

"MI5 are not going to let newsmen get hold of secrets like this."

"You hope they're not. But this isn't *their* secret, it's ours.

What will they care if your Boy Scout comes a cropper? They'll be delighted. It would teach us a lesson. And why would they be so fussy about newspapermen getting the story? If it made headlines that said we were treading on their territory, it would suit their book."

"I'm not sure I want to listen to this anymore," said Bret huffily. This was Bret getting ready for his knighthood—loyal servant of Her Majesty and all that. "I trust MI5 to be just as careful with secret information as we are."

"So do I, if it's *their* information. But this is not their information. This is a message—a message from you; not a message about one of their operations but about one of ours. What's more, it was given out on a Friday evening in what is a transparent trick to hamper any efforts they might make to stop us. How can you believe they'll play it your way and help you score?"

"It's too late now," said Bret. He took two ice cubes from a container that was painted to look like a side drum from the band of the Grenadier Guards, complete with battle honors, and dropped them into his drink. Bret could make one drink last a long time. It was a trick I'd never mastered. He offered ice to me but I shook my head. "It's all approved and signed for. There's not going to be any pussyfooting about trying to infiltrate them. There's an office in Cambridge which contains files on the whole network. It's coded, Stinnes says, coded to read like normal office files. But that shouldn't be a big problem. We're putting a man in there this evening. He's coming here to meet you."

"Beautiful, Bret," I said sarcastically. "That's all I need—for your tame gorilla to get a good look at me before he gets rolled in a carpet and shipped to Moscow."

Bret permitted himself a ghost of a smile. "It's not that kind of operation, Bernard. This is the other side of the job. We'll be in England. If there's any interference, we'll be putting the handcuffs on those bastards, not the other way around."

I weakened. I should have remained cynical about it, but I weakened because I began to feel that it might prove as simple as Bret Rensselaer said it would be. "Okay. What do you want me to do?"

"Run him up to Cambridge and play nurse." So that was it. I should have guessed that you don't get invited to Bret's for nothing. My heart sank into my guts. I felt the way some of those girls must have felt when they realized there were more works of art that lined the stairs all the way to Bret's bedroom. He saw it in my face. "Did you think I was going to try to do it myself?"

"No, I didn't."

"If you really think I can do it, Bernard, I'll try." He was restless. He got up again and poured more gin for me. It was only then that I realized that I'd gulped the rest of my drink without even noticing that I'd done so. "But I think our man deserves the best help we can find for him. And you're the best."

He went back and sat down. I didn't reply. For a moment we both sat there in that beautiful room thinking our own thoughts. I don't know what Bret was thinking of, but I was back to trying to decide what his relationship with my wife had been.

At one time I'd felt sure that Fiona and Bret had been lovers. I looked at him. She was right for him, that very beautiful woman from a rich family. She was sophisticated in a way that only wealthy people can be. She had the confidence, stability, and intellect that nature provides for the first-born child.

The suspicion and jealousy of that time, not so long ago, had never gone away, and my feelings colored everything I had to do with Bret. There was little chance I would ever discover the truth of it, and I was not really and truly sure that I wanted to know. And yet I couldn't stop thinking about them. Had they been together in this room?

"I'll never understand you, Bernard," he said suddenly. "You're full of anger."

I felt like saying that that was better than being full of shit, but in fact I didn't think that of Bret Rensselaer. I'd thought about him a lot over the past few months. First because I thought he was jumping into bed with Fiona and now because the finger of treason was pointed at him. It all made sense. Put it all together and it made sense. If Bret and Fiona were lovers, then why not co-conspirators too?

I had never faced an official enquiry, but Bret had tried to make me admit that I'd been in league with my wife to betray the Department's secrets. Some traces of the mud he'd thrown had stuck to me. That would be a damned smart way to cover his own tracks. No one had ever accused Bret of being a co-conspirator with Fiona. No one had even suspected that they were having a love affair. No one, that is, except me. I had always been able to see how attractive he'd be for her. He was the sort of man I'd had as rivals when I'd first met her; mature, successful men, not Oxbridge graduates trying to hack a career in a merchant bank, but men much older than Fiona, men with servants and big shiny cars who paid for everything by just signing their name on the bill.

It was very dark in the room now and there was a growl of thunder. Then more thunder. I could see the clock's brass pendulum catching the light as it swung backward and forward. Bret's voice came out of the gloom. "Or is it sadness? Anger or sadness—what's bugging you, Samson?"

I didn't want to play his silly undergraduate games, or sophisticated jet-set games, or whatever they were. "What time is this poor bastard arriving?" I said.

"No fixed time. He'll be here for tea."

"That's great," I said. Tea! Earl Grey no doubt, and I suppose Bret's housekeeper would be serving it in a silver teapot with muffins and those very thin cucumber sandwiches without crusts.

"You talked to Lange," he said. "And he bad-mouthed me the way he always does? Is that it? What did he say this time?"

"He was talking about the time you went to Berlin and made him dismantle his networks."

"He's such a crook. He's still resenting that after all these years?"

"He thinks you dealt a blow to a good system."

"The 'Berlin System,' the famous 'Berlin System' that Lange always regarded as his personal creation. It was Lange who ruined it by bringing it into such discredit that London Central sent me there to salvage what I could from it."

"Why you?" I said. "You were very young."

"The world was very young," said Bret. "Britain and the U.S. had won the war. We were going to be arm in arm together while we won the peace too."

"Because you were American?"

"Right. An American could look at what was going on in Berlin and be impartial about it. I was to be the one who went there and unified the Limeys and the Yanks and made them into a team again. That was the theory; the fact was that the only unification came from the way they all hated and despised me. The Berlin intelligence community got together just to baffle and bamboozle me. They led me a merry dance, Bernard; they made sure that I couldn't get to the people I wanted, get the documents I wanted, or get competent office help. I didn't even have a proper office, did you know that? Did Lange tell you how he made sure that no German would work for me?"

"The way I heard it, they gave you a big apartment and two servants."

"Is that the way Lange tells it? By now he probably even believes it. And what about the Russian princess?"

"He mentioned her."

"The real story is that those bastards made sure the only office space I had was shared with a clerk who went through my files every day and told them what I was doing. When I tried to get other accommodation they blocked every move I made. Finally I contacted a friend of my mother's. She wasn't young, she wasn't a princess, and she had never been in Russia, although her mother was distantly related to White Russian aristocracy. She had the big apartment in Heerstrasse, and by offering half of it to me she was able to prevent it being commandeered for use by some other Allied military outfit. I used that place as an office and I got her neighbor to do my typing."

"Lange said she was a Nazi, your friend."

"She'd lived in Berlin right through the war and her folks had been murdered by the Bolsheviks, so I guess she didn't go around waving any red flags. But she had close friends among the July twentieth conspirators. When Hitler was blown up in 1944 she was taken in for questioning by the SD. She spent three nights in the cells at Prinz Albrecht Strasse. It was touch and go whether they sent her to a camp, but there were so many suspected persons to be detained that they grew short of cells to hold them, so they let her go."

"There was a row about Lange's brother-in-law," I said.

"Damn right there was. If Lange had learned how to keep his head down and his mouth shut, maybe it wouldn't have blown up like that. But Lange has to be the big man on campus. And he particularly resented me because I was a fellow American. He wanted the exclusive title of tame Yank, and he'd got a lot of leeway playing that role. The office let him get away with all kinds of tricks because they thought it was just another example of good old Yankee know-how and the unconventional American way of tackling things."

"So he resigned?"

"It was tough for him, but he'd been told enough times about that woman he married. There was no way I could ignore an SS man living in Lange's parlor while I was lowering the boom on guys who'd done nothing more than joining the party to save their school-teaching jobs."

I didn't answer. I tried to reconcile Bret's version of these events with Lange's burning hatred. "They were not good times," I said.

"Did you ever hear of CROWCASS?" said Bret.

"Vaguely. What is it?"

"Right after the fighting ended, SHAEF started building a file of suspected war criminals. CROWCASS was the Central Registry of War Criminals and Security Suspects. Maybe it was a muddle, the way everyone said it was afterwards, but at the time CROWCASS was gospel, and Lange's brother-in-law had his name on that registry."

"Did Lange know that?"

"Sure he did."

"When did he find out?"

"I don't know when he found out, but he knew about the brother-in-law having served in the Waffen-SS before he got married. I know that because I found in the file a copy of the letter he'd been sent warning him not to go ahead. And all ex-members of the SS and Waffen-SS were automatically arrested unless they'd already faced an enquiry and been cleared. But Lange didn't care about any of that. He was playing the American card again. He let the British think he'd got special dispensation from the Americans and vice versa. He's a slippery one; I guess you know that."

"Didn't you know it?" I said.

"I know that, and I knew it then. But everyone was telling me what a wonderful network he was running. They wouldn't let me see anything he was producing, of course—security wouldn't permit. So I just had to take their word for it."

"He brought us some good people. He'd been in Berlin before the war. He knew everybody. He still does."

"So what was I to do?" said Bret defensively. "His goddamned brother-in-law was running round with a *Kennkarte* that identified him as a payroll clerk with a building company. It had a denazification stamp. He liked to tell everyone he'd been a Navy medic. He was picked up brawling in a bar in Wedding. He was stinking drunk and still fighting when they took him downtown and threw him into the drunk tank. They put these drunks under the cold showers to cool them off, and a cop who'd got hit on the nose began wondering how this Navy medic came to have an SS blood-group tattoo under his arm."

Outside, the river and the fields beyond were obliterated by gray mist and rain was beating against the window. Bret was lost in the shadows and his voice was impersonal, like a recording machine delivering some computer judgment.

"I couldn't ignore it," he said. "It was a police report. It was delivered to the office, but no one there wanted a hot potato like that on their desk. They sent it right along to me. It was probably the only piece of paperwork that they forwarded to me in the proper way." I said nothing. Bret realized that his explanation was convincing and he pursued it. "Lange thought himself indispensable," said Bret. "It's tempting to think that at any time, but it was especially tempting for someone heading up several networks—good networks, by all accounts. But no one is indispensable. The Berlin System managed without Lange. Your dad put the pieces together."

"Lange thinks my father would have helped him. He thinks my father was deliberately moved out of Berlin so that you could go in there and get rid of him."

"That's crap and Lange knows it. Your dad had done very well in Berlin. Silas Gaunt was his boss and when Silas got a promotion in London he brought your father back to London with him. Nothing was ever written on paper, but it was understood that your dad would go up the ladder with Silas. He had a fine career waiting for him in London Central."

"So what happened?" I said.

"When Lange got sore, he tried to sell all his networks to the U.S. Army. They wouldn't touch him, of course."

"He had good networks," I said.

"Very good, but even if they'd been twice as good, I doubt if he could have sold the Counterintelligence Corps on the idea of taking them over."

"Why?"

"The CIC weren't concerned with what was happening in the Russian Zone. Their task was security. They were looking for Nazis, neo-Nazi groups, and Communist subversives operating in the West."

"So why not pass Lange on to some other department?"

"In those days the U.S. had no organization spying on the Russians. Congress wanted America to play Mr. Nice Guy. There were a few retreads from the old OSS and they were working for something that called itself the War Department Detachment, which in turn was a part of something called the Central Intelligence Group. But this was amateur stuff; the Russians were laughing at it. Lange tried everywhere, but no one wanted his networks."

"It sounds like a meat market."

"And that's the way the field agents saw it when the news filtered through to them. They were demoralized, and Lange wasn't very popular."

"So my father came back to Berlin to sort it out?"

"Yes, your dad volunteered to come back and sort it out even though he knew he'd lose his seniority in London. Meanwhile Lange was sent to Hamburg to cool off."

"But he didn't cool off?"

"He got madder and madder. And when your dad wouldn't take him back unless he completely separated himself from his Waffen-SS brother-in-law, Lange resigned."

"Are you saying my dad sacked Lange?"

"Look in the records. It's not top secret."

"Lange blames you," I said.

"To you he blames me," said Bret.

"He blames my father?"

"In the course of the years Lange has blamed everyone from the records clerks to President Truman. The only one Lange never blames is himself."

"It was a tough decision," I said. "SS man or no SS man, I admire the way Lange stood by him. Maybe he did the right thing. Turning his brother-in-law out onto the street would have wrecked his marriage, and that marriage still works."

"The reason Lange wouldn't turn his brother-in-law out was because that brother-in-law was making anything up to a thousand dollars a week in the black market."

"Are you kidding?"

"That fateful night the cops picked him up in Wedding, he had nearly a thousand U.S. dollars in his pocket and another thousand bucks in military scrip. That's what got the cops so excited. That's why I had to do something about it. It's in the police report; take a look at it."

"You know I can't take a look at it. They never put those old files onto the computer, and no one can find anything that old down in Registry."

"Well, ask anyone who was there. Sure, Lange was on the take from his brother-in-law. Some people said Lange was setting up some of his deals for him."

"How?" I said, but the answer was obvious.

"I don't know. But I can guess. Lange hears about a black-market deal through one of his agents. Instead of busting them, he cuts his brother-in-law into the deal."

"He'd never survive if he pulled tricks like that."

"Don't play the innocent, Samson, it doesn't suit you. You know what the city was like during those days. You know how it worked. Lange would just say that he wanted the black-market deal to continue because one of the dealers was an important Soviet agent. His brother-in-law would play the role of Lange's *stoolie*. They'd all make money with no chance of arrest. It's a foolproof system. No one could touch him."

There was a ring at the front door. I heard the housekeeper going down the hall.

"This will be our man for the break-in tonight," said Bret. "It will be like old times for you, Bernard."

And then through the door walked Ted Riley.

Chapter 15

WHY DID you get yourself into this crock?" I asked Ted Riley for what must have been the hundredth time. For the hundredth time he failed to give me any proper explanation. He was in no hurry. He was drinking Powers Irish whiskey, and it was having an effect upon him, for when he spoke his voice had the lilt of Kerry, a brogue that makes everything into a song. I remembered that voice from my childhood, and it brought back to me all Ted's stories.

There was the one about his grandfather piling his freshly cut peat into "stooks" and how, "in the soft pink light of each and every morning," he found that some of his peat had been stolen. The thefts continued for years until one day Grandfather Riley tucked gunpowder into the turf and a neighbor's cottage burned to the ground. It was to avoid the violent retribution threatened by the injured man's relatives that the Rileys moved to County Kerry where Ted was born. How many of Ted's stories were true, how many embroidered, and how many invented just to amuse a wide-eyed little boy, I'll never know. But Ted was a part of my childhood, like climbing Berlin's rubble piles and ice skating on the Muggelsee.

"Ahhhh." Ted's yawn was a symptom of anxiety. For all God's creatures, fear brings a drowsiness, a self-preserving urge to snuggle down somewhere out of sight and go to sleep.

We were sitting in the sort of room in which I seem to have spent half my adult life. It was a hotel room in Cambridge, but this was not the Cambridge of Gothic spires or cloistered dons; this was a shopping street on the wrong side of town, a shabby hotel with cracked lino on the floor, a bathroom a long way down the hall, and a sink where a dripping tap had resisted all my efforts to silence it.

It was late evening, but we'd kept the room lights switched off. The curtain remained open and the room's only light came from the street lamps, the bilious yellow sodium glow reflected from the rain-wet road to make patterns on the ceiling. I could make out the shape of Ted Riley slumped on the bed, still wearing his damp raincoat. His hat was pulled down to cover his face. He only moved it back when he drank.

I was standing near the window, looking through the net curtain at the premises across the street. It was an old four-story building, its fascia stained and in places broken. According to the brass plates alongside the front door, it housed a firm of architects and an industrial designer as well as the solicitor's office we were to break into. On the top floor was the flat for the caretaker, but tonight according to Ted's research the caretaker was away visiting his son's family in London. The whole building was dark.

"Ah, now . . . ! You know . . . !" Ted said, and raised his glass to me. That was supposed to answer all my questions.

Ted Riley was trying to tell me that no matter how carefully he tried to explain things, I'd not understand. We were a generation apart, and what was more important, Ted's generation had fought a war while my generation had not. Ted was a friend of my father and everything in Ted's gesture told me that my father would have never asked him that question; my father would have known the answer. That's why Ted didn't reply. It was a convenient thing for Ted to believe.

I poured myself some more whiskey and took the bottle across to the bed. Ted held up his glass to me without removing the hat from his face. I poured him another good measure. He'd need it.

"Thanks, my boy," he said.

No matter how close I felt to Ted Riley, he saw me as the little boy who'd made good. Those who got their feet under a desk at London Central were regarded as a race apart by the men and women who had done the real work in those lonely places where the real work was done.

"When your man makes a suggestion, I'm in no position to turn it down," said Ted. "I'm employed on sufferance. The Department has told me so in those very words." He meant Bret of course, and Bret was "my man" because I'd accompanied him to Berwick House in his big car.

I stepped back to the window to watch the street. I didn't have to move far; the room was no bigger than a large cupboard. "That was a long time ago," I heard myself saying, just as everyone kept saying it to me when they thought I needed reassurance about my past. Time used to be the panacea for everything, but nowadays our sins are remembered on computers, and random-accessed memories do not fade.

A police car passed. Not quite slowly enough to be observing our target but not quite fast enough to be merely passing by. I decided not to mention it to Ted; he was jumpy enough already.

"There's no statute of limitations on blackmail," said Ted with no special bitterness in his voice. "It's written down somewhere in some secret file, to be used against me whenever I'm anything less than exemplary."

For a moment I thought there was some double meaning there. I thought he was telling me that I was in the same position. But that wasn't the Department's style. How can you blackmail anyone about something that's become common knowledge? No, just as Ted Riley's disgrace had been so assiduously concealed, so would any lingering suspicion about me be kept buried deep in the boneyard. I said, "For God's sake, Ted. Hams or cheese or booze or something . . . it's too long ago for anyone to care about it."

"I was young and very stupid. It wasn't so much the little black-market deals. Everyone was frightened that I'd been forced to reveal military information too. I never thought of it like that at the time."

"Not Dad," I said. "Dad would have trusted you with his life."

Ted grunted to show how silly I was. "Your dad signed the note for the enquiry. I could have kept it covered up until your dad found out. Your dad packed me off to London to face the music."

For a moment I felt sick. Ted was not only a very close colleague of my father, but a friend of the family. He was always in and out when we were living at Lisl Hennig's place. Ted was one of the family. Our German maidservant would keep a spare set of cutlery and a napkin handy just in case Ted arrived for dinner unannounced. "I'm sorry, Ted. I had no idea."

Ted gave another grunt. "I don't blame your dad; I blame

myself. Your dad made no secret of what he did to staff who broke the rules, and I was senior staff. Your dad did the only thing he could do. He made an example of me. I bear him no grudge, Bernard."

His voice was that of the slim young officer who'd so effortlessly hoisted me onto his shoulder and galloped down the corridor to put me into the bath. But in the gloom I could see that the voice was coming from a fat disappointed old man.

"Dad was bloody inflexible," I said. I went and sat on the bed. The tired old springs groaned and the mattress sagged under my weight.

"God rest him," said Ted. He stretched out and touched my arm. "You had the finest father anyone could wish for. He never asked us to do anything he wouldn't do himself." Ted's voice was strained. I'd forgotten that Ted was one of the sentimental breed of Irishmen.

"Dad was something of a Prussian at times," I said to ease the tension. Ted was getting to the kind of maudlin mood in which he'd start singing "Come back to Erin, mavourneen, mavourneen . . ." in the tear-jerking baritone that he always produced at the Christmas parties we used to have in the office in Berlin.

"Many a true word is spoken in jest," said Ted hoarsely. "Yes, your father was like some of those Prussians . . . the ones I liked. When the enquiry was held, it was your father who came to London and gave evidence on my behalf. If it hadn't been for what your dad said, I would have been kicked out of the service without a pension."

"Is that what happened to Lange?"

"Something like that," said Ted, as if he didn't want to talk about it.

"Was Lange on the take?"

Ted took his hat from his eyes in order to look at me and smiled. "Was Lange on the take? Lange was on the way to becoming the king of the Berlin black market by the time they booted him off to Hamburg."

"And my father didn't know?"

"Now you're comparing me with Lange. That's like comparing a first-time offender with Al Capone. I was just a kid, Lange was an old newspaperman who knew the ways of the world. Did you know that Lange was granted a personal interview with Hitler back in 'thirty-three when the Nazis first came to power? Lange was a mature sophisticated man. He knew how to cover his tracks and he could sweet-talk anyone into anything. Even your father came under his spell. But Lange was frightened of your father. It was only when your dad left Berlin for London that Lange pulled out all the stops. Rumors say he put a million marks into the bank."

"So much for rumors," I said. "Go and visit him now and you won't see much sign of it. He's living in a dilapidated dump off Potsdamer Strasse and drinking homemade wine. I felt so bad about him that I fiddled a small departmental payment for the information he gave me. Rensselaer saw the docket and started quizzing me about what Lange had said."

"Save your tears, Bernie. Lange did some terrible things in the old days—things I wouldn't like to have on my conscience."

"What things?"

"Lange's black-market friends were armed, and I don't mean with can openers. People got hurt, some even got killed. Lange stayed clear, but he knew what was happening when those toughs raided warehouses and hijacked Army trucks. And the crime figures prove it. When Lange went to Hamburg, things suddenly improved in Berlin."

"Was that why Lange was sent to Hamburg?"

"Sure. It was the only way they could prove his guilt. After that he never got a really good job again."

We sat there in silence, drinking. In an hour it would be finished and done with. I'd be in the car with Ted, roaring down the London road, and we'd be enjoying that slight hysteria that follows risky little games like this one.

I changed the subject. "So how is Erich Stinnes and his radio?"

"It all worked out just fine, Bernie. He listens to Radio Volga every morning."

"Radio Volga?"

"For the Soviet Armed Forces in Germany. It broadcasts all day every day up to ten o'clock at night, at which time all good Russian soldiers switch off and go to bed, except Saturday when it goes on until ten-thirty."

"It doesn't sound likely that the Army would be sending radio messages to a KGB officer."

"No, but until five o'clock every afternoon Radio Volga is relaying the Moscow Home Service Channel One. That could contain any messages the KGB ordered."

"What time?"

"As I say, he tunes in each morning. Or perhaps I should say that the timer you put on the electric plug shows electricity being used each morning at eight-thirty. Then he does his exercises and has a couple of cups of coffee before the interrogator comes."

"Is that the only station he listens to?"

"No, he plays with the buttons. It's a lovely toy, that little shortwave receiver. He amuses himself with it. East and West, Russian language, German language, and all sorts of Spanish-speaking stations, including Cuba. Of course, the only evidence we've got is the way he leaves the radio's tuning memory. Is he on the level, Bernie?"

"What do you think?"

"I've seen quite a few of them over the years that I've worked for the Debriefing Centre." He sat up, resting his elbow, and drank some of his whiskey. Ted was a serious drinker; he didn't just sip it, he gulped it down. "They're all a bit nervous. Some were terrified, some were just a little restless, but they were all nervous. But Stinnes is different. He's a cool customer, as calm as anything. The other morning I tried to ruffle his feathers. I put a glass of water and a slice of dry bread in front of him and told him to pack his bag, he was going to the Tower of London. I said we'd tumbled him. He just smiled and said it was bound to happen eventually. He's very cool."

"You think he's really still working for Moscow? Do you think it could all be an elaborate act to feed us misinformation? And we're swallowing it just the way he wants?"

Ted gave me a very slowly expanding smile, as if I was trying to put one over on him. "Now you're asking me something. That's what they call the sixty-four-thousand-dollar question. You're the brains now, young Bernard. You're the one who's supposed to be giving me the answers to questions like that one."

"He's handed us some good stuff," I said.

"Like this one tonight? Your man said we'll be able to pick up a whole network with the stuff we'll get out of that filing cabinet across the road."

"I don't like it, Ted. It's not our job, and Five know about it. If we get into hot water, there'll be precious little help from those bastards at the Home Office."

"Breaking and entering and stealing a couple of files? We've both done it plenty of times over there, Bernie. The only difference is that now we're doing it in England. It will be a piece of cake. I remember the time when you would have done a job like this in half an hour and come back looking for more work."

"Maybe," I said. I wasn't sure that I wanted to be reminded.

"Remember when I was sent back to Berlin to break into that big house in Heinersdorf? When you got the maid to let you wait in the front room? A Russian colonel's place it was. The dog took the arse out of your trousers when you climbed down from the bathroom window holding that box of photographs. And you rode the bike all the way back so that no one would see the hole in your pants. Your dad gave me hell for letting you do that."

"I was the only one thin enough to get through the window."

"Your dad was right. You were only a child. If those bastards had caught you and found out who your dad was, God knows what might have happened to you."

"It would have been all right. In those days no one could have guessed I was anything but a German kid."

"The things we did before they built that Wall! Those were the days, Bernie. I often think what a crazy childhood you had."

"We should get going," I said, looking yet again at my watch. I went to the window and opened it. It let cold air into the room but I could see better and hear better that way. I didn't want some squad of Special Branch detectives creeping up to grab Ted and show us what happened to people who poked their noses into Home Office territory.

"We've plenty of time, Bernie. No sense me hanging about in the doorway before the locksmith has got the door open. That's the way accidents happen."

"You shouldn't be doing this sort of job anymore," I said.

"I can do with the extra money," said Ted.

"Let me do it, Ted. You do backup."

He looked at me for a long time, trying to decide if I was serious. "You know I can't let you do it, old son. Why do you think your boss selected me to do it? Because Ted Riley has no reputation to lose. If the law grabs me, I'll do my act in court and the reporters won't even bother to ask me how I spell my name. If you got caught over there with your hands in the files, it might end up with questions in the House for the Prime Minister. I'd sooner get nabbed for doing it than answer to Mr. Rensselaer's fury at letting you do it for me."

"Then let's go," I said. I didn't like what he was saying, but he was entirely right. "The locksmith will be standing on the doorstep within three minutes."

Ted got to his feet and reached for his two-way radio. I did the same thing. "Is that okay?" I said into the microphone.

Ted had put the earplug in one ear and covered the other ear with his flattened hand. It was too dangerous for the loudspeaker to be switched on while he was working.

I repeated my test and he nodded to tell me he was hearing through the earpiece. Then he said, "Seems okay, old lad." His voice came through my handphone.

Then I changed the wavelength and called the car that was to collect him. "Taxi for two passengers?" I said.

Although I had the volume turned right down, the more powerful transmitter in the car came through loudly. "Taxi ready and waiting."

"Have you got everything?" I asked Ted. He was at the sink. The pipes made a loud chugging sound as the water flowed. Without removing his hat, he splashed his face and dried himself on the little towel hanging under the mirror.

Wearily he said, "Holy Mother of God, we've been all through that at least five times, Bernard." There were voices in the corridor and then sounds of two people entering the room next door. There was a clatter of the wardrobe door and the harsh swishing sound of coat hangers being pushed along a rail. The wardrobe backing must have been very thin for the sounds were loud. "Relax, son," said Ted. "It's a couple renting the room for an hour or two. It's that sort of hotel."

Yes, I was even more nervous than he was. I'd seldom played the part of backup man and never before to someone I knew and liked. For the first time I realized that it was worse than actually doing the job. It was that parental agony you suffer every time your children want to bicycle in the traffic or go away to camp.

Still in the dark, Ted buttoned up his coat and straightened his hat. I said, "If the lock proves difficult, I'll send the big cutters over to you."

Ted Riley touched my arm as if quietening a frightened horse. "Don't fuss, Bernard. Our man was in there only two days ago. He's a damned good man, I've worked with him before. He identified the type of filing cabinet and he's opened three of them since then. I watched him. I could almost do it alone."

"You'd better go now. You call me first, as soon as you're ready for the check calls," I said. I didn't watch him go; I went to the window to watch the street.

The rendezvous went like a training-school exercise. Our

tame locksmith arrived exactly on time and Ted Riley crossed the street and entered the door without a pause in his stride. The locksmith followed him inside, pulled the door closed, and fixed it so that it would remain firm against the test of any passing policeman.

He wouldn't be able to use the lift, so it was a long walk upstairs. But Ted was a pro: he'd make sure he didn't arrive out of breath, just in case there was a reception committee. Even using my pocket binoculars I couldn't see any sign of them entering the office. Ted would make sure they both kept away from the windows as much as possible. It was bad luck that the filing cabinets were on this outer wall.

They'd been inside a couple of minutes when Ted called me up. "Come back with hair on . . . ," he sang softly.

". . . you bald-headed bastard," I replied.

There had been no agreed identification, but more than once Ted had used his parody version of "Come Back to Erin" as recognition.

"It's going to be a piece of cake," Ted whispered.

"Street clear," I said.

It was more than three minutes before Ted called again. I was watching the time, otherwise I might have thought it was an hour or more. "Slight snag . . . but all okay. Add three."

"Street clear. Departure time add three."

The car was parked very close by; a few minutes this way or that wouldn't make much difference to them. I decided not to call the car crew until we were nearer to the rendezvous time.

It was five minutes before Ted came on the air again. I wondered what the hell was happening over there, but I knew how annoying such calls could be so I kept silent.

"It's not the same lock," said Ted. "The inside has been changed. We'll have to add ten." He sounded very calm and matter-of-fact, but I didn't like the sound of it.

"Cutters any good?" I offered. They could try going in through the back of the cabinet if all else failed. We had cutters that could go through almost anything.

"Not yet."

The rain continued. It was what Ted called "a soft day": steady drizzle that went on without end. There were not many pedestrians on the street and even the cars were infrequent. This was a good night to stay in and watch TV. That bloody Cambridge Constabulary car passed down the street again. Was it the same car showing interest in our target or was I seeing a succession of different cars on their way to and from the police station? I should have noted the registration.

"We've got suddenly lucky," said Ted's voice. He didn't enlarge on it. He kept the button pressed while he watched the locksmith working at the filing cabinet. I could hear the faint sounds of them working, sweating and straining to shift the cabinet: "We'll just look at the back of it." And then Ted was speaking to the locksmith: "Watch the wiring . . . it's wired! Holy Mother of . . ."

I was straining to see through the windows of the dark office. For a moment I thought they'd switched on the lights, for the two windows of the law offices lit up to become bright yellow rectangles. Then came the sound of the explosion. It was a deafening crash and the force of it clawed at me through the open window like a gale.

The law office windows dissolved into a shower of debris that, together with pieces of the two men, were showered out into the street.

"Taxi. Go. Go. Negative." It was the official way to say to scram to save yourself, and the car crew came back immediately with a reply.

"Please confirm." The voice was calm but I heard the engine start.

"Go. Go. Negative. Out."

I heard someone at the other end mutter "Good luck" as I switched off my radio. It was bad procedure but not one that I'd feel inclined to report: I needed all the well-wishers I could find.

From somewhere over the other side of town I heard a

police siren start up. I leaned out of the window and then threw the radio as far as I could toward the office. The windows were now dark again, except for the faint flicker of fire.

I buttoned my coat, put on my cap, and looked quickly round the room to make sure there was nothing left there to compromise us. Then I went downstairs to watch the police and fire service arrive.

The firemen arrived immediately after the first police car. And then an ambulance. The noise of their heavy diesel engines throbbed loudly. Batteries of headlights burned through the continuing drizzle of rain and reflected upon tiny bits of broken glass that were strewn all over the roadway and sparkled like ice. There were black pieces of charred paper and broken bits of wood, and things that I didn't care to inspect too closely. The fire engine's ladder moved slowly until it was positioned against the office windows, where a red glow was still to be seen. A fireman climbed it. There was a terrible smell of burning and enough smoke for the firemen to be using breathing gear.

The whole street was brightened as everyone drew back their curtains to watch the activity. By now the front door of the offices had been opened. The ambulance men pushed through the little crowd that had formed and went inside to look round. They didn't take a stretcher with them. They guessed they wouldn't be needing one.

It was three o'clock Sunday morning by the time I'd collected the car and driven back to Bret Rensselaer's place in Berkshire. Bret was fully dressed when he came to answer the door to me —he was quick to tell me that he'd never gone to bed—but he'd changed his clothes; he was now in roll-neck cashmere sweater and matching blue poplin pants. He'd been waiting for the phone call that would tell him everything had gone smoothly.

But when the phone call came, it told him that an explosion had killed two men in an office in Cambridge. The story was on the wire services. It was too late for the Sunday papers, but the national dailies would probably carry it on Monday. If a TV crew had got pictures, it might be on the evening bulletin.

"We need a break," said Bret. He'd put a drink in my hand and then devoted a lot of time to getting a second log burning in the fireplace. I crouched over it. I was cold.

"Yes, we need a rise in the price of beer or a bus drivers' strike to grab the headlines," I said. "But don't worry; a small explosion in the back streets of Cambridge isn't exactly front page stuff, Bret."

Bret pulled a little wheeled trolley over to the fire. On it there was a bottle of single-malt whisky that he'd brought out of the cupboard for me and a full jug of iced water. He sat on the fender seat and warmed his hands. The curtains were closed now, but I could hear the rain still beating on the glass, as it had been not many hours before when I'd sat here with Ted Riley, listening to Bret explaining how easy it was all going to be. "A booby trap," said Bret. "What bastards!"

"Let's not jump to conclusions," I said. I sat on the other side of the fender. I didn't like perching on fender seats; it was like trying to get warm on a barbecue—you cooked one side and froze the other. "Maybe it wasn't intended to kill."

"You said it was a booby trap," said Bret.

"It was a slip of the tongue."

"So what was it?"

"I don't know. It might have been no more than a device to destroy their secret papers. But a heavy-steel filing cabinet makes it into a bomb."

"They put a lot of explosive into it. Why not use an incendiary device?" asked Bret.

"We had an explosion like it in Berlin back in the old days. They'd only used a small charge, but the cabinet had some special fireproofing liner. When it went, it blew the side of the building out. It was worse than this one."

Why is he bugging me about all these details? I thought. Who cares about how big the explosive charge was? Ted Riley was dead.

"There's no chance that . . ."

"No chance at all. Two dead. You said the wire services had the story."

"They get it wrong sometimes," said Bret. "Will they be identified?"

"I didn't go in and look round," I said.

"Sure, sure," said Bret. "Thank Christ it wasn't you."

"Riley's an old-timer. He emptied his pockets and his clothes had no laundry marks. He made me check it with him. The other man I don't know about."

"The locksmith came from Duisburg. It was a German make. He was the expert on that sort of safe."

"They'd changed the inside of the lock," I said.

"I know," said Bret. He drank some of his tonic water.

"How could you know unless you had a monitor on the radio?"

Bret smiled. "I had someone monitoring the radio. There's no secret about that."

"Then why ask me the questions?"

"The old man is going to ask me a lot of questions and I want to know the answers. And I don't want to read the transcript to him; he can do that for himself. I need to hear what you've got to say."

"It's simple enough," I said. "Stinnes told the interrogator that there was some good stuff in that office. You sent Ted Riley in to get it. The filing cabinet was wired to destroy the evidence —bang. What difficult questions can the D-G ask, except why?"

"I don't blame you for feeling bitter," said Bret. "Ted Riley was a friend of your father, wasn't he?"

"Ted Riley was good at his job, Bret. He had the instinct for it. But the poor sod spent his life checking identity cards and making sure the burglar alarms were in working order. Just for one little lapse."

"He wasn't material for London Central, if that's what you are suggesting."

"Wasn't he? Who do you have to know to be material for

London Central?" I said. "Jesus, Bret, Ted Riley had more intelligence skills in his little finger than . . ."

"Than I have in my whole body? Or was it going to be Dicky? Or maybe the D-G?"

"Can I have another drink?"

"You won't bring Ted Riley back to life by pouring that stuff down your throat," said Bret. But he reached for the bottle of Glenlivet and uncapped it before handing it to me. I poured a big one for myself. I didn't offer Bret any; he was quite content with his tonic water.

"I had a talk with Ted Riley last night," I said. I stopped. The red lights came on in my skull. Everything warned me to be cautious.

"That must have been interesting," said Bret, keeping his voice just level enough for me not to get up and bust him in the nose.

"Ted told me that Stinnes is tuned to Moscow every morning at eight-thirty. Ted thought he was getting his instructions from them. Maybe one of the instructions they gave him was to tell us about the Cambridge cell and get Ted Riley blown into little pieces."

"Why are you telling me what Riley thought? Riley was just a security man. I don't need the opinions of security men when the interrogator is doing so well."

"So why didn't you send the goddamned interrogator to do the break-in last night?"

Bret held up a hand. "Ah, now I'm reading you loud and clear. You're trying to link the two events. Riley—despite the interrogator's satisfaction—sees through Stinnes and his misinformation scheme. So Riley has to be removed by a Kremlin-planned bomb. Is that what you're trying to sell me?"

"Something along those lines," I said.

Bret sighed. "You were the one who's been hyping Stinnes as if he was the greatest thing since sliced bread. Now your friend is killed and everything goes into reverse. Stinnes is the villain. And since Stinnes is virtually under house arrest, Moscow has to be the heavy. You really try my patience at times, Bernard."

"It fits," I said.

"So do a million other explanations. First you tell me the bomb was just to destroy the paperwork. Now you want it to be a trap to kill Riley. Make up your mind."

"Let's not play with words, Bret. The important question is whether Stinnes is playing a double game."

"Forget it," said Bret.

"I'm not going to forget it, Bret," I told him. "I'm going to pursue it."

"You landed Erich Stinnes for us. Everyone says that without you he wouldn't have come across to us."

"I'm not sure that's true," I said.

"Never mind the modest disclaimers. You got him and everyone gives you the credit for that. Don't start going round the office telling everyone they've got an active KGB agent in position."

"We'll have to take away the shortwave radio," I said. "But that will warn him that we're on to him."

"Slow down, Bernard. Slow right down. If you're blaming yourself for Ted Riley's death because you agreed to letting Stinnes have the radio, forget it."

"I can't forget it. It was my suggestion."

"Even if Stinnes is still active, and even if tonight's fiasco was the result of something arranged between him and Moscow, the radio can't have played a big part in it."

I drank some of the whisky. I was calmer now; the drink had helped. I resolved not to fight with Bret to the point where I flounced out and slammed the door, because I didn't feel I was capable of driving back to London.

When I didn't reply, Bret spoke again. "He couldn't send any messages back to them. Even if by some miracle he smuggled a letter out and posted it, there'd be no time for it to get there and be acted upon. What can they tell him that's worth knowing?"

"Not much, I suppose."

"If there's any conspiracy, it was all arranged before we got him, before he flew out of Mexico City. The use of that radio means nothing."

"I suppose you're right," I said.

"There's a spare bedroom upstairs, Bernard. Have a sleep; you look all in. We'll talk again over breakfast."

What he said about the radio made sense and I felt a bit better about it. But I noted the way he was going to bat for Stinnes. Was that because Bret was a KGB agent? Or simply because he saw in Stinnes a way of regaining a powerful position in London Central? Or both?

Chapter 16

As ALWAYS lately, the D-G was represented by the egregious Morgan. It was a curious fact that although Morgan couldn't always spare time to attend those meetings at which the more banal aspects of departmental administration were discussed, he could always find time to represent the D-G at these Operations discussions. I had always been opposed to the way the top-floor bureaucrats gate-crashed such meetings just to make themselves feel a part of the Operations side, and I particularly objected to pen pushers like Morgan listening in and even offering comments.

We were in Bret Rensselaer's room. Bret was sitting behind his glass-topped desk playing with his pens and pencils. Morgan was standing by the wall studying *The Crucifixion*, a tiny Dürer engraving that Bret had recently inherited from some rich relative. It was the only picture in the room and I doubt if it would have got there if it hadn't fitted in with Bret's black-and-white scheme. Morgan's pose suggested indifference, if not boredom, but his ears were quivering as he listened for every nuance of what was being said.

"This is a time to keep our heads down," said Dicky. He was wearing his faded jeans and open-necked checked shirt and was sprawled on Bret's black-leather chesterfield, while Frank Harrington was sitting hunched up at the other end of it. "We've stirred up a hornet's nest and Five will be swarming all over us if they think we're doing any sort of follow-up operation."

Dicky, of course, had been left out of the fiasco in which Ted Riley was killed, and he wasn't happy at the way he'd been bypassed, but Dicky was not a man to hold grudges, he'd told me that a million times. He'd be content to watch Bret Rensselaer crash full length to the floor and bleed to death, but it wouldn't be Dicky who put his dagger in. Dicky was no Brutus; this was a drama in which Dicky would be content with a non-speaking role. But now that Rensselaer wanted to organize a follow-up operation and possibly salvage some measure of success out of the mess, Dicky found his voice. "I'm against it," he said.

"It's a perfect opportunity," said Bret. "They've lost their records. It would be natural for Moscow to make contact." He rearranged the pens, pencils, paper clips, and the big glass paperweight like a miser counting his wealth.

"Is this what Stinnes is saying?" I asked.

Bret looked at me and then at the others. "I should have told you . . . ," he said. "Bernard has suddenly decided that Stinnes is here to blow a hole in all of us." He smiled, but the smile wasn't big enough to completely contradict this contention. He left that to me.

I was forced to modify that wild claim just as Bret knew I would be. "I didn't exactly say that, Bret," I said. I was sitting on the hard folding chair. I always seemed to be sitting on hard folding chairs; it was a mark of my low status.

"Then what?" said Frank Harrington. He folded his arms and narrowed his shoulders as if to make himself even smaller.

"I'm not happy with any of it," I said. I felt like telling them that I had enough evidence to support the idea that Bret should be put straight into one of the Berwick House hard-rooms pending an interior enquiry. But in the present circumstances any attempt to describe my reasoning, and my evidence, could only result in me being put there instead. "It's just a feeling," I said lamely.

"So what's your plan?" said Frank, looking at Bret.

"Stinnes says that a courier takes cash to pay the network. We know the KGB rendezvous procedure. We'll contact the network and I'll take them some money."

"Money? Who'll sign the chit for it?" said Dicky, suddenly sitting up and taking notice. Dicky could be very protective about German-desk funds being spent by anyone other than himself.

"It will come from Central Funding," said Bret, who was ready for that one.

"It can't come direct from Central Funding," said Morgan. "It must have the appropriate signature." He meant Dicky, of course, and technically he was right.

Bret wiggled his feet a little—his shoes were visible through the glass-topped desk—and ignored him. To the rest of us he said, "There's sure to have been cash and valuables lost in the explosion. And even if there wasn't, they'll want dough to cover their extra expenses. It's a perfect chance to crack them wide open."

"It sounds like bloody madness to me," said Morgan, angry at getting the cold shoulder.

"Do we know any of them?" said Frank vaguely.

Bret had been saving this one, of course, and Frank had fed him just the right cue. "Damn right we do! We know three of them in considerable detail; one is on the computer. I had a long session with Stinnes yesterday and I know exactly how it should be done."

Frank still had his arms folded. I realized that he was fighting the temptation to get out his pipe and tobacco; Frank found thinking difficult without the pipe in his hand, but the last time he'd smoked his pungent Balkan Sobranie here, Bret had asked him to put it out.

Frank said, "You're not thinking of trying this yourself, are you Bret?" He kept his voice level and friendly, but it was impossible to miss the note of incredulity and Bret didn't like it.

"Yes, I am," said Bret.

"How can you be sure that Bernard's wrong?" said Frank. "How can you be sure that Stinnes didn't send your two men into that booby trap? And how can you be sure he hasn't got the same kind of thing planned for you?"

"Because I'm taking Stinnes with me," said Bret.

There was a silence broken only by the sound of the D-G's black Labrador sniffing and scratching at the door. It wanted to get in to Morgan, who took it for walks.

"Whose idea was that?" said Dicky. There was a faint note of admiration and envy there. Like so many of the armchair agents up here on the top floor, Dicky was always saying how much he'd like to do some sort of operational job, although, like all the rest of them until now, he'd never done anything about it.

"Mine," said Bret. "It was my idea. Stinnes was doubtful, but my American accent will give me the cover I need. With Stinnes alongside me to give all the usual guarantees, they won't possibly suspect me as an agent working for British security."

I looked at him. It was a good argument. Whatever Bret Rensselaer looked like, it was not one of the ill-groomed spook hunters from MI5, and certainly not one of the Special Branch heavy-glove mob they took along to make their arrests legal.

"It might work," said Frank Harrington, without putting his heart and soul into it, "providing Moscow hasn't put out an alert for Stinnes." He looked at me.

"Nothing so far," I said.

Dicky shifted his weight and nodded. Then he ran his fingers back through his dry curly hair and smiled nervously. I don't know what Dicky was thinking except that anything that kept Bret busy was also keeping him off Dicky's back.

Only Morgan was upset at the idea. He scowled and said, "There's no chance of the D-G approving this one. Hell, Bret, the phone is still red hot with Five enquiring about the explosion." The dog, its scent of Morgan supplemented by the sound of Morgan's voice, renewed its scratching at the door. Morgan ignored it.

"You should never have told them," said Dicky, who could always be relied upon for excellent advice long after it was of any use.

But Bret was desperate. He knew his career was at stake. He needed a scalp, and breaking this network was the only scalp on offer. "I don't need any special permission. I'm going ahead anyway."

"I'd not advise that, Bret," said Morgan. He had both hands in his trouser pockets, and now he slowly walked across the room, staring reflectively at the toes of his shoes.

Bret resented the way in which Morgan used his position as the D-G's hatchet man to address all senior staff by their first name. It wasn't just the use of the first name, but the casual and overfamiliar way in which Morgan spoke that was so annoying. The Welsh accent could be a delight for reciting poetry, but it was an accent that could make even the friendliest greeting sound like a jeer. Bret said, "I had the backing of the old man for breaking into the law office. This is all part of that same job."

Morgan swung round and smiled. He had good teeth, and when he smiled he displayed them like someone about to brush them for a dental hygiene demonstration. Or someone about to bite. "And I say it isn't," he said.

There was only one way to settle it and Bret knew it. After a little give-and-take and a phone call, we all trooped down the corridor and into the Director-General's office. He was not very keen to see us, but Bret gently insisted.

The old man's office was in its usual muddle, though some

of the clutter had been tidied away. Despite the improvement we all had to stand, for there were books on the chairs and more piled on the floor.

Sir Henry Clevemore, the Director-General, was seated behind a small desk near the window. There wasn't much working space, for its top was occupied by photos of his family, including grown-up children with their offspring, and a vase of cut flowers. The D-G murmured his greeting to all of us in turn and then he listened solemnly to Bret. He didn't invite Morgan to comment, although Morgan was bouncing up and down on his toes, as he often did when agitated.

Bret took it very slowly. That was the best way with the D-G, if not to say the only way; he only understood when you explained everything very slowly. And if you could go on long enough you could wear him down until he agreed with whatever the request was, just to get rid of you. In all fairness, the old man needed a guardian like Morgan, but he didn't deserve Morgan. No one did.

It was while Bret was in full flow that a man came in through the door with a bundle of cloth under his arm. The D-G stood up, solemnly removed his jacket, and gave it to the newcomer who hung it on a hanger and put it into the wardrobe that was built into one wall.

Although Bret was disconcerted to the point of drying up, he resumed his pitch rather than let Morgan take over. But he now kept things very vague. "Don't worry about Bony," said the D-G, indicating the stranger. "He was with me in the war. He's vetted."

"It's rather delicate, sir," said Bret.

"I'll be gone in three minutes," said Bony, a short man in a tight-fitting gray worsted three-piece suit. He hung a partly made jacket onto the D-G and, apparently oblivious to us all, stood back to inspect the D-G's appearance. Then he made some chalk marks on the jacket and began to rip pieces off it the way tailors do.

"The lapels were rather wide on the last one," said the D-G.

"They are wide nowadays," said Bony. He wrote something into his notebook and, without looking up or interrupting his note taking, he said, "I've kept yours very narrow compared with what most people are wearing."

"I like them narrow," said the D-G, standing upright as if on parade.

"It's just a matter of your okay, Sir Henry," said Bret, in an effort to squeeze an approval from the old man while he was occupied with the details of his new suit.

"Two pairs of trousers?" said Bony. He put some pins between his lips while he tugged with both hands at the jacket.

"Yes," said the D-G.

"Isn't that a bit old hat, Sir Henry?" said Frank Harrington, speaking for the first time. Frank was very close to the old man. They'd trained together at some now defunct wartime establishment, and this was a mysterious bond they shared. It gave Frank the right to speak to Sir Henry in a way that no one else in the building dared, not even the Deputy.

"No, always do. Always did, always do," said the old man, stroking his sleeve.

"Gets damned hot, doesn't it?" said Frank, persisting with his ancient joke. "Wearing two pairs of trousers."

The D-G laughed dutifully, a deep resonant sound that might have been a bad cough.

"I feel we must continue," said Bret, trying now to press the meeting forward without saying anything that Bony might understand. "We've had a bad start, but we must go on and get something out of it."

"I'm coming under a great deal of pressure," said the old man, plucking at his shoulder seam. "I'll need more room under there, Bony." He pushed his fist under his arm to show where he wanted it and then stretched an arm high into the air to show that it constricted his movement.

Bony smoothed the material and sniffed. "You're not supposed to play golf in it, Sir Henry. It's a lounge suit."

"If we stop now, I fear we'll come out of it badly," said Bret.

"The trouble we ran into was simply a matter of bad luck. There was no actual operational failure." The operation was a success but the patient died.

Bony was behind the D-G now, tugging at the remnants of the half-made garment. "Keep still, sir!" he ordered fiercely, in a voice that shocked us all. Not Bret nor even Frank Harrington would have spoken to the D-G like that.

"I'm sorry, Bony," said the D-G.

Bony did not graciously accept the apology. "If we get it wrong, you'll blame me," he said, with the righteous indignation of the self-employed artisan.

"Have you brought the fabrics?" said the D-G. "You promised to bring the swatches." There was a retaliatory petulance in the D-G's voice, as if the swatches were something that Bony had failed to bring more than once in the past.

"I wouldn't advise the synthetics," said Bony. "They're shiny. That wouldn't suit a man of your position, Sir Henry. People would think it was a suit bought off the peg." Bony did all but shudder at the idea of Sir Henry Clevemore wearing a shiny synthetic ready-made suit.

Bret said, "We have excellent prospects, Sir Henry. It would be criminal to throw away a chance like this."

"How long do you want?" said the D-G.

Bony looked at him to see if he was asking about the delivery time of the suit, decided it wasn't a question for him, and said, "I want you to look at the wool, Sir Henry. This is the sort of thing for you." He waved samples of cloth in the air. They all seemed virtually identical to the material of the suit the D-G was wearing when we came in; virtually identical to the fabrics the D-G always wore.

"Two weeks," said Bret.

"You like it to go quickly," said the D-G.

Both Bony and Bret denied this, although it appeared that the D-G was addressing this accusation to Bony, for he added, "If everyone insisted on hard-wearing cloth, it would put you all out of business."

Bony must have been more indignant than Bret, for he got his rebuttal in first and loudest. "Now that's nonsense, Sir Henry, and you know it. You have suits you had from me twenty years ago, and they're still good. My reputation depends upon my customers looking their best. If I thought a synthetic material would be best for you, I'd happily supply it."

"Even one week might be enough," said Bret, sensing that his first bid was unacceptable.

"If synthetic material was the most expensive, you'd be selling that to me with the same kind of enthusiasm," said the D-G. He waggled a finger at the tailor like a little child discovering a parent in an untruth.

"Absolutely not," said Bony. The D-G delivered all his lines as if he'd said them many times before, but Bony responded with a fresh and earnest tone that was near to anger. The D-G seemed to enjoy the exchanges; perhaps this sort of sparring was what made the D-G order his suits from the indomitable Bony.

"I'll hold the barbarians at bay for a week," conceded the D-G. He didn't have to explain to Bret that the barbarians were at the Home Office or that after a week Bret's head might be handed over to them.

"Thank you, sir," said Bret and wisely ended the discussion.

But the D-G was not wholly concerned with the swatches of cloth that he was now fingering close by the window. "Who are you briefing for this job?" he asked without looking up.

Bony handed him a second batch of materials.

"I'm not very keen on that," said the D-G. He was still looking at the cloth and there were a few moments of silence while Bony and Bret tried to decide to which of them the remark was addressed. "But you are in charge so I suppose I'll have to let you decide."

"Yes, sir. Thank you," said Bret.

"If you want a shiny cloth, what about that?" said Bony, tapping one of the samples.

"I've no special desire for a shiny cloth," said the D-G

testily. "But I do want to try one of the synthetic mixtures."

Bret was edging toward the door.

Bony said, "They look good in the samples, but some of them don't make up very well."

"One wool and one mixture. I told you that at the beginning . . . the first fitting." He looked up to see Bret getting away and added, "You'll have to take . . . ," he nodded his head at me. He knew me well enough. On occasion I'd even had lunch with him. He'd seen me virtually every day at London Central for about six years, but still he couldn't remember my name. It was the same for most of the staff at London Central, yet still I found it irritating.

"Samson," supplied Bret Rensselaer.

"Samson. Yes." He smiled at me. "Take him with you. He knows how these things are done," said the D-G. The implication was that no one else present did know how such things are done, and he fixed me with a look as if to underline that that's exactly what he meant. He probably liked me; I had, after all, survived quite a few complaints from various members of the senior staff. Or perhaps he was just good at this thing they call management.

But now I wanted to protest. I looked at Bret and saw that he wanted to protest too. But there was no point in saying anything more. The D-G's audience had ended. Seeing us hesitating, he waved his cloth sample at us to shoo us away. "And keep in touch with Morgan," added the D-G. My heart fell and Bret's jaw tightened in rage. We both knew what that meant; it would give the pasty-faced Morgan carte blanche to master-mind the operation while using the name of the D-G as his authority.

"Very well, sir," said Bret.

And so I found myself inextricably linked to Bret Rensselaer's amateur attempt to infiltrate the Cambridge net. And I was the only person who suspected him of treason. For assistance we'd have Stinnes, whose name Bret had craftily kept out of the discussion—the only other person I couldn't trust.

Chapter 17

I'M SICK to death of hearing what a wonderful man your father was," said Bret suddenly. He hadn't spoken for a long time. The anger had been brewing up inside him so that even without a cue he had to let me have it.

What had I said about my father that had touched a nerve in him? Only that he hadn't left me any money—hardly a remark to produce such a passionate response.

We were in an all-night launderette. I was pretending to read a newspaper that was resting on my knees. It was 2:30 a.m., and outside the street was very dark. But there was not much to be seen through the windows, for this small shop was a cube of bright blue light suspended in the dark suburban streets of Hampstead. From the loudspeaker fixed in the ceiling came the soft scratchy sounds of pop music too subdued to be recognizable. A dozen big washing machines lined one wall. Their white enamel was chipped and scarred with the initials of the cleaner type of vandal. Detergent was spilled across the floor like yellow snow and there was the pungent smell of boiled coffee from a dispensing machine in the corner. We were sitting at the far end of a line of chairs facing the washing machines. Side by side Bret and I stared at the big cyclops where some dirty linen churned in suds. Customers came and went, so that most of the machines were working. Every few moments the mechanisms made loud clicking noises and sometimes the humming noises modulated to a scream as one of the drums spun.

"My father was a lush," said Bret. "His two brothers forced him off the board after he'd punched one of the bank's best customers. I was about ten years old. After that I was the only one to look after him."

"What about your mother?"

"You have to have an infinity of compassion to look after a drunkard," said Bret. "My mother didn't have that gift. And my brother Sheldon only cared about the old man's money. He told me that. Sheldon worked in the bank with my uncles. He would lock his bedroom door and refuse to come out when my father was getting drunk."

"Didn't he ever try to stop?"

"He tried. He really tried. My mother would never believe he tried, but I knew him. He even went to a clinic in Maine. I went in the car with him. It was a grim-looking place. They wouldn't let me past the entrance lodge. But a few weeks after he came back, he was drinking again. . . . None of them tried to help him. Not Sheldon, not my mother, no one. I hated to leave him when I went into the Navy. He died before I even went to sea." Bret looked at his watch and at the only other person there: a well-dressed man who'd been sitting near the door reading *Le Monde* and drinking coffee from a paper cup.

Now the man tossed the paper cup onto the floor, got to his feet, and opened the glass door to empty his machine and stuff his damp underwear into a plastic bag. He nodded to us before leaving. Bret looked at me, obviously wondering if that could be their first contact, but he didn't voice this suspicion. He said, "Maybe they won't buy it. We should have brought Stinnes inside here. Last year he made the cash delivery; that's why he knows exactly how it's done. They'd recognize him. That would be good."

I'd insisted that Stinnes remain in the second car. I said, "It's better this way. I want Stinnes where he can be protected. If we need him, we can get him in two minutes. I put Craig in to mind him; Craig's good."

"I still say we should have used Stinnes to maximum advantage."

"I don't want him sitting in here under the lights; a target for anyone driving past. I don't want him in here with a bodyguard. And we certainly don't want to give Stinnes a gun."

"Maybe you're right."

"If they're on the level, it will be okay."

"If they think we're on the level, it will be okay," Bret corrected me. "But they're bound to be edgy."

"They're breaking the law and you aren't; remember that. They'll be nervous. Stay cool and it will go smoothly."

"You don't really believe that; you're just trying to convince yourself," said Bret. "You've argued against me all the way."

"That's right," I said.

Bret leaned forward to reach inside the bag of laundry that he'd placed between his feet. He was dressed in an old raincoat and a tweed cap. I can't imagine where he'd found them; they weren't the kind of thing Bret would normally consider wearing. It was his first attempt to handle any sort of operation and he couldn't come to terms with the idea that we weren't trying to look like genuine launderette customers; we were trying to look like KGB couriers trying to look like launderette customers.

"Stinnes has been really good," said Bret. "The phone call went perfectly. He had the code words—they'll call themselves 'Bingo'—and amounts . . . four thousand dollars. They believed I was the regular contact coming through here a week early. No reason for them to be suspicious." He bent lower to reach deep enough in the bag to finger the money that was in a little parcel under the laundry. According to Stinnes, it was the way it was usually done.

I said nothing.

Bret straightened up and said, "You don't get too suspicious of a guy who's going to hand you four thousand bucks and no questions asked, right?"

"And that's what you're going to do?"

"It's better that way. We give them the money and say hello. I want to build them up. Next meeting I'll get closer to them."

"It's very confidence-building, four thousand dollars," I said.

Bret was too nervous to hear the sarcasm in my voice. He smiled and nodded and stared at the dirty laundry milling round in the machine.

"He got violent, my father. Some guys can drink and just get happy, or amorous. But my father got fighting drunk or else morose. Sometimes, when I was just a child, he'd sit up half the night telling me that he'd ruined my life, ruined my mother's life, and ruined his own life. 'You're the only one I've got, Bret,' he'd say. Then the next minute he'd be trying to fight me because I was stopping him having another drink. He took no account of my age; he always talked to me the way you'd talk to an adult."

A man came in through the door. He was young and slim, wearing jeans and a short, dark pea jacket. He had a bright-blue woolen ski mask on his head, the sort that completely hides the face except for eye slots and a hole for the mouth. The pea jacket was unbuttoned and from under it he brought out a sawed-off shotgun. "Let's go," he said. He was excited and nervous. He waggled the gun at us and moved his head to show that he wanted us to get going.

"What's this?" said Bret.

"Bingo," said the man. "This is Bingo."

"I've got it here," said Bret. He seemed to be frozen into position, and because Bret wouldn't move, the boy with the gun was becoming even more agitated.

"Go! go! go!" shouted the boy. His voice was high-pitched and anxious.

Bret got to his feet with the laundry bag in his hand. Another man came in. He was similarly masked, but he was broader and, judging from his movements, older, perhaps forty. He was dressed in a short bulky black leather overcoat. He stood in the doorway looking first at the man with the shotgun and then back over his shoulder; there must have been three of them. One hand was in his overcoat pocket, in his other hand he had a bouquet of colored wires. "What's the delay? I told you . . ."

His words were lost in the muffled bang that made the shop window rattle. Outside in the street there was a blast of flame that for a moment went on burning bright. It was across the road. That could be only one thing; they'd blown up the car. The second man tossed the bundle of colored wires to the floor. My God! Stinnes was in that car. The bastards!

Bret was standing when the car blew up. He was directly between me and the two men. The explosion gave me the moment's distraction I needed. I leaned forward enough to see round Bret. My silenced pistol was on my lap wrapped in a newspaper. I fired twice at the youngest one. He didn't go down, but he dropped the shotgun and slumped against the washing machines holding his chest.

"Get down, Bret!" I said, and pushed him to the floor before the other joker started firing. "Hold it right there," I shouted. Then I ran along the machines, and past the wounded man, kicking the shotgun back toward Bret as I went. I couldn't wait around and play nursemaid to Bret, but if he was a KGB man he might pick up the shotgun and let me have it in the back.

The older one didn't wait to see what I wanted. He went through a door marked STAFF before I could shoot at him. I followed. It was an office—the least amount of office you could get: a small table, one chair, a cheap cashbox, a vacuum flask, a dirty cup, and a copy of *The Daily Mirror*.

I went through the next door and found myself at the bottom of a flight of stairs. The door banged behind me and it was suddenly dark. There was a corridor leading to a street door. He hadn't had time to get out into the street that way, but he might have been waiting there in the darkness. Where was he? I remained still for a moment, letting my eyes adjust to the dark.

While I was trying to decide whether to explore the corridor, there was a sound of footsteps from the floor above. Then there was a loud bang. The flash lit the staircase, and lead shot rattled against the wallpaper. So this bastard had a shotgun too. The gun must have been under his buttoned coat; difficult to get at, that's why he'd had to run for it. That shot was just a warning, of course—something to show what was waiting for me if I climbed the stairs.

I wasn't looking for a chance to be a hero, but I heard his feet going up the next flight and I went up the first flight of stairs two at a time. I had rubber-soled shoes. He was making so much noise that he probably couldn't hear me. But as I halted at the next dark landing, his footsteps halted too. In the lexicon of hand-to-hand fighting, going up a dark staircase against a shotgun is high on the list of "don't-evers."

I was badly placed. Did he see me or did he guess where I was? He moved across the landing, aimed down the staircase, and pulled the trigger. There was a bang and a flash and the sound of him running. That was nasty; he was trying to kill me, now that his warning shot had gone unheeded. Bang! Jesus Christ! Another blast. I felt that one and I jumped back frightened and disoriented. For a moment I thought there must be two of them, but that was just a manifestation of my fear. So was the indigestible lump in my stomach.

I kept still, my heart pounding and my face hot. It was pitch dark except for a glimmer of light escaping from under the door of the office on the floor below me. I fancied I could see a pale blur where he was leaning over the balustrade trying to catch a glimpse of me. He must have taken the woolen mask off; too hot, I suppose. I kept very still, my shoulders pressed flat against the wall, and waited to see if he would do something even more stupid. Come on, come on, come on! Soon the police sirens would be heard and I'd be facing an audience outside in the road. On the other hand, so would he.

Sweat dribbled down my face, but my mouth was dry and rough like sandpaper. It was only with some effort that I breathed slowly and silently. The Department would gloss over the man I'd shot downstairs, especially if I wrote the report to make it sound as if I was protecting Bret. Protecting highly placed top-floor staff at London Central was not something the Department wanted to discourage. But they would not gloss over the inconvenience of untangling me from the clutches of the Metropolitan Police. Particularly not when our present relationship with the Home Office was decidedly turbulent.

Ah . . . keeping very still paid off! This was him. He leaned forward and the glint of light from the hall below caught his forehead. I am not a vindictive man, but I was frightened and angry. I wasn't going to let some hoodlum dynamite one of our cars and push a shotgun under my nose and try to kill me like they'd killed Ted Riley. This one wasn't going to slip away into the night. I raised my gun slowly and took careful aim. Maybe he saw me or the movement of the gun. He ducked back as I started to squeeze the trigger. Too late. I stayed very still, gun uplifted. I counted to ten and I was lucky. My inactivity encouraged him to lean forward again, this time more cautiously, but not cautiously enough. I pumped two shots into him. The silenced gun twisted in my hand and its two thuds were followed by a scream and a crash and the sound of a door banging, as he tumbled back into a room on the landing above me. They must have been using a room here. Maybe one, maybe all of them, had been upstairs waiting for us. That's why we got no warning from our men positioned across the street.

For a moment I hesitated. I wanted to look at their hideout but time was pressing and the consequences too serious. I ran downstairs, through the office—knocking the cashbox to the floor as I went—and pushed open the swing door into the launderette. Coins and paper money scattered over the floor; perhaps that would convince the cops it was a bungled robbery. It was blindingly bright under the fluorescent lights after the darkness of the stairwell, bright and steamy. I half closed my eyes to try to retain some of their adjustment as I went out onto the street.

The street was lit by the flames from the car. I saw a third man now. He was also dressed in a pea jacket. He was astride a motorbike and got it started as I brought the gun up and fired. But he was quick. And he was strong enough to swing the heavy bike round in a tight curve and open the throttle to roar away. I chanced one more shot at him, but after that I could see him only as a dark smudge against the fronts of the houses. Too dark, too much deflection and too much chance of putting a few rounds into someone's bedroom. So I went back into the launderette to see what Bret was doing.

Bret was doing nothing except holding his bundled-up laundry bag tight under his arm and watching the masked boy bleeding bright red frothy blood. The boy was still clamped over the washing machine, holding it tight as if he was trying to move it to another place. His feet were wide apart and there was blood on the white enamel, blood on the glass, and blood mingling with the spilled soapy water that had leaked onto the floor.

"He's had it," I said. "Let's go, Bret." I stuffed my gun back into my overcoat pocket. Bret was in shock. I gave him a short jab in the ribs to bring him back into the real world. He blinked and shook his head like a boxer trying to clear his brain. Then he got the idea and ran after me to where my car was parked on the corner.

"Stay in the car," I said, opening the door and pushing him into the front seat. "I've got to look at the others."

Bret was still holding the bag with the money and the laundry. He was like a man in a trance. As he settled into the car seat, the bag was on his knees and he had his arms round it tight, as if it was a baby. Across the road the Ford Escort in which Stinnes and the minder had arrived was still burning, although the flames were now turning to black smoke as the tires caught fire. "He's here," said Bret, meaning Stinnes.

"Shit," I said. Because, to my amazement, Bret was right. Stinnes had survived the bomb under the car. He was standing by the door of my Rover waiting to be let in. "Get in the back seat." His minder was standing close to him. It was only when they were awkwardly climbing into the back seat that I noticed they were handcuffed together. A minder that cuffs himself to his subject is a minder who takes no chances, but he'd saved Stinnes from certain death. Craig was huge and muscular; shackled to Craig, even King Kong would have to go where Craig went.

I started the car and pulled away before there was any sign of a police car. I suppose that respectable part of Hampstead doesn't attract a big police presence at three o'clock on a Tuesday morning. "What the hell happened?" I asked.

"I saw them coming," said Craig. "They were amateurs, real amateurs." He was very young, no more than twenty. "So I put the cuffs on and we got out." He had a simple outlook: most good minders are like that. And he was right; they'd behaved like amateurs, and that worried me. They'd even missed Craig and Stinnes escaping from the car. Amateurs. But the KGB didn't use amateurs in their hit teams and that worried me.

We passed a police car at Swiss Cottage. It was doing about seventy on the wrong side of the road, with the blue light flashing and the siren on. They were doing it the way they'd seen it done on late-night TV.

By this time Bret was coming back to life. "What was that you were saying, about how they would arrive very nervous?" he said. His voice was shaky; suddenly he'd experienced life at the sharp end of the Department and he was shocked.

"Very funny, Bret," I said. "Does that crack come before you thank me for saving your life or afterwards?" From behind us I heard young Craig coughing to remind us that the rear seats were occupied by people with ears.

"Saving my life, you son of a bitch?" said Bret in hysterical anger. "First you shoot, using me as a shield. Then you run out, leaving me to face the music."

I laughed. "That's the way it is being a field agent, Bret,"

I said. "If you'd had experience or training, you would have hit the deck. Better still, you would have taken out that second bastard instead of leaving me to deal with all of them."

"If I'd had experience or training," said Bret menacingly, "I would have read to you that section of the Command Rules that applies to the use of firearms in a public place."

"You don't have to read it to *me*, Bret," I said. "You should have read it to that bastard who came at us with the sawed-off shotgun. And to the one who tried to part my hair when I went after him upstairs."

"You killed him," said Bret. He was still breathing heavily. He was rattled, really rattled, while I was pumped with adrenaline and ready to say all kinds of things that are better left unsaid. "He bled to death. I watched him."

"Why didn't you give him first aid?" I said sarcastically. "Because that would have meant letting go your four grand? Is that why?"

"You could have winged him," Bret said.

"That's just for the movies, Bret. That's just for Wyatt Earp and Jesse James. In the real world, no one is shooting guns out of people's hands or giving them flesh wounds in the upper arm. In the real world you hit them or you miss them. It's difficult enough to hit a moving target without selecting tricky bits of anatomy. So don't give me all that crap."

"We left him to die."

"That's right. And if you had followed me upstairs with the shotgun I kicked over to you and tried to give me a little cover, you would have seen me kill another of those bastards."

"Is it going in your report?" said Bret.

"You're damn right it's going in my report. And so is the way you stood there like a goddamned tailor's dummy when I needed backup."

"You're a maniac, Samson," said Bret.

Erich Stinnes leaned forward from the back seat and said

softly, "That's the way it is, Mr. Rensselaer. What Samson did was just what I would have done. It's what any really good professional would have done."

Bret said nothing. Bret was clutching his bag and staring into space lost in his own thoughts. I knew what it was; I'd seen it happen to other people. Bret would never be quite the same again. Bret was no longer with us; he'd withdrawn into some inner world into which none of the stinking realities of his job would be allowed to intrude. Then suddenly he spoke softly, as if just voicing his thoughts: "And it was Sheldon he really loved. Not me; Sheldon."

"WELL, I don't want any of that in it," said Dicky. "It's not a report, it's a diatribe."

"Whatever you want to call it, it's the truth," I said. We were sitting side by side in the drawing room of the Cruyers' home. Dicky was wearing his "I Love New York" sweatshirt, jeans, and jogging shoes, with those special thick white socks that are said to lessen the shocks to the spine. We'd been watching the TV news to see if there was anything about the Hampstead shooting: there wasn't. The gas was hissing in the simulated coal fire and now the TV was displaying a rather unattractive foursome in punk outfits. For a moment Dicky's attention was distracted by them. "Look at those caterwauling imbeciles," he said. "Are we working our guts out just to keep the West safe for that sort of garbage?"

"Not entirely," I said. "We're getting paid as well."

He picked up the remote control and reduced the pop group to a pinpoint of light that disappeared with a soft plop. Then he took up my draft report again and pretended to read it afresh, but actually he was just holding it in front of his face while he thought about what to say next. "It's your version of the truth," he said pedantically.

"That's the only one I've got," I said.

"Try again."

"It's *anyone's* version of the truth," I said. "Anyone who was there."

"When are you going to get it through your thick head that I don't want your uncorrupted testimony? I want something that can go to the old man and not get me into hot water." He tossed the draft of my report on to the table beside him. Then he scratched his curly head. Dicky was worried. He didn't want to be in the middle of a departmental battle. Dicky liked to score his victories by stealth.

I leaned across from the armchair and picked up my carefully typed sheets. But Dicky gently took them from my hand. He folded them up and stuffed them under a paperweight that was handy on the other side of him. "Better forgotten, Bernard," he said. "Start again."

"Perhaps this time you'd tell me what you want me to say," I suggested.

"I'll draft something for you," said Dicky. "Keep it very short. Just the main essentials will be sufficient."

"Have you seen Bret's report?" I said.

"There was no report from Bret; just a meeting. Bret had to give a brief account of everything that's happened since he took over the Stinnes business." Dicky smiled nervously. "It wasn't the sort of stuff upon which careers are built."

"I suppose not," I said. An account of everything that had happened since Bret took responsibility for Stinnes would be one of unremitting disaster. I wondered how much of the blame Bret had unloaded onto me.

"It was decided that Stinnes should go back into Berwick House immediately. And Bret has to keep the old man informed of everything he intends to do about him."

"Berwick House? What's the panic? Everyone says the interrogation was going well since we moved him."

"No reflection on you, Bernard. But Stinnes was nearly killed. If it hadn't been for that fellow Craig, they'd have got him. We can't risk that again, Bernard. Stinnes is too precious."

"Will this affect Bret's appointment to Berlin?"

"They won't consult me on that one, Bernard." A modest smile to show me that they *might* consult him. In fact, we both knew that Morgan was depending upon Dicky's veto to stop Bret getting Berlin. "But I'd say Bret will be lucky to escape a suspension."

"A suspension?"

"It won't be called a suspension. It will be called a posting, or a sabbatical, or a paid leave."

"Even so."

"Bret's made a lot of enemies in the Department," said Dicky.

"You and Morgan, you mean?"

Dicky was flustered at this accusation. He got up from his chair and went to the fireplace so that he could toy with a framed photo of his boat. He looked at it for a moment and wiped the glass with his handkerchief before putting it back alongside the clock. "I'm no enemy to Bret. I like him. I know he tried to take over my desk, but I don't hold that against him."

"But?"

"But there are all kinds of loose ends arising out of the Stinnes affair. Bret has gone at it like a bull in a china shop. First there was the fiasco in Cambridge. Now there's the shooting in Hampstead. And what have we got to show for it? Nothing at all."

"No one tried to stop him," I said.

"You mean no one listened to your attempts to stop him. Well, you're right, Bernard. You were right and Bret was wrong. But Bret was determined to run it all personally, and with Bret's seniority it wasn't so easy to interfere with him."

"But now it *is* easy to interfere with him?"

"It's called 'a review,' " said Dicky.

"Why couldn't it be called a review last week?"

He sank down into the sofa and stretched his legs along it. "Because a whole assortment of complications came up this week."

"Concerning Bret?"

"Yes."

"He's not facing an enquiry?"

"I don't know, Bernard. And even if I did know, I couldn't discuss it with you."

"Will it affect me?" I asked.

"I don't think so, except inasmuch as you have been working with Bret while all these things have happened." He fingered his belt buckle. "Unless of course Bret blames you."

"And is Bret doing that?" I said. I spoke more loudly than I intended; I hadn't wanted my fears, or my distrust of Bret, to show.

As I said it, Dicky's wife, Daphne, came in. She smiled. "And is Bret doing what, Bernard?" she said.

"Dyeing his hair," improvised Dicky hastily. "Bernard was wondering if Bret dyes his hair."

"But his hair is white," said Daphne.

"Not really white. It's blond and going white," said Dicky. "We were just saying that it never seems to go any whiter. What do you think, darling? You ladies know about things like that."

"He was here the other evening. He had supper with us," said Daphne. "He's such a handsome man. . . ." She saw Dicky's face, and maybe mine too. "For his age, I mean. But I don't think he could be dyeing his hair unless it was being done by some very good hairdresser. It's certainly not obvious." Daphne stood in front of the fireplace so that we could get a good look at her new outfit. She was dressed in a long gown of striped shiny cotton, an Arab djellaba which the neighbors had brought back from their holiday in Cairo. Her hair was plaited, with beads woven into it. She'd been an art student and once worked in an advertising agency. She liked to look artistic.

"He'd have no trouble affording an expensive hairdresser," said Dicky. "He inherited a fortune when he was twenty-one. And he certainly knows how to spend it." Dicky had gone through his college days short of cash, and now he especially resented anyone having been young and rich, whether they were prodigies, divorcées, or pop stars. He looked at the clock.

"Is that the time? If we're going to see this video, we'd better get started. Have you got the food ready, darling?" Without waiting to hear her reply he turned to me and said, "We're eating on trays in here. Better than rushing through our meal."

Dicky had been determined to get a preview of the report I was preparing for submission to the D-G, but his command to bring it to him had been disguised as an invitation to supper, with a rented video of a Fred Astaire musical as a surprise extra.

"It's only soup and toasted sandwiches," said Daphne.

Dicky said, "I bought her one of those sandwich toasters. My God, I rue the day! Now I get everything between toasted bread: salami, cheese, ham, avocado, and bacon. . . . What was that mess you served the other day, darling—curried lamb inside a toasted *chapatti?* It was disgusting."

"It was just an experiment, darling," said Daphne.

"Yes, well, you didn't have to scrape all the burned pieces off the machine, darling," said Dicky. "I thought you'd set the whole kitchen on fire. I burned my finger."

He showed me the finger. I nodded.

"It's ham and cheese tonight," said Daphne. "Onion soup to start with."

"I hope you chopped the onion really small this time," said Dicky.

"He hates soup going down his chin," said Daphne, as though this was a curious aversion for which she could not account.

"It ruined one of my good ties," said Dicky. "And in the dark I didn't notice."

"Bret Rensselaer didn't spill his soup," said Daphne. "And he wears beautiful ties."

"Why don't you get the supper, darling?"

"The trays are all ready."

"And I'll get the video," said Dicky. He stood, hitched his trousers up, and retrieved my report from under the paperweight before he strode from the room.

"The video is on the machine," said Daphne. "He hates

saying he's going to the loo. He's such a prude about some things."

I nodded.

She stood by the kitchen door and said, "I'll go and get the food." But she made no move.

"Can I help you, Daphne?"

To my surprise she said yes. Usually Daphne didn't like visitors in her kitchen. I'd heard her say that many times.

I followed her. The kitchen had all been redecorated since the last time I'd been there. It was like a cupboard shop; there were cupboards on every available piece of wall space. All were made of plastic, patterned to look like oak.

"Dicky is having an affair," she said.

"Is he?"

She disregarded my feigned surprise. "Has he spoken with you about her?"

"An affair?"

"He relies on you," she said. "Are you sure he hasn't mentioned anything?"

"I've been with Bret Rensselaer a lot of the time lately."

"I know I'm putting you in a difficult position, Bernard, but I must know."

"He hasn't discussed it with me, Daphne. To tell you the truth, it's not the sort of thing he'd confide to me, even if it was true." Her face fell. "And I'm sure it's not," I added.

"It's your sister-in-law," said Daphne. "She must be as old as I am, perhaps older." She opened the toasting machine and pried the sandwiches out of it, using the blade of an old knife. Without turning to me she said, "If it was some very young girl, I'd find it easier to understand."

I nodded. Was this, I wondered, a concession to my relationship with Gloria? "Those sandwiches smell good," I said.

"They're only ham and cheese," said Daphne. "Dicky won't eat anything exotic." She got a big plate of previously prepared sandwiches from the oven. "Tessa, I mean. Your sister-in-law; Tessa Kosinski."

"I've only got the one," I said. And one like Tessa was more than enough, I thought. Why did she have to make everyone's life so bloody complicated?

"And she's a friend," said Daphne. "A friend of the family. That's what hurts."

"Tessa has been kind to me, helping me with the children."

"Yes, I know." Daphne sniffed. It wasn't the sort of sniff that fragile ladies used as a prelude to tears—more the sort of sniff Old Bailey judges gave before passing the death sentence. "I suppose you must feel a debt of loyalty." She put cutlery on the trays. She did it very carefully and gently, so that I wouldn't think she was angry.

"I'll do anything I can to help," I said.

"Don't worry about Dicky hearing us. We'll hear the toilet flush." She began to look for soup bowls and she had to open four of the cupboards before she found them. "They had an affair before." She was speaking to the inside of the cupboards. "Now, don't say you didn't know about that, Bernard. Tessa and I made up after that. I thought it was all finished."

"And this time?"

"A friend of mine saw them at a little hotel near Deal . . . Kent, you know."

"That's a strange place to go for . . ." I stopped and tried to rephrase the sentence.

"No, it was chosen as one of the ten best places for a lover's weekend by one of the women's magazines last month. *Harpers & Queen,* I think. That's why my friend was there."

"Perhaps Dicky . . ."

"He told me he was in Cologne," said Daphne. "He said it was top secret."

"Is there something you want me to do about it?"

"I want to meet your brother-in-law," said Daphne. "I want to talk to him about it. I want him to know how I feel."

"Would that really be wise?" I said. I wondered how George would react to an approach from Daphne.

"It's what I want. I've thought about it, and it's what I want."

"It might just blow over."

"It will. They all blow over," said Daphne. "One after another he has these girlfriends, and I wait for it to blow over. Then he goes off with someone else. Or with the same one again."

"Have you spoken to him about it?" I said.

"He says it's his money he spends, not mine. He says it's the money his uncle left him." She turned to me. "It's nothing to do with the money, Bernard. It's the betrayal. He wouldn't betray his country, would he? He's fanatical about loyalty to the Department. So why betray his wife and children?"

"Did you tell him that?"

"Over and over again. I've had enough of it. I'm going to get a divorce. I want George Kosinski to know that I'm naming his wife in a divorce action."

Poor George, I thought, that's all he needs to complete his misery. "That's a serious step, Daphne. I know how you feel, but there are your children . . ."

"They're at school. I only see them in the holidays. Sometimes I think that it was a terrible mistake to send them to boarding school. If the children had lived at home, perhaps Dicky would have had more to keep him from straying."

"Sometimes it works the other way," I said, more to comfort her than because I believed it. "Sometimes children at home make husbands want to get out."

"Will you arrange it?" she said. "In the next few days?"

"I'll try," I said. I heard Dicky upstairs.

Daphne had the trays all ready. "Could you open the wine, Bernard, and bring the paper napkins? The corkscrew is in the drawer."

As she held the refrigerator door open for me to get the wine, she said, "Wasn't that a surprise about Mr. Rensselaer? I'd always liked him." She closed the door and I waited for her as she pushed the hot sandwiches onto the serving plate with flicking motions so that she didn't burn her fingers.

"Yes," I said.

"Stealing a Cabinet memo and giving it to the Russians. And now they're saying he tried to get you all killed." She saw the surprise in my face. "Oh, I know it's still the subject of an enquiry, and we mustn't talk about it, but Dicky says Bret is going to have a job talking his way out of this one." She picked up all three trays after piling them one on top of the other. "It must be a mistake, don't you think? He couldn't really be a spy, could he? He's such a nice man."

"Come along, come along," shouted Dicky from the next room. "The titles are running."

"Dicky's such a mean pig," said Daphne. "He can't even wait for us before starting the film."

Chapter 18

YOU SAID you wouldn't be late." Gloria was in bed and my coming into the bedroom had wakened her.

"Sorry," I said. Our relationship had developed—or should I say degenerated?—into that of a married couple. She spent each weekend with me and kept clothes and makeup and jewelry in my house. To say nothing of countless pairs of shoes.

She sat up in bed and switched on the dim bedside light. She was wearing a black chiffon nightdress. Her pale blond hair was long enough to touch her shoulders. "Did you go on?"

"No, I didn't 'go on,' if you mean to a nightclub or fancy-dress party."

"You don't have to snap at me." There was enough light for me to see the neat way in which she'd folded her clothes before going to bed. It was a bad sign; such fastidious attention to detail was often a sign of her suppressed bad temper.

"Do you think I like spending the evening with Dicky?" I said.

"Then why stay so late?"

"He'd rented a video. I couldn't leave before it had finished."

"Did you have dinner there?"

"Supper; a sandwich and a cup of soup."

"I ate with the children. Doris cooked a meat pie."

"I wish you'd call her 'Nanny,'" I said. The nanny was young and I wanted to keep my distance from her. "She'll start calling me 'Bernard' next."

"You should have told me before. I can't suddenly change now," said Gloria. "She'd think she'd upset me or something." Her hair was falling over her face; she pushed it back with her hand, which she held to her head as if posing. "So it wasn't business?"

"Of course it was business. I told you that Dicky insisted that I bring the first draft of my report with me."

"Who else was there?"

I sat down on the bed. "Look, darling. If I'd mentioned you, Dicky would have included you in the invitation. We both know that. But didn't we agree that it's better to keep a low profile? We don't want everyone in the office talking."

"That depends what they're saying," said Gloria, who felt that we should be together every minute of our free time and especially resented being left alone for any part of the weekends.

I leaned forward and embraced her tightly and kissed her.

"What did you talk about?" she said.

"Bret is in trouble," I said.

"With the Department?"

"Dicky is the last of the big-time wishful thinkers. But even allowing for Dicky's exaggeration, Bret is facing the music for everything that's gone wrong with the Stinnes debriefing. Now they're going to start saying it's all been done on Moscow's orders."

"It's Bret's own fault, darling. He thought it was all so easy. You said that yourself."

"Yes, he's brought it on himself, but now they're going to heap everything they can think of on him. Whether he's KGB or not, they'll make him the scapegoat."

"Scapegoat's not the word," she said. "Scapegoats were released into the wilderness. You mean Bret will be delivered to MI5 as the person who's been usurping all their powers and functions. Not so much a scapegoat as a hostage. Am I right?"

"Perhaps consolation prize is the expression we're looking for," I said bitterly. I'd seen too many severed heads delivered to the Home Office under similar circumstances to be optimistic about Bret's fate. "Anyway, Bret is probably going to face more serious charges than that," I said.

She looked at me quizzically and said, "He's a KGB mole?"

"I don't know."

"But that will be the charge?"

"It's too early for charges. Maybe there won't be any. No one's told me anything, but there's been some sort of top-level meeting about Bret. Everyone is beginning to think he's working for Moscow. Dicky seems to have told Daphne. She thought I'd already been told, so she gave the game away."

"What a bombshell when the newspapers get the story," said Gloria.

I kissed her again, but she didn't respond.

"They should be shot," she said. "Traitors. Bastards." She didn't raise her voice, but her body stiffened in anger and the depths of her feeling surprised me.

"It's all part of the game."

"No, it's not. People like Rensselaer are murderers. To appease their social conscience they'll turn over men and women to the torture chambers. What swine they are!"

"Perhaps they do what they think is right," I said. I didn't exactly believe it, but that was the only way I could do my job. I couldn't start thinking I was part of a struggle of good against evil or freedom against tyranny. The only way I could work was to concentrate on the nuts and bolts of the job and do it as well as I could.

"Then why don't they go to Russia? They know it's not the kind of world we want or we'd have voted the Communists into power long ago. Why don't they just go to Russia?"

"Well, why don't they?" I said.

"They want their cake and eat it. They're always rich and well educated, aren't they? They want their privileged status in a rich West while they're appeasing their guilt about enjoying it."

"Are you talking about Bret?" I said. I stood up. "Or are you talking about my wife?"

"I'm talking about traitors," she said.

I went over to the wardrobe and opened it. Someplace there was a tweed suit that I hadn't worn for years. I sorted through the clothes until I found it, hung inside a plastic bag—Fiona put all my suits into plastic bags—and then I felt through the pockets. "I suspected Bret of having an affair with my wife. Did I ever tell you about that?"

"If you're looking for cigarettes, I threw them all out."

"I suddenly remembered leaving a packet in that tweed suit," I said. The suit brought back memories. The last time I'd worn it I'd been to a horse show with Fiona and my father-in-law. It was a time when I was working very hard at being nice to him. He'd won a prize for jumping over fences, and he took us all to a fancy restaurant on the river near Marlow. I ran out of cigarettes and my father-in-law wouldn't let me pay cash for some more; he insisted they be added to his dinner bill. The incident stuck in my mind because it was in the restaurant that I first heard that he'd set up trust funds for the children. He hadn't told me, and Fiona hadn't told me either. Worse still, he'd told the children but told them not to tell me.

"Yes, I threw them out. If there are cigarettes in the house, you'll start smoking again, you know that. You don't want to, do you?"

I closed the wardrobe door and abandoned the notion of a cigarette. She was right; I didn't want to start smoking again, but given my present level of stress I wasn't sure how long I'd be able to resist the temptation.

"You have to have someone to look after you," she said in a conciliatory tone.

"Once I was certain that Bret was having an affair with Fiona, I hated him. My hatred for him influenced everything I thought, said, and did." My need for a cigarette had abated. Even if I'd found a carton on my pillow, I wouldn't have bothered to open it. "It was only with great effort that I could listen to anything that was said about him without reprocessing it and distorting it. Now I've got that feeling under control. I don't even care if they *did* have an affair. I can look at Bret Rensselaer with a clear mind. When I tell you I don't know whether he's guilty, I mean exactly that."

"Jealousy, you mean. You were jealous of Bret Rensselaer because he's rich and successful and maybe had an affair with your wife."

"Yes," I said.

"That's natural enough, Bernard. Why shouldn't you be angry and prejudiced? Why should you be impartial to any man who treats you badly?"

"Are you going to tell me why?"

"Because you like to play God, Bernard. You killed two men the other night in the launderette. You didn't gloss over it. You told me. You told Dicky. I have no doubt it's in your report, with you taking unequivocal responsibility for their deaths. You're not an insensitive brute, you're not a thug or a killer. The only way you can cope with the guilt you suffer over those deaths is by convincing yourself that you observe the world round you with total objectivity. That's playing god, darling. And it's not the way to assuage your guilt. Admit that you're fallible, accept the fact that you're only human, admit that if Bret goes to the Old Bailey, you'll be delighted to see him get his comeuppance."

"But I won't be delighted. Not even a wronged husband wants to see the other man in the Old Bailey. And in Bret's case, I have no real evidence. As far as I know, Fiona was never unfaithful to me."

"If you don't hate him for betraying you, then hate him for

selling out to the Communists. In that sort of hatred I'll join
you."

"Your father was one of our agents, wasn't he?"

"How did you find out?"

"I just guessed. There always has to be some special reason
for the daughter of a foreign national to get into the Department."

"My uncle and my father . . . the secret police took my uncle
away. They killed him in the police station. They were looking
for my father."

"You don't have to talk about it," I said.

"I don't mind talking about it. I'm proud of him. I'm proud
of both of them. My father is a dentist. London sent him dental
charts—it was part of his regular correspondence with other
dentists—and he used the dental charts to identify agents. The
dental surgery was a perfect cover for messages to be passed,
and the secret police never succeeded in infiltrating the organization. But all the agents had met my father. That was the big
disadvantage—everyone in every cell knew my father. The police finally got his name from someone they picked up photo-
graphing the frontier. He talked. They made a mistake and
arrested my uncle because he had the same name. He managed
to keep silent until my father and mother got away. I hate the
Communists, Bernard."

"I'm going to have a drink," I said. I took off my jacket and
tie and kicked off my shoes. "Whisky. Would you like one?"

"No thanks, darling."

I went into my study and poured myself a stiff drink. When
I got back to the bedroom, Gloria had combed her hair and
plumped up the pillows. I went on undressing. I said, "Dicky
is having an affair with Tessa, and Daphne's found out about
them."

"She told you that?"

"A friend of hers saw them in a hotel."

"There are always wonderful friends who'll bring you bad
news."

"It's difficult, isn't it? You become a party to a secret and suddenly you have a terrible responsibility. Whatever you do is likely to be wrong."

"You're talking about that Cabinet memo, aren't you?"

"Perhaps I am."

"You did nothing," she said.

"It looks as though I didn't have to. The Department know about Bret. Daphne actually mentioned the Cabinet memo."

"What does she want you to do?"

"Daphne? She wants to talk to George. She says she's going to name Tessa in a divorce action."

"Is she serious?"

"You tell me."

"That would ruin Dicky's career, wouldn't it?"

"It depends. If it looked like it was becoming the messy sort of divorce that got into the newspapers, then the Department would get rid of Dicky very quickly."

"Does Daphne know that?"

"She's very bitter."

"She's put up with a lot."

"Has she?"

"You told me that Dicky was constantly unfaithful to her."

"Did I?"

"Of course you did. And everyone in the office has noticed the way he's been dandying up on certain evenings. And his wife is always phoning asking where he is."

"Everyone knows that?"

"All the girls know."

"Does his secretary talk about it?"

"You mustn't ask me questions like that, darling. I can't be the office stool pigeon."

"I don't like the idea of a secretary who talks about her boss. It's a short step from that to official secrets. . . ."

"Don't be pompous, darling. Dicky gives her a rotten time. I think she's wonderfully loyal under the circumstances."

Chapter 19

I DON'T KNOW whether Bret Rensselaer was officially ordered to keep away from Erich Stinnes or even discouraged from doing so, but obviously someone from the Department had to keep in touch with him. Had he been left at Berwick House and neglected, there was always the chance that London Debriefing Centre would encourage the Home Office to take him over.

When Stinnes suddenly stopped talking to the interrogator, the matter became urgent. I was sent to talk with Stinnes. There was a note initialed by Bret waiting on my desk. I don't know who chose me for the job, but I suppose there weren't many on the shortlist of suitable visitors.

It was pouring rain when I arrived at Berwick House. The formalities that had greeted Bret Rensselaer's Bentley on my previous visit were waived for my second-hand Rover. No pulling to the side after entering the outer gate—just a quick look at my card and a perfunctory salute.

There was no one to see that I parked in the visitors' marked space in the courtyard and no sign of the Governor or his Deputy anywhere. Instead of the main entrance I used the back door. The duty clerk knew me by sight and he swiveled the visitors' book for my signature and offered me his Parker pen. Judging by the blank spaces in the book they didn't have many visitors at Berwick House these days.

Erich Stinnes wasn't locked up. At certain specified hours he was permitted to exercise in the grounds. When it rained he could come down into the great hall and look through the leaded windows at the bare rosebushes. He had the freedom of the second floor, but I had to notify the key-room clerk that I was going up there. The clerk stopped eating his cheese sandwich long enough to write out the chit that permitted me to leave again. When he passed it to me the chit was marked with his greasy fingerprints. I'm glad that hadn't happened to Bret.

"Not like Notting Hill Gate, is it, Erich?" I said.

"It's good enough," he said. They'd moved him to Number 4, a large comfortable accommodation at the front. He had a sitting room with a sofa and two armchairs, a colored print of the Battle of Waterloo, and a medieval electric fire. He had a tiny "kitchen" too, although it was really no more than an alcove equipped with sink, cooking ring, some pans, crockery, and an electric kettle.

"Are you going to make me a cup of tea?" I said. "It's very warm in here—do you want me to open a window?"

"They will bring some tea at four," he said. "You must know that by now. No, don't open the window. I think I have a chill."

"Shall I get the doctor to look at you?"

"No doctors. I have a horror of them." His voice was flat and cold like his eyes. There was some sort of change in the atmosphere since our last meeting. He was suspicious of me and didn't bother to hide it.

"Still drawing landscapes?" I asked. I took off my raincoat and put it on a hook behind the door.

"There's not much else to do," he said. The whole building was well heated and it was warm in this room, but the electric fire was fully on, and in addition to his gray flannels and dark-green shirt Stinnes wore a heavy sweater. He was sitting on a big chintz-covered sofa and there were several London newspapers beside him. They'd been folded and refolded as if every word in them had been read.

He was able to be very still. It was not the easy stillness that comes with relaxation or the tense stillness that concentration produces, but something else—some quality that couldn't be defined, something that enabled him to remain always the onlooker no matter how involved he truly felt. He was always the sun; everything moved except him.

I took off my jacket and sat in the chair opposite him. "The interrogator went home early yesterday," I said. "And early the day before that."

"Some species of bird are born able to sing, but others have to learn to sing from their parents." There was no jocularity. It sounded like something he had ready to recite for me.

"Is that an ornithological fact or are you trying to tell me something, Erich?" In fact I knew it was true. Stinnes had told me before. He was fond of displaying such expertise.

"It was inevitable that you should try to find some way to blame me," he said.

"And which sort of bird are you, Erich? And how do we start teaching you how to sing?"

"I accepted your offer in good faith. I didn't promise to run your covert operations department and make it work properly."

"What *do* you see as your side of the bargain?" I said.

"I give the interrogator full and truthful answers to everything he asks. But I can't tell him things I don't know. I wish you'd explain that to him."

"Four men have died," I said. "You knew one of them: Ted Riley; he was with you in London. He was a personal friend of mine. People are angry."

"I'm sorry," said Stinnes. He didn't look very sorry, but then he never did look very anything.

"We were bounced, Erich. Both times we were bounced."

"I don't know the full details," he said. It was a very Russian response; he knew all the details.

"Both times we walked into a booby trap," I said.

"Then both times you were a booby."

"Don't get too damned smug," I said, and then regretted that he'd made me angry.

"Are you a professional or have you been behind a desk too long?" He paused, and when I didn't answer he said, "Don't toy with me, Mr. Samson. You know that Rensselaer is an amateur. You know he refused to let your Operations staff plan these meetings. You know that he did it that way because he wanted to show everyone that he could be a wonderful field agent."

It wasn't the reaction I'd expected. Stinnes showed no anger about Bret Rensselaer's actions even though they'd brought Stinnes near to being killed. In fact, his interpretation of the fiasco put Bret into the role of hero—an amateur, blundering hero, but a hero nevertheless. "Did you criticize these 'amateurish' ideas?" I asked.

"Of course I did. Didn't you?"

He had me there. "Yes," I admitted, "I criticized them."

"So would anyone with half an hour's field experience. Rensselaer is a desk man. Why wasn't he ordered to use your Operations planners? I urged him to do that over and over again."

"There were problems," I said.

"And I can guess what the problems were," said Stinnes. "Your boss Rensselaer is determined to make his name before the MI5 people take over my interrogation?"

"Something like that," I said.

"He's at the dangerous age," said Stinnes with studied contempt. "It's the age when desk men suddenly want to grab a final chance for glory."

There was a knock at the door and a middle-aged woman in a green apron brought in a tray of tea with buttered toast and a plate of sliced cake. "They do you very well in here, Erich," I said. "Do you get this sort of stylish tea every day or only when visitors come?"

The woman smiled at me but said nothing. They were all vetted people, of course; some of the domestic help were retired clerical staff from London Central. She set out the cups and teapot and left silently. She knew that even one word can destroy the mood of an interrogation.

"Every day," said Erich. There was a packet of five small cigars on the tray. I suppose it was his daily ration, but he seemed to have stopped smoking for there was a pile of un-opened packets on the mantelpiece.

"But you still don't like it here?" His uncooperative attitude toward the interrogator was what had brought me down here. There was obviously something he didn't like.

"You trust me well enough to act on my information and risk the lives of your agents, but you keep me locked up in case I run away." He drank some tea. "Where is it that you think I will run to? Will I run back to Moscow and face trial?"

I was tempted to tell him how vociferously I had opposed his being brought back to Berwick House, but that wasn't the way to do it. And in any case, I didn't want him to know how little effect my opinions had upon London Central's top-floor decisions. "So what sort of bird are you, Erich? You haven't answered that one yet."

"Let me out of here and I'll show you," he said. "Let me do what Rensselaer failed to do."

"Penetrate the Cambridge network?"

"They'll trust me."

"It's risky, Erich."

"The Cambridge network is the best thing I brought over to you. It's what delayed me in Mexico City. It's what forced me to go back to Berlin before coming over to you. Do you have any idea what risks I took to get enough information to pene-trate that network?"

"Tell me."

It was a sardonic reaction to his plea and he knew it. He said, "And now you want to throw it away. Well, it's your loss."

"Then why do you care?"

"Only because you are determined to blame me for disas-ters of your own making. Why should I be blamed? Why should I be punished? I don't want to spend month after month locked up in this place."

"I thought you liked it," I said.

"It's comfortable enough, but I'm a prisoner here. I want to live like a human being. I want to spend some of that money. I want to . . . I want to do all sorts of things."

"You want to see Zena Volkmann? Is that what you were going to say?"

"Have you seen her?"

"Yes," I said.

"Did she ask about me?"

"She thinks she did all the work, I got all the credit, and you got all the money."

"Is that what she said?"

"More or less."

"I suppose it's true." He took off his glasses and polished them carefully.

"I don't know that she did all the work, and I certainly didn't get all the credit. Other than that, I suppose it's true."

He looked at me but didn't smile at my allegation. "You needn't worry. If I am free, I won't go rushing off to find her."

"The love has cooled?"

"I'm fond of her. But she's another man's wife. I no longer have the stamina for that sort of love affair."

"But you have the stamina to try breaking into the Cambridge net?"

"Because it's the only way I'll ever be able to get free of you people."

"By giving us proof positive of your loyalty to us?"

"As I've told you, that network is the best prize I can offer you. Surely even you English will not want to keep me locked up after I deliver them to you?" These were his own agents, yet he said it without any sign of emotion. He was a cold-blooded animal.

"There is the problem of protecting you, Erich. You are a big investment. They put a bomb under your car last week."

"That wasn't intended for me. That was an accident. Surely you don't believe that they identified me?" He leaned back in the sofa and grasped his hands together and cracked the knuckles. It was an old man's gesture that didn't fit my picture of him. Was it this captivity that was aging him? He was a "street man" —his whole career had been based upon dealing with people. If he was allowed to try breaking the Cambridge net, at least he'd be doing the thing he was best at. Perhaps all betrayals— marital, professional, and political—are motivated by the drive to do what you're best at, no matter whom you're doing it for.

"You seem very certain," I said.

"I'm not paranoid, if that's what you mean."

I left it like that for a moment and drank some tea. "You're not smoking these days, I notice." I picked up the packet of cheroots from the tray and sniffed them. I hadn't smoked for ages. I put the cheroots down again, but it wasn't easy.

"I don't feel like smoking," he said. "It's a good chance for me to give up altogether."

I poured myself some tea and drank it without milk or sugar the way he drank his; it was awful. "How would you start?" I didn't have to explain what I meant. The idea of Stinnes trying to crack a Soviet network using his own methods was uppermost in both our minds.

"First, I've got to have my freedom. I can't work if you are going to have someone watching me night and day. I must be able to go to them completely clear of all your strings. You understand?"

"They're alarmed now," I said. "They must have been in touch with Moscow. Moscow might have told them about you."

"You have too much faith in Moscow. Just as we have always had too much faith in the efficiency of London Central."

"I'd stand very little chance of convincing my masters that you could bring that network home alone. They won't want to believe it; they'd consider it some kind of reflection upon their competence. They'd be afraid of another disaster and this time one in which we lost you too. Moscow is searching for you, Erich. Surely you must know that."

"Moscow doesn't put out alerts for defectors until there has been publicity about them. The policy is to play down such things in case other Soviet citizens get the same idea."

"You weren't just a defector," I said. "Your going dealt a big blow to them."

"All the more reason why they would keep quiet. Have your analysts reported anything yet?"

"I'll try and find out," I promised. Erich knew that my reply was an evasion, and yet there was no way I could keep him from guessing the right answer to that question. The analysts had been monitoring the East Bloc radio and TV and watching the press for anything that could relate to Erich Stinnes. And they'd especially scrutinized the restricted publications and given particular attention to the diplomatic and KGB radio traffic by means of which Moscow controlled its embassies and agents throughout the world. So far there had been nothing that could be recognized as a reference to Erich Stinnes or his enrollment by our Department. It was as if he'd disappeared into outer space. He smiled. He knew there had been nothing.

"I'd need only ten days, two weeks at the most. I know this network, and I'd approach it another way. If you were prepared to pick them up without evidence, I could give them to you in less than a week."

"No. Here on this side of the world we have this inconvenient necessity to provide the courts with clear evidence. Even then, the juries free half the people sent up for trial."

"Plant something on them. I'll give evidence."

"We haven't had a clear decision on whether we can use you in court yet," I said.

"If I agree . . ."

"It's not that easy. There are legal difficulties. My Department aren't empowered to handle this sort of prosecution. If you were cross-questioned in open court, it might become embarrassing."

"And your Home Office won't help? Why don't you change this antiquated system? The KGB is centrally controlled to work against the enemies within and the enemies without. Separate agencies—one working to locate foreign agents within

Britain and another to penetrate foreign countries—is cumbersome and inefficient."

"We like it a bit cumbersome and inefficient," I said. "An agency like the KGB can take over its government anytime it wishes."

"It hasn't happened yet," said Stinnes primly. "And it never will. The Party remains supreme and no one challenges its power."

"You don't have to proclaim the Party line anymore, Erich. We both know the Soviet Union is facing a crisis."

"A crisis?" he said. He leaned forward, elbows on knees, and hands clasped tight together. His pinched face was very pale and his eyes bright.

"There are urgent demands for incentives to be built into the declining economy. I don't have to tell you all that, Erich." I smiled but he didn't respond to my smile. I seem to have touched a nerve.

"And who is fighting against such reforms?" He hunched his shoulders more. I wondered exactly where Stinnes had placed himself in this struggle. Or was he still denying that there was one?

Well, if this was the only way to bring him alive, I'd pursue it. "The moribund Party officials—who meddle with the economy at grass-roots level and skim the cream from it. They don't want to be replaced by skilled factory managers, technical experts, and trained administrators, the only ones who might be able to create the kind of system of incentives that eventually produces an expanding economy."

"The Party . . ."

". . . remains supreme. Yes, you already said that."

". . . is close to the work force," said Stinnes. He was clearly agitated by my remarks.

"It's close to the work force because of the way in which the Party's come to a tacit agreement with them. The workers stay out of politics and the Party makes sure that no one has to work very hard. That was all right in Lenin's time, but it can't go on much longer. The Russian economy is a disaster."

Stinnes rubbed his cheek, seemingly alarmed at the idea. "But if they let the factories get rid of the lazy and hire only the hard workers, then they will be reintroducing into the system all the greed, fears, and strife of competitive capitalism. The Revolution will have been for nothing; they will have revived the class war."

"That's the problem," I said.

"The Party will stand firm against that kind of reform," said Stinnes.

"But the economy will continue to decline. And one day the Soviet generals and admirals will encounter resistance to their profligate spending on guns and tanks and ships. The economy won't be able to afford such luxuries."

"Then the military will throw in their lot with the reformers?" said Stinnes scornfully. "Is that your contention?"

"It's possible," I said.

"Not in your lifetime," said Stinnes, "and not in mine." He'd been leaning forward, eyes bright and active as he pursued the argument, but now he sighed and slumped back in the sofa. Suddenly, for a brief moment, I glimpsed a different Stinnes. Was it the heaviness that comes with constant pain? Or was Stinnes regretting the way he'd let me see a glimpse of what he really was?

"Why do you care, Erich?" I said. "You're a capitalist now, aren't you?"

"Of course I am," he said. He smiled, but the smile was not reassuring.

FROM Berwick House I drove straight back to London for a conference that was scheduled for half past five that afternoon. It was a high-powered departmental meeting that had already been going for nearly an hour. I waited in the anteroom and was called in just before six.

The Director-General—wearing one of his baggiest suits—

was in the chair. At the table there were Morgan, Frank Harrington, Dicky, and Bret Rensselaer. It wasn't exactly the full complement. The Deputy was attending to private business in the Bahamas and the Controller Europe was at a meeting in Madrid. The usual selection of booze was arranged on the side table, but everyone seemed to be keeping to Perrier water, except for Frank Harrington, who was nursing a large whisky in both hands and looking into it like a gypsy consulting a crystal ball. In deference to the D-G no one was smoking. I could see that this was putting Frank under some strain. He seemed to guess what I was thinking; he smiled and wetted his lips in the way he did when about to light his pipe.

"Ah . . . ," said the D-G. Twisting round to see me as Morgan ushered me into the conference room, he knocked his pencil off the table.

"Samson," supplied Morgan. It was one of his duties to remind the D-G of the names of the staff. So was retrieving things the D-G knocked to the floor without noticing.

"Ah, Samson," said the D-G. "You've just been to talk with our Russian friend. Why don't you pour yourself a drink."

"Yes, sir." The fluorescent lights were reflected in the polished tabletop. I remembered Fiona saying that fluorescent lighting made gin taste "funny." It was of course an insight into her pampered upbringing, a rationalization of why she didn't want to drink in cheap restaurants, corner bars, or offices. And yet I was never able to completely shed the suspicion that her theory might be true. I didn't let it interfere with my drinking, though.

While I poured myself a stiff gin and tonic I looked round the room. Sir Henry Clevemore seemed to be in good form today. Despite his wrinkled face and heavy jowls, his eyes were clear under those heavy lids, and his voice was firm. His sparse hair had been carefully arranged to make the most of it and today there was no sign of the trembling that sometimes made him stutter.

I wondered exactly what they'd been talking about. It was

unlikely that Bret had been asked any pointed questions at such a gathering; the D-G wouldn't have Dicky and Morgan along to witness Bret being put through the wringer. If I knew anything about the old man, if things came to the crunch he would stand aside as he had done before. He'd hand the whole business over to Internal Security and let them get their hands dirty. For the old man had a horror of disloyalty and he'd run a mile to get away from any sniff of it.

And certainly Bret showed no sign of strain. He was sitting next to the D-G and being his usual urbane shop-window-dummy self. Dicky was wearing a suede jacket as a sartorial concession to the D-G, Morgan was twitchy, and Frank looked bored. Frank could afford to look bored—he was the only one in the room who would probably remain unaffected if they opened an orange file on Bret. In fact, with Bret put on the back burner, Frank would probably be asked to stay on in Berlin. Knowing Frank and his vociferous requests for retirement, that would mean the offer of a bigger pension and a lot of fringe benefits to keep him happy.

"Did you record your interrogation?" Morgan asked me.

"Yes. But it wasn't exactly an interrogation," I said, pulling out a chair and sitting down at the other end of the table to face the D-G. "The recording is being transcribed now."

"Why wasn't it an interrogation?" said Morgan. "That was your instruction." Morgan brandished the notepad and pencil. He had on a new suit—dark gray, almost black, and tight fitting, with white shirt and stiff collar—so that he looked like the ambitious junior newspaper reporter that he'd been not so long before.

I didn't reply to Morgan, I stared into the D-G's red-rimmed eyes. "I went to Berwick House because the senior interrogator was getting nowhere. My task was to find out what the trouble was. I'm not a trained interrogator and I've very little experience." I spoke loudly, but even so, the D-G cupped his ear.

"What do you make of him?" said the D-G. The others were politely holding back, giving the D-G first go at me.

"He's sick," I said. "He seems to be in pain."

"Is that the most important thing you discovered?" asked Morgan, with more than a touch of sarcasm.

"It's something you aren't likely to get from the tape recording," I said.

"But is it of any importance?" said Morgan.

"It might be very important," I said.

"Do we have his medical sheet to hand?" the D-G asked Morgan.

Waiting until after Morgan had registered confusion, Bret answered. "He has consistently refused a physical. It didn't seem worth getting tough with him about it. But we've been taking it easy with him just in case."

The D-G nodded. The D-G, like many of the senior staff, was able to nod without making it a gesture of agreement. It was just a sign that he'd heard.

Encouraged by the D-G, I went quickly through my conversation with Stinnes, giving particular attention to his suggestion that he be allowed to break the Cambridge net.

Bret said, "I'd feel uneasy about releasing him in the mere hope that he could pull it off on his own."

"We're not achieving much by keeping him where he is," said Morgan. He tapped his pencil on the notepad. The way in which Morgan came to such meetings in the role of note taker for the D-G and then spoke to senior staff as an equal annoyed Bret. It annoyed other people too. I wondered if the D-G failed to understand that or simply failed to care. His ability to play one person off against another was legendary. That was the way the Department had always been run.

"I'm coming under a lot of pressure to transfer him to the Home Office people," said the D-G, pronouncing the final words with what was almost a shudder of distaste.

"I hope you won't give way to them," said Bret. He was very polite, but there was an edge in his voice that implied that the D-G would fall from grace if he succumbed to such pressure.

Dicky had consistently resisted any temptation to become

involved with the Stinnes debriefing, but now he said what was in everyone's mind. "I understood that we would hold him for the best part of a year. I understood that the whole idea was to use Stinnes as a way to measure our successes or failures over the past decade. I thought we were going to go through the archives with him."

Dicky looked at the D-G and Frank Harrington looked at Dicky. Frank Harrington would not emerge shiny bright from any close inspection of the Department's successes and failures. It was a maxim of the German desk that successes were celebrated in Bonn and rewarded in London, but failures were always buried in Berlin. Berlin was the one job you had to do sometime, but no one had ever built a career upon Berlin.

"That was the original plan," said Morgan. He looked at the D-G to see if he required more prompting.

The D-G said, "Yes, that was the original plan but we have had setbacks. More setbacks than you have yet heard about." Was that, I wondered, a reference to a pending enquiry for Bret? The D-G spoke very slowly and anyone replying immediately was likely to find himself speaking over him. So we all waited, and sure enough he spoke again. "It's something of a poker game. We have to decide whether to go on with our bluff, trust this Russian, and hope he can deliver the goods that will provide us with a strong bargaining position." Another long pause. "Or should we cut our losses and turn him over to MI5?"

"He's a highly experienced Soviet agent," said Frank Harrington. "And the KGB is a highly motivated organization. He didn't get to that position by failing to deliver the goods. If he says he can do it, I think we should take that seriously."

"Let's not just consider his ability, Frank," I said. "It's not just a matter of whether he can deliver or might fail to do so. We have to worry whether he's a KGB man still hot and active."

"Of course we do," said Frank hastily. "Only a fool would take him at face value. On the other hand, he's no damned use to us wrapped in tissue paper and stored away on the shelf."

"And in the long term?" enquired the D-G. I suppose he too realized that Frank couldn't possibly come out well from a systematic review of our activities, and he was curious to see Frank's reaction.

"That's for the historians," said Frank. "My concern is last week, this week, and next week. The strategy is all yours, Director."

The D-G smiled at this artful reply. "I think we are all of one mind," he said, although I had seen little evidence of that. "We must go for some sort of compromise."

"With Stinnes?" said Dicky. I never discovered whether it was supposed to be a joke, but Morgan smiled knowingly so perhaps he'd already told Dicky what was coming.

"A compromise with MI5," said the D-G. "I'm proposing that they appoint a couple of people to a committee so that we take joint control of the Stinnes debriefing."

"And who will be on the committee?" said Bret.

"You, Bret, certainly," said the D-G. "And I was going to have Morgan there to represent me. Would that suit you, Frank?"

"Yes indeed, sir. It's an admirable solution," said Frank.

"And what about German Stations?" said the D-G, looking at Dicky.

"Yes, but I would like to have Samson back working full time for me. He's been devoting a lot of time to the Stinnes business, and someone will have to go to Berlin next week."

"Of course, Dicky," said the D-G.

Bret said, "We might need him from time to time. He was the file officer on the Stinnes enrollment. The committee are sure to want to see him."

I suppose Bret now expected Dicky to say yes, of course, but Dicky knew how Bret would exploit such a casual agreement and so he didn't respond. Dicky was going to hold on tight to me. Trying to run his desk all on his own was biting into his social life.

The D-G looked round the table. "I'm so glad we're all agreed," he said. He'd obviously made this exact decision before the meeting began. Or Morgan had made it for him.

"Will Stinnes remain at Berwick House?" said Bret.

"Better you work out the details at the first meeting of the whole committee," said the D-G. "I don't want them to say we've presented them with a *fait accompli;* it will get things off to a bad start."

"Of course, sir," said Bret. "Who will have the chair?"

"I'll insist that you do," said the D-G, "unless you'd prefer not to do it that way. It would limit your voting."

"I think I should have the chair," said Bret. Bret was at his smoothest now, his elbows on the polished tabletop, his hands loosely clasped so that we could all see his signet ring and the gold wristwatch. It was all coming out well for him so far, but he wasn't going to enjoy hearing the way Stinnes described him as a blundering amateur when the transcription was sent upstairs. "How many of them will there be?"

"I'll sound them out," said the D-G. "Cabinet Office might want a say in it too." He looked round the table until he came to me. "You're looking very stern, young man. Have you any comments?"

I looked at Dicky. Whatever he'd told his wife about Bret being a KGB mole, Dicky was not going to stand up and remind the meeting about it. Dicky looked away from me and grew suddenly interested in the D-G. "I don't like it," I said.

"Why not?" interjected Frank, anxious to head off any chance of me being rude to the old man.

"They'll find some damned thing to use against us." There was no need to say who. They all knew I didn't mean Moscow.

"They're already well provided with things to use against us," said the D-G. He chuckled. "It's time for a compromise. I don't want to see us in direct conflict with them."

I said, "I still don't like it."

The D-G nodded. "No one here likes it," he said in a soft friendly voice. "But we have very little choice." He shook his head so hard that his cheeks wobbled. "No one here likes it."

He wasn't quite correct. Behind his lifted glass of Perrier water Morgan was loving every minute of it. He was stepping from office boy to an operational role without the twenty years of experience that usually went with such moves. It was only a matter of time before Morgan would be running the whole Department.

Chapter 20

U NMARRIED men are the best friends, the best masters, and the best servants," said Tessa Kosinski, my sister-in-law. She was undoing the wire to open a bottle of champagne, careful of her long painted fingernails. She flicked a piece of gold foil from her fingers and swore softly.

"Don't shake the bottle or it will go everywhere," I said. She smiled and without a word handed the bottle to me. "Who said that? Was it George?"

"No, Francis Bacon, silly. Why do you always think I'm totally ignorant? I may not have had Fi's brilliant career at Oxford, but I'm not an untutored fool." Her fair hair was perfect, as if she'd just come from the hairdresser, her pink dress revealed her bare shoulders, and she was wearing a gold necklace and a wristwatch glittering with diamonds. She was waiting for George to come home, and then they were going to the theatre and on to a party at the house of a Greek shipping magnate. That's the sort of life they led.

"I know you're not, Tessa. It's just that it sounded like something George might say." She was bright when she wanted to be. She knew that I was trying to get the conversation round to the subject of her men friends, but she deftly avoided it. The champagne wasn't so easy to open. I twisted the cork and, despite my warning to her, gave the bottle a little shake to help. The champagne opened with a loud bang.

"George is becoming a religious fanatic since we moved here," she said. She watched me pouring the champagne and said nothing when some spilled over onto the polished table.

"How did moving here affect him?" I put the bottle back into the silver bucket.

"We're so near the church now. Mass every morning without fail, darling—surely that's rather overwrought?"

"I've learned not to comment on other people's religion," I said cautiously.

"And he's become awfully friendly with a bishop. You know what a snob George is and he's so easily flattered."

"How do you know?"

"Now, now." She grinned. "I flatter George sometimes. I think he's very clever at business and I'm always telling him so."

"What's wrong with being friends with a bishop?" I asked.

"Nothing at all; he's an amusing old rogue. He sits up drinking George's best brandy and discussing the nuances of theology."

"That's not being a fanatic," I said.

"Even the bishop says that George is zealous. He says he must be trying to compensate for the lives of his two uncles."

"I thought his uncles were both priests."

"The bishop knows that; he was joking, darling. Sometimes you're as slow on the uptake as poor old George."

"Well, I think George is a good husband," I said, preparing the ground for the subject of her infidelities.

"So do I. He's wonderful." She got up and looked round the room in which we were sitting. "And look what he's done with this flat. It was a shambles when we first came to look at it. Most of the furniture was chosen by George. He loves going to the auctions and trying to get a bargain. All I did was to buy some of the fabrics and the carpets."

"It's a superb result, Tessa," I said. The cream-colored sofas and the pale carpet contrasted with the jungle of tropical plants that filled the corner near the far window. The lights were recessed into the ceiling to produce a pink shadowless illumination throughout the whole room. The result was expensive looking and yet austere. It was not exactly what one would expect to be the taste of George, the flashily dressed cockney millionaire. The whole flat was perfect and glossy, like a double-page spread in *House & Garden.* But it was lifeless too. I lived in rooms that bore the imprint of two young children: plastic toys in the bath, odd shoes in the hall, stains on the carpet, and dents in the paintwork. It was nothing less than tragic that George and Tessa had never had children. George desperately wanted to be a father, and Tessa doted on my two kids. Instead, they had this forbiddingly tranquil home in that bleak exclusive part of London—Mayfair. I'm not sure that either of them really belonged there.

"Give me another drink," said Tessa. She had this preposterous idea that champagne was the only alcohol that would not make her fat. She was like a small child in some matters, and although he grumbled about her behavior, George indulged her in such ridiculous notions. He was to blame for what he didn't like in her, for to some extent he had created this exasperating creature.

"I didn't intend to stay."

"George will be back at any time. He phoned from the workshop to say he was leaving." I took the bottle of vintage Bollinger from the solid-silver wine cooler and poured more for both of us. "Is the car going well?"

"Yes, thank you."

"George is sure to ask me if you like the car. He's taken a shine to you. I think he must have guessed the way you bully me about not looking after him properly." In Tessa's language that meant being unfaithful. Her vocabulary was brutally frank about everything except her infidelity.

"Then there's something we should talk about before he arrives," I said.

"Your girlfriend was looking absolutely stunning the other

night," said Tessa, getting to her feet. She walked over to the window and looked down at the street. "If George arrives soon, there's a place for him to park," she said. She came back to where I was sitting and, standing behind me, ruffled my hair. "I'm so glad you brought her. Where is she tonight?"

"She's at evening class," I said. I knew it would produce a hoot of laughter and I wasn't disappointed.

"Evening classes, darling? How old is she? She looks as if you might have kidnapped her from the fifth form."

"She's studying economics," I explained. "She's determined to go to Cambridge."

"What a coup that would be for an unlettered oaf like you, darling. A wife educated at Oxford and a mistress at Cambridge." She was still standing behind me, but when I tried to grab her wrist she ducked away.

"It's about you and Dicky," I said, determined to broach the subject.

"I knew that was coming. I could see it in your face," she said.

"You've worked hard to avoid talking about it," I said. "But there's something you ought to know."

"Don't tell me Dicky Cruyer is married or something awful like that," she said. She sank down in the soft chair, kicked off her gold evening shoes, and put her feet on the coffee table in such a way that her toes could touch the ice bucket.

"Daphne is furious," I said.

"I told him she'd find out about us," said Tessa calmly. "He's so careless. It's almost as if he wants everyone to know."

"A friend of Daphne's saw you at a hotel near Deal."

"I knew it," she said. She laughed. "Dicky packed both bags and forgot that I always leave my nightdress under the pillow . . . in case there's a fire or something. I unpacked when I got home, but at first I didn't notice the nightgown was missing. Then I absolutely panicked." She drank some champagne. She was enjoying the story, enjoying it more than I was. "You can imagine what I was thinking. Dicky had put his real address in the hotel register—he's such a chump—and I had visions of the hotel sending my wretched nightie to Daphne with a note saying she'd left it behind or something."

She looked at me, waiting for me to ask what she did next. "What did you do next?" I asked.

"I couldn't phone Dicky; he's furious if I phone him at the office. But I couldn't think how to put it to the hotel people. I mean, how can you explain that you don't want them to send your nightie back? Do you tell them to give it to Oxfam or say you've just moved house? It's impossible. So I jumped into my car and trundled all the way back to Deal again."

"Did you get it back?"

"Darling, it was an absolute riot. This lovely lady in the reception said she'd worked in big hotels all over Europe. No hotel ever returns nightgowns or articles of ladies' underwear to the address in the register, she said. They wait until there's a query about it. Then, darling, she showed me this immense cupboard full of flimsy garments left behind after weekends of illicit passion. You should have seen them, Bernard. I blushed at some of the things in that cupboard."

"So all was well?" I wanted to talk about her affair with Dicky, but I could see she was trying to spin things out until George got back and so avoid it.

"I said to this amusing lady that we should go into business and buy all these wonderful things from hotels and sell them. I even mentioned it to the people on this committee I'm on—it's a children's charity—but you should have seen their faces. They're all old fogies with tinted hair and fur coats. You'd have thought I'd suggested opening a brothel."

"You didn't explain to them exactly how you obtained this information?"

"I told them it had happened to a friend of mine."

"Not a very convincing subterfuge," I said.

"No, well, I'm not in that world, am I?" she said. That remark was aimed at me.

"It wasn't the nightdress. It was a friend of Daphne who saw you."

"And my mind has been buzzing ever since you said that just now. I can't think of any familiar face there that weekend."

"Daphne's talking about a divorce."

"She always says that," said Tessa. She flicked her hair back and smiled defensively.

"Always? What do you mean, always?"

"You know very well that I had a little fling with Dandy Dicky last year, or was it the year before? We talked about it one evening. I remember you were very toffee-nosed."

"If Daphne goes to a lawyer, it could become a rotten business, Tess."

"It will be all right," she said. "I know you mean well, Bernard darling. But it will be all right."

"If I believed that, I wouldn't be sitting here talking about it. But I know Daphne well enough to think she could be serious."

"Divorce? What about the children? Where would she live?"

"Never mind Daphne's problems. If she starts making a fuss, you'll have enough of your own. She wants me to introduce her to George."

"That's ridiculous," said Tessa.

"Dicky would be the real loser," I said. "Publicity such as a nasty divorce action would destroy his career."

"Don't say they'd fire him—I know that's not true."

"They probably wouldn't sack him, but he'd be posted to some lousy place on the other side of the world and left there to rot. The Department don't like publicity, Tessa. I don't have to draw you a diagram, do I?"

Her flippant attitude had changed now. She took her feet off the table and drank some champagne, frowning deeply as she considered her position. "George would be furious," she said, as if he'd be more furious about the publicity than about her infidelity.

"I thought you were trying to put your marriage together again," I said. "I remember you talking to me and saying that George was the most wonderful husband in the world and that all you wanted to do was to make him happy."

"I do, darling, I do. But it won't make him happy to be portrayed as the wronged husband and have his photo in all those lousy newspapers. I'll have to talk to Daphne. I must make her see sense. It would be insane for her to leave Dicky over such a stupid little thing."

"It's not a 'stupid little thing' to her," I said. "And if you start talking to her in that fashion, you'll only make things worse."

"What do you want me to say?"

"Don't make it sound as if you're doing it for me," I said testily. "I can't tell you what to say. But the only thing that Daphne will want to hear is that you're not going to see Dicky anymore."

"Then, of course; I'll tell her that."

"You've got to mean it, Tessa. It's no good just patching it over. . . . You're not in love with him or anything, are you?"

"Good heavens, no. Who could be in love with him? I thought I was doing Daphne a favor, to tell you the truth. I don't know how anyone can bear Dicky round them all the time. He's awfully wearing."

I listened to her protests with a healthy mistrust. I didn't know much about women, but I knew that such strenuous denials could sometimes be a sign of profound passion. "Tell her you're sorry. It's time you stopped all this nonsense, Tessa. You're not a child any longer."

"I'm not old and ugly," she said.

"No, you're not. Perhaps it would be better if you *were* old and ugly. George would remain loyal, no matter how old and ugly you were and you'd realize what a good husband you have."

"You men all stick together," she said sullenly.

"You make a lot of people unhappy, Tessa. I know you don't

see it like that, but you're a troublemaker. You had a rich father who gave you everything you ever asked for, and now you think you can have anything you want, no matter who it belongs to or what the consequences may be."

"You have a terrible tendency to play the amateur psychologist, Bernard. Did I ever tell you that?"

"I hate amateur psychologists," I said. She always knew how to needle me. I drank my champagne and stood up.

"Don't give me that injured-pride look, darling. I know you're trying to help."

"If you want me to talk to Daphne, I will. But I won't do it unless I get a sincere promise from you that the affair is at an end."

She stood up too. She came close and stroked the lapel of my jacket. Her voice was a purr. "You're very masterful, Bernard. That's a very attractive quality in a man. I've always said that."

"Do cut it out, Tessa. Sometimes I think that these love affairs of yours are staged to give you constant reassurance."

"Fi was always saying that. Father never praised us for anything at all. Fi didn't care, but I wanted a bit of praise now and again."

There was something in her voice that made me look at her more closely. "Have you heard from Fiona?" It was a wild guess. "A letter?"

"I was going to tell you, Bernard. Honestly I was. I was determined to tell you before you left this evening."

"Tell me what?"

"I saw Fi."

"Saw Fiona? When?"

"Just a few days ago."

"Where?"

"I have a dear old aunt who lives in Holland. We used to spend holidays with her. I always go and see her for her birthday. She used to come to us but she's too infirm to travel now." She gabbled nervously.

"Holland?"

"Near Eindhoven. She lives in a block of tiny flats built specially for elderly people. There's a doctor on call and meals if you want them. The Dutch do that sort of thing so well; it puts us to shame."

"And Fiona?"

"She came for the birthday meal. I almost fell over with surprise. She was sitting there as if it was the most natural thing in the world."

"What did you say?"

"What *could* I say, darling? My aunt knew nothing of Fiona going off to the bloody Russians. I didn't want to spoil the birthday for her. I just carried on as I had all the previous years."

"Was George with you?"

"George doesn't like family gatherings. That is to say, he doesn't like gatherings of my family. When it's *his* family, it's quite a different matter, and there are thousands of them."

"I see." If what George didn't like was Tessa's father, it's a feeling that I shared heartily. "Just you and Fiona and your aunt then?"

"She wants the children, Bernard."

"Fiona? My children? Billy and Sally?"

"They're her children too," said Tessa.

"Would you like to see her take them away?"

"Don't be like that, Bernard darling. You know I wouldn't. But she only wants them to spend a few weeks with her."

"In Moscow? In Berlin?"

"I don't know. For a holiday, she said."

"And if they go to her for a few weeks, how do we ever get them back?"

"I thought of that," said Tessa. She sipped her drink. "But if Fiona promises to send them back, she'll keep to it. It was the same when we were children, she'd never break her word in personal matters."

"If I was only dealing with Fiona it might be different," I

said. "But we're dealing with Soviet bureaucracy. And I wouldn't trust British bureaucracy as far as I could throw it, so the idea of delivering my kids to the mercies of the Soviet bureaucrats does not come happily to me."

"I don't understand."

"Those bastards want the kids as hostages."

"For Fiona?"

"Right now she's obviously in the first flush of excitement. The Russians let her out to the West and know she'll come back. But the chances are that feeling won't last. She'll become disillusioned with Soviet society. She'll find it's not the paradise she's been dreaming of all these years."

"Hostages?"

"When the kids are there, she'll discover that they can't return to the West all together. They'll make sure that she travels alone. She won't have any choice; she'll have to go back to the children."

"She's prepared to go through the courts to get custody."

"She told you that?"

"Over and over again."

"That's because she knows the Department for which I work won't tolerate it going to the courts. They'll press me to let her have custody."

"That would be disgusting."

"It's what they would do."

"The children have rights too. It would be wrong for a court to deliver them to the Russians without giving them a chance."

"Maybe I shouldn't say what they'd do before they've done it, but I'd say Fiona's chances are good."

"Bernard darling, do sit down for a moment. I didn't know how badly you'd take it. Do you want a whisky or something?"

"Thanks, Tess. No, I'll have some more champagne," I said. I sat down while she poured it for me.

"She said she doesn't want to row with you. She's still fond of you, Bernard, I can tell."

"I don't think so," I said. But did I really only want to hear myself contradicted?

Tessa sat down next to me. I could feel the warmth of her body and smell the perfume. It was a heavy exotic scent, suited, I suppose, for the sort of evening she had ahead of her. "I wasn't going to tell you this, but I think Fi is still in love with you. She denied it, but I've always been able to see through her."

"You're not making it any easier, Tessa."

"She must miss the children dreadfully. Couldn't it be that she simply wants to be with them for a short time each year?"

"It might be," I said.

"You don't sound very convinced."

"Fiona is a very devious person, Tessa. Truthful when it suits her, but devious. Surely I don't have to tell you that. Have you told anyone else about meeting Fiona?"

"Of course not. Fi said not to."

"Not even George?"

"Not even George. Cross my heart," she said and made the children's gesture of running a finger across her throat to swear it was true.

"And there was no one with her?"

"Just Fiona. She stayed the night. My aunt has a spare room. We talked half the night. Fiona had a rented car. She went to Schiphol next morning. She had to fly on to somewhere else . . . Paris, I think."

"Why couldn't she contact me?"

"She said you'd say that. She said it was better this way. I suppose her own people wouldn't suspect a stopover in Holland the way they would a visit to London to see you."

For a few minutes we said nothing. Then Tessa said, "She said she'd seen you."

"Since leaving?"

"At London airport. She said you had a brief chat."

"I'll have to ask you to forget that, Tessa. It was a long time back."

"Didn't you tell Dicky or anyone? That was silly, Bernard. Was that about the children?"

"Yes, it was. No, I didn't tell Dicky or anyone."

"I didn't tell Dicky about seeing my sister either," said Tessa.

"I was thinking about that, Tessa. You realize that this has a bearing on your relationship with Dicky?"

"Because I didn't tell him?"

"I don't want to discuss with you what Dicky does for a living, but surely you see that having an affair with you could lead to very bad trouble for him."

"Because of Fiona?"

"Someone who wanted to make trouble could connect Fiona to Dicky via the affair he's having with you."

"But equally they could connect Fiona with Dicky via the fact that you work for him."

"But I'm not regularly seeing Fiona."

"Neither am I, not regularly."

"That might be difficult to prove. And it might be that just one meeting with Fiona would be enough to make Dicky's bosses uneasy."

"My sister went to Russia. That doesn't make me a spy. And it doesn't make everyone I know a suspect."

"Perhaps it shouldn't, but it does. And in any case, Dicky can't be lumped together with all the other people you know . . . not in this context anyway. Dicky's contacts have to be specially scrutinized."

"I suppose you're right."

"I am."

"So what should I do?"

"I'd hate to see you mixed up in some damned espionage scandal, Tessa. I know you're an innocent, but many innocents get tangled up in these things."

"You want me to stop seeing Dicky?"

"You should make a clean break without delay."

"Write him a letter?"

"Absolutely not," I said. Why did women always feel the need to write letters when ending an affair?

"I can't just stop. I'm having dinner with him the day after tomorrow."

"You're sure Dicky doesn't know you saw Fiona?"

"I certainly didn't tell him," said Tessa. She was strident, as if she resented the advice I was giving her—and I suppose she did. "I told no one, no one at all. But if I just stop seeing him now, perhaps he'll guess there's something more to it."

"Have dinner with him and tell him it's all over."

"You don't think he'll ask me about Fiona?"

"I don't think so, but if he brings up the subject, you just say you haven't seen her since she left England and went to Berlin."

"You've got me worried now, Bernard."

"It will be all right, Tess."

"Suppose they know?"

"Deny seeing her. If the worst came to the worst, you could say you reported it to me and I told you to tell no one. You say you took that instruction literally."

"Wouldn't that get you into trouble?"

"We'll sort that one out when and if it comes. But I'll only help you if you're really serious about stopping this idiotic affair with Dicky."

"I am serious, Bernard. I truly am."

"There's a lot of trouble in the Department right now. There's a lot of suspicion being directed at everyone. It's a bad time to step out of line."

"For Dicky?"

"For anyone."

"I suppose they still think you had something to do with Fiona going away?"

"They say they don't, but I believe they do."

"She said she'd made a lot of trouble for you."

"Fiona?" I said.

"She said she was sorry about that."

"She was the one who ran."

"She said she had to do it."

"The children never mention her. It worries me sometimes."

"They're happy children. The nanny is a good girl. You give them a lot of love, Bernard. That's all children really need. It's what we needed from Daddy, but he preferred to give us money. His time was too precious."

"I'm always away or working late or some damned thing."

"I didn't mean that, Bernard. I didn't mean that love can be measured in man-hours. You don't clock in for love. The children know you love them. They know you work only in order to look after them; they understand."

"I hope they do."

"But what will you do about them? Will you let Fiona take them?"

"I'm damned if I know, Tessa," I said, and that was the truth. "But you must stop seeing Dicky."

Chapter 21

THE NEWLY formed committee that took charge of the Stinnes debriefing lost no time in asserting its importance and demonstrating its energies. For some of the newcomers the committee provided an example of Whitehall's new spirit of intradepartmental cooperation, but those of us with longer memories recognized it as just one more battlefield upon which the Home Office and the Foreign Office could engage forces and try to settle old scores.

The good news was that both Bret Rensselaer and Morgan spent most of each day in Northumberland Avenue, where the committee had its premises. There was a lot for them to do.

Like all such well-organized bureaucratic endeavors, it was established regardless of expense. The committee were provided with a staff of six people—for whom heated and carpeted office space was also provided—and all the paraphernalia of administration was installed: desks, typewriters, filing cabinets, and a woman who came in very early to clean and dust, another woman who came in to make tea, and a man to sweep the floor and lock up at night.

"Bret will build himself a nice little empire over there," said Dicky. "He's been looking for something to occupy himself with ever since his Economics Intelligence Committee folded." It was an expression of Dicky's hopes rather than his carefully considered prophecy. Dicky didn't mind if Bret became monarch of all he surveyed over there as long as he didn't come elbowing his way into Dicky's little realm. I looked at him before answering. There had still been no official mention that Bret's loyalty was in question, so I played along with what Dicky said. But I was beginning to wonder if I was being deliberately excluded from the Department's suspicions.

"The Stinnes debriefing can't last forever," I said.

"Bret will do his best," said Dicky.

He was wearing a denim waistcoat. He had his arms folded and was pushing his hands out of sight as if he didn't want any flesh to show. It was a neurotic mannerism. Dicky had become very neurotic since the night he'd had dinner with Tessa, the dinner at which she was supposed to tell him that they were through. I wondered exactly what had happened.

"I don't like it," I said.

"You're not there," said Dicky. "Thank your lucky stars that you're not running backward and forward for Morgan and Bret and the rest of them. I got you out of that one, didn't I?" He was in my miserable little office, watching me work my way through all the trays that he'd failed to cope with during the previous two weeks. He sat on my table and fiddled with the tin lid of paper clips and the souvenir mug filled with pencils and pens.

"And I'm grateful," I said. "But I mean I don't like what's happening over there."

"What is happening?"

"They're taking evidence from everyone they can think of. There's even talk of the committee going to Berlin to talk to people who can't be brought here."

"What's wrong with that?"

"They're supposed to be managing the Stinnes debriefing. It's not their business to go poking into everything that happened when we enrolled him."

"On principle?" said Dicky. He was quick to catch on when it was something to do with office politics.

"Yes, on principle. We don't want Home Office people questioning and passing judgment on our foreign operations. That's our preserve—that's what we've been insisting upon all these years, isn't it?"

"An interdepartmental squabble, is that how you see it?" said Dicky. He unbent a paper clip to make a piece of wire, then he looked round at the cramped little office that I shared with my part-time secretary as if seeing the slums for the first time.

"They'll want to question me; perhaps they'll want to question you. Werner Volkmann is coming over here to give evidence. And his wife. Where's the end of it? We'll have those people crawling all over us before that committee finishes."

"Zena? Did you authorize Zena Volkmann's trip to London?" He ran a fingernail up the corner of a bundle of papers, so that it made a noise.

"It will come out of committee funds," I said. "That's the first thing they got settled—where the money was to come from."

"Departmental employees going before the committee will not have to answer any question they don't consider relevant."

"Who said so?"

"That's the form," said Dicky. He threw the paper clip at my wastepaper basket but missed.

"With other departments, yes. But this committee is chaired

by one of our own senior staff. How many witnesses will tell him
to go to hell?"

"The D-G was obviously in a spot," said Dicky. "It's not
what he would have done in the old days. He would have bra-
zened it out and held on to Stinnes in the hope we'd get something good."

"I blame Bret," I said. I was fishing.

"What for?"

"He's let this bloody committee extend its powers too
widely."

"Why would he do that?" Dicky asked.

"I don't know." There was still no hint that Bret was suspect.

"To make himself more important?" persisted Dicky.

"Perhaps."

"The committee are stacked against him, Bernard. Bret will
be outvoted if he tries to step out of line. You know who he's
got facing him. He's got no friends round that table."

"Not even Morgan?" I said.

It was not intended as a serious question, but Dicky answered it seriously. "Morgan hates Bret. Sooner or later they'll
get into a real confrontation. It was madness putting them
together over there."

"Especially with an audience to watch them wrangling," I
said.

"That's right," said Dicky. He looked at me and chewed his
fingernail. I tried to get on with some paperwork, but Dicky
didn't budge. All of a sudden he said, "It's all over." I looked
up. "Me and your sister-in-law. *Finito!*"

What was I supposed to say—"I'm sorry"? Had Tessa told
him that I knew or was he just guessing? I looked at him to see
if he was serious or smiling. I wanted to react in the way he
wanted me to react. But Dicky wasn't looking at me; he was
looking into the distance, thinking perhaps of his final tête-à-
tête with Tessa.

"It had to end," said Dicky. "She was upset, of course, but

I was determined. It was making Daphne unhappy. Women can be very selfish, you know."

"Yes, I know," I said.

"Tessa's had a thing about me for years," said Dicky. "You could see that, I'm sure."

"I did wonder," I admitted.

"I loved her," said Dicky. This was all something he was determined to get off his chest and I was the only suitable audience for him. I settled back and let him continue. He didn't need encouraging. "Once in a lifetime, perhaps, you find yourself in a trap from which there is no escape. One knows it's wrong, knows people will be hurt, knows there will be no happy ending. But one can't escape."

"Is that how it happened with you and Tessa?" I said.

"For a month I couldn't get her out of my mind. She occupied my every thought. I got no work done."

"When was that?" Dicky getting no work done was not enough to give me a reference to the date.

"Long ago," said Dicky. His arms still folded, he hugged himself. "Did Daphne tell you?"

Careful now. The red-for-danger light was glowing inside my head. "Daphne? Your Daphne?" He nodded. "Tell me what?"

"About Tessa, of course."

"They're friends," I said.

"I mean did she mention that I was having an affair?"

"With Tessa?"

"Of course with Tessa." I suppose I was overdoing the innocence. He was getting testy now and I didn't want that either.

"Daphne wouldn't talk to me about such things, Dicky."

"I thought she might have poured her heart out to you about it. She pestered several other friends of ours. She said she was going to get a divorce."

"I'm glad it's turned out all right," I said.

"Even now she's still very moody. You'd think she'd be

overjoyed, wouldn't you? Here I've made Tessa unhappy—terribly unhappy—to say nothing of my own sacrifice. *Finito.*" He made a slicing movement of the hand. "I've given up the woman I truly love. You'd think Daphne would be happy, but no. . . . Do you know what she said last night? She said I was selfish." Dicky bared his teeth and forced a laugh. "Selfish. That's a good one, I must say."

"A divorce would have been terrible," I said.

"That's what I told her. Think of the kids, I said. If we split, the children would suffer more than either of us. So you never knew that I was having an affair with your sister-in-law?"

"You kept it pretty dark, Dicky," I said.

He was pleased to hear that. "There have been a lot of women in my life, Bernard."

"Is that so?"

"I'm not the sort of man who boasts of his conquests—you know that, Bernard—but one woman could never be enough for me. I have a powerful libido. I should never have got married, I realized that long ago. I remember my old tutor used to say that the trouble with marriage is that while every woman is at heart a mother, every man is at heart a bachelor." He chuckled.

"I have to see Werner Volkmann at five," I reminded him.

Dicky looked at his watch. "Is that the time? How that clock goes round. Every day it's the same."

"Do you want me to brief him before he sees the Stinnes committee?"

"The Rensselaer committee, you mean. Bret is very keen it's called the Rensselaer committee so that we'll keep control of it." Dicky said this in such a way as to suggest that we'd already lost control of it.

"Whatever it's called, do you want me to brief Werner Volkmann about what to say to them?"

"Is there something that we don't want him to tell them?"

"Well, obviously I'll warn him he can't reveal operating procedures, codes, safe houses . . ."

"Jesus Christ!" said Dicky. "Of course he can't reveal departmental secrets."

"He won't know that unless someone tells him," I said.

"You mean we should warn all of our people who are called to give evidence?"

"Either that or you could talk to Bret. You could make sure that each person called to give evidence is told that there are guidelines they must follow."

"Tell Bret that?"

"One or the other, Dicky."

Dicky slid off the table and walked up and down, his hands pushed into the pockets of his jeans and his shoulders hunched. "There's something you'd better know," he said.

"Yes?" I said.

"Let's go back to one evening just after you came back from Berlin with that transcript . . . the German woman who disappeared into the Havel last Christmas. Remember?"

"How could I forget."

"You were getting very excited about the radio codes she used. Am I right?"

"Right."

"Would you like to tell me that over again?"

"The codes?"

"Tell me what you told me that evening."

"I said she was handling material, selected material, for transmission. I said it was stuff that they didn't want handled by the Embassy."

"You said it was good. You said it was probably Fiona's stuff that this woman was sending."

"That was just conjecture." I wondered what Dicky was trying to get me to say.

"Two codes, you said. And you said two codes was unusual."

"Unusual for one agent, yes."

"You're beginning to clam up on me, Bernard. You do this sometimes, and it makes my life very difficult."

"I'm sorry, but if you told me what you were getting at, I might be able to be more explicit."

"That's right—make it my fault. You're good at that."

"There were two codes. What else do you want to know?"

"IRONFOOT and JAKE. You said that Fiona was IRONFOOT. And you said, 'Who the hell is JAKE?' Right?"

"I found out afterwards that IRONFOOT was a mistranslation for PIG IRON."

Dicky frowned. "Did you follow that up, even after I told you to drop it?"

"I was at Silas Gaunt's house. Brahms Four was there. I just casually mentioned the distribution of material and asked him about it."

"You're bloody insubordinate, Bernard. I told you to drop that one." He waited for my reply, but I said nothing and that finally forced him to say, "Okay, okay. What did you find out from him?"

"Nothing I didn't already know, but he confirmed it."

"That if there were two codes, there were two agents?"

"Normally, yes."

"Well, you were right, Bernard. Now maybe we see the killing of the Miller woman in another light. The KGB had her killed so that she couldn't spill the beans. Unfortunately for those bastards on the other side of the fence, she'd already spilled the beans . . . to you."

"I see," I said. I guessed what was coming, but Dicky liked to squeeze the maximum effect out of everything.

"So who the hell's JAKE, you asked me. Well, maybe I can now tell you the answer to that question. JAKE is Bret Rensselaer! Bret is a double and probably has been for years. We have reports going back to his time in Berlin. Nothing conclusive, nothing that makes firm evidence, but now things are coming together."

"That's quite a shock," I said.

"Damned right it's a shock. But I can't say you look very surprised, Bernard. Have you been suspicious of Bret?"

"No, I don't . . ."

"It's not fair to ask you that question. It makes me sound like Joe McCarthy. The fact is that the D-G is dealing with the problem. Now perhaps you realize why Bret is in Northumberland Avenue rubbing shoulders with those MI5 heavies."

"Has the old man delivered him to MI5 without telling him?"

"Sir Henry wouldn't do anything like that, especially not to one of our own. No, MI5 know nothing of this. But the old man wanted Bret out of this building and working somewhere away from our sensitive day-to-day papers while Internal Security investigate him. . . . Now this is all just between the two of us, Bernard. I don't want a word of this to go out of this room. I don't want you telling Gloria or anyone like that."

"No," I said, but I thought that was pretty rich since I'd already got the gist of it from Daphne. Daphne was a wife with no reason to be friendly to him, while Gloria Kent was a vetted employee who was handling the sensitive day-to-day papers that Bret wasn't seeing.

"Bret doesn't realize he's under suspicion. It's essential that he doesn't get wind of it. If he fled the country too, it would look damned bad."

"Will he face an enquiry?" I asked.

"The old man's dithering."

"Hell, Dicky, someone should talk to the old man. It can't go on like this. I don't know what evidence there is against Bret, but he's got to be given a chance to answer for his actions. We shouldn't be discussing his fate when the poor sod has been shunted off so that he can't find out what's going on."

"It's not exactly like that," said Dicky.

"What is it like then?" I asked. "How would you like it if it was me telling Bret that you were JAKE?"

"You know that's ridiculous," said Dicky.

"I don't know anything of the kind," I said. Dicky's face changed. "No, no, no . . . I didn't mean you might be a KGB agent. I mean it's not ridiculous to suppose you might be a suspect."

"I hope you're not going to make a fuss about this," said Dicky. "I was of two minds whether to tell you. Perhaps it was an error of judgment."

"Dicky, it's only fair to the Department and everyone who works here that any uncertainty about Bret be resolved as quickly as possible."

"Maybe Internal Security need time to collect more evidence."

"Internal Security always need time to collect more evidence. It's in the nature of the job. But if that's the problem, then Bret should be given leave of absence."

"Let's assume he's guilty—he'll run."

"Let's assume he's not guilty—he must have a chance to prepare some sort of defense."

Dicky now thought I was being very difficult. He moved his lips as he always did when he was agitated. "Don't get excited, Bernard. I thought you'd be pleased."

"Pleased to hear you tell me that Bret is a KGB mole?"

"No, of course not that. But I thought you'd be relieved to hear that the real culprit has been uncovered at last."

"The real culprit?"

"You've been under suspicion. You must have realized that you haven't had a completely clear card ever since Fiona went over to them."

"You told me that was all past history," I told him. I was being difficult; I know he'd only told me that to be encouraging.

"Can't you see that if Bret is the one they've been looking for, it will put you in the clear?"

"You talk in riddles, Dicky. What do you mean 'the one they've been looking for'? I wasn't aware they were looking for anyone."

"An accomplice."

"I still don't get it," I said.

"Then you are being deliberately obtuse. If Fiona had an

accomplice in the Department, then Bret would be the most natural person for that role. Right?"

"Why wouldn't I be the most natural?"

Dicky slapped his thigh in a gesture of frustrated anger. "Good God, Bernard, every time anyone suggests that, you bite their head off."

"If not me, then why Bret?"

Dicky pulled a face and wobbled his head about. "They were very close, Bernard. Bret and your wife—they were very close. I don't have to tell you the way it was."

"Would you like to enlarge on that?"

"Don't get touchy. I'm not suggesting that there was anything less than decorous in the relationship, but Bret and Fiona were good friends. I know how comical that sounds in the context of the Department and the way some people talk about each other, but they were friends. They had a lot in common; their background was comparable. I remember one evening Bret was having dinner at your place. Fiona was talking about her childhood . . . they shared memories of places and people."

"Bret is old enough to be Fiona's father."

"I'm not denying that."

"How could they share memories?"

"Of *places*, Bernard. Places and things and facts that only people like them know. Hunting, shooting, and fishing . . . you know. Bret's father loved horses, and so does your father-in-law. Fiona and Bret both learned to ride and to ski before they could walk. They both instinctively know a good horse from a bad one, good snow from bad snow, fresh foie gras from tinned, a good servant from a bad one . . . the rich are different, Bernard."

I didn't answer. There was nothing to say. Dicky was right, they had had a lot in common. I'd always been frightened of losing her to Bret. My fears were never centred on other younger, more attractive men; always I saw Bret as my rival. Ever since the day I first met her—or at least from the time I went to Bret and suggested that we employ her—I'd feared the attraction that he would have for her. Had that, in some way, brought about the very outcome I most feared? Was it something in my attitude to Bret and to Fiona that provided them with an undefinable thing in common? Was it some factor absent in me that they recognized in each other and shared so happily?

"You see what I mean?" said Dicky, when I hadn't spoken for a long time. "If there was an accomplice, Bret must be the prime suspect."

"One percent motivation and ninety-nine percent opportunity," I said, without really intending to say it aloud.

"What's that?" said Dicky.

"One percent motivation and ninety-nine percent opportunity. That's what George Kosinski says crime is."

"I knew I'd heard it before," said Dicky. "Tessa says that, but she said it about sex."

"Maybe they're both right," I said.

Dicky reached out to touch my shoulder. "Don't torture yourself about Fiona. There was nothing between her and Bret."

"I don't care if there was," I said.

Our conversation seemed to have ended and yet Dicky didn't depart. He fiddled with the typewriter. Finally he said, "One day I was with Bret. We were in Kiel. Do you know it?"

"I've been there," I said.

"It's a strange place. Bombed to hell in the war, everything rebuilt after the war ended. New buildings and not the sort that are likely to win prizes for architectural imagination. There's a main street that runs right along the waterfront, remember?"

"Only just." I tried to guess what was coming, but I couldn't.

"One side of the street consists of department stores and offices and the other side is big seagoing ships. It's unreal, like a stage set, especially at night when the ships are all lit up. I suppose back before it was bombed it was narrow alleys and waterfront bars. Now there are strip joints and discos, but they're in the new buildings—it's got an atmosphere about as sexy as Fulham High Street."

"They were after the shipyards," I said.

"Who were?"

"The bombers. It's where they make the U-boats. Kiel. Half the town work in the shipyards."

"I don't know anything about that," said Dicky. "All I remember is that Bret had arranged to meet a contact there. We went into the bar about eleven at night, but the place was almost empty. It was elaborately furnished—red velvet and carpet on the floor—but it was empty except for a few regular customers and a line of hostesses and the bartender. I never found out if the nightlife in Kiel starts later than that or doesn't exist at all."

"It's a beautiful place in summer."

"That's what Bret said. He knows Kiel. There's a big yachting event there every summer—Kiel Week—and Bret tries not to miss it. He showed me the pictures at the yacht club. There were big yachts with brightly colored spinnakers billowing. Girls in bikinis. *Kieler Woche*—maybe I'll take my boat there one year. But this time it was my luck to be there in the dead of winter and I've never been so cold in all my life."

What was all this leading up to, I wondered. "Why were you and Bret doing it? Don't we have people there? Couldn't the Hamburg office have handled it?"

"There was quite a lot of money involved. It was an official deal: we paid the Russians and they released a prisoner they were holding. It was political. A Cabinet Office request—very hush-hush. You know. It was going to be done in Berlin in the usual way, but Bret argued with Frank Harrington and finally it was decided that Bret would handle it personally. I went along to help."

"This was when Bret was still running the Economics Intelligence Committee?"

"This was a long time ago, when it was called the European Economics desk and Bret was officially only Deputy Controller.

But there's no reason to think this job had anything directly to do with that desk. I understood that Bret was doing this at the special order of the D-G."

"European Economics desk. That's going back a bit."

"Years and years. Long before Bret got his nice big office and had the decorator in."

"What are you going to tell me about him?" I said. I had the feeling that Dicky had come to a full stop.

"I was a complete innocent. I was expecting some well-dressed diplomatic official, but the man we met was dressed like a deckhand from one of the Swedish ferries, though I noticed that he arrived in a big black Volvo with a driver. He might just have come across the border—it's an easy enough drive." Dicky rubbed his face. "A big bastard he was, an old man. He spoke good English. There was a lot of small talk. He said he'd once lived in Boston."

"Are we talking about a Soviet official?"

"Yes. He identified himself as a KGB colonel. His documents said his name was Popov. It was such a memorable name that I've remembered it ever since."

"Go on, Dicky, I'm listening. Popov is a common enough Russian name."

"He knew Bret."

"Where from?"

"God knows. But he recognized him—'Good evening, Mr. Rensselaer,' he said, as bold as brass."

"You said the place was empty. He could have guessed who you were."

"There were too many people there for anyone to come in through the door and assume one of them was Mr. Rensselaer."

"How did Bret respond?"

"There was a lot of noise. It was one of these places where they have disco music switched up so loud it bends your eardrums. Bret didn't seem to hear him. But this fellow Popov obviously knew Bret from some other time. He was chatting away, as friendly as can be. Bret went rigid. His face was like one of those Easter Island stone carvings. Then I suppose his friend Popov noticed he was alarmed. Suddenly all the bonhomie was switched off. Bret's name wasn't mentioned after that; it was all very formal. We all went into the washroom and counted the money, tipping all the bundles of bills into a sink and repacking the case. When it was done Popov said good night and departed. No signature, no receipt, no nothing. And no 'Good night, Mr. Rensselaer.' This time it was just 'Good night, gentlemen.' I was worried in case we hadn't handled it right, but they released the man the next day. Have you ever had to do a job like that?"

"Once or twice."

"They say the KGB keep the cash. Is that true?"

"I don't know, Dicky. No one knows for sure. We can only guess."

"So how did he know Bret?"

"I don't know that either," I said. "You think he knew Bret from somewhere else?"

"Bret's never done any field work."

"Maybe he'd paid money over in the same way before," I suggested.

"He said he hadn't. He told me he'd never done anything like that before."

"Did you ask Bret if he knew the Russian?"

"I was a new boy; Bret was senior staff."

"Did you report it?"

"That the KGB man had called him 'Mr. Rensselaer'? No, it didn't seem important. It's only now that it seems important. Do you think I should tell Internal Security?"

"Take your time," I advised. "It sounds like Bret has got enough questions to answer for the time being."

Dicky forced a smile even though he was chewing his nail. Dicky was worried; not about Bret, of course, but about himself.

Chapter 22

W<small>E WERE</small> celebrating the anniversary of Werner and Zena's marriage. It was not the exact date, but Gloria had offered to cook dinner for the Volkmanns, who were in London to appear before the committee.

Gloria was not a great cook. She prepared veal chops followed by a mixed salad and a shop-bought cake that said ZENA AND WERNER CONGRATULATIONS in chocolate.

Not without some misgivings, I'd allowed the children to stay up and have dinner with us. I would have preferred them to eat with Nanny upstairs, but it was her night off and she had made arrangements with friends. So the children sat at the table with us and watched Gloria playing hostess in the way their mother had so recently done. Billy seemed relaxed enough—although he only picked at the chocolate cake, which was unusual—but Sally sat through the meal pinch-faced and silent. She watched Gloria's every move and there was tacit criticism in the way she was so reluctant to help pass the dishes down the table. Gloria must have noticed, but she gave no sign of it. She was clever with the children: cheerful, considerate, persuasive, and helpful but never maternal enough to provoke resentment. Gloria took her cue from Nanny, consulting her and deferring to her in such a way that Nanny was forced into Fiona's role while Gloria became a sort of super-nanny and elder sister.

But Gloria's subtle instinct for handling the children let her down when she took the cushioned dining chair that Fiona had always used at table. She sat at the end of the table so that she could reach the hot plate and the wine. For the first time the children saw Fiona replaced and perhaps for the first time they faced the idea that their mother was permanently lost to them.

When, after tasting the cake and toasting Zena and Werner in apple juice, Gloria took the children upstairs to change into pajamas and go to bed, I was half inclined to go with them. But Zena was in the midst of a long story about her wealthy relatives in Mexico City and I let the children go. It was a long time before Gloria returned. Billy was in his new pajamas and carrying a toy crane that he felt he must demonstrate for Werner.

"Where's Sally?" I asked when I kissed Billy good night.

"She's a little tearful," said Gloria. "It's the excitement. She'll be fine after a good night's sleep."

"Sally says Mummy is never coming back," said Billy.

"Never is a long time," I replied. I kissed him again. "I'll come up and kiss Sally."

"She's asleep," said Gloria. "She'll be all right, Bernie."

Even after Billy was in bed and Zena had finished her long story, I worried about the children. I suppose Sally felt she had no one she could really confide in. Poor child.

"How did you remember the date of our marriage?" Zena Volkmann asked me.

"I always remember," I said.

"He's a liar," said Gloria. "He made me phone Werner's secretary and ask."

"You mustn't give away all Bernie's secrets," Werner told her.

"It was a wonderful surprise," said Zena. The two women were sitting on the sofa together. They were both very young, but they were as different as two young women could be. Gloria was blond, fair-skinned, tall, and big-boned, with that rather slow tolerant attitude that is often the sign of the scholar. Zena Volkmann was small and dark, with the coilspring energy and the short fuse of the self-made opportunist. She was dressed expensively and adorned with jewelry; Gloria was in tweed skirt and roll-neck sweater with only a small plain silver brooch.

Werner was in a mood for reminiscence that evening, and

he'd related story after story about the times we'd spent together in Berlin. The two women had endured our remembered youthful escapades with fortitude, but now they'd had enough. Gloria got to her feet. "More coffee? Brandy?" she said. She poured the last of the coffee for me and for Werner. "You do the brandy, Bernard. I'll make more coffee and tidy away."

"Let me help you," said Zena Volkmann.

Gloria said no, but Zena insisted on helping her to clear the table and load the dishwasher. The two women seemed to be getting along well together; I could hear them laughing when they were in the kitchen. When Zena came back to collect the last plates from the table, she was wearing an apron.

"How did it go, Werner?" I asked when finally there was a chance to talk to him. I poured my precious vintage brandy, passed him his coffee, and offered him the jug. But Werner resisted the suggestion of cream in his coffee. I poured the rest of it into my cup. "Cigar?"

"No thanks. If you can stop smoking, so can I," said Werner. He drank some coffee. "It went the way you said it would go." He had given evidence to the committee.

He slumped back in his chair. Despite his posture, he was looking very trim—Zena's strict diet routine was having an effect—but he looked tired. I suppose anyone would look tired if they were married to Zena as well as giving evidence to the committee. Now Werner pinched his nose between his thumb and forefinger as he always did when he concentrated. But this time his eyes were closed, and I had the feeling he would have liked to go right off to sleep.

"No surprises?" I asked.

"No bad surprises. But I wasn't expecting to see that damned Henry Tiptree on the committee. That's the one who gave you so much trouble. I thought he was attached to Internal Security."

"These Foreign Office attachments float from department

to department. Everyone tries to unload them. The committee is probably a good job for him; it keeps him out of the way."

"Bret Rensselaer is the chairman."

"It's Bret's final chance to be the golden boy," I joked.

"I heard he was in line for Berlin after Frank retires."

"I heard the same thing, but I could tell you a few people who'll do everything they can to stop him getting it."

"Dicky, you mean?"

"I think so," I said.

"Why? Dicky would become Bret's boss. Isn't that what he's always wanted?"

Even Werner didn't fully understand the nuances of London Central's command structure. I suppose it was uniquely British. "The German desk is senior to Berlin Resident in certain respects, but has to defer to it in others. There is no hard-and-fast rule. Everything depends upon the seniority of the person holding the job. When my dad was Berlin Resident, he was expected to do as he was told. But when Frank Harrington went there, from a senior position in London Central, he wasn't going to be taking orders from Dicky, who'd spent a lot of his departmental career attached to the Army."

"Dicky should never have had his Army service credited to his seniority," said Werner.

"Don't get me started on that one, Werner," I said.

"It wasn't fair. It wasn't fair to you, it wasn't fair to the Department, and it wasn't fair to anyone who works for the German desk."

"I thought you were a supporter of Dicky's," I said.

"Only when you try to tell me he's a complete buffoon. You underrate him, Bernie, and that's where you make a bad mistake."

"Anyway, Dicky will probably oppose the idea of Bret getting Berlin. Morgan—the D-G's hatchet man—hates Bret and wants Dicky to oppose it. Dicky will do as Morgan wants."

"Then you'll get it," said Werner with genuine pleasure.

"No, not a chance."

"Why? Who else is there?"

"A lot of people will be after that job. I know Frank keeps saying it's the Siberia of the service and the place where careers are buried, and all that may well be true; but everyone wants it, Werner, because it's the one job you've got to be able to say you did."

"You have enough seniority, and you're the only one who has the right experience. They can't pass you over again, Bernie. It would be absurd."

"The way I hear it, I'm not even going to be shortlisted."

"See the D-G," suggested Werner. "Get his support."

"He doesn't even remember my name, Werner."

"What about Frank Harrington? You can count on him, can't you?"

"They won't listen to what Frank says about who should take over. They'll want a new broom in there. A strong recommendation from Frank would probably be counterproductive." I smiled; "counterproductive" was one of Dicky's words, the sort of jargon I used to despise. I was going soft behind that desk.

Werner said, "Did Frank Harrington oppose the idea of letting MI5 people sit on the Stinnes committee?"

"I was there, Werner. Frank just said 'Yes, sir,' without discussion or argument. He said it was 'an admirable solution.' He's close to the D-G. The D-G must have told Frank what he intended and got his support beforehand."

"Frank Harrington said okay? Why? It's all a mystery to me," said Werner. He stopped pinching his nose and looked at me, hoping for a solution.

"The D-G wants Bret out of the Department. There's a lot of discussion about Bret right now. Hysterical discussion."

Werner looked at me for a long time. He was wearing his plastic inscrutable mask and trying not to look smug. "This is a new development," he said, unable to keep the note of triumph out of his voice. "I seem to remember a Christmas party when you'd come back from Lange—your head was filled with suspicions of Bret Rensselaer." He was grinning. Only with effort was he able to keep his voice level now, as though he wasn't poking fun at me, just retelling the story.

"I only said that all the leads should be investigated."

Werner nodded. He knew I was retreating from my former position as prosecutor and it amused him. "And now you don't think that?"

"Of course I do. But I hate to see the way it's being done. Bret is being railroaded. And I especially don't like the way he's being isolated. I know how it feels, Werner. Not so long ago I was the one whose friends were crossing the street to avoid me."

"Did you take it any further? Did you report your suspicions?"

"I was with Uncle Silas for the weekend . . . this is some time back . . . before Christmas. Brahms Four was there. I asked him about the receiving end of the intelligence over there."

"You told me all that. But what does he know about it?" said Werner scornfully.

"Not much, but as I told you, it was enough to convince me that the Miller woman was running two agents."

"In London Central? Make up your mind, Bernie. Are you still trying to prove that Bret is a KGB man or not?"

"I don't know. I go round and round in circles. But there *were* two agents: Fiona was coded PIG IRON, the other was JAKE. Brahms Four confirmed that, Werner."

"No, no, no. If Bret was feeding material back to Moscow . . . it doesn't bear thinking about. It would mean they knew about all the Brahms Four material as soon as we got it . . ."

"So we have to find out if Moscow was monitoring the Brahms Four material all the time we were getting it."

"How would you discover that?"

"I just don't know if we could. It would be a hell of a task to go through the archives, and I'm not sure how the D-G would react to a suggestion that we do it."

"It would look damned funny if they forbade you going to the archives, wouldn't it?"

"They wouldn't have to say they didn't trust me," I said. "They could simply point out how difficult it would be to ascertain that from the archive material. They'd also point out that if the KGB had a good source, they wouldn't compromise it by acting on every damned thing they got. And they'd be right, Werner."

"I can't believe that Moscow knew what Brahms Four was telling us all those years and let him get away with it. Even if Bret *was* monitoring the stuff for them."

"Finally they let Brahms Four escape," I said.

"They didn't exactly let him escape," said Werner. "You rescued him."

"*We* rescued him, Werner, you and me together."

"If Bret was reporting to Moscow, Brahms Four would still be in East Berlin."

"They had no warning, Werner. I made sure Bret didn't know what I was going to do. And until the last minute when you came to London and told Dicky, no one at London Central knew I was going to pull Brahms Four out."

"Your wife knew; she ran. She could have told Bret."

"Not enough time," I said. "I thought of that, but there wasn't enough time for Bret to find out and get a message to Moscow."

"So Bret is suspect and the D-G has put him on ice while he decides what to do about it?"

"It looks that way," I said.

"Only the Miller woman knows the truth, I suppose," said Werner. There was some unusual expression in his face that made me look at him closely.

"And she's in the Havel," I said.

"Suppose I told you that I'd seen the Miller woman?"

"In the morgue? Did she come out at Spandau locks?"

"She's not dead," said Werner smugly. "I saw her looking fit and well. She's a clerk. She works in the Rote Rathaus."

The Red Town Hall was the municipal centre for East Berlin, a massive red-brick building near Alexanderplatz, which, unlike so much around it, had survived for well over a century. "Alive and well? You're sure?"

"Yes, I'm sure."

"What's it all about then? Who is she? Was it all a stunt?"

"I found out a little about her—I have a friend who works there. Everything she said about her father living in England and about being married and so on seems to be true. I couldn't actually check her out, of course, but the story she gave you was true, as far as her identity is concerned."

"She just forgot to mention that she was a resident of the Democratic Republic and worked for the government."

"Right," said Werner.

"What luck that you spotted her! I suppose they thought she was tucked well away from us in that place. There wasn't much likelihood of anyone who'd seen her on this side going into an office in the East Berlin town hall."

"It was a million to one chance that I had to go there again. I remembered her because she once helped me with a tricky problem. An East German truck I use broke down in the West on a delivery trip. I went round in circles trying to find someone who had the necessary permissions to tow it from West to East. That was a year or more ago. Then, last week, I was in there again getting my ration cards."

"And she didn't recognize you? She must have seen you that night they arrested her and I got her to give me a statement."

"You did the interrogation. I waited outside. I only caught sight of her very briefly. I knew I'd seen her somewhere before, but I couldn't think where. I mean, it's not the sort of face you never forget. Then, after I'd given up and stopped thinking about her, I walked into the Rathaus and saw her sitting at her desk. This time I took a close look at her."

"She was no amateur, Werner. She made her suicide attempt convincing enough to get herself slammed into the Steglitz Clinic."

"Suicides in police cells—cops get very nervous about such things, Bernie. I looked into it. He was a young cop on duty at night. He played it safe and sent for an ambulance."

"And then they covered their tracks by taking her from the Steglitz Clinic and running the ambulance into the water."

"It must have been a diversion while another car took her across to the East."

"It worked all right," I said. "When I remember spending my Christmas Eve standing on that freezing cold wharf, waiting for them to lift that bloody vehicle . . ."

"I hope you're not going to suggest trying to get hold of her again. We couldn't grab her, Bernie, not there in the Mitte. They'd have us in the bag before we even got her to the car."

"It would be difficult, wouldn't it?"

"It wouldn't be difficult," said Werner. "It would be impossible. Don't even think about it."

"You'd better put all this in writing, Werner."

"I've got it drafted out. I thought I'd wait until I came to London so I could check with you first."

"I appreciate that, Werner. Thanks."

We sat for a few minutes drinking the coffee and not saying anything. I was fully occupied in trying out all the configurations that this new piece of the jigsaw puzzle presented.

Then Werner said, "How does this affect Bret?"

"You didn't tell the committee anything about this Miller woman being alive, did you?"

"You said not to tell them departmental secrets. This seemed like a departmental secret."

"So secret that only you and I know of it," I said.

"That's right," said Werner.

"Why, Werner? What the hell was it all about? Why did they use the Miller woman to pick up the material?"

"Suppose everything she told you was exactly true. Suppose she had been a radio operator handling the material from Bret

Rensselaer and the stuff from your wife. Suppose Fiona pulled her out when she went over to them. The Miller woman decides she's getting too old for espionage and tells Moscow that she wants to get out of the business—she wants to retire. Fiona encourages her because the Miller woman knows too much. So they find her an easy little job issuing licenses in the town hall. It happens all the time, Bernie. Probably she has a small pension and card for the *Valuta* shops so that she can buy Western goods. Everything is lovely, everyone is happy. Then one day, at short notice, they need someone to go to Wannsee and pick up the package. They need someone who has the right sort of papers for coming over to the West side of the city. It seems like a routine task. Little likelihood of danger. She'll only be in the West for a couple of hours, and she won't be searched by anyone on the West side when she goes through with the package." He fiddled with his coffee spoon, pushing it backward and forward. "Or perhaps it's not a one-off. Perhaps she does a lot of little jobs like that to eke out her salary. Either way, I have no trouble believing it. There's nothing that doesn't fit together."

"Maybe not. But that's not the way I'd treat someone like her. Imagine that *we* had been running a truly remarkable source in the KGB offices in Moscow. Would we let a case officer or radio operator for that agent go back over there for ten minutes, let alone a couple of hours? You know we wouldn't."

"The KGB are different," said Werner. He drove the spoon round the table, cornering recklessly when it came to the fruit bowl.

"Maybe they are, but my supposition isn't complete yet. What if they not only had one remarkable source but *two* remarkable sources? And one of them still in place, Werner—a source right in London Central still going strong. Are the KGB so different that they'd still let the Miller woman go and put her head in a noose? Would they take a chance on her being arrested and telling us enough to blow their other agent?"

"It's no good trying to think the way they think. That's the first thing I had to learn when I started dealing with them. They don't think like us. And you're being wise after the event. They had no idea that we were going to move in on that party at Wannsee. To them it must have seemed like the most routine and safe assignment possible." Werner tried to drink from the cup he'd already emptied. Even when he knew it was empty, he tipped his head right back to get the final drips. He hadn't touched his brandy.

"I still find it difficult to believe they'd take the risk," I said.

"What risk? Our people risk everything when they go through the Wall. They risk the detailed inspection of documents, the guards watching every move they make and listening to everything they say. There are the secret marks made on the passports and traveling papers. Everyone going East is scrutinized under a microscope no matter who they are. But what do their people risk when they come to spy on the West? No one crossing to our side is inspected very closely. Being a KGB agent is one of the safest jobs going. We're a walkover, Bernie. That woman's job was a sinecure. It was a million-to-one chance that she was swept up by the arrest team."

"And even then she got away with it."

"Exactly. All she had to do was make some gesture at suicide and she's conveniently moved to the Steglitz Clinic, all ready for the rescue. Damn it, Bernie, why are we so soft?"

"If you are right, Werner, it means that the KGB don't know what she divulged to us about the radio codes."

Werner turned the cup in the saucer and thought about that and didn't answer.

I pressed him. "Would they have put her right back into that job at the Rathaus if she'd admitted to giving us a confession?"

"Probably not."

"She didn't tell them, Werner. I'd bet on that. Perhaps they were impressed by their own efficiency. Maybe they were so pleased at themselves for rescuing her so swiftly and smoothly that it never occurred to them that they were already too late."

"I know what you're thinking," said Werner.

"What am I thinking?"

"That she can be turned. You think we should blackmail her, threaten to tell the KGB that she confessed . . ."

"And get her to work for us? A tired old woman like that? What would she tell us . . . all the latest dope on the ration-card issues? All the town hall gossip? No, Werner, I wasn't thinking of turning her."

"What then?"

"I don't know."

Werner changed the subject. "Do you remember that terrible place under the rubble in Koch Strasse, where the old man made the model planes?"

"The bearded one who built a workshop out of bits of packing cases?" I remembered it well. We were kids; the "old man" was probably no more than thirty, but there were lots of very elderly thirty-year-olds in Berlin at that time. He'd been a combat engineer in an armored division, a skilled fitter who scraped a living by selling model aircraft to the conquerors. Even as a child I'd seen the irony of him sitting in the bombed rubble of central Berlin and making so lovingly the model B-17 bombers that the American airmen bought as souvenirs. He was a fierce-looking man with a crippled arm. We called him "Black Peter" and when we went to watch him working he'd sometimes let us help him with sandpapering or boiling up the smelly animal glue.

"Did you know that the cellar he lived in was part of the prison cells under Prinz-Albrecht-Strasse?" Prinz-Albrecht-Strasse was the guarded way in which German adults of that time referred to Gestapo headquarters.

"I thought the Gestapo building was on the Eastern side."

"I was there last week with a friend of mine, a photographer who's doing a magazine article—photos of the graffiti on the Wall. Some of it's very funny."

"Only from this side," I said. "Drink your brandy, Werner. It was a Christmas present from Uncle Silas."

"Anyway, I walked back to look at the place where we used to visit Black Peter. It's all been leveled. They're building there. I found a big billboard that had fallen on its face. I picked it up and it was a notice—in four languages, so it must be old— saying YOU ARE NOW STANDING ON THE SITE OF THE GESTAPO PRISONS WHERE MANY PATRIOTS DIED."

"Is Black Peter's cellar still there?"

"No, the bulldozers went over it. But there in the middle of the rubble someone had placed a small bunch of flowers, Bernie."

"Near the sign?"

"The sign was face down. Someone had gone out to that desolate place and put an expensive bunch of flowers on the ground. No one walks across that empty site from one year to the next. How many Berliners know that that heap of rubble is the old Gestapo prisons. Can you imagine someone taking flowers out there to remember someone . . . ? After all these years. Fancy someone still doing that, Bernie. Like a secret little ritual. It made me shiver."

"I suppose it would," I said. I was slightly embarrassed by the depth of Werner's feelings. "It's a strange city."

"Don't you ever miss it?"

"Berlin? Yes, sometimes I do," I admitted.

"It's an amazing town. I've lived there all my life and yet I still discover things that astound me. I wish my father had lived a little longer. . . . I couldn't live anywhere else," said Werner. For him and for me, Berlin represented some part of our fathers' lives that we still hoped to discover.

I said, "And you're the one who keeps talking about retiring to live in the sun."

"Because Zena would love it, Bernie. She's always talking about living somewhere warm and sunny. I suppose we will one day. If it made Zena happy, I could put up with it."

"Talking of bouquets, do you remember that day we trailed Black Peter to see where he was going?"

"I don't know who was more frightened, him or us," said Werner.

"Us," I said. "Remember how he kept getting off his bicycle and looking back?"

"I wonder how much he paid for that big bunch of flowers."

"A week's work at least," I said. "Did you know it was the Jewish cemetery?"

"Didn't you?"

"Not at the time," I said.

"Every Jew knows it." For a moment I had forgotten how Werner's Jewish father had survived the Nazi regime by digging graves in a Jewish cemetery, a job no "Aryan" was permitted to do. "The Jewish school and the Jewish old-age home were there too. Grosse-Hamburger-Strasse was the heart of Berlin's old Jewish quarter, dating back hundreds of years."

"Yes, I knew the Jewish old-age home. That was where Berlin Jews were taken and held, prior to being transported to the East."

"It's strange that they chose such a very public place," said Werner. "In other cities the Jews were assembled at railway sidings or empty factory sites. But here they were right in the city centre, a short step from Unter den Linden. From the neighboring apartment blocks and office buildings the roll calls and loading could be seen by hundreds of local people."

"He chained his bicycle to the gate, I remember, and you said Black Peter couldn't be a Jew, he was in the Army."

"Then we saw that the graves were marked with *crosses,*" said Werner. "There must have been two hundred of them."

"The way he put the flowers on the grave I guessed it was a relative. He knelt at the grave and said a prayer. He knew we were watching by then."

"I could tell he wasn't a Jew when he crossed himself," said Werner, "but I still didn't realize what it was all about. Who could have guessed that they'd bury all those SS men in the old Jewish cemetery?"

"The bodies were from the fighting round the S-Bahn station Börse. The first order the Red Army gave, when the fighting stopped, was to start burying the corpses. I suppose the old Jewish cemetery in Grosse-Hamburger-Strasse was the nearest available place."

"The Russians were frightened of typhus," said Werner.

"But if the cemetery was very old, it must have been full," I said.

"No. In 1943 it was all dug up and the graves destroyed. Berlin was declared *judenrein*—cleared of Jews—about that time. The cemetery grounds stood empty from then until the end of the fighting."

"I thought he was going to kill you when he caught you." He'd hidden behind some bushes and grabbed Werner as we were leaving.

"I was always a little scared of him; he was so strong. Remember how he used to bend those bits of metal when he was making stands for the planes?"

"We were just kids, Werner. I think we liked to pretend he was dangerous. But Black Peter was miserable and starving, like half the population."

"He was frightened. I think he must have found out your father was an English officer."

"Do you think Black Peter was with his brother in the SS?" I asked.

"Do SS men say prayers? I don't know. I just believed everything he told us at the time. But if he wasn't in the fighting with his brother, how would he have known where he was buried."

I said, "Remember the evening we went back there and you brought a flashlight to see the name on the grave?"

"They weren't real front-line soldiers . . . clerks from Prinz-Albrecht-Strasse and police headquarters, cooks, and Hitler Youth. What terrible luck to be killed when the war was so nearly over."

"I wonder who decided to give them all proper markers with name, rank, and unit."

"It wasn't the Red Army," said Werner, "you can bet on that. I go past there sometimes. It's a memorial park nowadays. Moses Mendelssohn's grave is there and they've given him a new stone."

"I suppose we shouldn't have followed him. He never forgave us for finding out his little secret. We weren't welcome in his cellar after that." From the kitchen I heard the sound of the dishwasher starting. It was a very noisy machine and Gloria only switched it on when she was finished. "The ladies are coming with more coffee," I said.

"I'll talk to her," said Werner, as if he'd been thinking of the Miller woman all the time. "Maybe it will come to nothing, but I'll try."

"Better do nothing, Werner. It's a departmental problem; let the Department solve it. No sense in you getting into trouble."

"I'll sound her out," said Werner.

"No, Werner. And that's an order."

"Whatever you say, Bernie."

"I mean it, Werner. Don't go near her."

Then Gloria came in holding a jug of fresh coffee. She said, "What have you men been talking about?"

"What we always talk about: naked girls," I said.

Gloria thumped me between the shoulder blades before she poured out coffee for all four of us.

Zena Volkmann laughed; she was excited. She was hardly into the room before she said, "Werner, Gloria has been showing me an antique American quilt that Bernard bought for her. Can we buy one, Werner dearest? Appliqué work—a hundred and fifty years old. I've got the address of the shop. They cost an absolute fortune, but it would look wonderful on our bed. It would be a sort of anniversary present for us."

"Of course, my darling."

"Isn't he a perfect husband?" said Zena, leaning over and cuddling Werner and planting a kiss on his ear.

"Remember what I said, Werner. For the time being, do nothing."

"I remember," said Werner.

"If you don't want that brandy, Werner, I'll drink it."

Chapter 23

GLORIA expressed her love for me with such desperate intensity that I was frightened by it. Was it, I wondered, the unique passion that she wanted it to be? Was it the one and only chance for us both to find everlasting happiness? Or were these ideas just a measure of her youth? She could be so many different people: amusing companion, shrewd colleague, sulky child, sexy bedmate, and concerned mother to my two children. Sometimes I saw her as the fulfillment of all my hopes and dreams; at others I saw in her just a beautiful young girl balanced on the edge of womanhood and myself as a self-deluding middle-aged lecher.

It is liberating to be in love, and Gloria showed all the exhilaration that dedicated love provides. But to *be* loved is something quite different. To be loved is to suffer a measure of tyranny. For some the sacrifice comes easily, but Gloria could be possessive in a single-minded way that only the very young and the very old inflict upon their loved ones. She couldn't understand why I hadn't invited her to live with me permanently in my home in Duke Street. She resented every evening I didn't spend with her. When she was with me she resented the hours I spent reading, because she felt it was a pleasure we couldn't share. Most of all, she resented the trips abroad I had to make, so that I often deferred telling her about them until the last moment.

"Back to Berlin," she said peevishly when I told her. We were standing in the kitchen after Zena and Werner had gone back to their hotel.

"It's not my idea," I said. "But Berlin is my desk. There's no one else who can go in my place. If I put it off this week, I'll have to go next week."

"What's so urgent in Berlin?"

"Nothing is urgent there. It's all routine, but some of the reports can't be adequately covered in writing."

"Why not?" There was something, some anxiety, in her voice that I didn't recognize. I should have been warned by that but I prattled on.

"It's better to listen at length over a glass of beer. Sometimes the asides are more valuable than the report itself. And I have to see Frank Harrington."

"One long booze, is it?"

"You know I don't want to go," I said.

"I don't know anything of the kind. I hear you talking about Berlin with such love and tenderness that it makes me jealous. A woman can't compete with a city, darling." She smiled a cold and unconvincing smile. She was not good at hiding her emotions; it was one of the things I found attractive about her.

"It's where I grew up, sweetheart. When Werner and I get together, we talk of our childhood. Doesn't everyone reminisce when they see old school friends again? It was my home."

"Of course they do, darling. You don't have to be so defensive about such a dirty old whore. How can I really be jealous of an ugly, chilly heap of bricks?"

"I'll be back as soon as I can," I said. Before switching off the hall and kitchen lights, I switched on the light at the top of the stairs.

It was dark, the glimmer of light just enough to make a halo round her pale yellow hair. As I turned to speak with her she flung her arms round me and kissed me furiously. I could never get used to embracing this young woman who was almost as tall as I am. And when she hugged me there was a strength within her that I found exciting. She whispered, "You do love me, don't you?" I held her very tight.

"Yes," I said. I'd given up denying it. The truth was that I didn't know whether I loved her or not; all I knew was that I missed her dreadfully when I wasn't with her. If that wasn't love, I'd settle for it until love arrived. "Yes, I love you."

"Oh, Bernard, darling"—her cry of joy was almost a shout.

"You'll wake the children," I said.

"You're always so frightened of waking the children. We won't wake them, and if we do, they'll go back to sleep again. Come to bed, Bernard. I love you so much."

We tiptoed upstairs and past the children and the nanny. Once in the bedroom I suppose I should have switched on the overhead light, but I went to the bedside table to switch on that light instead. That's why I stumbled over the large and heavy suitcase that had been left at the foot of the bed. I lost my balance and fell full length to the floor with enough noise to wake up the whole street.

"What the bloody hell is that?" I shouted, sitting on the carpet and rubbing my head where I'd cracked it against the bedstead.

"I'm sorry, darling," said Gloria. She switched on the bathroom light to see better and helped me to my feet.

"What is it? Did you leave it there?" I didn't want to be helped to my feet; I just wanted her not to make the bedroom into an obstacle course.

"It's mine," she said in a whisper. For a moment she stood looking at me and then went into the bathroom and began putting cream on her face to remove her makeup.

"Good God, woman! Where did it come from?"

For a long time she didn't reply, then she pushed the door open and said, "It's some things of mine." She'd taken off her sweater and her bra. She washed her face and began brushing her teeth, staring at herself in the mirror over the sink as if I wasn't there.

"Things?"

"Clothes and books. I'm not moving in, Bernard, I know you don't want me to move in with you. The case is there only until tomorrow; then it will be gone." She had taken the toothbrush from her mouth so that she could speak and now she stood looking at herself in the mirror, talking as if to her own image and making the promise to herself.

"Why did you have to leave it in the middle of the bedroom? Why bring it up here at all? Couldn't it go under the stairs?" I started to undress, throwing my clothes on the chair. One shoe hit the wall with more force than I intended.

She finished in the bathroom and reappeared, wearing a new frilly nightdress I hadn't seen before. "The bathroom is all yours," she said. And then, "Mrs. Dias, your cleaning woman, has to get into that cupboard under the stairs to get the vacuum cleaner."

"So what?"

"She'd ask me what it was, wouldn't she? Or ask you what it was? And then you'd fuss about it. I thought it was better in here. I put it under the bed; then I had to get some things from it. I meant to push it back under the bed again. I'm sorry, darling. But you're a difficult man."

"It's okay," I said, but I was annoyed and unable to conceal my annoyance.

This silly accident with her suitcase spoiled the mood for both of us. When I came from the bathroom she was curled up in bed, the pillow over her head, and facing away. I got into bed and put an arm round her shoulders and said, "I'm sorry. I should have looked where I was going."

She didn't turn to face me. Her face was in the pillow. "You've changed lately, Bernard. You're very distant. Is it something I've done?"

"Nothing you've done."

"Is it Dicky? He's been like a bear with a sore head these last few days. They say he's given up his lady friend."

"You know he was seeing Tessa Kosinski?"

"You told me," said Gloria. She was still talking to her pillow.

"Did I?"

"A friend of Daphne's saw them in a hotel. You told me all that. I know you were worried about it."

"It was madness."

"Why?" she said. She turned her face toward me. She knew the answer, but she wanted to talk.

"Tessa is the sister of an intelligence official who is now working for the KGB. It would be okay for Dicky to have normal social contact with her. It would be okay for Dicky to be seeing her in the course of his job. But treason and infidelity have too much in common. Dicky was meeting Tessa secretly, and that sort of thing makes Internal Security very, very nervous."

"Is that why he gave her up?"

"Who told you he gave her up?"

"Sometimes I think you don't even trust me, Bernard."

"Who told you he gave her up?"

A big sigh. "So *she* gave *him* up."

"Why did you think it was his idea?"

"Falling over suitcases makes you paranoid, did you know that, darling?"

"I know that, but answer my question anyway."

Gloria stroked my face and ran a finger over my mouth. "You've just told me that Dicky had everything to lose from the relationship. Naturally I concluded that he would be the one to end it."

"And that's the only reason?"

"He's a man; men are selfish. If they have to choose between their job and a woman, they'll get rid of the woman. Everyone knows how men are." It was of course a reference to her fears about me.

"Tessa gave Dicky the push, but Dicky likes to tell it his way: strong-willed Dicky who knows what's best for both of them and brokenhearted Tessa trying to put the pieces of her life back together."

"He is like that, isn't he," said Gloria. "He's the worst sort of male chauvinist pig. Does Tessa really love him?"

"I shouldn't think so. I don't think she knows whether she loves him or not. I suppose he amuses her; that's all she asks. She'd go to bed with almost anyone she found amusing. Sometimes I think perhaps Tessa is incapable of loving anyone."

"That's a rotten thing to say, darling. She adores you and you've told me a thousand times that you could never have managed without all the help she's giving you."

"That's true, but we were talking about love."

"I suppose you're right. Love is different."

"They're not in love, Dicky and Tessa," I said. "If they were really in love, there would be nothing that could keep them apart."

"Like me pursuing you?" She hugged me.

"Yes, like that."

"How could your wife have let you go? She must be mad. I adore you so much."

"Tessa saw Fiona," I said suddenly. I hadn't meant to tell her, but she was involved. It was better that she knew what was happening. There always came a point at which the job and one's personal life overlapped. It was one of the worst things about the job, telling lies and half-truths about everything. For a womanizer I suppose these things come more easily.

"Your wife came here?"

"They met in Holland, at their aunt's house."

"What did your wife want?"

"It was the aunt's birthday. Both sisters visit her every year to celebrate it."

"She didn't go just for that, Bernard; she wanted something."

"How do you know?"

"I know your wife, Bernard. I think about her all the time. She wouldn't go to Holland to visit her aunt and see her sister except for a very good reason. She must have wanted something. Not a departmental something—there would have been other ways to tackle that; something from you."

"She wants the children," I said.

"You mustn't let them go," said Gloria.

"Just for a holiday, she said. Then she'll send them back." I was still trying to convince myself that it was as simple as that. I was half hoping that Gloria would encourage that belief, but she didn't.

"What mother could send her children back, not knowing when she'll see them again, if ever? If she goes to such trouble to arrange to see them, she'll never want to give them up again."

Gloria's opinion didn't make me feel good. I felt like getting up and having another drink, but I resisted the idea; I'd had enough already. "That's what I think," I said. "But if she goes through the courts for custody, she might well get them. I'm going to get a legal opinion about it."

"Are you going to tell your father-in-law?"

"I just can't decide. She's asking politely, and only asking that they go on holiday with her. If I refuse that request, a court might see that as refusing reasonable access. That would count against me if she pursued the matter and wanted custody."

"Poor darling, what a worry for you. Tessa told you this last week when you went there for drinks?"

"Yes," I said.

"You've been in a rotten mood ever since. I wish I'd known. I was worried. I thought perhaps . . ."

"What?"

"You and Tessa," said Gloria.

"Me and Tessa?"

"You know how much she'd like to get you into bed."

"But *I* don't want to go to bed with *her*," I said.

"Now who's shouting loud enough to wake up the children?"

"I like Tessa, but not like that. And anyway, she's married to George. And I've got you."

"That's what makes you so interesting to her. You're a challenge."

"Nonsense."

"Did you tell Werner about Fiona meeting Tessa? Did you tell him she wants the children?"

"No."

"But Werner's your best friend."

"He couldn't help. He'd only worry himself sick. I didn't think it was fair to burden him with it."

"You should have told him. He'll be angry that you haven't confided in him. He's easily hurt, anyone can see that."

"It's best this way," I said, without being really sure it was best.

"When are you testifying before the committee?" she said.

"I don't know."

"There's a rumor that you've refused to go."

"Oh, yes."

"Is it true?"

"No, it's not true. Dicky told me that the committee had scheduled a time to hear evidence from me, but I said that I would need written orders."

"To go before the committee?"

"I want written orders that specify what I can tell them."

"And Dicky won't give you that?"

"He wouldn't even give Werner guidelines to what he could reveal."

"He refused?"

"He dithered and changed the subject. You know what Dicky's like. If I'd asked him one more time, he would have developed a head cold and been taken home on a stretcher."

"Everyone else is giving evidence. Aren't you going rather far, darling?"

"These are not our people on the committee."

"They are MI5."

"I am not authorized to tell MI5 anything and everything about our operations."

"You're just being pigheaded." She laughed as if pleased I was giving someone else trouble rather than her.

"It's not just a matter of a combined committee: we've had those before, plenty of them. But it looks as if Bret has been shunted off onto that committee while they decide whether he should face an enquiry. If Bret is suspect . . . if Bret might turn out to be a KGB agent, why should I go over there and fill in the blanks for him?"

"If Bret is really suspect, the people on that committee must know," said Gloria. "And in that case, they'll make sure that you provide no evidence that would matter if it got back to the Russians."

"I'm glad you think so," I said. "But they're more devious than that. I suspect that the Stinnes committee want to use me as a blunt instrument to beat Bret across the head. That's the real reason I won't go."

"What do you mean?"

"That committee isn't called the 'Stinnes committee'—it's called the 'Rensselaer committee.' Was that a Freudian slip? Anyway, it's a good name because that committee isn't primarily interested in Stinnes except as a source of evidence about Bret. And if they finally get me over there, they won't want to know about how we enrolled Stinnes—they'll be asking me questions that might trap Bret."

"If Bret is guilty, what's wrong with that?"

"Let them provide their own evidence. They think I'll play ball with anything they want. They think I'll cooperate in order to prove that I'm whiter than the driven snow. Dicky more or less told me that. He said I should be pleased that suspicion has fallen on Bret because now they'd be less inclined to believe I was helping Fiona."

"I'm sure he didn't mean that," said Gloria.

"He meant it."

"You're determined to believe that the Department don't trust you. But there are no restrictions on you, none at all. I bring the daily sheets up from Registry. If there was any restriction on what you could see, I would know about it."

"Perhaps you're right," I said. "But there's still an undercurrent of suspicion. Perhaps it's just a way of keeping me under pressure, but I don't like it. And I don't like Dicky telling me that Bret's being convicted will let me breathe easy."

"Do you think the committee was convened by the Director-General as a way to investigate Bret Rensselaer?"

"The committee was the brainchild of someone higher up the ladder. The old man wouldn't be arranging for MI5 to help us wash the dirty linen unless he was ordered to do it that way."

"Higher up the ladder?"

"I see the hand of the Cabinet Office in this one. The Coordinator of Intelligence and Security is the only man who can tell both us and Five what he wants done. The D-G made it sound like his own idea so that the Department wouldn't feel humiliated."

"Humiliated by having MI5 investigate one of our people?"

"That's my guess," I said.

"If Bret is guilty, does it matter how they trap him?"

"If he's guilty. But there's not enough solid evidence for that. Either Bret is a super-agent who never makes a bad mistake or he's being victimized."

"Victimized by who?"

"You haven't seen at close quarters the sort of panic that develops when there's talk of an agent infiltrating the Department. There's hysteria. The other day Dicky was remembering all sorts of amazing ramifications of a trip to Kiel he made with Bret. Dicky was turning Bret's reaction to a KGB man into conclusive evidence against Bret. That's how the hysteria builds up."

"They say that where Bret went wrong was in the launderette," said Gloria.

"At first I thought so too. But now I'm inclined to see it as evidence in Bret's favor. The kid who came through the door shouted 'Go' to us. Why did he do that, unless he thought Bret was Stinnes? He was expecting someone to run off with them.

Everyone is trying to believe that it was something Bret arranged to eliminate Stinnes, but that doesn't make sense. It was planned as an escape; I see that now. And don't forget that Bret could have picked up that shotgun and killed me."

"And the bomb under the car?"

"Because they thought Bret was in the car."

"And you say that clears Bret?"

"I told you, those hoods were trying to spring Stinnes."

"Or to kidnap him," said Gloria.

"Not on a motorcycle. A back-seat passenger has to be willing to go along."

"If Bret is completely innocent, there's so much else to explain. What about the Cabinet memo that Bret sent to Moscow?"

"There's evidence that Bret's copy got to Moscow. But there was only one copy of that memo in the Department. Why shouldn't Fiona have sent a photocopy to Moscow? She had access."

"And then used it to frame Bret?"

"I'm only saying that all the evidence against Bret is circumstantial. We aren't certain that Moscow ever got the report that followed the memo. There isn't one really good piece of it that nails Bret beyond doubt."

"You can't have it both ways, Bernard. You say they put the bomb under the car in which Stinnes was sitting because they thought Bret was inside it. Either Moscow is going to immense trouble to frame Bret or else they tried to kill him. But those two actions are incompatible."

"Both actions would benefit Moscow. If that bomb had killed Bret, the Department would be in an even worse state of panic. As it is now, they have Bret under observation, they have a measure of control over who he sees and what he does. Everyone feels that if Bret is guilty, he'll fall prey to the interrogator, especially with Stinnes inventing some difficult questions for him. They're comforting themselves with the idea that Bret will cooperate fully with the investigation to avoid a long jail sentence. But if Bret was dead, things wouldn't look so rosy. There'd be no way to pull the chestnuts out of the fire. We'd have to be digging out all the material he'd handled, supervetting all Bret's contacts, and doing the same sort of complicated double-thinking that we did when Fiona went over there.''

"If a dead Bret is worse for us than a live Bret, why haven't they tried again?''

"They don't have hit teams waiting in the Embassy, sweetheart. Such killings have to be planned and authorized. A hit team has to be briefed and provided with false documentation. It all went wrong for them at the launderette, so now there will probably be some KGB officials arguing against trying again. It will take time.'' What I didn't say was that Fiona might be one of the people arguing against another attempt on Bret's life, for I suspected that Bret's life might depend upon what she decided.

"Do you think Bret knows he's in danger?''

"This is just one theory, Gloria. It could be wrong; Bret might be the KGB mole that everyone thinks he is.''

"Will they *make* you go before the committee?''

"The D-G won't want to go back to the Cabinet Office and say I'm being difficult, and yet the Coordinator is the only one who can order me to do it. I think the D-G will decide it's better to delay things and hope the committee will decide it can manage without me. In any case, I've got a breathing space. You know what the Department is like; if the committee insists on me attending, they'll have to put it in writing. Then I'll put my objections in writing too. In any case, nothing will happen until I come back from Berlin.''

"When are you going?'' said Gloria.

"Tomorrow.''

"Oh, Bernard. Couldn't it wait a week? There's so much I wanted to talk about with you.''

"Is there?'' I said, fully alerted. There was something in her voice, a plaintive note I recognized. "Is it something to do with that suitcase?''

"No," she said, quickly enough to indicate that she really meant yes.

"What's in it?"

"Clothes. I told you."

"More clothes? This house is full of your clothes now."

"It's not." Her voice was harsh and she was angry. And then, more rueful: "I knew you'd be beastly."

"You remember what we agreed, Gloria. We are not going to make this a permanent arrangement."

"I'm just your weekend girl, aren't I?"

"If that's the way you want to think about it. But there are no other girls, if that's what you mean."

"You don't care about me."

"Of course I do, but I must have just a bit of wardrobe space. Couldn't you take a few things back to your parents . . . and maybe rotate things as you need them?"

"I should have known you didn't love me."

"I do love you, but we can't live together, not all the week."

"Why?"

"There are all sorts of reasons . . . the children and Nanny and . . . well, I'm just not ready for that sort of permanent domestic scene. I must have breathing space. It's too soon after my wife left." The words came out in a torrent, none of them providing any real answer for her.

"You're frightened of the word 'marriage,' aren't you? That really frightens you."

"I'm not even divorced yet."

"You say you're worried about your wife getting custody of the children. If we were married, the court would be more sympathetic to the idea of you keeping them."

"Perhaps you're right, but you can't get married before you're divorced, and the court will not look favorably upon a bigamist."

"Or look favorably upon a father living with his mistress. So that's the reason?"

"I didn't say that."

"You treat me like a child. I hate you."

"We'll talk about it when I come back from Berlin. But there are other people involved in such a decision. Have you considered what your parents are likely to say to you if you moved in here?"

"What they'd say to you—that's what concerns you, doesn't it? You're worried about what my parents are going to say to you."

"Yes, I am concerned about them."

She began to cry.

"What's wrong, darling?" I said, although of course I knew what was wrong. "Don't be in such a hurry about everything. You're young."

"I've left my parents."

"What's that?"

"All my things are in the suitcase—my books, my pictures, the rest of my clothes. I had a terrible row with my mother, and my father took her side. He had to, I suppose. I understand why he did it. Anyway, I've had enough of them both. I packed my things and left them. I'm never going back."

I felt sick.

She went on: "I'm never going back to them. I told them that. My mother called me names. She said awful things about me, Bernard."

She was crying more seriously now and her head fell onto my shoulder and I could feel the warm wet tears on my bare skin. "Go to sleep, sweetheart. We'll talk about it tomorrow," I said. "The plane doesn't leave until lunchtime."

"I'm not staying here. You don't want me, you've told me that."

"For the time being . . ."

"I'm not staying here. I have someone I can go to. Don't worry, Bernard. By the time you come back from Berlin all my things will be out of here. At last I can see you as you really are."

She was still limp in my arms, still sobbing with a subdued

and desolate weariness, but I could hear the determination in her voice. There was no way she was going to stay except on promise of marriage and that was something I couldn't bring myself to give. She turned over to face away from me and hugged herself. She wouldn't be comforted. I remained awake a long time, but she went on sobbing very quietly. I knew there was nothing I could do. There is no sadness to compare with the grief of the young.

Chapter 24

BERLIN IS a somber city of gray stone. It is an austere Protestant town; the flamboyant excesses of South German baroque never got as far as Prussia's capital. The streets are as wide as the buildings are tall, so that the cityscape dwarfs people hurrying along the windswept streets, in a way that the skyscrapers of Manhattan do not overwhelm the human figure. Even Berlin's modern buildings seem hewn from stone, their glass façades mirroring the gray sky, monolithic and forbidding.

Inside Lisl Hennig's hotel the furniture had the same massive proportions that characterized the city. Solid, stately, and uncompromising, the oak tables, the heavy mahogany wardrobes, and the elegant Biedermeier cupboards and china cabinets of peach and pear wood dominated the house. Even in my little room at the top of the house, the corner cabinet and the chest of drawers, the carved chair and the bed built high upon several mattresses left little space to move from window to door.

I always slept in this room. It was the one I'd occupied as a child, when my family had the top floors assigned to them by the British Army of Occupation. From this window I'd floated my paper airplanes, blown soap bubbles, and dropped water bombs into the courtyard far below. Nowadays no one else wanted to use this dark cramped little box room so far from the bath. So the dark-brown floral patterned wallpaper remained, and over the tiny fireplace there still could be seen the framed engraving of medieval Dresden that Lisl Hennig had put there to hide the marks where Werner's air gun had been fired at a drawing of Herr Storch, the fat mathematics teacher. Storch had been a dedicated Nazi, but he had somehow managed to evade the denazification procedures and get his job back after the war.

I moved the picture to show Werner that the marks were still there. "Spat! spat! spat!" said Werner, firing an imaginary pistol at the place where the drawing of Storch had once been.

"You've got to hand it to him," I said without mentioning Storch by name. "He stuck to his views."

"He was a Nazi bastard," said Werner without rancor.

"And he did little to hide it," I said. The sky was black with storm clouds and now the rain began, huge drops of water that hit the glass with loud noises and made patterns on the dirty windowsill.

"Storch was cunning," said Werner. "He rephrased all his Nazi claptrap into anti-British and anti-American tirades. They could have put him inside for spreading Nazi ideas, but the British and the Americans kept telling everyone how much they believed in free speech. They couldn't do much about Storch." Werner was standing by the fireplace, fidgeting with the china figure of William Tell that had been relegated to this room after a maid had dropped it into the sink while cleaning it. The pieces had been stuck together with a glue that had oozed to make brown ridges around the arms and legs.

I'd been trying to find some suitable opportunity to tell Werner about Tessa's meeting with my wife and about her request for the children, but the right moment didn't come. "Do you ever see him? Herr Storch, do you ever see him?"

"He got married again," said Werner. "He married a widow

who had a watchmaker's shop in Munich." Werner was dressed in a dark-gray worsted jacket and the corduroy trousers that the Germans call *Manchesterhosen.* His shirt was green and with it he wore a green polyester tie with little red horses. On the hook behind the door he'd hung a tired old gray raincoat. I knew he had an appointment with some East Bloc bank officials that afternoon, but even if he hadn't told me, I would have guessed he was going over to the East; he always wore such proletarian clothes when going there. His long black coat with its astrakhan collar and the kind of tailored wool suits he preferred, to say nothing of his taste in shoes, would have been too conspicuous in the streets of East Berlin.

"Trust Storch to fall on his feet."

"He made your life hell," said Werner.

"No, I wouldn't say that."

"All that extra homework, and always making you come out to the front of the class and do the geometry at the black-board."

"It was good for me. I was top for mathematics two years running. My dad was amazed." There was a crash of thunder and a blue flash of lightning.

"Even then, old Storch kept on at you."

"He hated the English. His son was killed fighting in the Libyan Desert. He told the boys in the top class that the English had shot all their prisoners."

"That was just propaganda," said Werner.

"You don't have to spare my feelings," I said. "There are bastards everywhere, Werner. We both know that."

"Storch didn't have to take it out on you."

"I was the only *Engländer* he could get his hands on."

"I've never heard you say a bad word about old Storch."

"He was a tough-minded old bastard," I said. "He must have known that one word to my dad about him having been a storm trooper would have got him kicked out of his job, but he didn't seem to care."

"I would have squealed on him," said Werner.

"You hated him more than I did."

"Don't you remember all that poisonous stuff about Jewish profiteers, and the way he stared at me all the time?"

"And you said, 'Don't look at me, sir, my father was a gravedigger.'"

"That was when old Herr Grossmann was away on sick leave, and Storch did the history lessons." A long roll of thunder sounded as the storm moved over the city and headed for Poland, such a short drive down the road. Werner scowled. "All Storch knew about history was what he'd read in his Nazi propaganda—about how the Jewish profiteers had made Germany lose the war and ruined the economy. They should never have let a bigot like that take the history class."

"I think I know what you're going to say, Werner."

Werner sat down on the sagging armchair, smiled at me, and, although I knew what was coming, he said it anyway. "One man was the very worst scoundrel, he told us. Already rich— he amassed a second fortune in a few months. He borrowed from the central bank to buy coal mines, private banks, paper mills, and newspapers. And he paid back the loans in money so devalued by inflation that this whole spread cost him almost nothing."

"Hugo Stinnes," I said. "It sounds like you've been looking at the encyclopedia, Werner. Yes, I was thinking of that long passionate lecture from old Storch only the other day."

"So why would some Russian bastard with a KGB assignment choose a name like Stinnes as an operating name?"

"I wish I knew," I said.

"Hugo Stinnes was a German capitalist, a class enemy, obsessed by the threat of world Bolshevism. What kind of joke is it for a Russian KGB man to choose that name?"

"What kind of man would choose it?" I said.

"A very, very confident Communist," said Werner. "A man who was so trusted by his KGB masters that he could select such a name without fear of being contaminated by it."

"Did you only think of that now?" I asked.

"Right from the time I first heard the name it seemed a curious choice for a Communist agent. But now—now that so much depends upon his loyalty—I think of it again. And I worry."

I said, "Yes, the same with me, Werner."

Werner paused and, using his little finger, scratched his bushy eyebrows. "When the Nazi party sent Dr. Goebbels to open their first office in Berlin, they used that little back cellar in Potsdamer Platz that belonged to Storch's uncle. It was a filthy hole; the Nazis called it 'the opium den.' They say Storch's uncle let them have it without paying rent and in return Storch got a nice little job with the party."

I looked at the rain as it polished the roofs of the buildings across the courtyard. The roofs were tilted, crippled, and humpbacked, like an illustration from "Hansel and Gretel." My mind was not on old Herr Storch any more than Werner's was. I said, "Why not use his real name—Sadoff—why use a German name at all? And if a German name, why Stinnes?"

"It raises a lot of questions," said Werner as his mind went another way. "If Stinnes was planted solely as a way of giving us false information, then the Miller woman was used only to support that trick."

"That's not difficult to believe, Werner," I said. "Now that we know she wasn't drowned in the Havel, now that we know she's safe and well and working for the East German government, I've changed my mind about the whole business."

"The whole business? Her collecting that material from the car at the big party in Wannsee? Did she want to get arrested that night when we set it up so carefully and were so pleased with ourselves? Was that confession she gave you at some length—was it all set up?"

"To implicate Bret? Yes, the Miller woman made a fool of me, Werner. I believed everything she told me about the two code words. I went back to London convinced that there was another agent in London Central. I disobeyed orders. I went and talked to Brahms Four. I was convinced that someone in

London Central—probably Bret—was a prime KGB agent."

"It looked that way," said Werner. He was being kind, as always. He could see how upset I was.

"It did to me. But no one else was fooled. You told me again and again. Dicky turned up his nose at the idea, and Silas Gaunt got angry when I suggested it. I even began to wonder if there was a big cover-up. But the truth is that they weren't fooled by her and her story, and I was."

"Don't blame yourself, Bernard. They didn't see her. She was convincing, I know."

"She made a fool of me. She had nicotine stains on her fingers and no cigarettes! She had inky fingers and no fountain pen! She drowns, but we find no body. How could I be so stupid! A clerk from East Berlin; yes, of course. Everyone in London Central was right and I was wrong. I feel bad about that, Werner. I have more field experience that any of those people. I should have seen through her. Instead I went round doing exactly what they wanted done."

"It wasn't like that, Bernie, and you know it. Silas Gaunt and Dicky and the rest of them didn't argue with you or give any reasons. They wouldn't believe your theory because it would have been too inconvenient to believe it."

"Then Posh Harry gave me documents that supported the idea that there was a mole in London Central."

"You're not saying Posh Harry was in on it?"

"I don't think so. Posh Harry was a carefully selected go-between. They used him the way we've used him so often. That was probably Fiona's idea."

"It's the very hell of a complicated scenario they had," said Werner, rubbing his face. "Are you sure that you've got it right now? Would it be worth them going to all that trouble? When you got Stinnes out of Mexico City, you nearly got killed doing it. A KGB man from the Embassy was shot."

"That shooting was an accident, Werner. Pavel Moskvin was the one who gave me a tough time in East Berlin. If Stinnes is a plant, then Moskvin is the man behind it. I can't prove it, of course, but Moskvin is the sort of hard-nosed Party man that Moscow has monitoring and masterminding all their important departments."

"You think Moskvin planted him without any contacts or case officer or letter drop? You think Stinnes is all on his own?"

" 'Solitaries,' the Russians call them; agents whose real loyalties are known to only one or two people at the very top of the command structure. The only record of their assignment is a signed contract locked in a safe in Moscow. Sometimes when such people die, despised and unlamented, even their close relatives—wife, husband, children—aren't told the real story."

"But Stinnes left his wife. He'd even had a fight with her."

"Yes," I said, "and that convinced me that he really wanted to come over to the West. But the fight was genuine—his story false. We should have allowed for that possibility, I suppose."

"So now you think Stinnes is a solitary?" said Werner.

"For them the solitary isn't so unusual, Werner. Communism has always glamorized secrecy; it's the Communist method: subversion, secret codes, cover names, secret inks, no agent permitted to contact more than two other agents, cells to make sure that one lost secret doesn't lead to the loss of another. All these things are not exclusively Russian, and not peculiar to the KGB; this sort of secrecy comes naturally to *any* Communist. It's part of the appeal that worldwide Communism has for the embittered loner. If my guess is right, Moskvin is the only other person who knows the whole story. They probably didn't tell the truth to the snatch team that hit the launderette. The KGB would reason that just one extra person knowing the real story would increase the risk of us discovering that Stinnes was a plant."

"A man who sacrificed himself? Is Stinnes that sort of man?" said Werner. "I'd marked him down as a hard-nosed and ambitious opportunist. I'd say Stinnes is the sort of man who sends others off to sacrifice themselves while he stays behind and gets the promotions."

Werner had hit upon the thing that I found most difficult to reconcile with the facts. Right from the time when Stinnes started talking about coming over to the West I'd found it difficult to believe in his sincerity. The Stinneses of the KGB didn't come West—not as defectors, not as agents, and especially not as solitaries who'd spend the rest of their days unrewarded, unloved, and uninvolved with the job, acting out a role in which they had no belief. As Werner said, Stinnes was the sort who dispatched others to that kind of fate.

"When Moscow wants him back, they'll find a way to get him," I said.

"I'll go along with your theory," said Werner grudgingly. "But you won't convince many others. They like it the way it is. You tell me London Central have practically written Bret off. The Stinnes committee are just getting into their stride. If what you say about Stinnes is correct, they're all going to wind up with egg on their faces, a lot of egg on their faces. You'll need some solid evidence before going back there and trying to convince them that Stinnes is a plant. That's a combined-services committee, and they're telling each other that Stinnes is the greatest break they've had in years. You'll have a lot of trouble convincing them that they've fallen for a KGB misinformation stunt."

"More than just a stunt, Werner," I said. "If Stinnes blows a big hole in London Central, forces the Department to compromise with Five, spatters a little blood over me, and has Bret facing a departmental enquiry, I'd call that a KGB triumph of the first order."

"I've been in front of that committee," said Werner. "They'll believe what they want to believe. Rock that boat and you'll be the one who falls into the water and drowns. I'd advise you to keep your theories to yourself. Keep right out of it, Bernie."

There was more thunder, fainter now as the storm abated, and trickles of sunlight dribbled through the cloud.

"I *am* keeping out of it," I said. "I told Dicky I wouldn't go to the committee without detailed written instructions."

Werner looked at me wondering if it was a joke. When he realized it wasn't, he said, "That was silly, Bernie. You should have done what I did. You should have gone through the motions: smiled at their greetings, laughed at their little jokes, accepted one of their cigarettes, and listened to their idiot comments while trying to look enthralled. You refused? They'll regard you as hostile after that. What are they going to think if you go to them now and say that Stinnes is a phony?"

"What are they going to think?" I said.

"They're going to resurrect all their darkest suspicions of you," said Werner. "Someone on that committee is sure to say that you might be a KGB agent trying to rescue Bret and trying to wreck the wonderful job that the Stinnes debriefing is doing."

"I brought Stinnes in," I said.

"Because you had no alternative. Don't you remember the way certain people said you were dragging your feet?" He looked at his watch, a stainless-steel one, not his usual gold model. "I really must be going."

He had plenty of time, but he was nervous. Werner made a lot of money from his completely legitimate banking deals, but he was always nervous before going East. Sometimes I wondered if it was worth it. "Where's your car?"

"It's just a quick one. Some signatures to show that goods have arrived over there. The quicker I get the receipts, the quicker I get paid, and with bank charges the way they are . . . I'll go over on the S-Bahn. Once I arrive at Friedrichstrasse, it's only five minutes."

"I'll walk down to Zoo Station and see you onto the train," I said. I still hadn't told him about Fiona and the children.

"Stay here, Bernie. You'll get wet."

When we went downstairs, Lisl Hennig was sitting in the dining room. It was a large airy room overlooking the gloomy courtyard. The paneling had been painted cream and so had some of the cupboards. There was an old Oriental rug to cover worn lino just inside the doorway, and there were framed prints on the walls—scenes of German rural life—and one tiny picture that was different from the rest. It was a George Grosz drawing, a picture of a deformed soldier, a war veteran made grotesque by his injuries. It was full of rage and spite and despair so that the artist's lines attacked the paper. Lisl was sitting near the drawing, at a table near the window. She was always there about noon. On the table there was the usual pile of newspapers. She couldn't live without newspapers—she was obsessed by them, and woe betide anyone who interrupted her reading. Her mornings were always spent in going through them all, column by column: news, adverts, gossip, theatre, concert reviews, share prices, and even the classified adverts. Now she had finished her papers; now she was sociable again.

"Werner, darling. Thank you for the beautiful flowers, *Lieb-chen.* Come and give your Lisl a kiss." He did so. She looked him up and down. "It's freezing cold outside. You won't be warm enough in that raincoat, darling. It's terrible weather." Did she recognize Werner's clothes as those he wore when visiting the East? "You should be wearing your heavy coat."

She was a big woman and the old-fashioned black silk dress with a lacy front did nothing to disguise her bulk. Her hair was lacquered, her once-pretty face was heavily but carefully painted, and there was too much mascara on her eyelashes. Backstage in a theatre her appearance would have gone un-remarked, but in the cold hard light of noon she looked rather grotesque. "Sit down and have coffee," she commanded with a regal movement of her hand.

Werner looked at his watch, but he sat down as he was told. Lisl Hennig had protected his Jewish parents, and after Werner was orphaned she brought him up as if he was her one and only son. Although neither of them displayed much sign of deep affection, there was a bond between them that was unbreakable. Lisl commanded; Werner obeyed.

"Coffee, Klara!" she called. *"Zweimal!"* There was a re-sponse from some distant part of the kitchen as her "girl" Klara

—only marginally younger than Lisl—acknowledged the imperious command.

Lisl was eating her regular lunch: a small piece of cheese, two wholemeal wafers, an apple, and a glass of milk. Except for her, the dining room was empty. There were about a dozen tables, each set with cutlery and wineglass and a plastic rose, but only one table had linen napkins and this was the only one likely to be used that lunchtime. Not many of Lisl's guests ate lunch; some of them were semipermanent residents, out at work all day, and the rest were the kind of salesmen who couldn't afford lunch at Lisl's or anywhere else. "Did you bring me what I asked you to bring me?" Lisl asked Werner.

"I forgot, Lisl. I am very sorry." Werner was embarrassed.

"You have more important things to do," said Lisl, with that smile of martyrdom that was calculated to twist the knife in poor Werner's wound.

"I'll get it now," said Werner, rising to his feet.

"What is it?" I said. "I'll get it for you, Lisl. Werner has an important appointment. I'm walking up to Zoo Station. What can I bring back for you?" In fact, I guessed what it was; it was an eyebrow pencil. Whatever other elements of her makeup Lisl found necessary, none compared with the eyebrow pencil. Ever since her arthritis made shopping difficult for her, Werner had been entrusted with buying her makeup from the KaDeWe department store. But it was a secret, a secret with which even I was not officially entrusted; I knew only because Werner told me.

"Werner will get it for me. It is not important," said Lisl.

Klara brought a tray with a jug of coffee and the best cups and saucers, the ones with the sunflower pattern, and some *Kipfel* on a silver platter. Klara knew that the little crescent-shaped shortcakes were Werner's favorite.

A man in a smart brown leather jacket and gray slacks came into the dining room and deposited his shoulder bag on a chair. It was at the table where the linen napkins had been arranged. He smiled at Lisl and left without speaking.

"Westies," explained Lisl, using the Berlin word for tourists from West Germany. "They eat lunch here every day."

"The family with the grown-up sons; I saw them in the lobby," said Werner. Even without hearing an accent, Berliners were always able to recognize such visitors, and yet it was hard to say in what way they were any different from Berliners. The faces were more or less the same, the clothing equally so, but there was something in the manner that distinguished them from "Islanders," as the West Berliners referred to themselves.

"They hate us," said Lisl, who was always prone to exaggerate.

"Westies hate us? Don't be silly," said Werner. He looked at his watch again and drank some coffee.

"They hate us. They blame us for everything bad that happens."

"They blame you for their high taxes," I said. "A lot of West Germans begrudge the subsidies needed to keep Berlin solvent. But all over the world big cities are funded from central government."

"There is more to it than that," said Lisl. "Even the word 'Berlin' is disliked and avoided in the Bundesrepublik. If they want a name for a soap or a scent or a radio or a motorcar, they might name such things 'New York' or 'Rio' or 'Paris,' but the word 'Berlin' is the universal turnoff, the name that no one wants."

"They don't hate us," said Werner. "But they blame us for everything that happens in the cold war. No matter that Bonn and Moscow are making the decisions—Berlin takes the blame." Werner was diplomat enough to take Lisl's side.

"I don't know about that," I said. "Bonn gets more than its fair share of knocks and pays out more than its fair share of money."

"Does it?" said Lisl. She was unconvinced. She hated to pay her taxes.

I said, "Conveniently for the D.D.R., there is only one Germany when someone wants German money. Reparations to

Israel didn't come from both halves of Germany—only from the West half. After the war the debts incurred by Hitler's Third Reich were not shared—only the West half settled them. And now, whenever the D.D.R. offers to set free political prisoners in exchange for money, it's the West half that pays the ransoms to the East half. But when anyone anywhere in the world wants to express their prejudice about Germans, they don't tell you how much they hate those Germans in the East—who suffer enough already; all anti-German feeling is directed against the overtaxed, overworked Westies, who prop up the overpaid, incompetent bureaucrats of the Common Market and finance its ever-increasing surplus so it can sell more and more bargain-priced wine and butter to the Russians."

"Bernard has become a Westie," said Lisl. It was a joke, but there was not much humor there. Werner gobbled the last *Kipfel* and got up and said goodbye to her. Lisl didn't respond to our arguments or to our kisses. She didn't like Westies even when they had lunch every day.

With Werner, I walked along Kantstrasse to Zoo Station. The rain had stopped, but the trees dripped disconsolately. There was more rain in the air. The station was busy as usual, the forecourt crowded, a group of Japanese tourists taking photos of each other, a man and woman—both in ankle-length fur coats—buying picture postcards, a boy and girl with stiff dyed hair and shiny leather trousers singing tunelessly to the strumming of a guitar, French soldiers loaded with equipment climbing into a truck, two arty-looking girls selling pictures made from beads, an old man with a pony collecting money for animal welfare, a young bearded man asleep in a doorway, an expensively dressed mother holding a small child at arms length while it vomited in the gutter, and two young policemen not noticing anything. It was the usual mix for Zoo Station. This was the middle of the Old World. Here were Berlin's commuter trains and here too were trains that had come direct from Paris and went on to Warsaw and Moscow.

I went inside with Werner and bought a ticket so that I could accompany him up to the platform. The S-Bahn is Berlin's ancient elevated railway network and the simplest way to get from the centre of West Berlin (Zoo) to the heart of East Berlin (Friedrichstrasse). It was chilly up there on the platform; the trains rattled through, bringing a swirl of damp air and a stirring of wastepaper. The stations are like huge glass aircraft hangars, and like the tracks themselves they are propped up above street level on ornate cast-iron supports.

"Don't worry about Lisl's eyebrow pencil," I told Werner. "I'll get that for her on the way back."

"Do you know the color she wants?"

"Of course I do. You're always forgetting to get them."

"I hope you're wrong about Stinnes," said Werner.

"You forget about all that," I said. "You get over there and get your papers signed and get back. Forget about me and the Department. Forget all that stuff until you get back."

"I think I might stay the night," said Werner. "There's someone I must see in the morning, and there are long lines at the passport control if I come through when everyone's coming back from the opera."

A Friedrichstrasse train came in, but Werner let it go. I had the feeling that he didn't want to go over. That was unusual for Werner; he might get jumpy, but he never seemed to mind going over there. Sometimes I had the feeling that he liked the break it made for him. He got away from Zena and lived his own bachelor life in the comfortable apartment he'd created over a truck garage. Now he lingered. It was a perfect chance for me to tell him how Fiona had gone to Holland and talked to Tessa about having the children with her. But I didn't tell him.

"Where will you eat tonight?" I said, as my contribution to the kind of conversation that takes place at railway stations and airports.

"There are some people I know in Pankow," said Werner. "They've invited me."

"Do I know them?" I said.

"No," said Werner. "You don't know them."

"What time tomorrow?"

"Don't fuss, Bernie. Sometimes you're worse than Lisl."

The train arrived. "Take care," I said as he stepped into it.

"It's all legit, Bernie."

"But maybe they don't know that," I said.

Werner grinned and then the doors closed and the train pulled away. It felt very very cold on the platform after the train had departed, but that might just have been my imagination.

Chapter 25

AT MIDNIGHT the front door to Lisl Hennig's hotel was locked. That had always been the routine, ever since I could remember. Any hotel guest who occasionally returned after that time was given a key on request. Any guest frequently returning after that time was asked to find another hotel.

Guests arriving there after midnight without a key had to tug the old bellpull. You couldn't hear the bell from outside in the street and sometimes guests made a great deal of noise before they got in. I couldn't hear the bell from my little garret room at the very top of the house. Lisl could hear the bell. She slept downstairs—she'd been sleeping downstairs ever since her arthritis had got really bad. Lisl never went down to open the door, of course; just that one flight of stone stairs, from the salon to the front hall, was something she didn't attempt very often. One of the servants opened the door if the bell rang. They took it in turns. Usually it was Klara, but on that night after Werner went over to the East it was Richard, a youngish man from Bremen who worked in the kitchen. Klara was not out that night, of course—she was in bed and asleep and awakened by the bell as always. But when she was off duty, she was off duty, and she just turned over and forgot about it.

So it was Richard who went down to the front door when the bell sounded at 2:30 a.m. It was dark and still raining, and Richard took with him the wooden bat used for flattening slices of veal to make Wiener schnitzels. As he said afterwards, he knew that there were no guests still not back and he wanted something to defend himself with.

So it was Richard who woke me up out of a deep sleep in which I was dreaming about old Mr. Storch, who was making me recite a poem about Hitler. It was a silly dream in which I knew no poems about Hitler except a rude one which I was frightened to tell Mr. Storch.

"A gentleman to see you, sir," said Richard, having shaken me by the shoulder and put Storch and my classmates to flight. "There's a gentleman to see you." He said it in English. I suspected that he'd got it from one of those film butlers because he had exactly the right accent and inflection whereas the rest of his English was appalling.

"Who?" I said. I switched on the bedside light. Its yellow plastic shade made patterns on the wall and its light made Richard look jaundiced and ferocious.

"It's me." I put my glasses on and looked toward the doorway. It was Bret Rensselaer. I could hardly believe my eyes. For a moment I thought it was all a part of my dream. I got out of bed and put on my dressing gown.

"My God, Bret, what are you doing in Berlin?" I said. "It's okay," I told Richard. "It's a friend of mine."

As Richard left and closed the door, Bret stepped into the light. He was hardly recognizable. This wasn't the Bret I knew. His dark overcoat was so soaked with rain that it was dripping pools onto the ancient carpet. There was mud on his shoes. He had no necktie and his shirt was dirty and open at the throat. His staring eyes were deep sunk into his ashen face and he needed a shave badly.

"You look like you could do with a drink," I said, opening the corner cupboard where I had a bottle of duty-free Johnnie

Walker and some glasses. I poured him a big shot of whisky. He almost snatched it from me and drank a couple of gulps.

"I had to find you, Bernard. You're the only one who can help me."

Was this really Bret Rensselaer? I never thought I'd see the day when Bret was asking anyone for help, let alone asking me. "What's wrong, Bret?"

"You're the only one I can trust anymore."

"Sit down," I said. "Get out of that wet coat and take the weight off your feet."

He did as I told him, moving with the shambling robotic pace of the sleepwalker. "They'll go for you too," said Bret.

"Start at the beginning, Bret," I said.

But he was too tired to understand. He didn't look up at me; he was slumped on the chair studying his muddy shoes. "They arrested me." He said it very quietly so that I had to lean close to him to hear.

"Who did?"

"A team from Five . . . it was all kosher. They had all the documentation . . . even a chit from the Deputy with the two authorized signatures."

"Morgan had signed?"

"Yes, Morgan had signed. But it's not all Morgan's doing; they've got a whole file on me."

I poured myself a drink while I pulled my thoughts together. Was Bret admitting to me that he was a KGB mole? Had he come to me convinced that I was a KGB agent too? And how the hell was I going to find out? I sipped the drink and felt the warmth of it slide down my throat. It didn't make my thinking any clearer, but it was waking me up in the best possible way. "What now?" I said tentatively. "How can I help?"

"It all began when the committee went down to Berwick House," said Bret, as if he hadn't heard my question. "Some of them wanted to be present at an interrogation. There had been a lot of argument about whether Stinnes was really cooperating or just playing us along. Ladbrook was there. Ladbrook's straight, you know that."

I nodded. Ladbrook was the senior interrogator. He kept out of office politics as much as possible.

"We used one of the big downstairs rooms; there wasn't room for everyone in the recording room." Bret held out his glass for another drink. I poured him one, a small one this time. He didn't drink it right away. He swirled it round in his hands. Bret said, "The interrogation was concerned with codes and communications. I wasn't listening all that closely at first; I figured that it was all stuff I'd heard before. But then I realized that Stinnes was offering some goodies. Five had one of their communications boffins assigned to the committee just for that sequence, and he got excited. He didn't jump up and down and sing 'Rule, Britannia!' but he might have if there'd been more legroom."

"Stuff you hadn't heard before?"

"Really good material, Bernard. Stinnes started out by offering us the whole signals procedures at the Embassy, and the boffin from Five asked some questions that Stinnes answered easily and unequivocally. This was a different sort of Stinnes I was seeing; he was smooth and charming and polite and deferential. He cut a hell of a good figure with them. Jokes too. They were even laughing, and Stinnes was more at ease than I'd ever seen him before. Then one of the Five people said it was a pity that he hadn't given us some of this material a few weeks earlier because there were sure to be signals alterations anytime now, in the light of Stinnes changing sides. And Stinnes calmly said that he'd told me all this stuff in the first days I saw him."

"And you denied it?"

Bret's voice was shrill. "He never gave us any of that hard intelligence. He didn't give it to me, he didn't give it to Ladbrook, and he didn't give it to you."

"So what was your reaction?"

"I'm the chairman of that lousy committee. What am I supposed to do, call myself to order and appoint a subcommittee?

I let it roll. What could I do, except sit there and listen to all that crap."

"And they swallowed it?"

A thought struck Bret Rensselaer. "He didn't tell you any of that stuff, did he? Codes and communications? Embassy contact lists? Foreign country routings? Signals room security? Did he tell you any of that? For God's sake . . ."

"No, he didn't tell me any of that," I said.

"Thank Christ for that." He wiped his brow. "There are moments when I wonder if I'm tipping off my trolley."

"They arrested you?"

"That wasn't until two days later. From what I heard afterwards, it seems that the people from Five got together that night for some kind of council. They were excited, Bernard, and convinced. They hadn't seen Stinnes before. All they knew about him was this smooth, dynamic guy who's falling over himself trying to give away Soviet secrets. What are they supposed to think except that I've been sitting on him?"

"And Ladbrook?"

"He's a good man, Bernard. Apart from you, Ladbrook is the only person who can see what's really going on. But that won't make any difference. Ladbrook will tell them the truth, but that won't help me."

"What will he say?"

Bret looked up with alarm and annoyance. I had become the interrogator now, but there was nothing he could do about that; I was his last hope. "He'll say that Stinnes has given us only operational material."

"Good operational material," I said. It wasn't a statement, it wasn't a question; it was a bit of both.

"Wonderful operational material," said Bret sarcastically. "But every time we acted on it, things seemed to go unaccountably wrong."

"They'll say that was your fault," I said. And to some extent it *was* his fault: Bret had wanted to show everyone what a fine field agent he might have made, and he'd failed.

"Of course they will. That's the brilliance of it. There is just no way of proving whether we did it wrong or if it was material arranged to fail right from the word go."

I said, "Stinnes is a plant. A solitary. His briefing must have been lengthy and complex. That's why it took so long to get him to move. That's why he went back to Berlin before coming out to Mexico again."

"Thanks, buddy," said Bret. "Where were you when we needed you?"

"It's easy to see it now," I admitted. "But it looked okay at the time. And some of the stuff was good."

"Those early arrests in Hannover, the dead-letter drops, the kid in our office in Hamburg. Yes, it was good, but it wasn't anything they couldn't spare."

"How did they arrest you?"

"Five sent two men from K7 who searched my house. That was Tuesday . . . no, maybe Monday . . . I've lost all track of time."

"They found nothing?"

"What do you think they found?" said Bret angrily. "A radio transmitter, invisible ink, and one-time pads?"

"I just want to get the facts straight," I said.

"It's a frame-up," said Bret. "I thought you were the one person who'd see that."

"I do see it. I just wanted to know if there was anything planted at the house."

"Shit," said Bret. He went pale. "Now I remember!"

"What?"

"They took a suitcase out of the loft."

"What was in it?"

"Papers."

"What papers?"

"I don't know, typewritten paper, reams of it. They took them away to examine them. There were several pieces of baggage in the loft. I thought they were all empty."

"And now one is full of papers. Any recent visitors to the house?"

"No, none. Not for weeks."

"No repairmen or telephone wiring?"

"A man came to fix the phone, but that was okay. I had our own engineers out the next day to check the house."

"Check the house for bugs and wires, not check the house for suitcases full of papers."

He bit his lip. "I was a fool."

"It sounds as if you were, Bret. They would put your phone on the blink and then turn up."

"That's right. They arrived just after I had trouble—they said they were in the street, working on the lines. It was a Saturday. I said I didn't know you guys work on Saturdays."

"The KGB work a long week, Bret," I said.

"He can't sustain it," said Bret, hoping that I would agree. He was talking about Stinnes. I didn't answer. "It's a bravura performance and the committee are eating out of his hand right now. But he can't sustain it."

"When did they arrest you?"

"First the senior grade officer from K7 came to my home. He told me I wasn't to leave the house."

"Your house?"

"I wasn't to go to the office. I wasn't even to go to the shops in the village."

"What did you say?"

"I couldn't believe my ears. I told him to remain in the room with me while I phoned the office. I tried to get the D-G, but Sir Henry was on a train going to Manchester."

"Clever Sir Henry," I said.

"No, it was genuine enough. His secretary tried to reach him with messages at both ends."

"Are you crazy, Bret? Five send a K7 search and arrest team to pick up a senior officer, and the D-G just happens to have another appointment that he can't break and no contact number? Are you telling me the D-G wasn't in on the secret?"

Bret looked at me. He didn't want to believe they could do that to him. Or that they would want to. Bret didn't just happen to be born in England like the rest of us—Bret was an Anglophile. He loved every blade of bright green grass that Shake-speare might have trodden on. "I suppose you're right," he said at last.

"And you skipped?"

"I left a message saying that I urgently wanted an appointment with the D-G and gave my phone number. I said I'd stay by the phone and wait for the call."

"And then you took off. That was good, Bret," I said with genuine admiration. "That's what I would have done. But they'll have you on the airline manifest even if Immigration didn't identify you."

"I have a friend with a Cessna," said Bret.

He needn't have told me that, and I felt reassured that he was prepared to fill in the details. "Did they leave anyone outside the house?" Bret shrugged. "Do you think they tailed you?"

"I changed cars."

"And the watchers don't run to anything that could follow a Cessna, so they'll be trying to trace the plane landing."

"I flew to Hamburg and then came on by car. I rented the car in a false name. Luckily the girl at the counter didn't read the driving license carefully."

"You can't win them all, Bret. You forgot about the computer on the autobahn entrance point. They even get traffic violators on that one."

"I'm innocent, Bernard."

"I know you are, Bret. But it's going to be tough proving it. Did anyone say anything about a Cabinet memo?"

"Cabinet memo?"

"They're trying to lock you up tight, Bret. There is a Cabinet memo; the numbered copy is the one to which you had access. It's been to Moscow and back again."

"Are you serious?"

"And a lot of people have been told about it since then."

"Who?"

"I was singled out to be shown a copy, and so was Dicky

Cruyer. You can bet there were others. The implication is that the full report went to Moscow too."

"I should have been told."

"You're not wrestling only with Stinnes," I said. "You've got the whole of Moscow Centre to contend with, and they've spent a lot of time working on it."

He drank a tiny sip of whisky as if he didn't trust himself any longer. He didn't ask what it was all about or anything like that. He'd had a lot of time to think what it was all about. He must have known by that time that his chances of getting out of it and becoming Mr. Clean again were very slim. The sea was rough. Bret was going down for the third time and there was every chance he'd take me with him. "So what do I do, Bernard?"

"Suppose I said, 'Turn yourself in'?"

"I wouldn't do that."

"Suppose *I* turned you in?"

"You wouldn't do that," said Bret. He looked away from me, as if meeting my eyes would increase the chances of my saying I would turn him in.

"What makes you so sure?" I said.

"Because you're an egomaniac. You're cynical and intractable. You're the only son of a bitch in that Department who'd take the rest of them on single-handed."

It wasn't exactly what I wanted to hear, but it was sincere enough and that would have to do. "We don't have a lot of time. They'll trace you right to this room. Getting into Berlin without leaving a track is almost impossible, unless you come in from the East, in which case no records are kept."

"I never thought of it like that," said Bret. "That's crazy, isn't it?"

"Yes, it is, but we don't have time to write to Ripley about it. We don't have time to do anything very much. I'd say that London Central will trace you to Berlin, and maybe to me at this hotel, within two or three days."

"Are you saying what I think you're saying?"

"Yes. We'll have to talk to Frank. The only other course is

for you to leave town very quickly. Why did you come here, Bret?"

"I decided that you were the only person who could help."

"You'll have to do better than that, Bret," I said.

"And I have money here," he said. I continued to stare at him. "And a gun."

"Honesty is the best policy, Bret," I said.

"You knew, did you?"

"Not about the money. But when a senior officer does anything unusual in Berlin I like to know, and there are people who know I like to know."

"Who the hell told you about the gun?"

"Buying a gun is very unusual, Bret," I said. "Especially for a man who can sign a docket and get one across the counter from Frank Harrington."

"So Frank knows too?"

"I didn't tell him."

"Will Frank turn me in?"

"Let's not tempt him too much. Suppose I go along and talk to him while you stay out of sight?"

"I'd appreciate that."

"Frank could defy the Department for weeks, and if Five sent anyone here, Frank has authority enough to have them refused entry at the airport. If we got Frank on our side . . ."

"It would start looking good," said Bret appreciatively.

"Not good, Bret, but a bit less bloody doomy."

"So you'll see Frank in the morning?"

"I'll see Frank now. We haven't got enough time for luxuries like night and day. And at night we won't have his secretarial staff to get an eyeful of you and me talking to him. If we see him on his own and he says 'No deal,' we might persuade him to forget he ever saw us. But once his secretary enters it in the appointment diary, it will be more difficult to deny."

"He'll be asleep." Bret obviously thought it would prejudice our chances of success to wake Frank from a deep dreamless slumber.

"Frank never sleeps."

"He'll be with a girl? Is that what you mean?"

"Now you're getting warmer."

Chapter 26

FRANK Harrington, Berlin Resident and head of Berlin Field Unit, was not asleep. He was sitting on the floor of the large drawing room of his magnificent house at Grunewald surrounded by records. On every side of him there were piles of Duke Ellington records while music played on his hi-fi. "Frenesi"—it was a lush orchestral arrangement into which the vocalist sang: "A long time ago I wandered down into old Mexico . . ." Or was it something quite different? Was it just that I still felt bad about the way in which I'd contrived that the Stinnes enrollment had taken place in Mexico, rather than in Berlin where Frank would have got a measure of the credit? Whatever the music, I still felt guilty at having deprived Frank of that "mention" and self-conscious about asking him for help in matters arising from that same event. ". . . Stars were shining bright and I could hear romantic voices in the night . . ."

Frank's valet, the inscrutable Tarrant, showed me in. He was wearing his dressing gown and his hair was slightly disarranged, but he gave no sign of being surprised by this visit in the small hours of the morning. I suppose Frank's frequent love affairs had provided Tarrant with enough surprises to last a lifetime.

"Bernard," said Frank very calmly, as if I often visited him in the small hours. "What about a drink?" He had a record in his hand. Like all the other records it was in a pristine plain-white jacket with a number written in the corner. He hesitated before placing it on one of the piles, then he looked up at me. "Whisky and water?"

"Yes, please. Shall I help myself?"

There was a cut-glass tumbler on the drinks trolley, some ice cubes in it not yet melted, and traces of bright lipstick on its rim. I picked it up and sniffed at it. "Campari and orange juice," said Frank as he watched me. "Still playing detectives, Bernard?"

There had been another visitor—obviously female—but Frank did not supply her name. "Force of habit," I said. Campari and orange juice was one of Zena Volkmann's favorite drinks.

"It must be urgent." He didn't get up from where he was sitting in the middle of the carpet. He reached for his pipe and tobacco pouch and for the big ashtray that was already half filled with ash and unburned tobacco.

"Yes," I said. "It was good of you to let me come right away."

"You didn't give me much chance to decline." He said it ruefully. Had he sent her away on my account or was she waiting for him upstairs in the bedroom? Was it Zena Volkmann or just some girl he'd met at a frantic Berlin party as he met so many of the females with whom he got entangled?

"The Stinnes committee have gone mad," I said.

"Don't sit there!" It was a shout, almost a cry of pain. "They're my very earliest ones. I'd die if one of those was damaged."

"This is your Ellington collection, is it?" I asked, looking at the records everywhere.

"The only chance I get is at night. I'm shipping them to England. I have to have them valued for the insurance. It's not easy to put a price on the rare ones."

I paused politely and then said again, "The Stinnes committee have gone crazy, Frank."

"It happens," said Frank. He was still sitting the way he'd been when I came into the room. Now he charged his pipe, packing the bowl with the shreds of tobacco and pushing them down with his fingertip. He did it very, very carefully as if to show me that it was a difficult thing to do.

I said, "Stinnes seems to have convinced them that Bret Rensselaer is some kind of KGB mole. They put him under house arrest."

"And what do you want me to do?" said Frank. He didn't light his pipe. He rested it against the ashtray while he read the label on another record, entered details of it into a loose-leaf notebook, and placed it on the appropriate pile.

"Did you know that was going to happen?"

"No, but I should have guessed that something like it was in the wind. I've been against that damned committee right from the start." He sipped at his drink. "We should have turned Stinnes over to Five and let it go at that. These combined committees always end in a power struggle. I never saw one that didn't."

"Stinnes is driving the wedge in deep, Frank." I didn't remind him that he'd showed no sign of being against the committee when I'd seen him with the D-G.

Frank picked up his pipe while he thought about it. "House arrest? Bret? Are you quite sure? There was talk of an enquiry, but arrest . . . ?" He lit the pipe with a match, holding the bowl inverted so that the flame could get to the tightly packed tobacco.

"A witch-hunt has started, Frank. It could cause permanent damage to the Department. Bret has a lot of friends, but he has implacable enemies too."

"Lange?" Was that a gibe at me? He puffed at the pipe as he looked at me, but he didn't smile.

"Some more influential than Lange," I said. "And even worse is the way that people—even senior staff—are trying to find evidence to confirm Bret's guilt."

"Are they?" He didn't believe that.

"Dicky dug up some half-baked story about being in Kiel with Bret when a KGB man recognized him."

"And it wasn't true?"

"It was entirely true. But if Dicky had taken the trouble to look up Bret's report on the incident, he would have found it completely and adequately explained by Bret. People are jittery, Frank, and that brings out the worst in them."

"People are jittery since your wife went over. It was the enormity of that that shook the Department to its foundations."

"If you . . ."

"Don't get angry, Bernard." He held up a hand and ducked his head as if warding off a blow. It was Frank's pleasure to play the role of vulnerable ancient to my role of bellicose son. "I'm not putting any blame on you, but I am stating a fact."

"Bret is here. He's here in Berlin," I said. "And he's in bad shape."

"I rather thought he might be," said Frank. He puffed his pipe again. He'd lost interest in sorting his record collection now. Even when the Ellington music stopped, he didn't put another one on the player. "I don't mean in bad shape; I mean I thought he might be in Berlin."

"How?" If Frank knew officially about Bret's arrival, the report would go through regular channels and be in London by noon the following day.

"Why else would you be here in the middle of the night? It's surely not in response to a phone call from Bret in London. Bret must be here; there's no other explanation."

"He thinks they'll put out a departmental alert for him."

"Surely it hasn't come to that," said Frank calmly.

"I think it might have done, Frank. The old man was not available when Bret was put under house arrest."

"And you think that's a bad sign?"

"You know the D-G better than anyone, Frank." Frank puffed his pipe and didn't comment on his possible knowledge of the Director-General's way of going to ground when his senior staff were to be arrested.

Eventually Frank said, "What could I do for Bret? Supposing I wanted to do anything?"

"We should neutralize Stinnes. Without him the whole action against Bret will collapse."

"Neutralize him? What do you mean by that?"

"We thought Stinnes was a mediocre agent in a dead-end job. All our records and enquiries pointed to that. But I think that was all cover. I think Stinnes is one of their most reliable people. They might have been grooming him for this one for ages."

"Or it might be that your wife's arrival over there gave them the necessary extra information that made his job possible."

"It would be foolish to deny that possibility," I said without getting angry. "The timing points to Fiona. She might have been the trigger, but the background must have been started long ago."

"Neutralize him?"

"How we do it doesn't really matter, but we must persuade Moscow that Stinnes is no longer their man and in place."

"You're not leading up to an XPD? Because I won't go along with that."

"I don't want him killed. The best solution would be to make Moscow believe that Stinnes is really turned and working for us."

"That might take some time," said Frank.

"Exactly. So let's not try that. Let's tell them we know about Stinnes, that we have him under lock and key and are giving him a bad time."

"What sort of bad time?"

"A damned bad sort of bad time," I said.

"Would they care?"

"How would we feel if it was one of ours?" I said.

"If they were roughing him up, we'd do everything we could to get him out."

"And that's what they'll want to do," I said. "Everything suggests that Stinnes is a sick man. He sits around holding himself as if he's in pain, he resists all attempts to make him have a physical examination, and he's stopped smoking. . . . Of course, that could all be an act."

"What is it you're expecting me to do?"

"There's something else you should know, Frank," I said. "The Miller woman is alive and well and working across the city in the Red Town Hall."

"Are you sure?"

"Werner spoke with her."

"He should have reported it."

"He went back to take another look."

"So that was it," said Frank half to himself.

"What?"

"There's something *you'd* better know. They're holding Werner Volkmann. He was arrested last night in East Berlin and taken to Babelsberg."

"Babelsberg?"

"It's a part of the old film studios. The Stasis use it when they want to be beyond any possible Protecting Powers jurisdiction that might apply to the inner parts of the city. We can't send a military police patrol into Potsdam the way we can to the rest of Berlin."

"Poor Werner."

"You guessed it was Zena: the Campari and orange—that's her drink. I sent for her as soon as I got the report."

"How is she taking it?" I said.

"The same way Zena takes everything," said Frank. "Very, very personally."

"Where did it happen?"

"The Red Town Hall. He was talking to someone over there and asking too many questions. One of my people saw the van draw up outside the Town Hall and he recognized Volkmann being put in. Later it was confirmed by one of our inside people who saw the police report."

"Have they charged him?"

"I know nothing except what I've told you. It only happened last evening."

"We'll have to do something, Frank."

"I know what you're thinking, Bernard, but that's impossible."

"What is?"

"Exchanging Werner for Stinnes. London Central would never wear it."

"Is it better that we deliver Bret back to London and let Stinnes send Five to trample all over him?" I said.

"Bret is innocent. Very well; I believe Bret is innocent too. But let us not overreact. You're not really telling me you think he'll be tried and found guilty and sent to prison?"

"Moscow has produced fake evidence. God knows how much of it there is."

"Fake evidence or no fake evidence, it won't send Bret to jail and you know it."

"They won't even send him for trial," I said. "They never do send senior staff for trial, no matter what the evidence against them. But Bret will be retired and discredited. Bret has a very exaggerated sense of loyalty—you know what he's like. Bret couldn't live with that."

"And what if I bring Stinnes here without authority? What will happen to me?"

Well, at least Frank had reached the necessary conclusion without my drawing him a colored diagram. Frank's authority was confined to Berlin. The only way we could do anything to help Bret in the short term was by bringing Stinnes here. "You're close to retirement, Frank. If you overstep the mark, they'll get angry but they won't take it out on you. Especially when they realize that you've saved them from a fiasco."

"I'm not going to lose my bloody pension for some hare-brained scheme of yours," said Frank. "It's not within my power."

"See Bret," I said. "He's waiting outside in the car. See Bret and you might change your mind."

"I'll see Bret. But I won't change my mind."

I WOULDN'T have convinced him without Bret Rensselaer. It was the mangled patrician figure that moved Frank Harrington to throw the rule book out the window and send two of his heavies to England to get Stinnes. There was paperwork too. Stinnes hadn't yet been given any sort of travel document other than the stateless person's identity card. That was valid for traveling, but it required some hastily done backup with scribbled signatures.

Just to create a smoke screen Frank left a message with the D-G's personal secretary and sent a telex to London that said Stinnes was to be questioned in connection with the detention of a departmental employee in East Berlin. The name of Werner Volkmann was not mentioned and the proposed venue of the Stinnes questioning was left vague.

The other half of the procedure was more straightforward. I found Posh Harry in Frankfurt. When he heard that there was a well-paid job for him he got the next plane for Berlin.

I met him in the Café Leuschner, a big barn of a place near the remains of the Anhalter Bahnhof, that weed-bedecked chunk of railway terminal that has been left standing in the middle of the city like a rich man's folly in some Old-World garden.

The big café was made to look even larger by the row of gilt-framed mirrors. They lined the wall, and the marble countertop with all the glinting bottles and glasses was tilted by the reflections.

As a kid I'd always liked to sit at the counter rather than at the tables. In those days the chairs were old bentwood ones, painted olive green, the only color of paint that one could get in the city. The furniture at Leuschner's café—like so many other painted things of that time—exactly matched the trucks of the U.S. Army.

Leuschner's used to be my Saturday treat. It was the high point of my week. I'd meet my father at his office, and with him in his best uniform we'd walk to Leuschner's for one of Herr Leuschner's ice creams that only kids were allowed to buy. Then one day my father discovered through an informer that the ice cream came from U.S. Army supplies. He was going to report it, but my mother dissuaded him on account of the way old Herr Leuschner was always feeding hungry kids for nothing. But my father wouldn't take me there after that.

Now it was Leuschner's son, Willi, behind the bar. We'd been kids together. Not Wilhelm, not Willy, but Willi. I remembered how exasperating he'd always been about adults getting his name right. Willi had the same kind of big mustache his father had worn—the same sort of mustache the Kaiser had worn, and many of his subjects too, until people started thinking that big curly mustaches made you look like a Turk.

The young Leuschner greeted me as I entered. "How goes it, Bernd?" he said. He had that manner bartenders learn—an arms-length friendliness that reserved the right to toss you into the street should you get drunk.

"Hello, Willi. Has Posh Harry been in?"

"Not for a long time. He used to come in a lot—he brought some good business too—but he shares an office in Tegel now. He likes to be near the airport, he said, and I don't see him so much."

It was then that Posh Harry arrived. He arrived at the appointed time; he was a very punctual man. I suppose, like me, he'd learned that it was a necessary part of dealing with Germans.

He was wearing a superb camel-hair overcoat and a gray trilby. They didn't go well together, but Posh Harry had swagger enough to carry off anything. He could have come in wearing a baseball cap and creased pajamas and Willi Leuschner would still have greeted him with the awed respect I heard in his voice this time. "I was just saying how much we like to see you here, Herr Harry." Even Willi didn't know Posh Harry's family name; it was one of Berlin's best-kept secrets. When Posh Harry replied, it was in flawless German and the chirruping Berlin accent.

It was Willi who showed us to a quiet table at the back. Willi was shrewd; he could recognize those customers who wanted to sit near the window and drink wine and those who wanted to sit at the back and drink whisky. And those who wanted to sit somewhere where they couldn't be overheard. To get those seats you had to drink champagne; but German champagne would do.

"We want to set up a meeting, Harry," I said when Willi had served us our *Sekt,* written the price of it on a beer mat which he slapped on the table, and gone back to his place behind the bar.

"Who's 'we'?" said Posh Harry, toying with the beer mat in such a way as to ensure that I could see what it was costing me.

"Not too many of those big questions, Harry. Let's get the details right and you collect the money, okay?"

"That's the way I like to do it," said Harry. He smiled. He had the wide toothy smile of the Oriental.

"We're holding a KGB man; he has the working name of Stinnes. We caught him in a red-hot situation."

"Am I permitted to ask what is a red-hot situation?"

"We caught him mugging a little old lady in a sweet shop."

"Is this on the level, Bernie?" Now it was the serious face and low sincere voice of the professional. I could see why he did so well at it; he could make you think he really cared.

"No, a lot of it is not on the level, but our KGB friends will know what's what. You tell them that we're holding Stinnes in a hard-room and that we're kicking shit out of him."

"You want me to say you personally are involved?"

"Yes, you tell them that Bernie Samson is kicking shit out of Erich Stinnes, on account of the way he was held in Norman-nenstrasse last year by this same individual. Revenge, tell them."

An old man came in. He was wearing tails complete with top hat, and playing a concertina. He was a famous Berlin character —the "Gypsy Baron," they called him. In the cafés along the Ku-damm he played the music the foreign tourists liked to hear

—Strauss, Lehár, and a selection from *Cabaret*—but this was a place for Berliners, so he kept to their kind of schmalz.

"And?"

"And you felt they should know about it."

"Okay." He was a master of inscrutable faces.

"Let them chew it over for five minutes and then say that London Central are finished with this character. London Central will be handing him over to Five unless some better offer came up from somewhere else—like Moscow."

"When?" said Posh Harry, reaching for the dripping-wet bottle from the ice bucket and pouring more for us both.

"Very soon. Very, very soon. There is no chance that Five would deal with Moscow, so time is vitally important. If they were interested in having Stinnes back, you could get me to a meeting to discuss his release."

"Here?" He used a paper towel to mop up the ice water he'd dripped over the table.

"His release here in Berlin. But first I want the meeting," I said.

"With?"

"With my wife. And whoever she wants to bring along."

"What's the deal, Bernie? You release the Russkie—what do you want in return? Or is kicking shit out of Russkies something you're giving up for Lent?"

"They'll know what I want in return. But I don't want that anywhere on the record, so don't even start guessing," I said. "Now, in the course of conversation, you'll make sure they know that Bret Rensselaer has been given an important promotion and a special job. You don't know exactly what it is, but it all came about because he was the one who brought Stinnes down. He was the one who nailed him to the wall. Got it?"

"It's not difficult, Bernie. It's a shame to take the money."

"Take the money anyway."

"I shall."

"The meeting is to be over this side. I suggest the VIP suite on the top floor of the Steigenberger Hotel. It's good security;

there's room to move . . . car parking is where you can see it . . . you know."

"And the food is excellent. That might appeal to them."

"And the food is excellent."

"They'll probably want to send someone to inspect the room."

"No problem," I said.

"Timing for the exchange?"

"We'll have their man Stinnes available in the city."

"I mean . . . you'll want to do this immediately the meeting ends, won't you? This is not one of those fancy setups where they come over the bridge for the TV cameras ten days later?"

"Immediate. And complete secrecy; both sides."

"Your wife, you say? I'll go over there today. Maybe I could wrap up this whole deal by the weekend."

"Good thinking, Harry. I'll be at Lisl Hennig's this evening. Phone me there anyway; let me know what's happening. Have you got the phone number?"

"Are you kidding? Your wife, eh?" The concertina player finished playing *"Das war in Schöneberg im Monat Mai . . ."* and took a bow. Posh Harry eased his chair back and applauded loudly. He smiled at me to show how happy he was. It was a bigger smile this time; I could count his gold teeth.

"She'll be the one to talk to, Harry."

"I think I can find her."

"If I know her the way I think I do, she will have planned the whole business; she'll be sitting by the phone waiting for you to call." I got to my feet. I'd said enough.

"It's like that, is it?"

"The script is all written, Harry. We just have to read our parts."

Harry pulled a bundle of paper money from his back pocket and paid for the champagne. The tip was far too generous, but the Department would pay.

"That material I gave you—was it good?" he asked.

"It was *Spielmaterial,*" I replied.

"I'm sorry about that," he said. "Some you win, some you lose, and some . . ."

". . . some get rained out," I finished for him.

He shrugged. I should have guessed that he had had no real faith in it; he'd given it to me for nothing. That was not Posh Harry's style.

Chapter 27

LISL SAT where she could see the flowers. It was a vast display of different blooms—more than I could put names to—and arranged in a basket tied with colored ribbon. The flowers had obviously come from some expensive florist. They were the ones Werner had brought for her. Now the petals were beginning to fall. Werner was not demonstrative, but he was always giving Lisl flowers. Sometimes, according to his mood, he would spend ages choosing them for her. Even his beloved Zena was not treated with such care in the matter of flowers. Lisl loved flowers, especially when they came from Werner.

Sometimes, when she smiled, I could see Lisl Hennig the beautiful woman I'd met when I first came to Berlin. I was a child then, and Lisl must have already been almost fifty years old. But she was a woman of such beauty that any man would be at her call.

Now she was old, and the commanding manner that had once been a part of her fatal attraction was the petulance of an irritable old woman. But I remembered her as the goddess she'd once been, and so did Lothar Koch, the shrunken little retired bureaucrat who regularly played bridge with her.

We were sitting in Lisl's "study," a small room that had become a museum of her life. Every shelf and cupboard was crammed with mementos—china ornaments, snuffboxes, and an abundance of souvenir ashtrays. The radio was playing Tchaikovsky from some distant station that faded every now and again. There were only three of us playing bridge. It was more fun this way, Lisl said, whenever we were bidding and deciding which hand would be the dummy. But Lisl liked company, and there were only three of us because Lisl had failed to find a fourth despite all the cajoling of which she was capable.

The counters for which we played were stacked up high. Lisl liked to play for money no matter how tiny the stakes. When she was a young girl she'd been sent to a finishing school in Dresden—a favored place for wealthy families to send their grown-up daughters—and she liked to affect the manners of that place and time. But now she was content to be the *berlinerisch* old woman she truly was, and there was nothing more *berlinerisch* than playing cards for money.

"It's big business nowadays," said Herr Koch. "Since 1963 those East Germans have made almost three billion Deutschemark in ransoms."

"I bid one spade," said Lisl, staring at her cards. "Three billion?"

"No bid," said Koch. "Yes, three billion Deutschemark."

"One heart," I said.

"You can't do that," said Lisl.

"Sorry," I said. "No bid." Why had they suddenly started talking about political prisoners held in the Democratic Republic?—they couldn't have heard about Werner. Lisl finally bid two spades.

"About fourteen hundred people a year are ransomed by the Bonn government. None of them are criminals. Mostly they are people who have applied for exit permits and then been heard to complain about not getting them."

"They must be mad to apply for an exit permit," said Lisl.

"They are desperate," said Koch. "Desperate people snatch at any chance however slim."

Lisl put a queen of hearts on Herr Koch's king. From now on she'd be trumping hearts unless I missed my guess. I knew she didn't have the ace; I had it. I played low; it was Koch's trick. Perhaps they wouldn't exchange Werner for Stinnes. Perhaps we'd have to pay to get Werner back. Would they sell him or would they prefer a big show trial with lots of publicity? Perhaps I'd handled it badly. Perhaps I should have let the KGB think that Stinnes had fooled us completely; then they wouldn't risk spoiling it by publicizing Werner. Could they put Werner on trial without revealing the Miller woman's role in framing Bret Rensselaer?

Koch led with an ace of clubs. I knew Lisl would trump it and she did, using a three. That was the way with cards and with life: the smallest of cards could beat an ace if you chose the right moment.

Lisl picked up the trick and led a four of spades. She must have a handful of trumps.

"You should have bid a grand slam," said Herr Koch sarcastically. He was smarting at having his ace trumped.

"The people are priced according to their worth," said Lisl, continuing with the conversation as if to appease Koch.

"A university don can cost us up to two hundred thousand Deutschemark," said Koch. "A skilled worker about thirty thousand."

"How do you know all this?" I asked him.

"It was in the *Hamburger Abendblatt,*" said Lisl. "I lent it to him."

"The government of the Democratic Republic have a bank account in Frankfurt," said Koch, without acknowledging the loan of Lisl's Hamburg newspaper. "Prisoners are delivered two weeks after payment is received. It is a slave trade." Then Lisl led a heart from the dummy hand so she could trump it. My hearts were useless now that Lisl had none. You can only fight in the currency that your opponent shares. I played my jack of hearts.

"Play your ace, Bernard," she urged. She knew my ace was useless too. Lisl laughed. She loved to win at cards.

Lisl led a small trump and lost the trick to Herr Koch.

"You lost that one," I said. I couldn't resist it.

Herr Koch said, "She doesn't care. The dummy has no trumps."

"You'll never teach him bridge," said Lisl. "I've been trying to explain it to him since he was ten years old."

But Koch persisted. "She brought out a trump from you and a trump from me."

"But she lost the trick," I said. "You won it with your jack."

"She removed the potential dangers." Koch turned over the cards of the trick and showed me the ten and the jack which we'd played. "Now she knows that you have no trumps and she'll slaughter you whatever you play."

"Let him play his way," said Lisl ruthlessly. "He's not subtle enough for bridge."

"Don't be fooled by him," said Herr Koch, talking to Lisl as if I wasn't present. "The English are all subtle, and this one is subtle in the most dangerous way."

"And which is that?" said Lisl. She could have simply laid her hand full of trumps on the table and we would have conceded all the remaining tricks to her, but she wouldn't deprive herself of the pleasure of winning the game one trick at a time.

"He doesn't mind us thinking he is a fool. That is Bernard's greatest strength; it always has been."

"I will never understand the English," said Lisl. She trumped, picked up the trick, smiled, and led again. Having said she didn't understand the English, she proceeded to explain the English to us. That was *berlinerisch* too; the people of Berlin are reluctant to admit to ignorance of any kind. "If an Englishman says there's no hurry, that means it must be done immediately. If he says he doesn't mind, it means he minds very much. If he leaves any decision to you by saying 'If you like' or 'When you like,' be on your guard—he means that he's made his requirements clear, and he expects them to be precisely met."

"Are you going to let this slander go unchallenged, Bernard?" said Koch. He liked a little controversy, providing he could be the referee.

I smiled. I'd heard it all before.

"Then what of us Germans?" persisted Koch. "Are we so easygoing? Tell me, Bernard, I want your opinion."

"A German has no grays," I said, and immediately regretted embarking on such a discussion.

"No grays? What does this mean?" said Koch.

"In Germany two cars collide; one driver is guilty and therefore the other is innocent. Everything is black or white for a German. The weather is good or the weather is bad, a man is sick or he is well, a restaurant is good or it is terrible. At the concert they cheer or they boo."

"And Werner," said Koch. "Is he a man without grays?"

The question was directed at me, but Lisl had to answer. "Werner is an Englishman," she said.

It was not true, of course; it was an example of Lisl's impetuous delight in shocking and surprising. Werner was about as un-English as any German could be, and no one knew that better than Lisl.

"You brought him up," I said. "How could Werner be English?"

"In spirit," said Lisl.

"He adored your father," said Herr Koch, more in order to reconcile the difference of opinion than because it was true.

"He admired him," I said. "It's not quite the same thing."

"It was your mother who first took a liking to Werner," said Lisl. "I remember your father complaining that Werner was always upstairs playing with you and making a noise. But your mother encouraged him."

"She knew you had the hotel to run," I said. "You had enough to do without looking after Werner."

"One day I'll go to England and see her again. She always sends a card at Christmas. Perhaps next year I'll go and see her."

"She has a spare room," I said. But I knew in fact that

neither Lisl nor my mother would endure the rigors of the airplane journey. Only the very fit could cope with the airlines. Lisl had not yet forgotten her uncomfortable trip to Munich five years ago.

"Your father was so formal with little Werner. He always spoke to him as to a grown man."

"My father spoke to everyone in exactly the same way," I said. "It was one of the things I most liked about him."

"Werner couldn't get over it. 'The *Herr Oberst* shook hands with me, Tante Lisl!' It would have been unthinkable for a Wehrmacht colonel to shake hands and talk so solemnly with a small child. You're not listening, Bernard."

No, I wasn't listening any longer. I'd expected both of them to say I was German, but such an idea had never entered their heads. I was devastated by the rejection so implied. This was where I'd grown up. If I wasn't German in spirit, then what was I? Why didn't they both acknowledge the truth? Berlin was my town. London was a place my English friends lived and where my children were born, but this was where I belonged. I was happy sitting here in Lisl's shabby back room with old Herr Koch. This was the only place I could really call home.

The phone rang. I was sure it was Posh Harry. Lisl was shuffling the cards and Herr Koch was calculating the scores for the hundredth time. The phone rang unanswered several times, then stopped. "Are you expecting a phone call, Bernard?" enquired Lisl, looking at me closely.

"Possibly," I said.

"Klara answers if I don't pick it up. It's probably a wrong number. We get a lot of wrong numbers lately."

What if Posh Harry's approach was rejected? I would be in a very difficult position. Even if Bret Rensselaer was innocent, that didn't prove that the rest of my theory was correct. Stinnes might be genuine. It was then that I began to worry that Stinnes might not be informed about the whole structure of Moscow's plot to discredit Bret Rensselaer. Suppose Stinnes was a kamikaze sent to blow London Central into fragments but had never been told the details of what he was doing? Stinnes was the sort of man who would sacrifice himself for something in which he truly believed. But what did he truly believe? That was the question that had to be answered.

And what would I do in Fiona's position? She was holding all the cards; all she had to do was sacrifice Stinnes. Would she believe that I'd tumbled to their game? Yes, probably. But would she believe that I could convince London Central of the real truth? No, probably not. Bret Rensselaer was the element that would decide the way Fiona jumped. I hoped Posh Harry got that bit of the story right. Maybe Fiona wouldn't believe that I could persuade the fumbling bureaucrats that Stinnes was making a fool of them; but Bret and I together—she'd possibly believe that the two of us combined could do it. Bret and I combined could do anything, in Fiona's opinion. I suppose the kind of man she really wanted was some incongruous and impossible combination of the two of us.

"Drinkies?" said Lisl in what she imagined was English. Without waiting for a reply she poured sherry for all of us. I didn't like sherry, especially the dark sweet variety that Lisl preferred, but I'd been pretending to like it for so long that I didn't have the courage to ask for something else.

It was nine-thirty when the call came through. I was a hundred and fifty points behind Lisl and trying to make two hearts with a hand that wasn't really worth a bid. Lisl answered the phone. She must have realized that I was waiting for my call. She passed it to me. It was Posh Harry.

"Bernard?" They would be monitoring the call, but there was no point in disguising who I was; they would know that already.

"Yes?"

"I've been talking."

"And?"

"They'll come back to me in one hour."

"What do you think?"

"She asked me if Bret will be at the meeting."

"It could be arranged."

"They might make it a condition." I looked at Lisl and then at Herr Koch. They were both giving very close attention to their cards in that way people study things when they're trying to look as if they're not eavesdropping.

"Bret's in charge; make that clear," I said.

"I'll tell them. They will come equipped, you realize that." That meant armed. There was no way we could prevent that; we had no right to search Russian cars or personnel crossing into West Berlin.

"Okay," I said.

"Guaranteed safe passage and return for the woman?" That was Fiona, frightened that we might arrest her. But by now they'd no doubt provided her with all the paperwork that made her a Soviet citizen, a colonel in the KGB, and probably a Party member too. It would be a legal nightmare getting her arrested in West Berlin where the U.S.S.R was still a Protecting Power with legal rights that compared to the British, French, and American ones. In the U.K. it would be a different matter.

"Guaranteed for the whole party. Do they want it in writing?" I said.

"They don't want it for the whole party—just for the woman," said Posh Harry. It seemed a strange thing to say, but I gave it no special thought at the time. It was only afterwards that it had any significance.

"Whatever they want, Harry."

"I'll phone you back," he said.

"I'll be here," I said.

I rang off and returned to the bridge game. Lisl and Herr Koch made no reference to my phone call. There was a tacit understanding that I was employed by some international pharmaceutical company.

We played another rubber of bridge before Posh Harry phoned back to tell me that everything was agreed on for the meeting in the Steigenberger Hotel. Even by the end of his negotiations Posh Harry didn't know that they were holding

Werner in custody. It was typical of the KGB; nothing was told to anyone except what he needed to know.

I phoned Frank Harrington and told him they'd agreed but would need some kind of written guarantee that the woman would be allowed to return unhindered.

Frank grunted his agreement. He knew the implications, but made no comment about Fiona or the Department's interest in arresting her. "They are here in saturation levels," said Frank. "KGB watchers have been coming through the crossing points for the last two hours. I knew it was going to be an affirmative."

"KGB? Coming through to the West?"

"Yes, they've been sniffing round ever since you got here. They probably saw our friend arriving." He meant Bret.

"And their friend too?" I said. I meant Stinnes; he'd arrived that afternoon.

"I hope not," said Frank.

"But both are secure?"

"Very secure," said Frank. "I'm not letting them out." Frank had both men accommodated at his official mansion in Grunewald. There was half a million pounds' worth of security devices built into that place. Even the KGB would have trouble getting at them there. After a pause Frank said, "Are you equipped, Bernard?"

I had a Smith & Wesson that I left in Lisl's safe, together with some other personal things. "Yes," I said. "Why?"

"A KGB hit team went through about thirty minutes ago. It was a reliable identification. They don't send a hit team unless they mean business. I can't help worrying that you might be targeted."

"Thanks, Frank, I'll take the usual precautions."

"Stay where you are tonight. I'll send a car for you in the morning. Be very careful, Bernard. I don't like the look of it. Eight o'clock okay?"

"Eight o'clock will be very convenient," I said. "Good night, Frank. See you in the morning." I'd turned the radio down while talking on the phone; now I made it louder. It was a

Swedish station playing a Bruckner symphony; the opening chords filled the room.

"You people in the pill business work late," said Lisl sarcastically when I rang off.

Herr Koch had held his ministerial job throughout the Nazi period by not giving way to curiosity or being tempted to such impetuous remarks. He smiled and said, "I hope everything is in order, Bernard."

"Everything is just fine," I told him.

He got up and went to the radio to switch it off.

"Thank you, darling," said Lisl.

"Bruckner," explained Herr Koch. "When they announced the disaster at Stalingrad, the radio played nothing but Beethoven and Bruckner for three whole days."

"So many fine young boys . . . ," said Lisl sadly. "Put on a record, darling. Something happy—'Bye, Bye, Blackbird.' "

But when Herr Koch put a record on, it was one of his favorites, *"Das war in Schöneberg im Monat Mai . . ."*

"Marlene Dietrich," said Lisl, leaning back and closing her eyes. *"Schön!"*

Chapter 28

THEY'RE coming through Checkpoint Charlie now." I recognized the voice that came through the tiny loudspeaker, although I couldn't put a name to it. It was one of the old Berlin Field Unit hands. He was at the checkpoint watching the KGB party coming West for the meeting. "Three black Volvos."

I was using my handset radio to monitor the reports. I heard someone at this end say, "How many of them?"

Standing alongside me in the VIP suite of the Steigenberger

Hotel, Frank said, "Three Volvos! Jesus Christ! It's a bloody invasion!" Frank had committed himself, but now that it was actually happening he was nervous. I'd told him to have a drink, but he'd refused.

"All of a sudden it's green," said Frank, still looking out of the window to the street far below us. "Berlin, I mean. The winters always seem as if they'll never end. Then suddenly the sunshine comes and you notice the chestnut trees, magnolias, flowers everywhere. The gray clouds and the snow and ice are gone, and everywhere is green." That's all he said, but it was enough. I realized then that Frank loved Berlin as I loved it. All his talk of wanting to get away from here, to retire in England and never think about Berlin again, was nonsense. He loved it here. I suppose it was his imminent retirement that had made him face the truth; packing up his Ellington records, separating his personal possessions from the furniture and things that belonged to the residence, had made him miserable.

"Three drivers plus nine passengers," said the voice.

"Who is that?" I asked Frank. "I recognized the voice, I think."

"Old Percy Danvers," said Frank. It was a man who'd worked here in my father's time. His mother was German from Silesia, father English: a sergeant in the Irish Guards.

"Still working?"

"He retires next year, just a few months after me. But he's remaining here in the city," said Frank wistfully. "I don't know how the office will manage without Percy."

"Who's getting Berlin when you go?" I asked. I sipped the whisky I need to face them. Would Fiona really come?

"There was talk of Bret taking over."

"That won't happen now," I said.

"I don't care who comes here," said Frank. "As long as I get away."

I looked at him. Now both of us knew it wasn't true. Frank smiled.

Then Bret Rensselaer came back from the phone, and I said,

"Nine of them; they just came through Checkpoint Charlie. They'll be here at any time." Behind Bret there was a German kid—Peter—who'd been assigned to provide Bret's personal protection. He was a nice kid, but he took it too seriously and now he wouldn't let Bret out of his sight.

Bret nodded and joined us for a moment at the window before sinking into one of the soft gray suede armchairs. The VIP suite at the Steigenberger runs the whole length of the building, but the entrance to it is inconspicuous, and many of the hotel's residents don't even know it exists. For that reason the suite is used for top-level meetings both commercial and political and by publicity-shunning tycoons, politicians, and film stars. There's a dining room at one end and an elegant office area at the other. In between there's a TV lounge, sitting room, bedrooms, and even a small room where the waiters can open champagne and prepare canapés.

Champagne and canapés were ready for the KGB party, but higher on the list of priorities were the extra locks, the security devices, and doors that close off this part of the top floor and the suite's private lift that would enable the KGB delegates to arrive and depart without mixing with the other hotel guests.

"What is their weakest point?" said Bret, speaking from behind us as if talking to himself. Bret had recovered some of his confidence by now. He had the American talent for bouncing back; all he'd needed was a hot shower, clean linen, and the sports pages of the *Herald Tribune*.

I didn't answer, but Frank said, "Fiona."

"Fiona?" Did I hear resentment in Bret's voice? Was there a proprietorial tone that came from some affection Bret still had for her? "Fiona is their weakest point? What do you mean, Frank?"

Frank turned round and went and sat in the armchair opposite Bret. Ever since I'd brought Bret into Frank's house in Grunewald there had been a distance, almost a coldness, between the two men. I couldn't decide to what extent it was a latent hostility and to what extent it was embarrassment, a sign of Frank's concern for the humiliation that Bret was suffering.

Frank said, "She is a latecomer to their organization. Some of them probably still view her with suspicion; no doubt all of them have some kind of hostility toward her."

"Is that view based upon received reports?" said Bret.

"She's a foreigner," said Frank. "Putting her in charge over there means that everyone's promotion expectations are lessened. Compare her position with ours. We've all known each other many years. We know what we can expect from each other, both in terms of help and hindrance. She is isolated. She has no long-term allies. She has no experience of what actions or opinions can be expected from her colleagues. She is constantly under the microscope; everyone round her will be trying to find fault with what she does. Everything she says will be examined, syllable by syllable, by people who are not in sympathy with what she's doing."

"She's a Moscow appointment," said Bret. Again there was some indefinable note of something that might have been affection or even pride. Bret looked at me, but I looked at my drink.

Frank said, "All the more reason why the staff in her Berlin office will resent her."

"So what are you proposing?" Bret asked Frank.

"We must give her the opportunity to negotiate while separated from the rest of her people. We must give her a chance to speak without being overheard."

"That won't be easy, Frank," I said. "You know why they send such big teams. They don't trust anyone to be alone with us."

"We must find a way," said Frank. "Bernard must move the chat onto a domestic plane. There must be something he could talk to her about."

"Talk about the kids," said Bret. I could cheerfully have throttled him, but I smiled instead.

"She might have thought all this out for herself," said Frank, who also knew Fiona well. "She might get time alone with us by some ruse of her own."

"And what about us?" said Bret. "What's our weakest point?" Peter, his bodyguard, watched Bret all the time and tried to follow the conversation.

"That's easy," said Frank. "Our weakest point is Werner Volkmann." Frank's dislike of Werner was based upon the affair Frank had had with Werner's wife, Zena. Guilt breeds resentment; Frank disliked Werner because he'd cuckolded him.

"Werner's name hasn't even been mentioned," said Bret. "At least, that's what Bernard told us."

"I'm sure Bernard told us the truth," said Frank. "But they're holding Werner Volkmann, and Werner is Bernard's very closest friend. They know what we want in return."

"What we are *pretending* to want in return, Frank," I said. "Our real benefit is revealing to London Central that Stinnes is Moscow's man who's trying to frame Bret and make trouble for everyone else. We have to do that without Moscow realizing what our true purpose is. Making them release Werner is a convenient smoke screen."

Frank smiled at what he regarded my rationalization. He thought Werner was my real motive for setting this one up. But Frank was wrong. I wouldn't let either of them discover my real motive. My real motive was my children.

"BERNARD!" All of a sudden my wife came walking through the door. "What a glorious suite. Did you choose it?" A cold smile, just in case anyone thought she was sincere.

She stood there as if expecting the usual kiss, but I hesitated, then extended my hand. She shook it with a mocking grin. "Hello, Fi," I said. She was dressed in a gray woolen dress. It was simple but expensive. She was not living like a worker, but like the ones who told the workers what they were allowed to do.

"Hello Frank; hello Bret," she said. Fiona smiled at them and shook hands. She was in charge of the party and she was determined to show it. This was her first official visit to the West. Looking back afterwards I realized that despite our reassurances, she was wondering if we were going to arrest her. But she carried it off with the same brisk confidence with which she did everything. Her hair was different. She'd let it grow and taken it back into a sort of bun. It was the sort of hair style that Hollywood might provide for a Communist official in the sort of movie where she takes off her glasses, lets her hair down, and becomes a capitalist in the last reel. *Ninotchka.* But I saw no sign of Fiona shedding the chrysalis of Communism. Indeed, if appearances were any guide, it seemed to suit her.

After everyone had shaken hands with everyone, a waiter—that is to say, one of our people, armed but dressed as a waiter—served drinks. Frank offered champagne. He'd bet me five pounds that they wouldn't accept it. He'd got some Russian white wine in the cooler anticipating that they'd ask for something like that, just to be difficult. But Fiona said champagne would be wonderful, and after that, they all said they'd have champagne. Except me; I had another scotch.

There were not nine of them in the room. Two armed KGB men were in the lobby, another was assigned to help the drivers make sure no one tampered with the cars, and someone was supervising the use of the private lift. There were three actual negotiators and two clerks. The only one I knew, besides Fiona, was Pavel Moskvin, whose path kept crossing mine. He shed his ankle-length black overcoat and dumped it onto the sofa. He stared at me. I smiled and he looked away.

There was a much younger man with their party, a blond man of about twenty-five, wearing the kind of suit that KGB men wore if they couldn't get out of Moscow. He must have been on the teaching machines, for his German and English were perfect and accentless and he even made little jokes. But he was very much in Fiona's pocket and he watched her all the time, in case she wanted something done. Alongside him was the third negotiator, a white-haired man who did nothing but frown.

"I hope you agree that time is the vital factor," said Bret. It was his show; Frank had agreed to that right from the start. Bret had most to lose. If the meeting was going to become a fiasco, then Bret would have only himself to blame. And no doubt Frank would toss him to the wolves in a desperate attempt to save himself. Where would Frank's explanation leave me? I wondered.

"Yes," said Fiona. "May we take notes?"

Bret said, "So we thought we'd break the meeting up into one-to-one discussions. The prime discussion will be about your man Stinnes. We can discuss procedure at the same time, in the hope that we'll reach agreement. Are you the senior officer?"

"Yes," said Fiona. She drank some champagne. She knew what was coming, of course, but she kept very serious.

"Our senior negotiator is Mr. Samson," said Bret.

There was a long silence. Pavel Moskvin didn't like it. He'd not touched his champagne, which was going flat on the dining table. He showed his hostility by folding his arms and scowling. "What do you think, Colonel Moskvin?" Fiona asked. *Colonel* Moskvin, was it . . . look out, Major Stinnes, I thought.

"Better we all stay together," said Moskvin. "No tricks."

"Very well," said Bret. He motioned for them to sit at the circular dining table. The waiter topped up the glasses. The blond youth put his chair behind Fiona so that he could sit with his notepad on his knee.

"What is it you want?" said Moskvin, as if trying to take over from Fiona, who sat back and said nothing. His folded arms strained his jacket across the back and showed where he had a pistol stowed under his armpit.

"We have your man Stinnes," said Bret. "It was a good try but it failed. So far we've held the press at bay, but there's a limit to how long we can do that." The blond youth translated for Moskvin. Moskvin nodded.

"Is that why you brought him to Berlin?" said Fiona.

"Partly. But the Germans have newspapers too. Once the

story breaks, we'll have no alternative but to hand him over to the DPP and then it's out of our hands."

"DPP?" said Moskvin. "What is this?" Obviously he could understand enough English to follow most of what was said.

"The Director of Public Prosecutions," said Bret. "The British state prosecutor. It's another department. We have no control over it."

"And in return?" said Fiona.

"You've arrested Werner Volkmann," I said.

"Have we?" said Fiona. It was very Russian.

"I haven't come here to waste time," I said.

My remark seemed to anger her. "No," she said with a quiet voice that throbbed with hatred and resentment. "You have come here to discuss the fate of Erich Stinnes, a good and loyal comrade who was shamelessly kidnapped by your terrorists, despite his diplomatic status. And who, according to our sources, has been systematically starved and tortured in an attempt to make him betray his country." Fiona had quickly mastered the syntax of the Party.

It was quite a speech and I was tempted to reply sarcastically, but I didn't. I looked at Frank. We both knew now that I was right, and I could see the relief in Frank's face. If the official KGB line was going to be that Erich Stinnes had been kidnapped, starved, and tortured, Stinnes would be reinstated in his KGB rank and position. Even the most thick-skulled men in London would then have to accept the fact that Stinnes had been planted to make trouble.

"Let's not make this meeting a forum for political bickering," I said. "Werner Volkmann for Major Stinnes; straight swap."

"Where is Comrade Stinnes?" said Fiona.

"Here in Berlin. Where's Werner?"

"Checkpoint Charlie," said Fiona. It was strange how after all these years the Communists still used the U.S. Army name for it.

"Fit and well?"

"Do you want to send someone over to see him?" she asked.

"We have someone at Checkpoint Charlie. Shall we agree to do that while we go on talking?" I asked. She looked at Moskvin. He gave an almost imperceptible nod.

"Very well. And Comrade Stinnes?" said Fiona. I looked at Bret. The exchange was Bret's worry.

"We have him here in the hotel," said Bret. "But you must nominate one of your number to see him. One. I can't let you all go." Good old Bret. I didn't know he had it in him, but he'd pipped that one on the wing.

"I will go," said Fiona. Moskvin was not pleased, but there was little he could do about it. If he objected, she'd send him and then she'd still have a chance of speaking to me in private.

ERICH Stinnes was in a suite along the corridor. Frank's men had virtually abducted him from Berwick House waving authorizations and a chit signed by Bret in his capacity as chairman of the committee, a position which technically he still held. But I took us to an empty suite next door to the one where Stinnes was being held.

"What's the game?" said Fiona. She looked round the empty rooms; she even rummaged through the roses looking for a microphone. Fiona was very unsophisticated when it came to surveillance electronics. "What is it?" She seemed anxious.

"Relax," I said. "I'm not going to demand my conjugal rights."

"I came to see Stinnes," she said.

"You came because you wanted a chance to talk in private."

"But I still want to see him," she said.

"He's down the corridor waiting for us."

"Is he well?"

"What do you care if he's well?"

"Erich Stinnes is a fine man, Bernard. I'll do what I can to prevent his dying in prison." Stinnes feigning illness was a part of their plan. That became obvious now.

"Don't worry," I said. "We both know that Erich Stinnes is as fit as a fiddle. He'll go home and get his chestful of medals."

"He's a good man," she said, as if convincing me of it was important to her. She didn't deny that he was fit. His sickness was all part of the scenario—Fiona's touch no doubt; a way to give Stinnes an easier time.

"We haven't got time to waste talking about Stinnes," I said.

"No, you've come to talk about your precious Werner," she said. Even now that she'd left me, there was still an edge of resentment in her voice. Did all wives fear and resent the friendships that had come before marriage?

"Wrong again," I said. "We have to talk about the children."

"There's nothing to talk about. I want them for a holiday. It's not much to ask. Did Tessa speak to you?"

"She did. But I don't want you to take the children."

"They're mine as much as yours. Do you think I'm not human? Do you think I don't love them as much as you do?"

"How can I believe you love them the way I love them when you've left us?"

"Sometimes there are allegiances and aspirations that go beyond family."

"Is that one of the things you're going to explain to little Billy when you take him round the Moscow electric stations and show him the underground railway?"

"They're my children," she said.

"Can't you see the danger of taking them with you? Can't you see the way in which they'll become hostages to your good behavior? Isn't it obvious that once they're there you'll never again be allowed to come West all together? They'll always keep the children there to be sure you do your duty as a good Communist and return East as every good Soviet citizen must."

"What of their life now? You're always working. Nanny spends her life watching TV. They're shunted from your mother to my father and back again. Soon you'll take up with some other woman and they'll have a stepmother. What sort of life is that? With me they could have a proper home and a stable family life."

"With a stepfather?"

"There is no other man, Bernard," she said very softly. "There will be no other man. That is why I need the children so much. You can have other children, dozens of them if you wish. For a man it's easy—he can have children until he's eighty —but I'll soon be past the suitable age for motherhood. Don't deny me the children." Like all women she was tyrannized by her biology.

"Don't take them to a country which they won't be able to leave. Fiona! Look at me, Fiona. I'm saying it for your sake, for the children's sake, and for my sake too."

"I have to see them. I have to." Nervously she went to the window, looked out, and then came back to me.

"See them in Holland or Sweden or on some other neutral ground. I implore you not to take them to the East."

"Is this another one of your tricks?" she said harshly.

"You know I'm right, Fi."

She wrung her hands and twisted the rings on her fingers. Her marriage band was there still and so was the diamond I'd bought with the money from my old Ferrari. "How are they?" It was a different voice.

"Billy's got a new magic trick and Sally is learning to write with her right hand."

"How sweet they are. I got their letters and the drawings. Thank you."

"It was Tessa's idea."

"Tess has grown up suddenly."

"Yes, she has."

"Is she still having those stupid love affairs?"

"Yes, but George is reading the riot act to her. I think she's beginning to wonder if it's worth it."

"What's the trick?"

"What trick?"

"Billy's."

"Oh! You cut a piece of rope into two halves and then make it whole again."

"Is it convincing?"

"Nanny still can't work it out."

"It's in the family, I suppose."

"I suppose so," I said, although I wasn't sure what sort of trickery she was referring to, or whether she meant my sort of trickery or her own.

"Will they arrest me if I come to England on my old passport?" she asked.

"I'll find out," I promised. "But why not see the children in Holland?"

"You'd better not become an accessory, Bernard."

"We are conspiring together right now," I said. "Which of our masters would tolerate it?"

"Neither," she said. It was a concession, a minuscule concession, but the first one she'd made.

"I miss you, Fi," I said.

"Oh, Bernard," she said. Tears welled up in her eyes. I was about to take her into my arms but she stepped back from me. "No," she said. "No."

"I'll do what I can," I said. I don't know exactly what I meant and she didn't ask; it was no more than an abstract noise that intended comfort and she accepted it as such.

"They won't let Werner go," she said. She looked round the room, anxious about being recorded.

"I thought it was agreed."

"Pavel Moskvin has the power of decision. He's in charge of these negotiations, I'm not."

"Werner did nothing of any importance."

"I know what he was doing. The Miller woman's been under permanent surveillance since last week. We were waiting for Werner to make contact."

"The Stinnes operation is all washed up. It's finished, discredited, done for. What Werner said to the Miller woman is of no importance."

"Keep calm. I know. But I'm under orders."

"No Werner, no Stinnes," I said.

She said nothing, but her face was white and tense and she was breathing in that way she did when stress got too much for her.

I said, "Moskvin killed the little MacKenzie kid in the safe house in Bosham."

She shrugged.

"What did he have to do that for?" I persisted. "MacKenzie couldn't swat a fly without reciting the Miranda warnings."

She looked at me and gave a deep sigh. "You'll have to take him out, Bernard."

"What?" I said.

Petulantly and with a gabbled haste that was not typical of her she said, "You'll have to take him out—Moskvin."

For a moment I was speechless. Was this my wife speaking? "How? Where?"

"It's the only way. I've got Werner down to the bus park at Checkpoint Charlie. I told Moskvin that you might want to see him waving to be sure he was fit and well. That was before you got Moskvin's agreement to your sending your man over there."

"How will you explain it?" I said.

"Rid me of that man and I won't have to explain anything."

I still wasn't sure. "Kill him, you mean?"

She was nervous and excited. Her answer was shrill. "People get killed. It wouldn't be the first time that someone was killed at the Wall, would it?"

"No, but I can't start shooting at a delegation like yours. They're likely to bring up the tanks. I don't want to be the man who starts World War Three. I'm serious, Fi."

"You must do it personally, Bernard. You mustn't order anyone else to do it. I don't want anyone else to know it was discussed by us."

"Okay." I heard myself agreeing to it.

"Promise?" I hesitated. "It's Werner; your friend," she

said. "I'm doing everything I can. More than I should." Because it suited her, I thought. She wasn't doing it for Werner, or even for me. And what was she doing anyway? I was going to be the one putting my neck on the block. And now she wanted to deprive me of the chance of explaining it to my masters.

"I promise," I said desperately. "Put him and Stinnes in the last car and let me ride with them. But the children stay with me. That's a condition, Fi."

"Be careful, Bernard. He's a brute."

I looked at her. She was very beautiful, more beautiful than I ever remembered. Her eyes were soft and the faint smell of her perfume brought memories. "Stay here, Fi," I said. "Stay here in the West. We could fix everything."

She shook her head. "Goodbye for the last time," she said. "Don't worry, I'll send Werner back. And I won't take the children from you for the time being."

"Stay."

She leaned forward and kissed me in a decorous way that would not smudge her lipstick; I suppose they'd all be looking at her for such signs. "You don't understand. But one day you will."

"I don't think so," I said.

"Let's go and see Comrade Stinnes," she said. And now her voice was hard and resolute once more.

Chapter 29

I'D ALLOWED for a lot of varied possibilities arising from my meeting with Fiona, but her demand that I kill Pavel Moskvin, one of her senior staff, caught me unawares. And yet there could be no doubt that she was serious. As Bret and Frank had already agreed just a few minutes before the meeting, my friendship with Werner was damned important to me. If killing a hood like Pavel Moskvin could rescue Werner from a prospect of twenty years in a *gulag,* I wouldn't hesitate. And Fiona knew that.

But there were a lot of unanswered questions. I found it difficult to accept Fiona's explanation at face value. Would she really ask me to kill Moskvin just so she could keep to her side of the bargain? It seemed far more likely that Moskvin was an obstacle to her ambitions. But it was difficult to believe that Fiona would go that far. I preferred to think that her desire to have him dead came from somewhere higher up in the echelons of the KGB—Moscow Centre, in all probability.

But why didn't they try him, sentence him, and execute him for whatever he'd done? The obvious answer to that was *blat,* the Russian all-purpose word for influence, corruption, and unofficial power. Was Moskvin the friend or relative of someone that even the KGB would rather not confront? Was getting rid of him in the West—and so attributing his death to the imperialists—a clever scheme whereby Moscow kept their hands clean? Probably.

Werner Volkmann was still in the roadway on the wrong side of Checkpoint Charlie—our man could see him clearly from the observation post on Koch Strasse. According to what was being said on the radiophone, Werner was wearing his gray raincoat and pacing up and down, accompanied by a guard in civilian clothes.

As arranged with Fiona, I was in the last of the three KGB Volvos when they pulled away from the front of the Steigenberger. There were plenty of policemen there, some in civilian clothes, but not so many that the KGB party attracted any more attention than would the departure from the hotel of any minor celebrity. At the front of the line of three black Volvos there were a white VW bus, an unmarked police vehicle, and a motorcycle cop. Behind us there was another white VW bus containing Frank Harrington, Bret Rensselaer, and three members of the Berlin Field Unit. It was our communications van, two whip-lash antennas and an FM rod on the roof.

The convoy of cars moved out into the traffic and past the famous black, broken spire of the Memorial Church, incongruously placed amid the flashy shops, outdoor cafés, and swanky restaurants of the Kurfürstendamm. There were no flashing lights or police sirens to clear our way. The cars and their two escorting buses eased into the lanes of slowly moving traffic and halted at the traffic signals.

I turned my head to see the white van behind us. Frank was in the front seat, next to the driver. I couldn't see Bret. The cars followed the motorcycle cop, keeping a distance between them so that it didn't look as if we were all together. We attracted less attention that way.

Along Tauentzienstrasse the traffic thinned, but we were stopped by red lights at the big KaDeWe department store. The lights turned green and we began rolling forward again. Then someone stepping into the road threw a plastic bag of white paint at the car I was in. Whether this was part of Fiona's plan or the action of some demonstrator who'd seen the Volvos—with their D.D.R. registration plates—parked outside the Steigenberger, I never discovered. Neither did I ever find out if Pavel Moskvin had been prepared by stories of danger and possible attempts on his life. But as the bag of white paint hit our car and splashed across the windscreen, the driver hit the brakes. It was then, without any warning, that Pavel Moskvin opened the door and jumped out into the road. I slid across the seat and scrambled out after him as the traffic raced past. A red Merc hooted and almost ran over me; a kid on a motorbike swerved round Moskvin and almost hit me instead.

Moskvin ran for the old U-Bahn station that stands in the middle of the traffic there at Wittenbergplatz. I was a long way behind him. There were cops everywhere. I heard whistles and I noticed that one of the other black Volvos had stopped on the far side of the traffic circus.

Obviously Moskvin didn't know the city well. He ducked into the entrance to the U-Bahn, expecting some escape route, but then, realizing he would be trapped, he dashed out again and raced into the fast-moving traffic, jumping between the cars with amazing agility. He ran along the pavement pushing and striking out with his fists to punch people out of his way. He was a violent man whose violence provided a spur for his energy, and, despite his bulk and his middle age, he ran like an athlete. It was a long run. My lungs were bursting and my head spun as I pounded after him.

He turned to see me. He raised an arm. There was a crack and a scream. A woman in front of me doubled up and fell to the ground. I ducked to one side and ran on. Moskvin kept running too. He raced toward Nollendorfplatz. In Kleiststrasse the tracks of the railway emerge from under the roadway and occupy the centre median of the street. He climbed the railings, ran across the tracks, and jumped down the other side. I did the same. I stood on the railings trying to see where he was, thankfully gulping air as my heart pounded with exertion. Bang! There was another shot. I felt the wind of it and jumped down out of sight. Was he, I wondered, heading for the Wall? It wasn't far away; the vast arena of floodlights, barbed wire, mines, and machine guns at Potsdamer Platz was close. But how would he try to get across? Were there some secret crossing places which the KGB used and we didn't know about? We'd suspected it for ages but never found one.

I got my second wind and kept pounding after him. He had to go to Nollendorfplatz unless he had a safe house in this street. Then I saw him. And on the other side of the street—the wrong side of the street—one of the VW vans was grinding its way through the oncoming cars. Now there was a blue light flashing on its roof. No siren though. I wondered if Moskvin could see the light. Frank and his BFU detachment were trying to get to the other side of the Platz and cut him off. I saw old Percy Danvers jump out of the white VW bus and start running. But Percy was too old.

Nollendorfplatz was a big traffic intersection, a circus where fast-moving traffic circulates. The centre of the intersection is filled by the ancient iron structure of the station, raised on stilts above the street. The rusty old railway tracks emerge from under Kleiststrasse and slope gently up to it.

I saw Moskvin again. A car flashed its headlights and another one hooted loudly and then I glimpsed him leaping through the traffic to the middle of the road and the entrance to the station. There were two stations here: the modern underground and the old elevated one it replaced. Had he changed his mind? Was he going to duck down into the U-Bahn, the underground railway, and hope to get aboard a train and leave us behind? A slim hope. But then he raced up the rattling iron steps of the elevated railway station. The bloody fool thought he'd get a train up there. Or perhaps he thought he'd jump down and run along the elevated tracks and cross the Wall the way the elevated trains did from Lehrter Bahnhof to Friedrichstrasse.

I got a clear view of him now. He was halfway up the iron staircase and there was no one in the way. I fired twice. He jumped, but my pistol hand was shaking after the exertions of the chase and I didn't hit him. Across the road Percy Danvers was trying to get ahead of him. Good old Percy; I had to find out what kind of pills he'd been taking.

Then I heard two more shots from the street and I could see the white VW. It bumped as it came riding up onto the pavement. Its doors opened and men jumped out. Frank Harrington was among them, a pistol in his hand. And so was Bret, gung ho and full of fight.

What's Frank doing with a gun? I thought—he doesn't know one end of a gun from the other. Had Frank worried that the Steigenberger meeting might have ended with us all being marched off by the KGB at gunpoint? Frank had always been a bit of a romantic.

I ran into the old elevated station. It was darker in here. I got to the foot of the next staircase and kept close to the wall as I climbed up to the platform. Now there was a volley of shots. They came from across the street. Police perhaps, or people from the other VW bus, but I couldn't see it and I couldn't see any of the three black Volvos either.

Moskvin's feet clattered on the steps. There was a shout as he elbowed someone out of his way. A man carrying a cast-iron bust of the Great Elector fell, the bust hit the stairs with a loud clang, bounced, and broke. I was close behind Moskvin now. At the top of the stairs he stopped. He had realized that the elevated station wasn't a station at all; it had long since been in use as an antique and junk market. This bright yellow train never went anywhere; its doors opened onto little shops and the platform was a line of stalls displaying old clothes, toys, and slightly damaged valuables. The destination boards said BERLINER FLOHMARKT.

He turned and fired at random. I could see the consternation on his face. I fired too. Both of us were being jostled by a terrified crowd. There was a thud and a crash of breaking glass and the bullets zinged off into nowhere.

Moskvin was still hoping that the elevated train tracks would provide him with an escape route. He fought his way through the crowds. There was panic now, screams and shouts. A woman fell and was trampled underfoot. Moskvin turned and fired two shots blindly into the crowd to cause maximum crush that would impede his capture. There was blood spurting. Antique furniture was knocked over, a cut-glass light fell to the floor, a case full of old coins tipped up and the contents went everywhere. A bearded man tried to retrieve the coins and was knocked over.

Through the "trains" of the *Flohmarkt* I caught a glimpse of the other platform. Frank and his party were there. They were making better progress on that side since they weren't moving in the ferocious and terrible wake of Moskvin. "Stay back, Bernard!" It was Bret's voice calling from the other platform. "We'll take him."

They had marksmen with proper weapons. It made sense to

let them move forward rather than my heading into Moskvin's gun sights.

There was the noise of breaking glass and then I saw that Bret was trying to climb up onto the roof of the train. From there he would see the end of the platform, and Moskvin. But Moskvin saw him first. He fired and Bret lost his balance, slid, toppled, and went to his knees before falling to the ground with a loud scream of pain.

I edged forward, more slowly now. Outside in the street below there was a racket of police sirens and some confused shouting. I saw Moskvin again and again, but he was dodging behind the stalls; there was no way of getting a clear shot at him. His hat had fallen off and his close-cropped hair was little more than stubble. He looked older now, a fierce old man whose eyes gleamed with hatred as he turned once and stared directly at me, daring me to step into the open and do battle with him.

When he got to the end of the platform he was alone. The frightened shoppers had scrambled past him and fled down the steps to shout in the street. He saw the tracks that led to the next elevated station. Did he know that one was a market too? Perhaps he no longer cared. As he turned to face me, he saw Frank and the party that had edged their way down the other side. There was a confusion of shooting, the sound echoing like a drum roll in the confined space.

There was only one way Moskvin could go. He climbed onto a bench and pushed aside old Nazi uniforms and some military helmets adorned with eagles. Then he kicked at the dirty windows using the immense strength that comes to those with nothing to lose. The glass and wooden frames smashed into fragments under the kicks from his heavy boots, and he jumped through the shower of broken glass.

He landed down on the train tracks with a force that made his knees bend, and one hand was stretched out to recover his balance. But in an instant he was upright again and running eastward. His ankle-length black overcoat was flapping out like the wings of some wounded crow and his pistol was held high in the air, proudly, like the flaming torch of an Olympic runner.

"Hold your fire!" It was Frank Harrington's voice. "He can't get away, the bloody fool."

But there was the sound of two shots and the black crow stumbled. Yet he had within him the energy and determination of a dozen ordinary men. He ran: one, two, three, four paces. But when he went down again the wings had flapped for the last time. His gun fell from his hand. His face was screwed up into an expression of rage. He clawed desperately at the rails trying to get up again, but, failing, he rolled over and, face upward, bled.

From the station at the other end of the tracks there came the sound of Oriental music. It was the Türkischer Basar, and today it was crowded.

Everyone kept under cover as training rules demand. But I heard someone shout, "Where's that bloody doctor!" It was an English voice calling from the other platform. "Mr. Rensselaer is hurt bad."

Then Frank's voice: "Everyone stay exactly where they are; everyone!" Then he said it again in German.

I kept under cover too, as Frank commanded. It was his show now: Berlin was Frank's town. I was half inside the entrance to one of the little shops. I put my head out enough to see round the sliding door. I could see Moskvin. He hadn't moved. Frank Harrington went out there alone. He was the first person to get to him. I saw him bend over the body for a moment, take his pulse, and then drag an old fur coat right over him. Pavel Moskvin was dead, just as Fiona wanted him. Everything was quiet now except for the Turkish music and Bret's cries of pain.

Chapter 30

I T WAS night. There was a loud, regular, clicking noise, but it was too dark to see where it was coming from. I could only just see Frank. He was sitting on a hard wooden bench.

"We have to be thankful for small mercies," said Frank Harrington. "At least they released Werner Volkmann. They might have kicked up an unholy row when one of their senior staff got killed."

"Yes, they released Werner." I'd just come up from the morgue where Pavel Moskvin was in a drawer in a chilled room with a label tied to his toe. I sat down on the bench.

"Even though we didn't guarantee the safety of that party, I was expecting all hell to break loose. I thought there might have been an official protest."

"Then I've got news for you, Frank," I said. "The ballistics report says that Pavel Moskvin was not killed by one of our rounds." I tossed the mangled piece of metal into the air and caught it.

"What?"

"They said they'd put the report on your desk."

"I haven't been back to the office."

"Three of our bullets hit him, but the one that killed him came from a Soviet-caliber gun." I offered him the round, but he wouldn't take it. Frank was curiously squeamish about fire-arms.

"What the hell?" said Frank. "And why use one of their own guns?"

"Someone over there wanted him dead, Frank. And they wanted us to know that." It was, of course, Fiona's little touch —a way of turning attention away from me, and thus away from her too.

"That's why there's been no protest?"

"And why Werner was released as promised," I said. I hadn't told Frank about my conversation with Fiona and her request that Pavel Moskvin be "taken out." Now it had become evident that the KGB hadn't relied upon us; they'd had their own marksman chasing Moskvin. I suppose they would have had too much to lose had we taken him alive.

"Good grief," said Frank. "There's never a clean ending, is there?"

"That's why we have files, Frank."

"So Moskvin was intended to die," mused Frank. "That explains the KGB hit team we identified. I thought they might be after you."

I said, "Stinnes will return in triumph. Moskvin represented a threat to him. I overheard a conversation between them once. Moskvin was out to get Stinnes."

Our voices were hushed. It was night and we were in the Steglitz Clinic, a part of the hospital of the Free University, the same place from which the Miller woman had been rescued after her pretended attempt at suicide. It has been a terrible night and Frank Harrington's lined face showed how badly he was taking it. Old Percy Danvers, one of Frank's best people and his close friend, was dead. Pavel Moskvin had shot him through the head. That happened in Kleiststrasse before they even got to the flea market and the gun battle in the station. Young Peter—Bret's bodyguard—was badly hurt.

We were waiting for Sheldon Rensselaer to arrive. Bret was in the intensive care ward and not expected to live beyond the weekend. His brother Sheldon was flying in from Washington on a U.S. Air Force flight. Sheldon Rensselaer had a lot of influence in Washington.

"And his wife?" I asked. Ex-wife, I meant. Bret's wife had started spending her alimony years ago.

"Yes, they finally found her. Apparently she winters in Monte Carlo."

"She's coming?"

"She sent three dozen roses."

"Perhaps she doesn't realize how bad Bret is."

"Perhaps," said Frank in a voice that meant she knew.

"Poor Bret," I said.

"He didn't recognize me," said Frank. He was waiting to see Bret again and still wearing the white medical gown they'd given him to go into the ward.

"He wasn't really conscious," I said.

"I should have stopped him getting up on that train. He saw the kid hit and felt he had to do something."

"I know," I said. Frank was reproaching himself unnecessarily for what had happened to Bret. "Did you talk to London?" I asked him, in order to change the subject.

"The old man was not in the best of moods," said Frank.

"We got him off the hook," I said. "We got them all off the hook. Without what you did, those stupid bastards would still be believing all that crap Stinnes was feeding them."

"But they're not admitting that," said Frank.

"How can they deny it? Last night the monitoring service picked up an item about Stinnes being honored in Moscow."

"We both know we stopped London making complete idiots of themselves, but they're closing ranks and pretending they knew about Stinnes all the time. Even the old man said that there's valuable information to be obtained even from non-genuine defectors."

"And what about what they did to Bret?"

"They say he wasn't really under house arrest. They say the man who spoke with him was acting without official instructions."

"Balls," I said.

"And now the man in question is on duty somewhere and can't be reached."

"I bet," I said.

"I spoke to all of them. They're bastards, Bernard. I've often choked you off for saying so, but I take it all back." Everywhere was dark. A nurse came through the swing doors wheeling a trolley that was clanking with glass and stainless steel. She walked away slowly and eventually disappeared into the darkness that was at the end of a long corridor.

"And what about you, Frank?"

"I was in line for a K."

"So I heard." Frank had set his heart on that knighthood. Even though he pretended not to care, it meant a lot to him.

"The old man says it would be inappropriate to recommend that now, after I've so flagrantly disobeyed orders."

"But you saved them."

"You keep saying that," said Frank peevishly. "And I keep telling you that they don't see it that way."

"We couldn't have done it without you, Frank. You risked everything and we were proved right."

"There was talk of giving the K. to Bret instead," said Frank. "I don't know what will happen now."

"The surgeon said Bret won't live."

"The surgeon says no one can predict what a bullet wound like that will do. They've wrapped him in some kind of tinfoil trying to preserve his body heat. They're doing everything that can be done."

"You'll retire anyway?" I said.

"The old man has asked me to stay on here. There is the prospect of a K. in two years' time."

"What did you say?"

"I said you should have Berlin," said Frank. "But the old man said that you were lucky not to be facing grave charges."

Now that my eyes had become used to the gloom I could see the big electric clock over the door that led to the wards. It was the clock that gave that loud click every second. It was the only sound to be heard. "What time did they say his brother's plane would arrive?"

"I don't think he can possibly get here before four," said Frank.

"Sheldon was his father's favorite. Bret resented that. Did he ever tell you?"

"Bret didn't reveal much about his private affairs."

"Yes. I was surprised he confided in me."

"He knew he could trust you, Bernard, and he was right. He came to you at a time when there was no one else he could trust."

"I didn't know him very well," I said. "I'd always suspected that he'd had an affair with Fiona."

"He knew you didn't like him, but he came to you all the same. Bret was grateful for what you did. He told me that. I hope he told you."

"Neither of us did anything for Bret," I said. "It wasn't personal. It wasn't like you doing something for me or me doing something for you . . ."

"Or you doing something for Werner," said Frank artfully.

"It was for the good of the Department," I said, ignoring Frank's aside. "Bret was being framed, and those idiots in London were letting it happen. Something had to be done."

"There will be a big shake-up," said Frank. "Dicky is hoping to get the Europe desk, but there's not much chance of that, thank God. Bret might have got Europe if this hadn't happened. Morgan, the D-G's hatchet man, is getting some sort of promotion too."

"Is Bret in the clear now?"

"Yes. Bret without this damned bullet in his guts might have ended up as the golden boy all over again. Funny how things happen, isn't it?"

"Yes, very funny."

"I told the D-G that you should have a recommendation, Bernard. But it was no use. He's against it and I'm not in a position to do much for you at present, I'm afraid."

"Thanks anyway, Frank."

"Don't be disappointed, Bernard. This is a disaster averted, a Dunkirk for the Department. There are decorations galore and ennoblements and promotions for victories like Trafalgar and Waterloo; but there are no rewards for Dunkirks, no matter how brave or clever the survivors might be. London Central don't give gold medals to staff who prove they are wrong, and prove it with senior staff from Five looking on. They don't give promotions after finales like the last act of *Hamlet* with blood and gore on every side and the unexplained death of a senior KGB official, even if he wasn't given a safe conduct."

"But we saved them from making fools of themselves. We saved the D-G's job, Frank."

"Maybe we did. But there's more to be gained from giving bad advice when the result is a triumph, than from giving good advice when the outcome is a near disaster."

A doctor came through the door that led down the long corridor to the intensive care unit where a white-faced, motionless, unseeing Bret was wired into a roomful of life-support machinery: heart pumps, oxygen supply, and drip feeds. At his side attentive nurses watched dark monitor screens on which little electronic lines jumped, faltered, and flickered.

"Would you come?" said the doctor, a Turk with a strong accent and large mustache. "He might be able to recognize you this time."

"Thanks," said Frank to the doctor. To me he said, "Life is like show business—it's always better to put a fiver into a hit than five grand into a flop."

"We put five grand into a flop," I said.

"Give my best wishes to Werner," said Frank. "I wouldn't have let him down, Bernard. Even if you hadn't been here, twisting my arm, I wouldn't have let Werner down."

"He knows that, Frank. Everyone knows."

WERNER was waiting outside in Zena's car. He looked tired, but no more tired than I'd often seen him before. He was still wearing the old jacket and corduroy trousers. "I got your message," he said.

"Didn't I tell you not to go near that bloody Miller woman?" I said.

"You didn't know it was a stakeout?"

I let his question hang in the air for a moment; then I said, "No, I didn't know it was a stakeout, but I had brains enough to guess it might be."

"I just got back to my apartment here when the phone rang," said Werner. "It was your girl. She'd been trying to get you all day."

"My girl?" I knew he was talking about Gloria, of course, but I was annoyed that she'd phoned, and also that she'd got through to Werner.

"Gloria. She thought you might be staying with us. Rumors were going round in London. She was worried about you."

"What time was this?"

"Just now."

"In the middle of the night?"

"She was in some rotten little hotel in Bayswater. She couldn't sleep. She said you'd quarreled and she'd moved out."

"That's right."

"I told her to pack her things and get a cab and move back into your place."

"You did what?"

"You don't want the poor kid sitting in some crummy little doss house in Bayswater, do you?"

"Are you trying to break my heart, Werner? She's got enough money to check into the Savoy if Bayswater is so terrible."

"Don't be a bastard, Bernie. She's a nice kid and she loves you."

"Hold everything, Werner! Did you tell her that this was my idea, this moving back into my place?"

No answer.

"Werner. Did you tell Gloria it was my idea?"

"She thought it was your idea. I thought it was better that you sorted it out when you got back to London."

"You're a regular bloody matchmaker, aren't you, Werner?"

"You're crazy about her—you know you are. You should grab her while you have the chance, Bernie. It's no good you living in the hope that one day Fiona will come back to you."

"I know that," I said.

"You saw her today . . . yesterday, I mean. I saw her too. Fiona's changed, Bernie. She's one of them now. And she beat us at our own game. She's tough and she called the shots. She made fools of us all."

"What do you mean?" I said. I was weary and irritable. I wasn't asking that Werner thank me for getting him out, but neither was I welcoming his criticism.

"So take Stinnes. Are you still going to tell me he's sick?"

I didn't reply.

"Because I saw him after he arrived over there. I saw him light up a big Havana and make some crack about how pretending to be off tobacco was the worst part of the job. He didn't avoid the physical because he was very sick; he avoided it because he didn't want us to know how strong he was."

"I know," I said, but Werner had to go on about it.

"That was just one small part of the deception plan. By letting us think he was sick, he avoided any risk of us giving him intensive interrogation. He was treated with silk gloves . . ."

"Kid gloves," I corrected him.

"Just the way Fiona knew a sick man would be treated. She outwitted us at every turn. It's game, set, and match to Fiona, Bernie. It's no good you trying to pick a quarrel with me—it's game, set, and match to Fiona."

"Don't keep saying the same thing over and over again," I said.

"Don't keep saying the things *you don't like to hear* over and over again. That's what you mean, isn't it?"

"We came out of it intact," I said. "You're here, I'm

here, and the Department is still putting our salaries into the bank . . ."

"Face the truth, Bernie. See how fast her success has come. Do you remember that night we waited at Checkpoint Charlie in my old Audi? Zena was away somewhere and you were sleeping on my sofa. We were expecting Brahms Four to try. Remember? That was only a year ago, Bernie, and that was well before Fiona went over there. Look what she's done since then. Brahms Four is retired, Bret's economic department is closed down. She's smeared you so cleverly that it will take you years to get in the clear again. Bret's been facing some sort of enquiry. Stinnes stirred up all kinds of trouble for us with MI5 so that it may take years before the bad feeling is gone. And they've done it all so cheaply. Fiona is as arrogant and successful as I've ever seen a KGB senior grade officer—and I've seen plenty—while Stinnes is repatriated and will obviously use the knowledge and experience he's acquired to stage more operations against us. Face the facts, Bernie."

Werner turned the key and started the engine. It was a cold night and the car needed two or three tries before it came to life. He went down the slope and out past the gatekeeper. Berlin never goes to sleep and there was plenty of traffic on Grunewaldstrasse as we headed for his apartment in nearby Dahlem. He took it for granted that I would sleep on his sofa for what was left of the night, just as I took it for granted that Frank Harrington would phone me there to give me any instructions that came from London. It was like that with all of us. We all knew each other very well; too damned well at times. That's why, when we arrived outside his apartment and he switched off the engine, he said, "Admit it."

"Look at it another way," I said. "Fiona, one of the brightest and best-placed agents they've ever had, was flushed out and had to run for it so hurriedly that we lost little or no data. Brahms Four, a brave old man who for years supplied such good banking data and East Bloc forecasts that the Americans traded with us for it, was brought out safely . . ."

"Because you and I . . .," said Werner.

But I plowed on. "I survived their attempts to discredit me and even their loony hope that I'd run. I survived it so well that they had to rejig their resources to turn suspicion onto Bret. Okay, they were smart—I fell for it at first and so eventually did a lot of other people who had more data than I did and should have known better. But at the end of the road, Bret's reputation will have survived, and we proved flexible enough to bend the rules and even break them. The willingness to break rules now and again is what distinguishes free men from robots. And we spiked their guns, Werner. Forget game, set, and match. We're not playing tennis; it's a rougher game than that, with more chances to cheat. We bluffed them; we bid a grand slam with a hand full of deuces and jokers, and we fooled them. They were relieved to get Stinnes back and they didn't even try to sustain the fiction that he was really enrolled."

"Luckily for you," said Werner.

"Luckily for both of us," I said. "Because if they'd stuck to their story that Stinnes was a traitor, I'd now be on a plane to London, handcuffed to an Internal Security man and you'd still be on the wrong side of Charlie. Okay, there are wounds, and there will be scars, but it's not game, set, and match to Fiona. It's not game, set, and match to anyone. It never is."

Werner opened the door and, as the light inside the car came on, I saw his weary smile. He wasn't convinced.

A Note on the Type

The text of this book was set in a digitized version of a typeface called Baskerville. The face itself is a facsimile reproduction of type cast from molds msde for John Baskerville (1706–1775) from his designs. Baskerville's original face was one of the forerunners of the type style known to printers as "modern face"—a "modern" of the period A.D. 1800.

Composed, printed, and bound by
The Haddon Craftsmen, Inc., Scranton, Pennsylvania.
Designed by Virginia Tan.